Praise for *Queen Sugar*

"In *Queen Sugar*, two bulwarks of American literature—Southern fiction and the transformational journey—are given a fresh take by talented first time novelist Natalie Baszile. . . . [The novel] is a sensory experience, a tableau vivant that Baszile skillfully paints in a palette simultaneously subtle and bold. *Queen Sugar* is a bright and enticing reminder that, sometimes, you can go home." —*O, The Oprah Magazine*

"A nuanced evocation of contemporary black life." —*San Francisco Chronicle*

"Baszile infuses her novel with flickers of poetic detail and spot-on observations. . . . *Queen Sugar* gets props for its charming characters and enthralling, fully realized setting." —*The Atlanta Journal-Constitution*

"Reading this book is inhabiting, briefly, the backbreaking and brutal yet rewarding life that is sugarcane farming. . . . *Queen Sugar* is an impressive debut from a talented writer and a fascinating look into the world of the contemporary South." —*The Washington Independent Review of Books*

"Baszile, whose father arrived in California from Louisiana in 1954, knows the region well, and *Queen Sugar* yields a moving tale of contemporary Southern life." —*San Jose Mercury News*

"The confidence and intimacy of *Queen Sugar* come from its parallels with the author's life story. . . . Details gleaned through those experiences help create a story where readers can feel the aching muscles and sweat-drenched shirts. . . . With such a captivating first novel, Baszile has established herself as a bright new author worth keeping an eye on." —*Minneapolis Star Tribune*

"In her heartfelt and beautiful debut novel, Natalie Baszile tells a tale of the South that is as deeply rooted in time and place as it is universal. How do we make sense of family? Loss? The legacies passed down to us? These are the questions that Charley, a young widowed mother, grapples

with as she tries to save the sugarcane plantation that is her inheritance and which, unbeknownst to her, holds the answers to both her past and her future."   —Ruth Ozeki, *New York Times* bestselling author of
A Tale for the Time Being

"Natalie Baszile debuts with an irresistible tale of family, community, personal obligation, and personal reinvention. The world is full of things that keep you down and things that lift you up—*Queen Sugar* is about both and in approximately equal measure. Smart and heartfelt and highly recommended."

—Karen Joy Fowler, *New York Times* bestselling author of
We Are All Completely Beside Ourselves

"*Queen Sugar* is a gorgeous, moving story about what grounds us as brothers and sisters, as mothers and daughters, and all the ways we fight to save each other. Natalie Baszile's characters put brave roots into inhospitable ground, looking for a place, a person, a community to call home. I alternately laughed and wept as they failed each other, forgave each other, lost each other, found themselves. It's a wise, strong book, and I loved it. You will, too."

—Joshilyn Jackson, *New York Times* bestselling author
of *Someone Else's Love Story*

"After turning the last page of *Queen Sugar*, I already miss the gutsy, contemporary African American woman who ditches California and migrates to Louisiana to run her inherited cane farm. Natalie Baszile is a fresh, new voice that resists all Southern stereotypes and delivers an authentic knockout read."

—Lalita Tademy, *New York Times* bestselling author
of *Cane River* and *Red River*

"Raw with hardship and tender with hope, *Queen Sugar* digs deep to the core of a courageous young widow's life as she struggles to keep her farm in Louisiana's sugarcane country. Natalie Baszile writes with a bold and steady hand."   —Beth Hoffman, *New York Times* bestselling author
of *Looking for Me* and *Saving CeeCee Honeycutt*

ABOUT THE AUTHOR

Natalie Baszile has a master's degree in Afro-American Studies from the University of California, Los Angeles, and an MFA from the Warren Wilson Program for Writers where she was a Holden Minority Scholar. *Queen Sugar* has been made into a dramatic television series, produced for OWN by Warner Horizon Television. Baszile lives in San Francisco with her family.

QUEEN SUGAR

Natalie Baszile

PENGUIN BOOKS

PENGUIN BOOKS
An imprint of Penguin Random House LLC
375 Hudson Street
New York, New York 10014
penguin.com

First published in the United States of America by Viking Penguin,
a member of Penguin Group (USA) LLC, 2014
Published in Penguin Books 2015
This edition with a new introduction published 2017

A Pamela Dorman / Penguin Book

THE LIBRARY OF CONGRESS HAS CATALOGED THE HARDCOVER EDITION AS FOLLOWS:

Baszile, Natalie.
Queen sugar : a novel / Natalie Baszile.
pages   cm
ISBN 978-0-670-02613-5 (hc.)
ISBN 978-0-14-313273-8 (pbk.)
1. African-American women—Fiction.   2. Family life—Fiction.   I. Title.
PS3602.A8523Q44 2014
813'.6—dc23
2013036789

Printed in the United States of America
10 9 8 7 6 5 4 3 2 1

Set in Warnock Light
Text designed by Carla Bolte

Cover Key Artwork © 2017 Warner Bros. Entertainment Inc. All Rights Reserved.

For Hyacinth and Chloe

I have a field on my mind that needs plowing.

—Anne Wilkes Tucker

INTRODUCTION

❦ Fearless storytelling. It grips you from scene one, on the page or on the screen. Suddenly you care deeply for people you've never met, people whose lives you will come to realize are imagined with grit and vision, sacrifice and soul. You sense, as things deepen, that the storyteller put her life—her emotional life—on the line. She dares you to look at the darker parts of human nature, the parts most of us would rather ignore. In a fearlessly told story, you both lose yourself and find yourself. And long after you've turned the last page or watched the last credit roll, the story continues to unfurl in your mind.

Then there's this. A fearlessly told story can change the way you think—about yourself and about how we treat each other. It creates space for dialogue. It bridges the divide.

In creating the world of *Queen Sugar*—first in the novel and then in the hugely successful, multiseason television series on OWN, the Oprah Winfrey cable network—we wanted to offer you something different and something *necessary*. We wanted to celebrate African American life in all its richness and complexity. In *Queen Sugar*, you'll find people who feel familiar as memory—because they remind you, just as they reminded us, of people we all know: grandmothers, aunts and uncles, brothers and sisters, sons and daughters. Here are people with tender hearts and unbreakable spirits and also, yes, veins of anger and understandable flaws. Here are people whose lives aren't always represented in mainstream media. We wanted to celebrate the beauty of family and community, while shining a bright, frank light on the challenges we face—as a people and as a nation. We wanted to revel in the beauty and mystery of south Louisiana while not shrinking from its dark history.

This, we believe, is why the novel and the series have resonated so deeply with readers and viewers: because the *Queen Sugar* story is emotionally true. Yes, *Queen Sugar* is an African American story. But it is also an *American* story. The people you will meet in the novel and in the series—which cleaves to Natalie's original story and then, under

Ava's direction, flows beyond the covers of the book—are proud, hard-working people struggling to live on their own terms.

Moving from page to screen has been an unforgettable journey. Readers have become viewers, and viewers have become readers as they travel between the book and the series. But no matter how or where you enter, we hope more than anything that you take away this: a sense of hope and a feeling of connection to something much larger.

Because that is what fearless storytelling can do. Welcome to the novel, welcome to the series—welcome to the fierce, fearless story of *Queen Sugar*.

—Ava DuVernay and Natalie Baszile

ACKNOWLEDGMENTS

Thank you, first and foremost, to my family. To Hyacinth and Chloe, the lights of my life, and my husband, Warrington, who has always been in my corner. Thank you for believing in me. To my parents, Janet Baszile, a woman of extraordinary strength and wisdom, and my father, the late Barry Baszile, who was always willing to drive and more than happy to cook. To my sister, Jennifer, for the early-morning calls. To Aunt Vicie, Aunt Royanna, Antionette, Antonio, Uncle Dan, Marvin, Michelle, Pop and Aunt Dell, Uncle Sonny, Uncle Charles, and Aunt Mary—thank you for your huge hearts and for always welcoming me home. To Gig, Big Warrington, Shanga, Monique and Kala Parker for all the summers.

I am eternally grateful to my adopted Louisiana family, without whose help this book would not have been written. First, to Rene Simon—for your kindness, generosity, expertise, and unwavering support. You have been the best friend and guide I could have hoped for. To the Shea family: Stuart and Becky, Suzy, Maureen, Katie, Miss Barbara, and their families—thank you for helping with research and for making me feel welcome. A special thank you to Stephanie Shea—for your friendship, the birthday invitation, and the afternoon drive that changed everything. To Maggie, Aimee, James, Paul, and Grace Simon for always setting a place for me at your table. To Patricia France for my first Mardi Gras shoe and Mrs. Daniels for being a gracious New Orleans hostess. Thanks also to Gail Porter, Peter Patou, and Suzonne Stirling, for the wonderful meals and excellent conversation. To Chad and Clint Judice. To Cleveland Provost for your patience and quiet wisdom.

To my agent, Kimberley Witherspoon for believing in my work. To William Callahan for those first kind words. To Allison Hunter and Monika Woods.

A thousand thanks to my secret weapons: Dylan Landis—a true friend and brilliant surgeon—thank you for the thousands of hours, for never leaving my side, and for the pixie dust. To David Groff, who appeared at precisely the right moment—thank you sharing my vision, for your encouragement, and for always making time. To Jim Krusoe for your ability to offer the one, surprising suggestion.

I owe a tremendous debt to Warren Wilson's MFA Program for Writers. To Kevin "Mc" McIlvoy, David Haynes, Diana Wagman, Adria Bernardi, and Debra Spark for your guidance and outstanding teaching. To the members of the novel workshop, especially Diane Arieff and Larry Bingham who encouraged me to keep going, and to my fellow Wallies, Catherine Brown and Gabrielle Viethen. A special thank you to Ellen Bryant Voight and Peter Turchi for providing the beacon.

To my wonderfully supportive writing group: Louise Aaronson, Catherine Alden, Leah Griesman, Susi Jensen, Kathryn Ma, Bora Reed, Elana Shapiro and Suzanne Wilsey.

Thank you, dogs and cats at the San Francisco Writers' Grotto, for your friendship and wise counsel. Especially to Julia Scheeres, Laura Fraser, and Caroline Paul.

To Alison Hiraga and Barbara Brooks for being good friends and trusted readers.

To the Ragdale Foundation for providing much needed time and space, and Sylvia Clare Brown for her generosity. To my lovely Ragdale spouses, Rick Hilles, Raymond Johnson, Gregory Mertl, Robin Messing, Nancy Reisman, and Sarah Van Arsdale.

To the Virginia Center for the Creative Arts, and the generous souls at Hedgebrook, particularly Nancy Nordhoff, Vito Zingarelli, Amy Wheeler, and their staff for their radical hospitality.

To the wonderful, insightful, supportive folks at Penguin Random House: Pamela Dorman, Kiki Koroshetz, Beena Kamlani, Carolyn Coleburn, Holly Watson, Winnie De Moya, Paul Lamb, Nancy Sheppard, Roseanne Serra, Carla Bolte, Clare Ferraro, Kathryn Court, and the entire sales and marketing teams of both Viking and Penguin.

Finally, to Coach Flagler and to the late Charles Muscatine, who were there at the beginning.

JUNE

1

✿ Three days ago, Charley Bordelon and her eleven-year-old daughter, Micah, locked up the rented Spanish bungalow with its cracked tile roof and tumble of punch-colored bougainvillea and left Los Angeles for good. In an old Volvo wagon with balding tires and a broken air conditioner, they followed the black vein of highway—first skirting the edge of Joshua Tree, where the roasted wind roared in their faces, then braving the Mojave Desert. They pushed through Arizona and New Mexico, and sailed over the Texas prairie.

Twenty-four hours ago, they crossed into Louisiana where the cotton and rice fields stretched away in a lavish patchwork of pale greens and browns, and a hundred miles after that, where the rice and cotton fields yielded to the tropical landscape of sugarcane country.

Now it was the next morning, their first full day in Saint Josephine Parish. They hadn't seen a house or car since they turned off the Old Spanish Trail, and the road, which crossed over the Bayou Teche, was leading them farther away from town, farther out into the country, and Charley—who'd never seen real sugarcane before yesterday—thought she should have trusted her instincts; thought that if she'd just listened to the small voice that whispered *take the map*, they'd be there by now. Instead, she had listened to her grandmother, Miss Honey, with whom she and Micah now lived. "Put that away," Miss Honey had said at breakfast that morning as Charley spread the map over the kitchen table. "I know how to get there. Just let me get my purse." Now here they were—Charley and Micah and Miss Honey—wandering hopelessly, like three blind stooges, through south Louisiana's cane country, creeping down one ragged back road till it dead-ended in a grass-choked gulley before trying another, while the sun got hotter and the air grew soupier; burning up precious time as they searched for the turnoff that would lead Charley to her fields. She had inherited eight hundred acres of sugarcane land from her father, Ernest. For the last ten months, she had pored over more aerial photos and assessors' maps than she cared to count, signed documents and placed phone calls. She had planned what she could from a distance. The fields Charley had thought of for almost a year were out there—somewhere. Land she had to get ready for the harvest in October. God help us, she thought.

It was eight forty-five. Charley was supposed to meet Wayne Frasier at nine. The cup of Community Coffee, with its bitter note of chicory, had made her queasy. Maybe it was the coffee, but maybe not, Charley thought, as she remembered how her mother accused her of being a city girl and warned her not to make this move. Charley swore her mother was wrong, but now she thought maybe it was true. She was accustomed to measuring distance in freeway off-ramps, not hectares or miles, weighing things in pounds rather than bushels or tons. The only crop she had ever harvested were the Meyer lemons that hung lazily from the trees along her backyard fence. The only soil she ever tended came in bags from the Home Depot. She exhaled heavily. If she were a country girl, she thought, she could scan the horizon and know which of these godforsaken roads led to her fields. But she wasn't a country girl. Not even a little.

Charley turned to her window and caught a scent of Louisiana on the June breeze; the aroma of red clay, peppery as cayenne, musty as compost, and beneath it, the hint of mildew and Gulf water. She marveled at how different the landscape was from anything she'd known back in California: the stretch of Highway 5 between Los Angeles and San Francisco with its endless miles of almond and pistachio orchards, vast stretches of orange groves whose blossoms perfumed the air on early-spring mornings, rolling acres of grape vineyards, tomato and cotton fields, and of course, the uninterrupted miles of reeking cattle lots—all of it with the spiny silhouette of the Sierra Nevada, like a promise, along the horizon. Charley imagined Los Angeles, with its traffic and smog and relentless sprawl, and beyond it, the never-ending coastline and immeasurable Pacific, ridiculously beautiful in the honeyed light of a southern California afternoon. Now the vast Pacific had been replaced by an ocean of sugarcane: waist-high stalks and slender, emerald-green leaves with tilled soil between. Cane as far as her eyes could see.

Charley glanced at Miss Honey. Dressed in a butter-yellow polyester dress belted high on her waist, ginger stockings rolled like doughnuts around her ankles, and white orthopedic sandals, she sat in the passenger seat clutching her white leather purse. Charley wanted to ask if they were getting close, but remembered how, yesterday, Miss Honey scolded her for arriving three hours late. "Well, it's about time. You said noon," Miss Honey had said, standing on the top porch step. "I started to think y'all had changed your minds"; how Miss Honey had flicked that purple plastic fly swatter as if it were a riding crop, and reprimanded her for cutting her hair. "You used to have long, pretty hair," she'd said. "Good hair. Now you look like a man."

More minutes passed. A weather-beaten farmhouse set back from the road, a cluster of small wooden shacks in the distance that looked strangely familiar. Were they driving in circles?

"I'm sorry, Miss Honey," Charley said. "But are you sure this is the right way?"

"Of course I'm sure," Miss Honey said. "If that man Frasier said your place was off the Old Spanish Trail, then this is the way. This used to be an Indian road."

Micah, who had been fiddling with an ancient Polaroid camera Miss Honey had given her, reached over the backseat and tapped Miss Honey's shoulder. "You can't say Indian. It's Native American. Indian is offensive."

"Oh, really?" Miss Honey said without turning around. "Do you know any Indians?"

"Native Americans," Micah corrected. "Indians live in India."

Miss Honey laughed, though Charley thought it wasn't a laugh of delight or amusement. "Well, the Native Americans *I* know like to be called Indians," Miss Honey said, fingering her purse strap. "Bunch of 'em live in the woods behind my house." She turned to Charley. "They built a big casino with a Mexican restaurant and a fancy steak house over in Charenton. Lights up the whole sky at night."

Charley nodded, and was about to suggest they go gambling sometime, feed the slots or take their chances at blackjack, when Miss Honey said, "Nothing over there but a pack of jackals if you ask me. Jackals and sinners."

They drove on.

Out in the fields, a gaggle of laborers followed doggedly behind a tractor. Up ahead, the remnants of an old sugar mill—brick smokestacks, rusted corrugated siding, dust-caked windows—loomed over the cane.

Miss Honey dabbed her neck with a wad of tissue and smoothed her gray candy curls. "I can't stand riding in a car with no air-conditioning."

Charley nodded and added *tune-up* to the list of chores she'd tackle as soon as they got back to Miss Honey's and she was able to unpack.

"Baby," Miss Honey said, "look in that cooler and hand me a Coke." She raised her hand, palm side up, to her shoulder. Charley recognized the gesture. Her father held his hands the same way, right down to the fingers curved as though he were gripping a ball. "Hand me a boiled egg," he'd say during their cross-country drives to Saint Josephine when she was a girl. Or, "Reach in there and give me a couple of those cookies," and she'd root around in the cooler he'd packed until she found what he asked for, excited to put just the right thing in her daddy's hand.

Micah handed a bottle of Coke over the seat and Miss Honey twisted off the cap. She drew a small square packet from her purse, tore it open, and poured the contents—a tablespoon of powder the color and consistency of cornstarch—into the bottle. She swirled the mixture until a head of hissing foam rose along the glass.

"What's that?" Micah asked.

Miss Honey took a swig. "Stanback. I take it for my headaches."

Charley was no chemist, but she considered the properties of Coke—water, corn syrup, a healthy dose of caffeine—and guessed at the Stanback—aspirin for the pain, a little sugar to cut the bitterness, some type of amphetamine for an extra boost—and figured the combination would give quite a buzz. She wondered, as Miss Honey nursed the concoction, closed her eyes, and leaned back against the headrest, if her grandmother wasn't mildly addicted.

Micah leaned over the seat. "Can I try some?"

"Don't even think about it," Charley said, and both Micah and Miss Honey looked at her as if she'd just blurted out a string of swearwords. "I mean—I'm sure Miss Honey needs her medicine. There's water in the cooler if you're thirsty."

"Why your father bought land way out here is beyond me," Miss Honey said, a moment later. "If he wanted to own a business he should have bought something in town. Russell Monroe has been trying to sell his barbershop for two years. I know he'd have let it go for nothing. And I hear some rich white fella from New Orleans just bought the old bank building on Main Street. Gonna turn it into a snazzy hotel." She waved a dismissing hand toward the window. "There's no one out here but a bunch of crackers."

Charley felt her shirt clinging wetly to the knobs of her spine, and debated whether to tell Miss Honey how yesterday, soon after they crossed into the parish, she saw another car, a pickup, approaching fast in her rearview mirror. It rode her bumper, then slid parallel.

"Don't look," Charley had told Micah, though she couldn't help but look herself. The passenger, a white kid in a backwards baseball cap, stared at her for several long seconds, surveyed her car, then turned to the driver, who leaned forward. Charley turned her gaze back to the road, but the driver kept pace with her, even though he was driving in the opposite lane. She held her breath. Her hands shook. Finally, the pickup pulled ahead, glided in front of her, and for what felt like forever, she couldn't see anything but the lettering on the tailgate, the silhouettes of two naked ladies on the mud flaps. She eased her foot off the brake and fell back. The truck gunned its motor and seconds later it was gone, the glow of its brake lights disappearing as it rounded the curve. Were they in danger? Who could say, but for a moment, Charley wondered what her father had been thinking to leave her a sugarcane farm in south *bumfuck* Louisiana.

"You never know why people do what they do," Charley said now, speaking louder so Micah would hear. "You just have to assume they're doing their best." And then she repeated the lines she'd been saying for the last ten months, the lines that had become her mantra: "I think this move will be good for us. An adventure. A fresh start." Charley wasn't saying this just for Micah's sake, she was saying it for her own. Because the truth was, she needed this farm. It was the opportunity she'd been hoping for. Until now, her life hadn't gone the way she planned. She loved her job teaching art to inner-city kids, but it barely paid the bills or ate into the mountain of grad school loans. She drove a car that should have been scrapped for parts, and lived in a house she'd never own. She was thirty-four, and widowed, and may just have been a terrible mother. She needed this farm, wherever it was. She needed a second chance. She needed momentum. And a good shove.

"I reckon." Miss Honey dabbed her neck with her tissue again. "Don't get me wrong, I'm glad y'all are here. It's been too long. But sometimes, you go looking for adventure, all you find is disaster."

"What do you mean, 'disaster'?" Micah said. "What's going to happen?"

"It's just a saying," Charley said, but for good measure she decided not to mention the pickup or how, for the rest of the drive, she pulled over every time a truck came up behind them.

The paved road they'd been following led to a dirt path—a generous way to describe the strip of trampled ground deeply rutted with tread marks and grass growing up between. A wooden stake with the carved letter L leaned to one side.

Charley felt a rush of excitement, a warm tingling that spread over her arms and down her spine, causing her to feel a little light-headed. "This is it."

Dust billowed behind the Volvo until the path ended at a bank of trees. Woods stood tall and impassable to the left, but up ahead to the right sprawled open space. Charley's heart raced as she imagined what was out there: fields so splendidly verdant she'd feel short of breath just looking at them. Her father left the door open and she had stepped through it.

Charley parked. Then she, Micah, and Miss Honey made their way over the clotted ground.

"Holy moly!" Micah cried. "It's huge!" She took a picture with the ancient Polaroid, then hurled a stick far into the tangle of weeds and creeping vines.

"My God," Charley muttered. "This can't be." Across the field, wide and long as ten city blocks, stunted cane stalks dotted the earth, their straggly leaves a starved shade of pale green with deeply sunburned edges. Grass and weeds grew thick and matted between the rows, which were preposterously rutted with tire tracks. Even to Charley's untrained eye, it was clear no one had been out there in months. Where were the neatly tilled rows, the lush cane plants high as a man's shoulder? Where was the moist soil, dark and rich as ground French Roast? Under a morning sky coated with clouds gray as concrete, Charley stared out over fields that should have looked like the hundreds of lush acres she passed on the drive down, but didn't.

"I thought this Frasier fella was managing the place," Miss Honey said, raising her hand to shield against the glare.

"He was." Charley twisted her wedding ring absentmindedly. "Last time we talked, he said something about replacing a tractor belt."

"Well, I'd say he's got some explaining to do."

Charley consulted her watch. They were five minutes late. "You think he's been here and left already?"

"I couldn't tell you what he might do," Miss Honey said. "I don't know this Frasier from Adam's housecat."

"I know where we should put the cows," Micah declared, peering through her camera's viewfinder. "They can live out by those trees."

"This isn't that kind of farm," Charley said.

"But we can't have a farm without cows," Micah pressed. "What about goats?"

"No goats."

"Well, what then?"

Charley glanced at her watch again, then squeezed the bridge of her nose. "Sweetheart, why don't you walk around and take some pictures." White clouds, thick as mashed potatoes, drifted across the sky. Something that looked like a flat-winged bee bounced between the blossoming vines as hot air rose from the dirt.

"My feet are starting to swell," Miss Honey said. "I'll be in the car."

It was almost ten o'clock before an old Ford F-150 with a "Jesus is my co-pilot" license plate rambled down the road ahead of a long contrail of dust. George Strait's crooning voice wafted through the truck's open window. A white man sat behind the wheel.

"Thank God." Charley waved. She had imagined Frasier as older, early sixties perhaps, and stocky as a lumberjack. She had imagined a man wearing embossed cowboy boots and a cowboy hat with a cane leaf braided around the band. But the man who climbed down from the truck looked much younger. Years of physical labor had worn any possibility of fat from his frame. His NASCAR jersey had Dale Earnhardt's picture on the front and sun gilded his brown hair, which, at that moment, was wet. She walked over to greet him. "Mr. Frasier?"

"Miss Bordelon," Frasier said, in the same flat tone she recognized from the phone. "Sorry about the time. Some accident on the road."

"No, no, that's okay," Charley said, extending her hand. "It's nice to finally meet you. In person, I mean."

"Likewise." Frasier gave her hand a firm shake but didn't say anything more.

"I've been waiting a long time for this day." Charley gestured toward the fields. "It's good to see everything for myself. I'd have come down sooner, but I had to wait for my daughter to finish school. Now that I'm here, though, I'm ready to get down to business." She waited for Frasier to respond, but he didn't, so Charley, growing increasingly uneasy, plunged in deeper. "I know we talked about all the work to be done, but I have more questions. For starters, and I hope you don't take this the wrong way, I was looking at the fields and I noticed . . . Well, they don't look exactly like I thought they would." Like they *should.*

"Yeah, well." Frasier threaded his thumbs through his belt loops. He was hard-core Nashville and Grand Ole Opry. Jim Beam straight from the bottle.

"I don't mean to question your work," Charley said. "It's just that I passed plenty of other fields on my drive into town and they were so neat, so orderly, and I—"

"Thought yours would look better," Frasier said.

"Well, yes. But I don't want you to think I'm criticizing—"

"Actually, Miss Bordelon." Frasier looked at Charley with a pained expression, then straightened as though he'd practiced what he was about to say. "I won't be working for you."

"You won't be what?"

"I took another job."

"You *what?*"

Frasier fell silent. He looked down at the ground, then out over the fields.

"But when?" Charley said. "Why didn't you tell me?" She stared at Frasier. He had an honest face, the kind you'd want to see if you were stranded along the roadside with a flat tire late at night. "Are you working for someone else? Because if it's money, I don't have much, but I'm sure we can work something out." Without thinking, she touched her wedding ring again, a platinum band that had been pounded thin in back where the jeweler made it larger. Six angled prongs framed an enormous diamond that had belonged to Davis's mother before it became her engagement ring.

"My brother-in-law pulled some strings," Frasier said. "Got me a job on a rig."

"Rig?"

"Oil rig," Frasier said. "Out in the Gulf."

Charley twisted her ring so that the diamond pressed into her palm. "But I just talked to you two weeks ago. You didn't say anything about another job."

"I know. I wanted to try it out first."

"You're kidding, right? This is a joke. We're supposed to harvest this cane in October. We only have five months."

Frasier batted at the closest cane plant, then ripped a withering leaf from the stalk. "I've been working cane since I was sixteen, Miss Bordelon. I'm shamed to admit it, but I don't have a penny saved. If I bust a knee, what'll I do? Couple years back, Mr. LeJeune took—"

"Who?"

"Mr. LeJeune. The man who owned this farm before your daddy. When he got too sick to run this place himself, his kids stepped in. But they weren't really interested. They were off in New Orleans, riding on floats, going to balls, drinking Pimm's Cups at the Columns Hotel."

"I won't be riding on floats," Charley said. "And I've never heard of a Pimm's Cup. Mr. Frasier, please."

Frasier crumpled the cane leaf in his palm. "I had to beg 'em to plant enough cane last year and they hardly took care of the cane that was here. When LeJeune died, they scraped by until they sold. Your daddy convinced me we could bring this place back. But now he's gone too."

"But I'm here," Charley said. "Give me a chance."

Frasier shredded another cane leaf. "If I don't do something now, I'll run out of money before I run out of air. I don't want to be greeting folks at Walmart when I'm sixty-five."

"But I was counting on you. I've been *paying* you."

Frasier pulled two checks from his breast pocket, handed them to Charley, and she saw that they were the ones she'd mailed weeks ago. "I've asked around. Problem is, this time of year, anyone worth hiring has already signed on for a job."

Charley touched Frasier's jersey as if it were the hem of his royal robe. If he wore a ring she would have kissed it. She would have knelt if he'd asked her to. "Please, Mr. Frasier. Wait one season. You've put me in a terrible bind."

Frasier looked at her with great sympathy. "Your daddy was a good man," he said. "I never met him in person, but I could tell. And I can tell you're a good person too." He brushed his hands on his pants. "But two more months and I get my union card. I'll have benefits."

"We both know I can't run this place by myself. Please. I'm begging you."

"It only seemed right to tell you in person."

Charley looked out at her fields. The cane seemed to have withered even more in the hour since she arrived. Birds, whose chipper singing she hadn't noticed until now, seemed to mock her with their chatter. "All this time and you never said a word." A tremendous lump thickened in her throat and she turned away, willing herself not to cry. She fully expected Frasier to leave, but he waited patiently, hands wedged deep in his back pockets.

"If you'd like to go over things," he offered.

Somehow, Charley managed to write down the instructions he gave her: how to start the tractor; where to buy replacement parts, diesel, and fertilizer; what tools were in the shop; directions to the Ag station. She took notes, but had no idea what to do with them.

At last, Frasier looked openly at his watch. "I guess that does it." He turned to leave, stepping sure-footedly over the ruts and clumps of soil. At his truck, he paused. "It's good land. I hope you know that. Good luck to you, Miss Bordelon."

And then he was gone.

• • •

Once Frasier's truck disappeared, Charley walked unsteadily back to the car, where Miss Honey fanned herself with an envelope.

"How'd it go?"

"Fabulous," Charley said, sliding in. "He's a gem. A real man of his word." She held herself together long enough to slip her keys into the ignition. The engine turned over. But as she shifted into reverse, Charley thought about how much her life had slipped. Six hours ago, she felt like a girl getting ready for a dance, with lights and music and a new life stretched out before her like a red silk carpet. Now she was a girl who kept losing things: she lost her husband in a holdup he just had to resist and she almost lost her daughter. She lost her father to cancer, and now she was about to lose his strange and unexplained legacy, this sugarcane farm. She had a pad of notes she could barely read, her manager had quit, and she was out in the middle of God knew where. Charley stopped the car. She took a long, deep breath. Then she hid her face in her hands and sobbed.

"When you stood there for so long, I had a feeling," Miss Honey said. She rubbed Charley's back.

At the feel of Miss Honey's touch, Charley cried harder. "I'm sorry."

Miss Honey pressed a damp napkin from the cooler into Charley's hands. "That's okay, *chère*. Let it out," she said. "'Cause you got a big job ahead of you. And in a minute, you're gonna have to pull yourself together."

At the far edge of the field, Micah's yellow T-shirt and orange shorts flashed like banners against the brown earth as she started to run.

"Who'd Ernest buy this place from?" Miss Honey asked.

Charley wiped her eyes, watching her daughter approach. "Some family named LeJeune."

Miss Honey looked surprised. For a moment, it seemed as though she might say something, but she just nodded and let Charley collect herself.

"Look at these," Micah said, panting, as she reached the car. She handed four Polaroids through the window before she saw Charley's face. "Mom? Why are you crying? Miss Honey, what's wrong with my mom?"

Miss Honey opened a bottle of water and offered it to Micah. "Quiet, *chère*. You mamma's having a bad day."

2

In twenty-four hours he would be a fugitive; twenty-four hours, and the Chevy Impala would appear on the Phoenix Police Department's list of stolen vehicles. Ralph Angel considered his new identity as the car glided over the highway. He tugged at his collar, remembering the crisp white dress shirts he wore as a college student all those years ago; white shirts with natural shell buttons that cost most of his monthly allowance. But fingering his collar now, all Ralph Angel felt was the frayed cotton of his thrift-store button-down.

Behind Ralph Angel, his son, Blue, six years old, kicked the seat. "Can we go to the plaza on Sunday?"

"Why?"

"I want a churro," Blue said. "I didn't get one last time."

"So?" Ralph Angel stuck his arm through the window. How many times in the last four months had he and Blue walked to the plaza on a Sunday morning? He'd scrape together enough money for four warm churros wrapped in newspaper and a six-pack of Dos Equis, and they'd sit on the shaded grass listening to the mariachis play. They stayed all day and into the evening sometimes, Ralph Angel nursing his beer, Blue nibbling the long ropes of fried dough, the two of them watching red-lipped women dance with men in cowboy hats and boots. Those trips always ended the same way: back in the rented room, Blue asleep in his street clothes, the two of them sharing the soft mattress while Ralph Angel stared at the TV, waiting for sleep that rarely came. By midnight, he'd give in to the craving, slip out for a drink at the Piccolo Club or cruise Fifty-ninth Avenue to score some junk.

"When we get to Billings, maybe we can find a new treat," Ralph Angel said. "Something better than churros." But Blue was absorbed with Zach, the Power Rangers action figured he treated in mysterious and punishing ways. Ralph Angel heard Blue say, "Once a Power Ranger, always a Power Ranger," and make exploding sounds as he smashed Zach against the door hardware.

"Easy there, buddy," Ralph Angel said. "Maybe we'll get you a buffalo burger." Cowboys and buffalos, wasn't that what they had out there in Big Sky country? He imagined frontier towns, white men dressed in flannel and spurs. He imagined life in Billings: he'd stick out like a fleck of pepper in the salt.

Blue unfastened his seat belt, sat forward, and walked Zach across Ralph Angel's headrest. "Mystic source, mystic force," he said.

Ralph Angel heard clicking noises near his ear as Blue pressed the light on Zach's Dino Fire; heard Blue say, "Power ax," as he pressed the tiny weapon into Ralph Angel's cheek.

"Zach wants to know what else we'll eat," Blue said.

Ralph Angel thought for a moment. "How about huckleberry pie?" Cowboys always ate huckleberry pie.

Blue laughed. "Zach says we can eat huckleberry pie every day when you come home from work. We can have huckleberry pie for breakfast if we want."

"Sure, buddy. Whatever you say."

Billings, Montana, according to the article in *Money* magazine that Ralph Angel read in the emergency room last month when Blue jumped off a wall and sprained his ankle, was the seventh-best place in the country to live. In the accompanying photo, a man and a boy paddled a canoe. Their backs were turned, but you understood from the way they leaned forward in their matching life vests, the way they raised their oars in unison, with water like chips of crystal spilling back into the lake, that they were father and son. White, of course, rugged and sturdy, but still. Staring at the picture, Ralph Angel had been overcome. He could be that father. Blue could be that boy. They just needed to get to Billings.

But something felt wrong, which was why he was procrastinating; why it had been three days since they left Phoenix and he'd driven only as far as Flagstaff. If he turned around now, they would be back in Phoenix by midnight, no later than two. He could put Blue to bed, get Mrs. Abernathy across the hall to babysit while he returned the car. Only there was no home to go home to. Six months ago, the sheriff nailed an eviction notice on the door, set their clothes on the street. For the last four months, they had lived at the Wagon Wheel, a motel at the end of East Van Buren, where he paid for their room by the week. There was no job to wake up for, because he got fired.

"I'm hungry," Blue said. "What do we have to eat?"

Ralph Angel looked at the empty passenger seat. If Gwenna were here, she'd have thought ahead, packed sandwiches, drinks, and something sweet as a surprise. That was one of the things he loved about her; she always thought ahead, always scanned the horizon for problems, like a ship's captain stationed at the bow. "We'll stop soon," Ralph Angel said. "Just hold on." He glanced at the passenger seat again and braced himself against the twist of longing. There was no Gwenna to pack sandwiches or encourage him to look for another job; no Gwenna to reassure him everything would be okay because Gwenna was dead.

"Are we there yet?"

"Those four words," Ralph Angel said, "I don't want to hear them. Now sit back." He let his eye wander across the landscape, the sloping golden foothills dotted with ponderosa, and tried again to picture them in Montana. He'd rent a small house with a yard that opened onto a meadow. Blue and his friends would build a fort in the woods or by a lake if there was one close by, and when the boys got older, they'd stay out all weekend, camping and fishing the way boys liked to. He'd go to all of Blue's games—baseball and basketball—and sit in the bleachers with the other parents. "That's my kid," he'd say when Blue scored the winning basket. "That's my kid."

Ralph Angel glanced at the sudden movement in the rearview mirror. Zach wagged back and forth while Blue chanted, "Are-we-there-yet-Are-we-there-yet," like a drumbeat. He tried to ignore it, tried to focus on the road and their life in Billings, until finally he reached back, grabbed Zach, and held him out the window. He felt the sun warm his hand, smelled the clean scent of pine. "You done?" Except for the wind, the car was silent. After five long seconds he said, "Thought so," and passed the action figure back.

At Tuba City, Ralph Angel took a break. He pulled off the road and into the rest stop parking lot, wedging the Impala between two semis.

"Pop?"

Tourists on their way to or from the Grand Canyon filed through the double doors, headed toward the restaurant. Ralph Angel imagined them bent over burgers and fries.

"Stay in the car. I'll be back."

"But I'm hungry and Zach has to pee," Blue said.

"Tell him to hold it. Let me see what they've got in there. I'll be back in a second." Ralph Angel tucked in his shirt and zipped his jacket halfway. He scanned for Highway Patrol, then fell in line with people entering the building.

Inside, the air was heavy and smelled like doughnuts. There was a restaurant, a minimart, and beyond, a row of fast-food counters. His stomach seized at the thought of day-old grease, of plates smeared with ketchup, cigarette butts tucked into wadded napkins. The summer before he went off to college, he'd worked briefly as a dishwasher at the Waffle House just outside town, and had been surprised and horrified by what people did with their food. "People are animals," Eddie the busboy said, stacking dishes on the stainless steel sink, and Ralph Angel had agreed. Now he closed his eyes as the nausea swelled, then passed. When it was gone, he watched the swirl of people moving through the lobby: women in capri pants and visors, men in cargo shorts and fanny packs, kids Blue's age, running giddily across the tiled floor.

Surprisingly, the minimart was empty, peaceful as a library. As Ralph Angel entered, the young woman behind the counter looked up from her magazine. She wore bright pink lipstick and her mouth reminded Ralph Angel of the wax lips he chewed as a kid. He flashed a smile.

"Water?" he asked.

She pointed to a bank of refrigerators on the far wall, then went back to her reading.

Ralph Angel gave a cheerful thumbs-up, then made his way down the aisle, being sure to walk deliberately. He wanted the girl to see he had a goal, he was a man who wanted water. When he reached the back wall, he slid the glass doors open and felt the rush of cold air, like a light slap in the face, looked for the cheapest bottled water and took two. Glancing toward the front of the store, he saw that the girl's head was down, still reading. She tucked a strand of hair behind her ear in the slow, unconscious way women did when they were preoccupied.

Beside him, the refrigerators hummed steadily, and Steely Dan's breezy hit "Rikki Don't Lose That Number" wafted in from the food court, over the echoes of families chattering, and coins jingling, and cashiers calling out people's orders. They were the sounds of summer. For a few seconds, as Ralph Angel stood listening, it seemed to him that the day was filled with possibility, as if a yolky, glowing ball hovering over the rest stop was suddenly cracked open, spilling warmth and light down on all those inside. For a moment he felt it, like a faint pulsing: the lightness that came with a few lazy summer months, the quiet joy in being connected to people you loved and who loved you. But then it faded, and he was flooded with the awesome knowledge that he was all alone—no mother, no father, no Gwenna. Just him and Blue.

And so, as he walked up the aisle toward the register, Ralph Angel plucked items off the shelf: Tiger's Milk bars, Snickers, Slim Jims—whatever he touched—and dropped them into his sweatpants, because he had to feed his boy, because raising his son was the only thing he was good at, and he would do whatever it took. The wrappers crackled as they slid down his leg and came to rest above the ankle elastic. The urge to take inventory, like a trick-or-treater, surged within him.

At the counter, his heart pounding, Ralph Angel managed to hold up the bottles of water. "You got a bathroom in here?" he asked, tossing two crumpled dollars on the counter.

The girl's mangy blond hair was swept up in a giant butterfly clip. She was like the young, fast white girls in Phoenix who hung out at the park; girls who laughed in his face, cussed him out just for fun.

"Down the hall next to Roasters." She scanned the bottles, dropped them into a plastic bag, and held it out to him.

"Cool. Thanks."

As Ralph Angel turned to leave, the corner of the Tiger Milk bar slipped out of his pants leg, dragged on the floor with a *sushing* sound.

"What's that?" the girl asked, pointing. She leaned across the counter.

Ralph Angel glanced down at the triangle of shimmery gold foil. He looked at the girl.

"Dude," she said, her face darkening, "are you fucking boosting?" She looked right at him, not through him or past him the way so many people did, but right into his eyes, her gaze direct, searing.

Ralph Angel opened his mouth, but before any words could come, the girl stepped backward, felt for the phone mounted on the wall.

"It was an accident," Ralph Angel managed. "I don't know what I was thinking." He approached the counter, his hands out where she could see them, then reached in his pocket and pulled out a small roll of bills. "Jesus, just give me a minute." His hand trembled as he unfolded a twenty and a wad of singles. "This is all I've got. I swear."

The girl stared at the money.

"I was saving it for gas," he continued. "I've got my kid with me, see? Just let me pay. I got my kid. He's in the car."

The girl eyed him, then glanced up at the video equipment mounted on the ceiling.

Ralph Angel saw his pixilated self on the monitor. "I swear it's true." He pointed at the big picture window behind her, to one of the minivans at the edge of the lot rather than the Impala. "There, that green van. The one with the kid behind the wheel."

A couple walked in. Matching shirts, matching sneakers. Ralph Angel heard the woman say, in a nasally midwestern tone, "We should buy some of these garlic chips for the kids."

Ralph Angel let his hands fall to his sides. "What's gonna happen to him if I get hauled off to jail? His mama's dead. Just let me pay up. You won't ever see me again."

He knew the girl was weighing her choices, marked the moment, by the blink of her eyes, when she decided against him.

And in that next moment, Ralph Angel made his own decision. No use trying to convince some thick-necked security guard he actually *had* enough cash to buy the food he stole, that his kid really *was* in the car, even if it wasn't the car he pointed out to the girl. And what about the car? How would he explain that he rented it for a couple days, just to get around town, but that somehow those couple days had turned into a couple weeks? That the rental place had sent a dozen demand letters threatening to alert the police if he didn't bring the car back? That his grace period expired *today*, and that by this time tomorrow he'd be wanted for grand theft auto?

Ralph Angel lunged forward. He swept the money off the counter, bolted from the store, back through the crowded lobby, the plastic bag with the water bottles in it swinging at his side, the stolen food shaking up and down against his leg, the girl's cry "Stop that guy" echoing behind him. He pushed through the glass doors, stumbled out into the heat and the blinding sunlight. At the Impala, he dived behind the wheel, jammed the key into the ignition, and tore out of the lot.

"Pop!" Blue squeezed himself into the front seat. Christ, he thought it was a game.

"Sit back. Get down. Be quiet."

Ralph Angel was back on the highway before he drew a breath, the clean, hard desert all around him, the rest stop shrinking to miniature in his rearview mirror.

The Colorado Plateau.

Juniper and ponderosa.

The unfurling road.

A tap on his shoulder.

"I'm still hungry, Pop," Blue said. "And Zach really, really, really has to pee."

"Aw, shit," Ralph Angel said, remembering his promise. "Use this." He dropped a dented foam cup over the seat. "And here," he said, tossing back the Tiger's Milk bar and Slim Jims. "Those should hold you till we can stop again."

Blue whimpered as he struggled with the cup. After a minute he said, "Now what?"

"Now what, *what*?"

"The cup. It's full."

"Well, throw it out, for Christ's sake." Ralph Angel pressed the button for Blue's window and felt the tug on his headrest as Blue pulled himself forward. In his mirror, he saw his son blinking as he held the cup up to the wind.

"Oh, no," Blue cried. "Aw, Pop."

Ralph Angel glanced quickly behind him. Blue's shirt and pants were drenched, the cup overturned. Urine streamed down the door, a dark spot the shape of some distant continent, spreading over the burgundy upholstery. "Goddamnit!"

"It was an accident!" Blue said, his small voice quaking.

"Goddamn, Blue!"

"Pop, I'm wet."

"Motherfuck!" Ralph Angel said. "Well, what do you want me to do about it? I'm driving. Can't you see I'm trying to drive?" The whole world seemed to be spinning, the road ahead all zigzaggy and wavy in the mid-morning light.

Silence again from the backseat, followed by muffled sobbing.

Ralph Angel thought of the father and son in the canoe and knew that man would react differently. He would be patient. He would be kind. And then there was the memory of himself as a kid: the envelope of deep sleep, the vague awareness of liquid warmth flowing from him, and the shame as he stripped the reeking sheets off the bed. Ralph

Angel glanced in the mirror. Why did it seem like the kid always got the brunt of whatever he was feeling? "Hey, look, sorry I yelled," Ralph Angel said. "I didn't mean it." He unzipped his jacket. "Take off those clothes and throw them up here. You can wear this till I find a place to rinse them."

Blue handed his wet clothes over the seat, the sweat jacket he wore now draped like a tent from his shoulders to his knees. He sat back, peeled the Slim Jim from its plastic wrapper, and stuffed the whole thing in his mouth. He chewed, swallowed hard, then reached for the Tiger's Milk bar.

"Go easy, there, buddy, slow down," Ralph Angel said. "You're going to make yourself sick."

Almost an hour since he ran from the rest stop. Ralph Angel pinched a minidoughnut from the wrapper and took a bite, the chocolate coating, waxy and flavorless, stuck to his teeth. He fixed his gaze on the horizon and thought about Miss Honey. If she hadn't called, if she'd just stayed out of his business, he could have gotten by on the money in his pocket, made due till Gwenna's next social security check. But she *had* called, with news that Charley was coming down, and not just visiting but coming down for good, to work some sugarcane land their father left her.

"How much land?" he'd asked. The last time he saw his kid sister, she was twelve or thirteen. It was hard to imagine her being old enough to run anything.

"Plenty," Miss Honey had said. "Come home."

But by then, things had turned around for him and Blue. They weren't sleeping in the car anymore—he'd sold it. They had a room. Blue was back in school. He hadn't found a job yet, but he was optimistic, he had prospects. "There's nothing for me in Saint Josephine," he'd said. He knew it and she knew it too. Besides, the last time he was home, things hadn't gone so well.

But Miss Honey was like a dog with a bone. "Why not?" she'd

pressed. "I know Charley would love to see you. You could help her with the farm. It would have made your daddy happy to know his children were close."

"If my daddy was so concerned with my welfare, why didn't he leave half the farm to me?" He hadn't expected to get much, maybe a few thousand dollars. He couldn't believe Charley got everything.

"Well, if you'd paid him back like I told you, maybe you would have gotten more."

"Jesus, 'Da. Get off my case. What happened between my daddy and me wasn't only my fault."

"Just think about it," Miss Honey had said.

Blue nudged Ralph Angel's shoulder with Zach's feet. "I'm tired of being in this car. It's not fun anymore."

"Your pop's got a lot on his mind." Ralph Angel turned on the radio, tuned it to a rap station. "You know this song, don't you? You can sing along if you want."

Blue sat back. He recited the lyrics—girl trouble, police searches, paparazzi—and bobbed his head to the beat.

"There you go. Nice, buddy. Now sit tight while I work things out."

Evening was rising. Ralph Angel unplugged the GPS tracking device and stuffed it under his seat. He looked down at Blue, sitting crossed-legged on the passenger seat now, unbelted and still wearing his sweat jacket. Gwenna would chew him out for letting Blue eat all that junk. She'd give him hell for not bringing extra clothes.

"You figure things out yet, Pop?" Blue scooted forward and locked Zach in the glove box.

If he took the back roads, he'd avoid the highway patrol; he wouldn't have to worry about them punching in his license plate and seeing that the car was stolen. It would be a slower drive, but he could be there in a week, ten days tops. Ralph Angel looked through his side window. He'd liked being out west, wished things had turned out different. Phoenix, Billings—maybe someday he'd come back and give them another go.

He hadn't wanted to show up in Saint Josephine till he was back on his feet, hadn't wanted to show up till he had something to brag about. But 'Da's call had been like holding a flame to a pilot light.

"Pop, you going to answer me? Have you worked things out?"

"Yeah, I think so." Seven days of driving. Ten tops. By all rights, half that farm was his. And even if he'd fucked things up and couldn't get it for himself, he'd get it for Blue. "Buckle up," Ralph Angel said, and he squeezed Blue's shoulder, thinking of the man and the boy in the canoe. He made a U-turn in the road, eased the car up to eighty, set the cruise control.

"Are we going back?"

The sun had sunk below the horizon, the last of its crown blazing fiery gold above the pine. "I got a better idea," Ralph Angel said, and flipped on his high beams. "We're going to Saint Josephine, buddy. We're going home."

3

🌿 At the sound of Charley's car, two dogs lounging under the screened porch dragged themselves into the sunlight, and the smaller dog, a scruffy terrier mix with fur like pipe cleaner bristles, barked and ran toward her. Charley greeted him cheerfully but gave him a wide berth as she pocketed her key and crossed the unfenced yard.

Like so many country houses she'd seen in the last few days, this one sat on brick pillars a few feet off the ground, surrounded by a collar of packed red dirt, and beyond, a wall of neatly groomed sugarcane. It was a tidy little house with stepping-stones, a screened porch, and window boxes overflowing with glossy yellow daylilies and deep purple irises. Finding that the porch door was locked, Charley cupped her hands, pressed her nose to the screen. In the late-morning sun, she could just make out two rocking chairs angled toward each other, as though the people who lived there preferred talking to each other rather than watching for cars or passersby.

"Hello?" Charley called, then she walked around the side of the house where bamboo trellises sagged under the weight of okra and tomatoes. An old Ford pickup sat parked on the grass. "Hello?" Charley called again. "Anybody?"

The bigger dog loped toward her just then, his long whip of a tail swinging. He was the color of raw sugar and slobber hung from his black muzzle in long, foamy ropes. Charley froze as he circled her, but when he whined and galloped back toward the front door, she followed.

Behind the screened porch a door creaked open. "Who's there?"

"I'm looking for Prosper Denton," Charley said, climbing the steps again. It was exactly what Miss Honey had warned her *not* to do. "You don't just drop in on Prosper," Miss Honey had said as they drove from the disastrous meeting with Frasier, heat rising off the fields and making the road undulate. According to Miss Honey, Prosper Denton ran the farms of the biggest white farmers around before he retired.

"If he's retired why should I see him?" Charley had asked.

"You don't *see* him," Miss Honey had said, ominously. "You *call* him. Tell him what happened." She had his number in her book. "But I'm telling you, if he agrees to meet with you, you can't go over there forgetting yourself. You can't come apart like a ball of twine that's hit the floor."

"My name is Charley Bordelon," Charley said now. "I'm Miss Honey's granddaughter." She waited for the man to respond, to throw the door open at the mention of Miss Honey's name, but he didn't. In fact, he didn't move at all. "I'm sorry to drop in unannounced. I tried calling yesterday but your phone just rang."

"What can I do for you, Miss?" His tone was cautious.

"I'd like to talk to you about sugarcane." Charley wished he'd step outside so she could see him, so he could see *her*. He would see the dark crescents of fatigue under her eyes, crescents she'd tried (and failed) to conceal with makeup. He would notice that she had made an extra effort to look nice: ironed her skirt, finally sewn that button on her blouse; that she was wearing *heels*, for Christ's sake, and white nylons even though it was eighty degrees and her crotch was beginning to sweat, but worn them anyway because it seemed the proper Southern thing to do. But he didn't come outside. "I understand you're an expert." Charley took a half step closer. "I'm in a bit of trouble."

"What kind of trouble?"

"I own some acreage out near the Old Spanish Trail." Charley paused. "My manager quit."

"What manager would that be?"

"Wayne Frasier."

"Frasier manages LeJeune's operation."

"He used to," Charley said. "My father bought it from the LeJeune family. When he passed last year, he left it to me."

The man said nothing.

"I tried to phone—" Charley began, but mercifully, the screen door opened and she stood face to face with Prosper Denton. Brown skin smooth as a new baseball glove. Head shiny as a gumball. He could have been in his late fifties, Charley thought, if his sagging jowls and neck hadn't told the real story.

Denton appraised her over the tops of his bifocals, then elbowed the screen door open. "Maybe you better come in."

The kitchen was tight but tidy. Shellacked homemade cabinets, dishrags folded neatly over a gleaming sink. Denton pulled a chair out from the kitchen table and motioned for Charley to sit. Someone must be taking good care of him, Charley thought, because his overalls and short-sleeved button-down were not only pressed but starched. Only his black brogans with their frayed laces and run-down heels were scuffed and dusty—probably as old was he was.

"You'll have to forgive me," Denton said, some of the gruffness fading from his tone, "I'm a bit lost in this kitchen when my wife's not here." He set a glass of lemonade in front of Charley, then tore a square of paper towel, folded it in half for a napkin.

Denton struck Charley as the kind of man who never wasted energy on extra movement or idle chitchat. He was foursquare Sonny Boy Williamson and Sister Rosetta Tharpe, a Silvertone guitar, *older* than old school.

He sat in the chair across from her. "So."

"I apologize for not calling," Charley said for the third time, and took a sip of lemonade. It was fresh-squeezed, with the perfect amount of sugar and not a hint of pulp. If summer had a taste it would be this. She could drink the whole pitcher. But when she looked up, Denton was waiting and not looking any friendlier. Charley set her glass on the table. Better get right to the point.

"My dad owned a lot of rental property back in Los Angeles." Charley pictured the four units in Paramount whose front doors all opened onto a small courtyard filled with palm trees and ferns, the duplex in Culver City around the corner from the Italian bakery, the condo in Long Beach with a view of the *Queen Mary*. "He believed real estate was the only thing worth buying. 'Real estate is the horse you need to ride,' he always said. When he died, I thought his lawyer would give me a list of properties. Instead, he said I'd inherited a farm."

Back up, she'd told the lawyer the day after the funeral. *Eight hundred what?*

Acres of sugarcane, the lawyer had repeated, lifting the sheet of paper from the file. *Two hundred acres of plant cane and another six hundred of something called first-year stubble.* He'd rubbed his chin.

"My dad waited years for the farm to come up for sale." Charley told Denton. "It had to be these acres. When it finally came up, he sold all his properties for the down payment."

But that's impossible, she'd told the lawyer. Her father was still living in the Long Beach condo, had lived there ever since he and her mother divorced. Gently, the lawyer explained that her father had rented it back from the new owners.

Charley connected the beads of condensation that had formed on the outside of her glass. She told Denton about Frasier quitting and returning her money. She described her fields. "Until ten months ago, I thought sugar grew on the baking aisle at the supermarket. Right below the chocolate chips and the sprinkles." As Charley spoke, she searched Denton's face, waited for him to do something—nod in agreement, shake his head in disgust, sigh with exasperation—but he just sat there, leaning forward with his elbows on his knees, staring at the floor. "According to Frasier," Charley said, "all the best managers are taken. He says I'll have trouble finding help so late in the season."

Denton sat back. "Frasier's right. You're already three months behind. Even if you find someone, they might sell you a lot of promises. Might say all you need to do is get out there with a cultivator, clean up the rows. They'll spray some Roundup on them weeds, charge you twenty thousand dollars, then disappear."

"Oh my God," Charley said, and saw a corresponding flicker on Denton's face.

"If Frasier ain't been doing his job, getting ready for grinding is gonna be like licking honey off a blackberry vine." He rubbed his hand over his bald head. "Back when I was running Simoneaux's plantation, I'd see LeJeune's wagons at the mill. His fields were yielding one, maybe two hundred tons an acre. You don't get that kind of tonnage without working that land right, working it all the time."

Keep talking, Charley prayed. The more he talked, the more he might care. "Please go on."

"Frasier ain't been working your fields, you probably down to twenty, thirty tons. Maybe less. You might be lucky to get five tons an acre. That's hardly worth your time." Denton paused. "Shame those LeJeune kids didn't do better by their daddy's land."

"So where do I start? How can I catch up?"

Denton ticked off the tasks. His nails were clean and short, except his pinkie nails, which were half an inch long and filed to points, as though he used them to scoop things or pick locks. "First you got to test your soil, run your drains," he said. "You needed to start off-barring way back in March, and the time for laying-by has almost passed. If I remember right, LeJeune's got a lot of three eighty-four out there, which tends to lodge. He might even have some five forty, which is like candy to them borers."

"Off-barring? Laying-by? Borers?" With every word Denton spoke, Charley felt herself pulled farther out to sea.

"What kind of equipment you got?"

"Frasier said something about a new belt for a tractor," Charley managed, "but I'm not sure what he meant."

Denton frowned deeply. "What do you mean, you're not sure?"

"He went over the list, but everything sounded the same." Charley exhaled. "Maybe I can just buy what I need."

"I don't know what kind of money you got, Miss, but a new tractor's a hundred thousand. Combine'll set you back two fifty."

"Two fifty what?" Charley could only stare at him. "Two hundred and fifty *thousand*?"

"That's for last year's model." Denton scratched the tuft of hair below his lip. "I'm not trying to frighten you, but you're an easy mark. You're young, you're not from around here, you've never worked cane, and frankly, you being a woman's gonna work against you."

"What difference does my being a woman make?"

"And colored on top of it?" Denton clasped his hands together as if in prayer, and rested his head against them. He was silent for a long moment. "You got to know what you're getting into here, Miss Bordelon. This ain't no game." He pushed away from the table and stood at the counter. "Tell you a quick story. Few years ago, a farm went up for sale. There was a black farmer, Malcom Duplechain, thought he'd put in a bid. He already owned three hundred acres out near Bienville. Real good land. His daddy owned it and maybe his daddy's daddy before that, but he wanted to grow his operation, wanted to get real big like some of these white farmers you see around. Duplechain and another colored fella decided to go in together. Property went up for sale, Duplechain put in his bid. Now, the bids were supposed to be sealed." Denton wadded his paper towel and tossed it on the table. "I'll give you one guess what happened."

"I don't know," Charley said. "They got outbid?"

"Yeah," Denton said, as if that much was obvious. "But by how much?"

Charley shrugged. "Ten thousand? Fifty thousand?"

Denton shook his head mournfully. "A hundred dollars, Miss Bordelon. Pocket change. Now, how do you think that happened?"

"I get it."

But Denton shook his head again. "I'm not sure you do. This down here makes inside baseball look like a cakewalk. You can't come down here thinking the field's wide open. You gotta *know* this thing. You got to *live* it. I've been in this business all my life." He sat down again. "Now, I can't sit here and say every white farmer's the same. That'd be like me saying all us black folks was the same. I know some whites that are real decent people.

"One grinding, I had thirty-two rows left to cut when my combine went out on me. Mill was closing up the next day and all that cane would've been lost. Know who cut those rows for me? A white farmer. My neighbor, Wilson Lapine. But it's hard enough when you're born into this game. What you're trying to do?" Denton let his head drop and rubbed his temples. "Your cane's gotta be thirteen notches high come the end of August if you want to be ready for grinding, and from what you're telling me, I don't see how that's gonna happen."

Charley closed her eyes and struggled to hold herself steady. She breathed deeply, fighting back the tears that burned her eyes and the tightening in her throat. She exhaled, and a weight, as though someone had laid a sack of cement on her breast, settled across her chest. She thought of Miss Honey—*Can't fall apart like a ball of twine*—and opened her eyes. "Mr. Denton, I know this is a lot to ask. You've already been so generous." Charley touched her ring, pressed her fingertip against one of the prongs. If she sold it, she could pay Denton whatever he demanded—maybe not forever, but for as long as it took to learn what she needed to know. "I wonder if you'd work with me, for pay, of course. I could use your help."

She waited.

Denton rubbed his hands together thoughtfully. "I'm flattered Miss Honey sent you out here to talk to me, Miss Bordelon. Your grandmother's no fool. She knows her onions. And I hope some of what I've said makes sense."

"It does," Charley said. "All of it."

Denton stared through the kitchen window. "I turned seventy-one back in April. This is the first time in sixty years I haven't had to get up before dawn to go to work. I got a little garden out there I like to mess around in. And when I'm not doing that, I like to go fishing." He turned to look at Charley, the expression on his face more open than she'd seen, as if he were searching for something. "You like to fish, Miss Bordelon?"

"My dad liked to fish," Charley said. "On weekends sometimes, he'd go down the beach near his house and catch abalone. Or he'd take his fishing pole and climb out to a rock way out in the surf." She could still see him standing there, a lone figure perched on top of the huge boulder, the ocean churning and crashing all around him while she played in the sand. They'd have fried fish and corn for dinner. "But me? I never tried it."

"Well, you ought to," Denton said. "It's peaceful. Nothing but you, your thoughts, and that fish. Everything else falls away." He paused, his shoulders slumping a tiny bit. "You're a smart young woman, Miss Bordelon. I feel for you, I really do. But I'm retired." Someone had mounted an Audubon clock above the sink, with birds—an American goldfinch, a Carolina wren, a hermit thrush—positioned at each hour. For a few seconds they sat listening to the clock's gentle ticking, and when the second hand reached the quarter hour, the clock chimed happily with a different bird's song. "Maybe you oughta sit this one out," Denton said, raising his head to look at Charley as the idea seemed to come to him. "Get a feel for things and, in a year, see if it's still for you. Who knows? You might decide to sell."

"I'm afraid it's not that simple." Charley glanced down at her lap. She had a run in her nylons, right above the knee, and the dark skin of her thigh shone through like a gash where the white threads were pulling apart. She thought back to her conversation with the lawyer that day in his office. *I don't mean to sound ungrateful*, she'd said, knowing that ungrateful was exactly how she sounded, *but are you saying there's no money? Nothing? Just some farm in Louisiana? There was money at a local bank in Saint Josephine*, the lawyer explained, *but it was entirely for operating expenses. Other than that, no, there was no money.* Even now, after all these months, the truth was hard to accept. Her father had sold every piece of property he owned to buy what amounted to a vacant lot.

Sitting across the table from Prosper Denton in a kitchen that smelled faintly of homemade bread, coffee, and freshly picked tomatoes, Charley tried to make Denton appreciate her predicament. "I can't sell," she said. "My father put the land in trust, I don't know why, but if I run it, I get the profits after the bank is paid. If I walk away, the land goes to charity." Charley felt a space open inside her as she thought about her father's other favorite saying: "I give you what I want you to have"—which sometimes sounded intensely generous and sometimes rang with fierce control.

The lawyer, looking like an old owl behind his mahogany desk, had said, *Your father was a good man. He was trying to provide for you.* He put up a hand to stop Charley's protestation. *You've got a million dollars' worth of presumably good land down there. I suggest you bone up. Get in touch with this man.* He slid a folder across the desk. On the front was a sticky note with a name, Wayne Frasier, and a number. *He's sort of a caretaker,* the lawyer said. *Managed the property for the sellers and, from what I understand, he agreed to work for your father.* She had flipped through the documents and photographs. *Handle this right,* the lawyer said, standing up and showing her to the door, *and your great-great-grandkids will never have to worry.* His final words convinced her. Charley had thought of Micah and Micah's children. And even as she reeled at the news of her inheritance, loving and resenting her father all at the same time, she knew what she would do.

Charley looked at Mr. Denton. "So you see, sitting out isn't an option. And selling is out of the question."

"Give yourself a chance to think on it," Denton said. "You might feel different in a day or two."

Charley nodded vacantly. He might as well have patted her head, might as well have told her all she needed was a long soak in the tub or a good night's sleep and she'd come to her senses.

Denton reached to refill her glass, but Charley covered it with her hand. "No, thanks, I'm fine." She folded her paper towel over, then over again. "My father sold everything he had to buy that land."

"Lot of farmers wanted that place." Denton's face brightened with admiration. "Must have come in with a strong offer."

"A million, one twenty," Charley said. "He had nothing left."

Denton whistled. "That's fourteen hundred an acre."

"Yes, it is. And at the end of the year, the bank is going to want its first payment. So I can't afford to 'think on it,' as you say."

Denton looked at Charley. "I wish I could help you."

And so, Charley stood. The conversation was over. Denton had shut her down before she got started and she wasn't in the mood for more talk. She carried her glass to the sink and rinsed it before he could object, then grabbed her backpack. "Thanks for your time."

Denton looked startled, but he led her to the door. "I can only tell you what I know to be true, Miss Bordelon."

Beyond the screen door, the yard was bright, the clouds overlapping like leopard spots against the flat sky, and Charley braced herself for the heat. The dogs, stationed at their post, looked up expectantly as she pushed through the screen door, and followed her to the car as if it were their duty. She pulled out of the yard, the dogs chasing alongside her, the narrow country road unwinding like thread from a spool, the sugarcane seeming taller and even grander than when she arrived. Charley gripped the wheel and noticed how her diamond ring glowed as it reflected the sunlight. So many things she didn't know, so many obstacles she couldn't see, so many challenges she couldn't even *imagine*, and no one to guide her.

Even before Charley saw them, she knew, from the garlicky smell that hung in the living room, that Micah and Miss Honey were cooking.

"You got up and out early this morning," Miss Honey said as Charley tossed her backpack on the table.

"Mom," Micah said. "Miss Honey's teaching me how to make Dirty Rice."

"I went to see Prosper Denton," Charley said.

Miss Honey's eyes narrowed, but then she turned her attention back to the cutting board with the chopped onions piled like a mound of confetti. "He knew you were coming?"

"He thinks I should sit out for a year. Either that or sell. Which I can't."

"Hmm." Miss Honey tapped Micah. "Baby, hand me that spoon."

In the vacant lot next door, some of Miss Honey's dresses and two of Micah's shirts hung stiffly from the clothesline. "Don't take this wrong," Charley said, "but how, exactly, did you think Denton could help me?"

Miss Honey's lips pursed. She kept her eyes on the cutting board, continued to chop, but said, "Last month, folks over in Pointe Olivier needed their water tower taken down. Whole thing was rusted out and waiting to fall. Problem was, they couldn't find anyone for the job. Power lines all around it, and every engineer they called swore they couldn't say for sure where it was gonna land. Everybody screaming it couldn't be done."

Charley went to the refrigerator, took out a Coke, wishing it were a beer, and twisted off the cap.

"So a couple men from the city called Mr. Denton," Miss Honey continued. "That same day he drove out to take a look. Walked around that tower a couple times, sketched out his plan on a napkin, then looked those men from the city right in the eye and said, 'I can do it.' Showed them exactly where that tower would fall. He sent those boys up there to make the cuts, attached the cables, got in the tractor, and before anyone could say Jackie Robinson, that tower came down, just like he said. Didn't kiss even *one* of those power lines."

Miss Honey called Micah over to the stove where ground beef sizzled in the iron skillet. She handed her a wooden spoon with burn marks along the handle, and told her to adjust the flame—not too high or the meat would burn; not too low or it would get soggy. "The secret to good cooking is knowing how to follow the recipe till you feel comfortable," she said. She covered the skillet with a plate, muting the sizzling. "Once you understand how the ingredients work together, *then* you can go off on your own. Till then, you're just wasting good food and everybody's time."

4

❧ Fred's Hometown Discount in Lafayette had everything you needed to make your house a home. Charley and Micah were on their way to buy sheets and an air mattress, and had just pulled away from Miss Honey's when Micah asked, "Is Miss Honey poor?"

Charley looked at Micah. Poor was bricks of government cheese in the freezer, she thought; poor was celebrities holding hands in the music video and singing "We Are the World" for starving children in Africa. She could spend a lifetime at Miss Honey's and not think the word *poor*, and yet she understood why Micah asked. Saint Josephine was not Los Angeles. Why, just yesterday on her way to the farm, she spotted, way back in the woods, a rusted Airstream trailer marooned in a murky puddle. Graffiti was spray-painted in crooked blue letters across its front, and a tattered American flag, instead of curtains, hung in the window. Even Miss Honey's house, which stretched from the broken sidewalk in front all the way to the woods out back, was nothing more than one hundred and twenty feet of raggedy tacked-on rooms, one after another like a line of boxcars.

"Miss Honey doesn't have a lot of money, that's true," Charley said, "but no one's ever gone hungry in her house." Poor but not hungry. That was the phrase her father used whenever he described his childhood. Charley always took it to mean there was so much more to life than just money. There were family and friends, there was good, satisfying work, and knowing you had a place on this earth where you were loved and there was nothing to prove. Charley looked both ways at the end of the block even though no cars were coming. "What do *you* think?"

Micah held up the Polaroid. She surveyed the street through the viewfinder. "Everything in this town is broken," she said. "Why is everyone black? Why do they stare every time we drive down the street?"

Charley laughed. "You'll get used to it." She thought back on their lives in LA with its wild mix of people: blacks, whites, Latinos and Asians, East Indians and Middle Easterners, no one staring at anybody.

At the edge of town, as Main Street fed into the two-lane and they picked up a little speed, Micah lowered her camera. She pressed her back against the passenger door and stared at Charley. "Are we poor because we live here now?"

"The Quarters"—the side of town where Miss Honey and most of the other black residents lived, a neighborhood that was *literally* over the railroad tracks—couldn't have been farther from what Micah had known. The streets were sloppily paved, the sidewalks cracked. On the narrow houses, paint curled away from sun-bleached clapboard. Battered couches and rusty lawn chairs seemed to clutter every porch.

Charley shivered despite the sun shining through her window. Were they poor? She had two hundred and thirteen dollars after paying for the trip to Saint Josephine. Davis was so young when he died—just thirty-two—he barely had life insurance. She had a master's in art history, which she'd still be paying for after Micah finished college, and nothing set aside for retirement. And though she didn't want to admit it, she couldn't have afforded to rent a house down here if she'd wanted to, had prayed Miss Honey would offer them a place to stay. And now, if she couldn't find a manager, if she couldn't whip her fields into shape and harvest a decent crop, she'd have squandered her father's investment. Charley took a breath, twisted her wedding ring. "Not poor. Not exactly." *Not yet*, she thought.

Ahead of her, Spanish moss hung in curtains from the live oaks, softening the light that fell through the branches and lent the road a hazy glow.

Micah opened the glove box, took out the map, and fanned herself. Seconds later, she kicked off the fleece-lined, shin-high suede boots she insisted on wearing despite Charley's warning that it wasn't boots weather, and propped her bare feet on the dash. She groaned. "It's *so hot.*"

"I tried to tell you."

Micah looked at her sideways, then reached to fiddle with the air conditioner.

Charley was just about to remind her that it was broken, tell her to leave it alone, when Micah's sleeve rode up her arm, revealing her scar. An impulse shot through Charley and she brushed her hand over it.

"Stop it," Micah said, pulling away. "I hate when you do that."

Charley withdrew her hand, placed it back on the wheel. "Sorry," she said, lamely, unable to reprimand Micah for her sharp speech. She could rationalize part of it: hormones. All the eye rolling, the crossed arms, and the sulking, even that clicking sound Micah made with her tongue to convey impatience or general disgust, it was part of growing up—that's what the parenting books said, anyway. And she had flickering memories of herself at Micah's age; remembered how sometimes the mere sound of her mother's voice made the hair on her arms prickle, it was that grating; or how, downstairs in the garage after school one day, she burst into tears for no reason she could think of. Just burst into tears, shoulders shaking and nose running, as she stood there beside shelves of laundry detergent and paper plates and her mother's old tennis rackets. So why get on Micah's case when she knew it was just a phase?

But then there was the other part; the part that had nothing to do with hormones and everything to do with her guilt. And for the next few minutes, as she drove, Charley cursed for not catching herself before she touched Micah's scar, for not thinking the moment through. Micah's accusatory tone, her rejection, stung, for sure, but it could never match her own lacerating self-loathing, her own sickening shame.

Charley reached for the map. "We're here," she said, unfolding it and spreading it in the space between them, "and we're trying to get there. You can be our guide."

Micah drew the map closer, traced the road with her finger. She was quiet for a while, then said, "I want to go home."

"Not again." Charley was pleading. They had had this conversation—
if you could call it a conversation with all the tears and pouting—a hundred times in the last ten months, like actors in a play.

Micah folded the map's corner. Vinton, Sulpher, and Lake Charles
disappeared into crisp accordion pleats. "I want to live with Lorna."

Lorna was Charley's mother, Micah's grandmother, back in Los Angeles. She took Micah shopping, to the children's symphony, and to tea
at the Ritz Carlton on her birthday. Last summer she took Micah to
Martinique and promised they would fly to Paris when Micah turned
fifteen. Lorna's house, a stately property with a towering wrought-iron
gate out front, a gurgling cherub fountain, and olive trees lining the
courtyard, was filled with framed pictures of the two of them. Charley
was happy the two were close, was happy Lorna could provide for Micah in a way she simply couldn't on her nonprofit salary; and yet, lately,
Charley felt a stab of jealousy whenever Micah mentioned Lorna's
name.

"I still don't understand why I have to—" Micah began.

"My God," Charley cut her off. "What can I tell you? That ship has
sailed. I'm not discussing it." She brushed Micah's hand from the
wrecked map as Welsh, Jennings, and Crowley vanished into its
creases. "I'm going to need that if you don't mind."

"Fine." Micah shoved the map off her lap. It crumpled in the well beneath her feet.

Beyond the window, the landscape rushed by. How could there be so
many shades of green? Cane fields the bright green of a new pippin apple, while the grass was almost jade, the woods the deep green of raw
spinach, and the reflection of the sunlit trees along the bayou a vibrant
chartreuse.

"You know, I'm not trying to torture you," Charley said, and studied
her hands, which had swollen in the heat. With difficulty, she twisted
her wedding ring off her finger and dropped it into the empty ashtray.
"Just think, Micah, how great it'll feel to walk across fields we own."

"I don't want to walk across fields. I want to live in a city, with side-walks and a swimming pool."

"We never had a pool."

"Stop joking. It's not funny." The wind tossed the flyaway strands of Micah's braids. She brushed them out of her face and said, "You promised there'd be kids."

"I know," Charley said. "Don't worry, we'll find them." She forced brightness into her voice. "It's south Louisiana. It's *Catholic*, for God's sake. Trust me, we'll find kids."

"What if they don't like me?"

"Of course they'll like you. You're smart and funny, and besides, you're from California. People always want to know kids from California."

"Sure. *Malibu*, California." Micah picked at the flaking upholstery. "*Beverly Hills*, California." She rubbed her arm absentmindedly, and then, in a voice so quiet Charley could barely hear her, said, "Kids can be mean."

The dark feeling lapped inside Charley and she steeled herself against it. Of course, Micah was right. Kids could be mean. But what choice did she have? She had come down here. Her father had left this door open and it was the only open door in her life.

Charley turned on the radio. The bandleader sang in a Cajun twang, and feeling her spirits rising, she tapped her hand lightly against the dashboard. The bass and drums, the button accordion's high whine, the rolling emerald fields and the sapphire sky. "Just wait, Micah. You'll see what I mean. It'll all be good when the farm's up and running." As she spoke, Charley's heart quickened. One song ended and another began. She stuck her head through the window and shouted, surprising even herself. "'Oh, summer has clothed the earth in a cloak from the loom of the sun!'"

"Oh my God, Mom. Shut up!" Micah sank low in her seat.

"Relax," Charley said, "it's a beautiful poem." She stuck her head through the window and yelled again. "'And a mantle, too, of the skies' soft blue, And a belt where the rivers run.'"

"Please, Mom! I'm not kidding. You're embarrassing me." Micah sank even lower and rode like that for a few minutes. Then, seeing Charley's ring in the ashtray, she fished it out and held it up to the light, then slipped it onto her index finger. "Why do you wear this?"

"It reminds me of Daddy," Charley said, though in truth, after four years, she struggled to remember Davis's face. She recalled more easily the smell of his shirts, like coffee and ink, the easy sound of his laugh, and the feeling of being with him in the kitchen as he cooked on Sundays—the Grateful Dead blasting from the portable speakers, the counters overrun with spices, the recipe for some curry dish he found in a magazine splattered with oil. She rubbed her heat-swollen index finger, indented where the wedding ring had pressed into it.

Micah slid the ring off her finger and jiggled it in her cupped hands. Charley started to grab it, but stopped herself. She silently counted to twenty.

"Okay, time's up." She reached over. "Let me have it back."

But Micah twisted away. "I just want to hold it."

"No. Give it back."

"*Tu me fais chier,*" Micah said under her breath, and pressed her closed fist to her chest.

"I didn't send you to that school to learn how to swear," Charley said, and wondered, not for the first time, how she ever let Davis talk her into enrolling Micah at the Lycée.

"It was nothing," Micah said, then, under her breath, *"Merde."*

Charley slapped the wheel. "Don't *merde* me."

"I want to go back," Micah said, then added with more certainty, "Lorna will send me a plane ticket."

Charley let the threat pass.

"You're just jealous," Micah said.

"That's ridiculous. Jealous of what?"

"You're a fish."

Charley would have laughed had Micah not been glaring so fiercely.

"Lorna and I are sharks," Micah spat. "Sharks are better. We rub our tongues along our teeth. Sharks *eat* fish."

Charley didn't take her eyes off the road. "And here I thought Lorna was teaching you which fork to use with your salad. I never guessed she was teaching you which fork was for stabbing me in the heart."

Micah covered her face with her hands. "I want to go home."

"This is your home. *I'm* your home."

Micah whispered something in French and shifted in her seat. She extended her right arm through the window as if to sift the breeze through her fingers, and Charley, alarmed, saw the diamond ring in Micah's palm as it reflected an instant of sunlight. She cried out exactly as Micah drew back her fist and threw. Charley caught a glimpse of the ring as it flipped in the wind and tumbled past the window. The Volvo careered off the road, onto the band of dirt edging the fields, a cloud of red dust swirling behind them. By the time Charley slammed on the brakes, they were hundred of yards farther along. Silence flooded the car.

"What the hell!" Charley cried. "What were you *thinking*?" But when she turned to Micah, her daughter met her gaze with an unapologetic glare. Charley kicked open the door. She stepped out into the moist air and ran back to where she believed the ring had landed. She waded into the cane, then dropped to her hands and knees, searching for her ring among the whispering rows. If she took her time and looked closely, Charley thought, channeled all her energy into her fingertips, she could find it. Down so far beneath the cane, the light took on an aqueous hue. Clumps of warm earth slipped through her fingers. Bits of soil lodged beneath her nails. She was so close to the ground she could taste it in the back of her throat; so far below the cane, the silence was amplified. But minutes passed and she couldn't find the ring.

"Mom!" Micah called from the road's shoulder. "I can't see you." She sounded scared.

Charley imagined Micah scanning fields that must've seemed to have swallowed her mother. "Go back to the car!" she yelled.

"But I'm scared." Micah's voice frayed. "I don't like it here."

Charley crawled deeper into the field.

"Please!" Micah begged.

"Get back in the car!" Charley was being cruel, she knew, and withholding. If Davis were there, he'd have told her as much. It was only a ring, he'd say. They could buy another some day, and even if they couldn't, it wasn't worth punishing their child. She was being like her mother, he'd say, attentive when she approved, cold as a stone when she didn't, and he'd challenge her to remember how it had felt to live with that kind of uncertainty. But Davis was gone. She was alone, and right now, cruelty felt deeply satisfying. Better than a back massage. Better than sex. The cane swayed above her and the sound of the rustling leaves was strangely soothing. Charley sat between the rows and buried her face in her hands. When the tears came, they flowed easily and she didn't try to stop them. Because it wasn't just the ring, or her dad, or Frasier; it wasn't Davis, or Denton, or even Micah. It was everything.

At last, Charley dried her face and waded back through the cane. She was shocked to see how far she was from the car. The road, in both directions, was empty. An image of the two white boys in the pickup flashed in her mind.

"Micah!" She ran to the car and was relieved to find Micah hiding in the small space behind the passenger seat, her head down and her arms raised above her head as if practicing for an earthquake drill. Charley opened the door and slid in behind the wheel. "Come on," she said. Her voice was still hoarse from crying. "Let's go."

"Did you find it?"

"No."

Micah stayed tucked.

"Come on," Charley said, and rested her hand lightly on Micah's back.

For a while they drove in silence. Gathering clouds cast shadows over the cane, and Micah, back in the passenger seat, sat with her head against the door, her eyes closed although Charley knew she wasn't sleeping.

"Mom?" Micah said, finally. She rubbed her own index finger. "I'm sorry."

Later that evening, Charley surveyed the bedroom, which wasn't much bigger than a pantry and felt even smaller with the double bed, their suitcases, and everything else they brought with them stuffed in Hefty bags dumped in the middle of the floor.

Micah flipped the switch, the motor kicked in, and the new air mattress they purchased from Fred's crackled to life and inflated in slow motion. When it was full, Micah said, "I'm going to find Miss Honey," and stepped across the mattress, bouncing like the first girl on the moon.

"Not too long," Charley said. "It's getting late."

Just over the threshold, Micah turned. "Mom, I'm really sorry about your ring."

"Me too."

"And Mom?"

"What?"

"You're not a fish."

In a moment, the screen door slammed, then slammed again. Charley pulled the curtain and saw the two of them on the swing—Miss Honey in her housedress and slippers, and Micah, snug beside her. In a few minutes, Micah's hair was loose and Miss Honey was brushing it—long strokes and quick gathering. There was a rhythm to it, and watching, Charley remembered the feel of Miss Honey's hands in her own hair all those years ago, the smell of Miss Honey's talcum powder, Cashmere Bouquet, which smelled of wood, and roses and maraschino cherries. She knew exactly how Micah felt. Charley watched awhile longer, then let the curtain fall. She wished she'd caught Micah by the elbow and pulled her close before she left the room. Wished she'd been able to say, *I'm sorry. I won't fail you twice.*

Charley's workshop—two thousand square feet of corrugated steel— sat on a patch of cleared ground just off the road that separated her north and south fields. An old John Deere tractor with a blown-out windshield and weeds twisting though the fender hulked out front. Rust-pocked chemical drums and stacks of cracked tires littered the side yard. The place had a postapocalyptic feel. It was a miracle the shop hadn't been bulldozed and hauled to the scrap yard. Inside, under brittle fluorescent lights, it was cool, a nice break from the heat, but the air reeked of diesel fuel with bitter undertones of dried grass and the slightly acrid scent of rat droppings.

In the tiny office, Charley sat at a desk piled high with farm bulletins and equipment manuals. She sorted through folders brimming with crumpled receipts and unpaid invoices. How Frasier managed to hold this ship together as long as he did was a mystery, Charley thought, and she guessed his departure was a small blessing. But she didn't know what half the bills were for, and even if she could identify the purchases, she couldn't find them in the shop.

"What the hell's Paraquat?" Charley said out loud. She balled the receipt and tossed it to the floor.

Around eleven o'clock, a sleek sedan with tinted windows and gleaming tires cruised up and parked. Charley heard the *ping, ping, ping* as the driver's door opened, and she was just stepping out of the office as a smooth-looking white man in crisp pale clothing rapped on the shop's metal door.

"Good morning," Charley said. "Can I help you?"

"Welcome to Saint Josephine, Miss Bordelon." He flashed a country- club smile and offered his hand, which sported a gold chunk of a class ring, then pulled a business card from his breast pocket. "I'm Jacques Landry."

"'Saint Mary's Sugar Cooperative,'" Charley read. She had driven past Saint Mary's sugar mill on her way to her farm and seen the original brick smokestacks draped with kudzu and the new, gleaming sugar warehouse. But other than noting that the air around Saint Mary's always smelled like malt balls, Charley hadn't paid much attention. She invited him in.

"So, you're the lucky owner of LeJeune's plantation," Landry said. "Congratulations. That's some fine land you've got out there." Landry was handsome the way a Chris-Craft motorboat was handsome—all good lines and varnished teak.

"Thank you," Charley said. "It's very—exciting."

"You're the name on everyone's lips," Landry said. He looked around the shop with bright-eyed interest, as if paintings, not tools, hung on the pegboard. "Miss Honey's granddaughter, all the way from Los Angeles to rescue LeJeune's plantation from ruin."

Landry was charming. The longer they talked, the more Charley felt like she was at a cocktail party. He laughed, asked her where she'd gone to college, what she'd majored in, when she'd married Davis, and what her mother did for a living. Slowly, it occurred to Charley that he was asking all the questions, and that she, tired of feeling desperate and alone on a sinking ship, was happy to answer him.

"So, how *are* things going for you, Miss Bordelon?" Landry sat on an arm of the beat-up couch and picked up an invoice, which Charley suddenly wanted to snatch back. "You doing all right? Have everything you need?"

No, she wanted to say. She had nothing. Please help. But she had already said too much: mentioned her student loans, her daughter's name and age. Landry was grilling her, wasn't he? And she had missed all the cues. "Why do you ask?"

"It's pretty quiet around here," Landry said, shrugging. "Sort of unusual this time of year. Most farmers are out cultivating their fields but it looks like you're barely finished laying-by." He sat with one foot crossed over the opposite knee, like a CEO in a boardroom, and now he wiggled his foot casually. "I noticed you've got some water hung up out near the back quadrant. Should probably get that pumped out soon. But listen to me, making suggestions. You probably know that already."

"You've been out in my fields?" Charley said.

"Took a little drive."

"Yes, well. I've had a few setbacks."

Landry picked up another invoice and scanned it. "Wayne Frasier. Yeah, I heard about that. Tough break."

"But I'll be fine," Charley said. "I've got some good leads."

Landry looked skeptical, but said, "I'm glad to hear it. Good people are hard to find, as I'm sure you know." He put the invoice down and stood.

"Is there something I can do for you?"

"No. I was just passing by. Saw your car out front, thought I'd stop in, see how you were doing." He scanned the shop once more, then turned to Charley with a broad grin. "I remember when old man LeJeune was still alive. Talk about a man who was suited to this business. Folks used to say he had cane syrup in his veins. I tell you, he poured his heart into this operation. Shame his kids didn't take better care of it."

"You're right," Charley said. She walked toward the metal door and slid it open.

"He had this car," Landry said, like a stand-up comedian about to deliver the punch line. "Great big Lincoln Continental. Had his man wash and wax it every Saturday. But would you believe he hardly drove it? Afternoons, rain or shine, right up till he got sick, he rode out to his fields on the back of a fifteen-hand Tennessee Walker." Landry sighed, almost dreamily. "I guess some people prefer the old ways."

His man, Charley thought.

"Thanks for stopping by," Charley said in what she hoped was a dry tone, and slid the metal door wider.

"Good luck, Miss Bordelon. You'll need it." Landry was almost over the threshold when he turned back. "One more thing. You ever think of selling this place?"

"It hadn't crossed my mind."

"Well, if it does, give me a call."

"And why would I want to sell?"

"Who knows?" Landry pointed to the card she held. "I'm just throwing it out there. You seem like a sensible young woman. It'd be a shame to see you get in over your head."

NeNee Desonier's trailer could have been the subject of a Dorothea Lange photograph, with its yellowing newsprint and strips of faded floral wallpaper clinging to the walls. In the places where there was neither newsprint nor wallpaper, gigantic watermarks, like seismographic readouts, stained bare plaster, which, over the years, Charley guessed, had turned from chalky white to burnt sienna. And NeNee herself should have been captured in a gelatin print. Her small dark face, etched with wrinkles, had a sinkhole in the middle where her top four teeth were missing. She was no taller than Micah, Charley thought, and probably ten pounds lighter. A bright green stocking cap swaddled her small head, and her faded housedress was so threadbare, it was a wonder it didn't disintegrate as she stood there.

But Charley was on a mission. The more she thought about Landry's intrusive questions, the way he seemed to prophesy her failure, the angrier she got. So when she found NeNee Desonier's name and address on an old pay stub in the files, she acted without thinking; got in her car and drove all the way out to Four Corners, the sleepy hamlet on the outskirts of the parish.

Now here she was, in NeNee's living room. "As I was saying." Charley smiled. NeNee did not. "I found your name on this piece of paper." She held out the pay stub.

NeNee glanced at it and nodded politely.

"How long did you work for Mr. LeJeune?"

NeNee held up four fingers, which meant either "four years *ago*" or "*for* four years," Charley couldn't tell.

"What kind of work did you do?" Charley asked.

NeNee offered another polite smile, but she looked increasingly nervous. Every few minutes she stole a glance at the front door.

Charley knew she should go. But she had driven all this way, was holding tight, like a child on a carousel, to the fantasy that NeNee Desonier was a seasoned manager like Denton, or a young, ambitious field hand on the lookout for an opportunity to run the show. At this point, she would have hired a middle schooler if he or she had worked cane before.

"*Ma petite-fille,*" NeNee said.

"What's that?"

NeNee pointed to the yard. The next second, a woman in her mid-forties, dressed in pink medical scrubs and sneakers, pushed through the front door. She saw Charley and stopped short. "Who are you?"

Charley introduced herself, offered her hand, but the woman regarded it suspiciously, then turned to NeNee and said something in what sounded like French, but wasn't quite. And suddenly, NeNee came to life. She chattered on, gesturing and occasionally pointing to Charley. The younger woman nodded, frowned, then glared at Charley over her shoulder. Finally, she turned.

"What do you want with my grandmother?"

"I thought—"

"Thought what?"

"I just thought, maybe she'd like to work for me." Charley started to explain about her farm, thought of explaining about Denton's refusal, but said only, "I own some acreage off the Old Spanish Trail—" when the woman cut her off.

"My grandmother is seventy-seven years old."

NeNee hobbled over to the rocker and sat down. She looked from Charley to her granddaughter, who, Charley realized, still hadn't said her name.

"I can see your grandmother is quite frail," Charley said. "I didn
alize until I got here. I was in the office, I mean, the shop, sorti
through stacks of papers and I found this." She held out the pay stub.

The woman glanced at the stub, then appraised Charley with a steely
gaze. "You ain't from around here."

"I'm from California."

"California," the woman said, as though California were a hostile
nation.

"But I live here now, with *my* grandmother. Not too far, as a matter of
fact."

"Excuse me, but have you ever worked cane?"

"No." Charley sighed. "I haven't."

The woman drew herself up. "Well, I have. And let me tell you, cane
work is the hardest, dirtiest, most backbreakin', thankless, low-paying
work there is. My family's worked cane for six generations, and after all
that, we ain't got nothin' to show for it. Just look at my grandmama's
house." She made a sweeping gesture. "She worked cane since she was
nine years old, and *this* is all she's got. Has she got any money saved?
Has she got a pension? Health care? Does she own anything but this
trailer and the little speck of sorry-ass ground it sits on?" Drops of sweat
spangled her hairline. "Those big cane farmers cut corners with her every chance they got."

Charley wanted to say that she was different, that she would offer
medical benefits, a retirement plan, even a small life insurance policy.
She wanted to look straight at the woman and ask, *How about you—
can I hire you?* But she had the overwhelming sense that she'd be digging a hole for herself.

"If it wasn't for social security," the woman fumed, "and the little bit
us grandkids scrape together each month, my grandmother would be
out on the road." The more she spoke, the thicker her accent grew. "And
here you come, pecking around like a spring chicken. Talking like
someone on the TV. Asking if she'll *work* for you?"

"I should go."

zile

...d be even worse to work for than a white man."

...y grabbed her backpack and stuffed the pay stub in the front ..., let herself out, and hurried down the steps. At the bottom, she ...ed. All she wanted was to find workers and get down to business. ...ques Landry was one thing—she should have expected that. But her own people? Who did they think she was? She looked back at the woman barring the doorway. "Sorry if I offended you or your grand-mother."

"I bet." And with that, the woman slammed the door.

5

❧ Four hundred miles to go. They were almost home. East of San Antonio, Ralph Angel saw a sign for Corpus Christi and got an idea. He merged off the interstate onto Highway 37. In the passenger seat, Blue continued his low, rumbling dialogue with Zach the Power Ranger, who was still imprisoned in the glove box. "'Cause we might get arrested," Ralph Angel heard him say. "So you have to stay inside and be very, very quiet."

Blue looked up and asked, "Are we there yet?"

"What did I say about that? Just wait. I have a surprise."

Eventually, the woods yielded to marshland, the two-lane road cutting a straight line through an expanse of gray water peppered with reeds and tufts of low, wiry grass. Egrets, white as porcelain, took flight from their rookeries, while in the distance a house balanced on stilts, lording over its watery homestead, and seeing all this, Ralph Angel felt something within him begin to shift. Like a page being turned.

Farther south, the road ended abruptly at the Intracoastal Waterway, the narrow channel stretching from the mouth of the Mississippi to the Rio Grande. A short wood dock jutted out into the water. Ralph Angel could see where the road picked up on the other side—not even sixty feet; they could almost swim across.

"What now?" Blue said.

"We wait."

It wasn't long before a ferry cruised up the channel. Cracked black buoys dangled from its rusted bow, paint curled away from the wheelhouse, but otherwise, nothing had changed; it was the same ferry as when he was a kid, and Ralph Angel, suddenly breathless with an old excitement, thought back to the day his daddy brought him to this very spot. A summer trip to the beach, just the two of them; a vacation he waited months to take, his father having called from California that September to say they would go someplace special when school got out. Ralph Angel had marked the days off the calendar, slogged through the long months until June finally arrived and his father, dashing in slacks and loafers, knocked on the front door. And while his father steered the Buick LeSabre with one hand, the other arm propped in the open window, he sang along to the cassette tape—Al Green's version of "People Get Ready"—as they cruised over the blacktop road. Ralph Angel bathed in the radiance of his dad's presence, so happy he thought he would burst.

And now, belching smoke, the same ferry rumbled up to the dock and idled. Ralph Angel smelled creosote and diesel fuel.

Blue grinned. "Can we ride on that boat?"

"You, me, and Zach."

Ralph Angel paid the one-dollar fare and steered the Impala onto the dock, then onto the ferry. For the few minutes it took to cross the channel, he and Blue stood on the creaky deck, Ralph Angel holding Blue's waist as he leaned over the side and spat in the water.

"It's a good boat, Pop," Blue said. He held Zach over the side, making sound effects as he pretended Zach could fly.

"Okay, that's enough," Ralph Angel said, but really, he didn't mind at all.

More miles of black road. A lone oil well seesawing. Then the marsh ended in a wavering wall of sea oats, and beyond it, a flat stretch of bone-colored sand, a sky the color of bleached driftwood washing out the horizon.

"Is this the surprise?"

Ralph Angel nodded as he killed the engine. "I came here with my daddy when I was a little boy," he said, and watched a seabird, squat as a crab apple, its beak thin as a sewing needle, skitter across the sand. How odd it felt to be back here after so many years, almost a lifetime, and yet here he was. He had a vague sense of his boyhood self separating from him now, standing beside him like a specter, so that he saw the landscape through two sets of eyes; felt the pull of old memories as if someone were tugging on his sleeve. He put a hand on Blue's shoulder. "You can get your feet wet if you want," which was exactly what his father had said to him.

A briny wind sprayed sand as Ralph Angel, kneeling, rolled Blue's pants up his spindly calves. "Not too far." He sat on the Impala's warm hood as Blue romped and galloped out to the pale brown surf, leaving a trail of flat-footed prints in the sand. The limp tide. A fringe of broken shells, froth, and plastic bottles left by the receding waves.

What he remembered most clearly was that they stayed at the beach all afternoon, that his father had set out a picnic with all his favorite things—salami between fluffy white slices of Evangeline Maid bread, Zapps potato chips, a can of Barq's root beer for each of them, a package of Big 60 cookies with lemon crème filling bought special from Winn-Dixie—and that the wind worried the blanket so much they finally took off their shoes and used them to anchor the corners. While they ate, his father told him about California: how in a single day you could drive from the beach where the sand was as fine as cornmeal out to the desert where cacti and bright orange poppies with petals thin as tissue paper blanketed the ground; how, at the lighthouse just south of the airport, you could watch whales spout plumes of spray as they migrated through the channel, their enormous backs glistening like sea monsters as they rolled through the swells; and how, on a clear September weekend, you could drive down to the pier and order a whole boiled crab, then sit with a brown bag on your lap, pick meat from the crab's body, and toss empty claws to the hovering gulls.

"When can I come live with you?" Ralph Angel had asked, flooded with longing. In those days, he lived with his mother, Emily, the girl his father had dated in high school, in a shabby little house in the back of town. But even then, at eight years old, while he didn't have a name for it, Ralph Angel could see that his mother was fragile; sensed that something within her was always on the verge of breaking loose, like a handle from a teacup. It was never a question of intelligence. She'd been class valedictorian with a full scholarship to LSU and plans to go on to law school until her pregnancy made that impossible; had taught herself German, and read every Louisiana history book shelved at the local public library. But she never seemed able to keep a job. "The office manager doesn't understand me," she'd say when she was fired from another law office where she worked as a paralegal, or later, "The staff has it in for me," after she cycled through every law firm from Saint Josephine to Baton Rouge, and worked as a file clerk.

"When you're older," his father had said.

"How much older?" The difference between months and years was still abstract and strange, but he had the sense that time was running out.

"We'll see," his father said. "Maybe next year. Right now I work all the time. I can't take care of you. I know your mama's a little different, but you're still better off down here." His father rolled over then, to nap in the sun, his legs crossed at the ankles, his flat feet dusted with sand.

But the next year, his father married a woman named Lorna, an ophthalmologist with her own practice, and a year after that, they had a baby girl named Charlotte, whom everyone called Charley for short, and who, merely by the fact of her presence, put an end to his father's visits, so that by the time Ernest finally sent for him, three years had passed. Meanwhile, Ralph Angel's mother, convinced the world was against her, stopped looking for work, grew paranoid (*They don't like me in that Winn-Dixie. They always make me wait. I'm not shopping there anymore.*) and reclusive. She drank.

The stick Blue found was as tall as he was. He dragged it over the sand, all the way back to the Impala. "Look. I can draw my name," he said, and gouged large letters at Ralph Angel's feet.

"It's time to go," Ralph Angel said, his thoughts turning to his trip to California. "Come on. Dry off."

"Can I bring it with me?"

"What do you need a stick for? You're going to poke your eye out."

But he'd had a hundred sticks just like it when he was a kid. Sticks and antique marbles, buttons and civil war bullets he found when they plowed up the cane fields. He'd come home with pockets bulging, and Miss Honey gave him old Kerns jars for his collections. "On second thought, why not. Just be careful with it. Let's go."

"I need to do one more thing."

"Okay, but hurry up."

Funny how much he still remembered: the airline ticket arriving in the mail with his father's handwritten instructions telling him what to do when he got to the New Orleans airport—how to check his suitcase at the counter, how to find his gate on the big TV screen, how the meal served on the plane would come on a small oval plate covered with foil, and he could pick what he wanted, chicken or beef. And if he behaved himself, the stewardess might pin a set of wings, just like the pilot wore, to his shirt.

"I've never been to California," his mother, Emily, had admitted, tearfully, as the attendant announced his flight was boarding. "I've never even been on an airplane." She'd pulled herself together long enough to see him off. "You be good out there. Mind your manners." Then she stood up, reached to hug him. And maybe it was because they were at the airport, where people were rushing to catch their flights, but for the first time, he saw how slowly she moved, how she had to concentrate on every step, how she seemed pained to raise her arms.

Excited as he was to be leaving he said, "I don't have to go. I could stay here with you." She was the best mother she could be.

Emily's lips trembled. "Boy," she said, finally, "stop talking nonsense and get on that plane." Her hands shook as she handed him his ticket.

Los Angeles was just like his father described—the bright blue sky, more cars than he'd ever seen—and he'd pressed his face to the window while his father drove to his new house, where Lorna and baby Charley waited. For the first month, things were easy as pie. He had his own room with a brand-new bed, new clothes, and a shiny new bike.

But being with his father in California was different from their time together in Saint Josephine. Jealousy sprouted quick as rye grass as Ralph Angel watched his father lavish attention on his new family, especially on baby Charley, just two and learning to talk. Charley, Charley, Charley. All anyone ever talked about was Charley. His plays for attention, minor offenses at first—his father's wallet swiped from the nightstand and tucked between the couch cushions, Charley's pacifier stuffed in the garbage disposal—became more serious: outbursts in class, schoolyard brawls, arguments with Lorna, until finally, claiming he was only trying to feed her, he filled a baby food jar with water and forced Charley to drink. The water flooded her mouth, bubbled from her little nose, and for a few terrifying seconds, even he was convinced she was drowning. "That's it," Lorna declared, and his father had no choice but to send him home. Back to the shabby house. Back to a mother whose condition had worsened.

Blue dropped to his knees, rolled in the sand, lay on his back and moved his arms and legs up and down like he was doing jumping jacks.

"What are you doing?" Ralph Angel said.

"Making an angel."

"This isn't snow."

"That's okay."

"Well, get up. You've got sand in your hair."

Blue stood and Ralph Angel brushed him off. Sand on Blue's neck. Sand down his shirt and in the waistband of his briefs. Sand in the folds of his pant legs.

Back on the road now, the stick poking through the back window, Ralph Angel said, "Stop scratching."

"But my hair itches."

"That's what I tried to tell you. We'll wash it when we get there."

"But it itches bad."

The sign outside the roadside café read LOST DOG: BLIND IN ONE EYE, MISSING RIGHT EAR. TAIL BROKEN. RECENTLY CASTRATED. ANSWERS TO THE NAME "LUCKY."

Ralph Angel laughed, thought: *I know the feeling.*

"What's so funny?"

"Nothing."

In the bathroom, Ralph Angel turned on the faucet, lay Blue faceup on the counter so his head hung over the sink. He pressed the dispenser till a half-dollar-size dollop of soap filled his palm.

"Close your eyes." A halo of lather surrounded Blue's face, his hair like the burrs caught on one's pant hem. Ralph Angel scrubbed till he felt the sand loosen.

"Ouch," Blue said. "That hurts."

Ralph Angel wiped soap away from Blue's eyes, out of his ears, then cupped his hand under the faucet so the warm water ran over Blue's scalp. "How's that?"

Blue smiled. "Better."

He dried Blue's hair with a paper towel, then looked into his son's face again, feeling the weight of Blue's head in his hand as the boy relaxed.

"I like being on this trip with you, Pop," Blue said. He yawned.

How *would* his life have been different if his father hadn't sent him back? If Charley had never been born? He couldn't say. How much of his mother was in him? He'd never know. But he could do everything he could think of for his boy. He could do that. "Thanks, buddy," Ralph Angel said, and sat Blue up on the counter. He wiped a drop of water that snaked down the boy's neck. "I do too. I like that it's just you and me."

6

It had been a week since Denton said no, and Charley still hadn't found a manager. She spent days scouring barbershops and roadside bars, oily garages and smoky pool halls—the places men gathered after work or on weekends to tell jokes, talk about their trouble on the job or with their wives; the places they went to feel like men, and where, if a desperate young woman who was trying to make her father proud happened to wander in, they wouldn't mind coming to her assistance. But no luck.

Now, exhausted and even more discouraged, Charley rolled over the railroad tracks into the Quarters. On the corner, a group of young men stood on the sidewalk: XXL plaid shirts and baggy jeans like gangsta rappers, hair braided in zigzag cornrows that made their hair look like puzzle pieces. They smoked pot and drank from brown paper bags, and as Charley rolled past and waved, they jerked their chins a tiny bit, like guards at a security checkpoint, and she debated whether to pull over and ask if any of them wanted a job.

Miss Honey's house was quiet. Must be at church, Charley thought, and went to her room to change out of her farm clothes—jeans, a plain short-sleeve blouse, and work boots—which made her look older and possibly a little butch, but which she believed helped make a good first impression, showed that she was serious, responsible, and not just some kid playing in the dirt. After a long day like today, it would feel good to sit out on the porch and watch the people pass, and maybe, for a minute, let her mind wander.

But when Charley stepped out of her bedroom into the living room, she saw Micah on the sofa. Micah's back was turned, her bare feet drawn up under her so that when she moved, the plastic slipcovers crackled. Micah pressed her ear to Miss Honey's phone, wrapped the cord around her finger, and at first Charley thought she was talking to a friend back home. But then she heard Micah say, "Hello, Lorna? Are you there?" Charley froze.

"It's me," Micah said. "Please pick up . . ." She waited, and when no one answered, her shoulders slumped with disappointment. "I'm just calling to tell you we made it. It's okay so far. Miss Honey says I can have a Coke anytime I want. She gave me Grandpa Ernest's old camera and is teaching me how to cook." Another pause. Thinking. "Mom went a little psycho the other day, but it wasn't her fault." Micah stopped talking, pushed the prongs on the cradle. *"Merde."* Hung up and redialed.

Charley held still. Last night after she bid Micah good night, her breath caught when the phone rang. She thought it might be Lorna. She waited for Miss Honey to call, heard Miss Honey's voice over the canned television laughter followed by the sound of the receiver being returned to the cradle. Charley had not spoken to her mother in two months, not since she stopped by her mother's house to outline her final plans, and the fact of not having her mother to consult felt like losing a limb.

"But it's the South," Lorna had said, as though moving to Louisiana were the same as moving to Siberia.

They stood in Lorna's newly remodeled kitchen. Charley looked around at the glistening travertine floors and polished marble countertops, the imported Italian tiles arranged in a swirling pattern behind the stove, the refrigerator large enough to store a whole side of beef, and she thought it was a kitchen she could never cook in. She took a sterling spoon from the drawer, stared into its silvery bowl at her upside-down face. "What's wrong with the South?" Her mother gave a little laugh that made Charley feel stupid for asking. Of course, she knew what was wrong. She had followed news coverage of the man dragged to his death behind a pickup truck in Texas, and the six black teenagers jailed in Louisiana on trumped-up charges.

"Come home," her mother had said. "Micah can take your old room.

She can go to your old school. Fine, if you insist on circling around that hellhole, but it's not fair to Micah."

"It's not a hellhole, Mother. It's an art program. And if I didn't work with those kids, no one would."

"I'm touched, but I'm not amused. I know your father thought it was noble, but I don't see anything noble about it. You've wasted enough time doing good for other people at your own expense."

"We're fine."

"You're not fine," her mother said. "You're a tenant. A tenant with a disconnected phone—don't even bother, I heard the recording. You drive a car I can hear two blocks away. How late is your rent? One month? *Two?* Fine, don't answer. But send Micah to me. I'll pay off those loans. I'll even buy you a new car. But only if she lives here."

Charley considered what Lorna could show Micah—the Louvre, the Met, safaris in Kenya. She considered the one thing, perhaps the only thing, she could now give her daughter, who was aching to stay in Los Angeles: the chance to see that even a woman in desperate straits could pull her own survival out of the ruddy earth.

"It's a generous offer, Mother, but we're going to Saint Josephine. I'm not changing my mind."

"How can you be so selfish?" Lorna grabbed the spoon from Charley and returned it to the drawer.

"What's that supposed to mean?"

"It's time to grow up, Charlotte. The child has been scarred once. Why drag her away from everyone she loves? Why drag her down to Louisiana, where she'll only suffer again?"

"That's not fair."

Now Charley waited to see if Lorna would answer the telephone.

"It's me again," Micah said. "I'd send you an e-mail, but Miss Honey doesn't have a computer. Anyway, I just wanted to say hi. I miss you. I don't have any friends yet. Okay, I think that's all. I love you." She replaced the receiver.

Part of Charley wanted to pounce on Micah for reporting back, wanted to grab her by the collar and shake her. But part of her understood how her daughter felt, so far from home. So, instead of scolding Micah about the call, Charley stepped into the room, said, "Hey there," brightly, as though she'd just ridden in on a Carolina breeze. She cleared a space next to Micah on the couch. "You get enough to eat? Because I can fix you something if you're hungry."

"I'm okay."

Miss Honey's couch was cluttered with cheap plush stuffed animals, the kind you won at a carnival. Charley picked up Tweety Bird, whose orange feet had faded and whose yellow plush rubbed off on her fingers. "I look at you sometimes and I can't believe how much you've grown," she said.

Micah shrugged.

For a minute, Charley struggled to think of more to say. Then, thankfully, she heard steps on the porch, the screen door squeaking open.

"Mother? Is anybody there?"

It was Violet, Charley's aunt, her father's only sister. Charley hadn't seen Violet since her dad's funeral.

"Well, it's about time," Charley said, going to the door. "I'd started thinking you were avoiding me."

Taller than Miss Honey, though not by much, hair slicked back into a cluster of lacquered curls more glamorous than Miss Honey's well-oiled ringlets; the same full figure and smooth butterscotch complexion. There was no mistaking Violet was Miss Honey's daughter.

"I've been helping out with Vacation Bible School," Violet said. She kicked off her shoes. "Rev's been working overtime since we got the new church. It's been all hands on deck. I haven't gotten a full night's sleep in weeks." She took a breath. "But look at you! Turn around, girl. Let me get a good look."

Charley spun in a small circle, happy to let Violet examine every inch of her. For the last ten months, she had lived almost entirely in her head, making plans, weighing her options, without anyone to act as a sounding board or confidante.

They embraced, and when they parted, Violet took Charley's face in her hands. "And your hair," she said, turning Charley's head to the side. "Girl, I love it."

"Miss Honey hates it," Micah said from the sofa.

"Well, I think it's wonderful. I say, good for you." Violet fingered her curls self-consciously. "I'd cut mine off if I had the face for it."

"God, I'm glad you're here," Charley said.

"And you," Violet said, pulling Micah to her feet. "Like a little woman. I think you've grown a foot taller. You like Saint Josephine so far?"

"I like Miss Honey's movies."

There were plenty of modern conveniences Miss Honey didn't have. She didn't have a computer. She didn't have a cell phone, or call waiting, or caller ID. She didn't have a coffeemaker or a blender, or cable or a satellite dish. But she did have a DVD player and enough old movies to fill the Library of Congress: war pictures (*The Bridge on the River Kwai*, *Battle of the Bulge*), westerns (*Escape from Fort Bravo*, *Saddle in the Wind*, *The Alamo*), and the deluxe twelve-pack box set of Shirley Temple classics.

Violet winked at Micah. "Well, she's got enough of them, that's for sure. But you can't stay inside all the time. Why don't you come to Vacation Bible School with me next week?"

Micah glanced at Charley. "No, thanks. I'm making a garden."

"A garden?" said Charley, and thought, *This from the kid who didn't like the feeling of Play-Doh between her fingers in preschool. This from the kid who won't squeeze toothpaste from the middle of the tube.* "Where did you get that idea?

"Miss Honey," Micah said. "She said I can use part of the empty lot next door."

"Well, that's creative," Violet said. "But I warn you, folks down here take their gardens very seriously."

Micah beamed.

"It's a terrific idea," Charley said, wishing she'd been the first one to offer encouragement. On warm summer evenings when she was a girl, she gardened for hours beside her father in the small yard behind his condo. There was nothing finer than the smell of fresh dirt and the feel of her bare feet in the warm grass. Sometimes, they gardened till it got dark, and Charley held the heavy-duty flashlight with its car-size battery and beam like a Broadway spotlight, while he bent over clay pots and raised beds. "Marigolds are on sale down at the hardware store," Charley said, remembering the ad in the morning's paper.

"I don't want flowers," Micah said. Her tone was matter-of-fact but she averted her eyes. "I'm having vegetables."

"Okay, vegetables then. Vegetables are good. We can start next weekend."

Micah hesitated. "I kinda want to do this myself."

"Oh. Well—of course," Charley said. "That's good. It'll give you something to do every day while I'm at the farm." She tried to ignore the little stab of pain under her breastbone and gave Micah's shoulder a congratulatory squeeze. But when she glanced at Violet, Violet offered her a sympathetic smile, one that said, *Don't worry, she still needs you.* Charley wondered how Violet, childless since her only daughter was killed in a car accident years ago, managed to get through the days.

Pots clanged in the kitchen.

"Mother?" Violet called, and they all filed out of the living room.

At the kitchen table, Miss Honey spooned leftovers onto plates. "Y'all come and eat. I can warm up some green beans if you don't think this is enough." The table was set for three.

"Hey, Mother," Violet said, and kissed Miss Honey's cheek. She washed her hands, then took the water pitcher from the refrigerator, and another place mat from the drawer. "Mother, I was just telling Charley how much I love her hair."

Miss Honey grunted. "She looks like a man."

"That's terrible," Violet said. "Now why would you say such a thing?" She stepped behind Miss Honey and swept the candy curls away from her face. "How 'bout it, Mother? You want a style like Charley's? We can do it right now. Quick, Micah, hand me some scissors." She winked at Charley.

"Get away from me with all that foolishness," Miss Honey said, batting Violet's hand away. "Go sit down."

They each pulled out a chair, Violet said grace, and after spreading her napkin across her lap, she reached across the table for Charley's hand and squeezed it. *"Beams of heaven, as I go. Through this wilderness below,"* she sang. Her voice was strong and warm, and she closed her eyes, gently rocked in her chair as she sang the chorus. When she stopped, a quietness and sense of lasting peace hung in the air.

"It's good to be here." Tears stung Charley's eyes as she bathed in the fading glow of Violet's voice. She could soak up Violet's warmth for a lifetime. She was the buttermilk pancakes to Violet's maple syrup, the white bread to Violet's bacon grease, and if she had a thousand more awful days like she'd had today, at least she had Violet to balance things out. "So what's this about a new church?" Charley said, wiping the corners of her eyes. She passed the French salad dressing to Violet.

"Girl, we finally did it. Found a place over on Chalmette, just off Third Street. It used to be a pool hall, but you'd never know it now. We've got new pews, new lights. Did most of the work ourselves. And the Rev? Charley, he's a new man. BP tried to talk him into staying, but you know what it's like when you hear the call."

"That's right," Miss Honey said, passing the rice dressing. "When God calls, you'd better answer."

"I guess that makes you First Lady of the church," Charley said.

Violet waved away the praise. "No sense getting bigheaded," she said, though she sat up a little straighter. "But look who's talking. You're a big land owner now."

"I wouldn't say all that."

"Now who's being modest? Eight hundred acres is nothing to sneeze at."

"More like eight hundred problems." In the last week, after Frasier and Denton, after Landry and NeNee Desonier's granddaughter, Charley had cursed her father's name more than once for pressing this so-called gift into her hands. Yesterday, at the shop, she'd almost torn up the maps and photographs, shredded the legal documents, and turned her back on the whole enterprise.

"Well, I think what you're doing is wonderful," Violet said. "If more black folks around here took a page out of your book, we wouldn't be in such a fix. We got all these smart, talented young men around here wasting away in the Bahamas."

"The Bahamas?"

"Prison," Miss Honey said. "That's what they call it."

"Call it anything they want, it's still the same." Violet shook her head. "All those young men. Stop 'em on the street, half will admit they've done time. Some have the nerve to be *proud* of it."

"Violet," Miss Honey said, her voice tightening. "You should watch dipping your finger into that Kool-Aid when you don't know the flavor. People go to prison for all sorts of reasons."

"I'm not saying they aren't good people, Mother. I'm just saying something's wrong when doing time is normal." She turned to Charley. "What do you think?"

Charley looked from Violet to Miss Honey. In the past week, she'd seen the way Miss Honey marched around town—calling to people she knew, asking why they hadn't been to church, reprimanding children she thought looked idle, telling them to tuck in their shirts, go home and put lotion on their ashy knees—and understood that Miss Honey considered Saint Josephine to be her own personal domain. Why, just yesterday she flagged down the mayor as he rolled through town in his red Cadillac Seville, and scolded him for not cutting the weeds by the playground. "Is something burning?" Charley said, and started to get up from the table. "I think I smell smoke."

"I still say something's happened to us black folks," Violet continued. "You may not want to hear it, Mother, but we both know I'm telling the truth. Just look at Ralph Angel." She paused. "No offense, Charley, I don't mean to speak ill of your brother."

At the mention of Ralph Angel's name, Charley felt emotions pass through her like shadows across a hillside as clouds drifted over. Even now, her foot stung from the time he aimed a stone at an egret at the water's edge, which it missed, hitting her so sharply, tears rushed to her eyes. At the time, she had thought it was an accident, but the way he always misbehaved with her made her wonder how much of an accident it really was. She remembered the look of hurt and bitter disappointment that darkened her father's face when, a few years later, he discovered Ralph Angel had continued to cash the tuition checks he sent, even though he'd dropped out of school.

"Stop right there, Violet," Miss Honey said. "I won't have you talking about Ralph Angel outside his name. Besides, he never went to jail."

"That's about the only thing he hasn't done," Violet said under her breath.

Charley was about to ask what else Ralph Angel had done, when Miss Honey cleared her throat, glancing at Micah.

"I know what that look means," Micah said. "It means you're about to talk about grown-up stuff and I have to leave the room."

"Every time he comes around, there's trouble." Violet turned to Charley. "The last time he was in town, three years ago, he and Mother got into an argument and he pushed her down."

"It was an accident," Miss Honey said.

"You broke your arm, Mother."

"He got overexcited. He's been that way since he was little."

Violet sighed, wearily. "When the doctor asked Mother what happened, she said she tripped over the laundry basket. I don't know why she always makes excuses for him."

"Can we go back, please?" Charley said. "He broke your *arm*?"

"Mother found some drug paraphernalia in the deep freezer," Violet said. "When she asked Ralph Angel about it, if he knew where it came from, he flew into a rage. 'Get out of my business,' he said. Mother grabbed his elbow, told him to calm down, think about Blue, the example he was setting. Well, that did it. Ralph Angel said, 'Don't tell me how to raise my kid,' and when she blocked the door, he pushed her down and she broke her arm. She waited two hours before she called me. And of course, I called Uncle Brother and John. By the time we got back from the hospital, Ralph Angel and Blue were gone."

Charley look at Miss Honey. "Is that how it happened?"

"I'm not talking about it," Miss Honey said. "All I know is, whatever problems Ralph Angel's got, he comes by them honest. Just look at his mother. Smart as a whip, but her head was never right."

"Where is Ralph Angel now?" Charley said. After the college tuition incident, his father had never mentioned his whereabouts, never mentioned him at all, come to think of it. And there'd been no mention of Ralph Angel in her father's will either, a fact that Charley had not thought of at the time, since they'd been out of touch for so many years, but that made her feel uneasy now. Had he really pushed Miss Honey down? Broken her arm? She had inherited a whole sugarcane farm while, at least to her knowledge, he had inherited nothing. What would he think about that?

"Last I heard, he was in Phoenix," Violet said, leaning closer. "Still drinking and messing with that pipe. But what do I know? Mother keeps up with him."

"Like I said, he comes by his troubles honest. We all got our cross to bear, Violet. Don't forget that. Last time I talked to Ralph Angel, he sounded better. Said he'd cleaned himself up."

"Well, good for him. Let him stay out there."

Miss Honey pointed an accusatory finger. "I'm booking you, Violet. Shame on you for bad-mouthing your own family."

"Fine, Mother. Whatever you say."

"Good grief," Charley said. "You two are at each other's throats over someone who isn't even here. Let me get us something to drink." She reached for the pitcher, even though every glass was still brimming with ice water. If Ernest had left any cash, she might offer to share it. Maybe she'd buy him a car. But there was only a farm, and only just barely.

Violet and Miss Honey retreated to their corners, and for a while they ate in silence. Then Violet took Charley's hand again and said, "The Rev and I are hosting an open house when we finish all the renovations. I hope you'll come."

"That reminds me," Miss Honey said. "We're having a family reunion in honor of Charley coming home."

"How thoughtful," Charley said. "Maybe after grinding. I need to work seven days a week till then."

"Awesome," Micah said. "I'll bake cookies."

"Next Saturday," Miss Honey said. "I've already called some of the family. Violet, I want you to help get the word out to the rest. Tell them eleven o'clock." She pointed to the baker's rack crammed with cookbooks. "Micah, you can bake all the cookies you want."

"I appreciate what you're trying to do," Charley said. "But the bills are stacking up, and I still haven't found a manager."

But Miss Honey had already pushed back from the table and started clearing the dishes. "Farm's waited this long, it can wait a few more days. Violet can start making calls right now. Micah, look in my purse and hand my address book to your aunt. And Violet, be sure to call Aunt Rose from Opelousas."

"Mother, did you hear what Charley said? She's got a lot to do right now."

Charley cast Violet an appreciative look.

"Besides," Violet continued, "I can't rearrange my schedule on such short notice. We've got choir practice next Saturday. The All-State competition is the end of this month."

"There, you see?" Charley said, trying to sound gentle and ministerial. "Later this summer would be better for everyone."

"'Can't rearrange your schedule on such short notice,'" Miss Honey muttered. She squirted dish soap in the sink, turned on the faucet. "Well, Violet, I guess you're a white lady now."

Violet sighed and let her fork dangle between her fingers. "For heaven's sake, Mother."

"Here I'm trying to plan something for Charley and you come telling me what I can and can't do?" Miss Honey plunged her hands into the soapy water.

"I drove all the way over here to visit Charley," Violet said. "Let's have a pleasant afternoon."

"Listen here, Violet. You're going to call the family like I told you, and you're going to cancel your practice."

"Mother," Violet said, quietly. "I may be your child, and I don't mean any disrespect. But there's nothing you can say that's going to make me cancel that practice." She folded her napkin primly. "I'd love to get the family together, but not next Saturday. No, ma'am."

Miss Honey turned the faucet off, and lather dropped from her arms as she waved toward the door. "If that's the way you're going to act, then get out of my house. I'm tired of looking at you."

"Mother, give Charley some time. Let her work things out on her farm before you go piling more on her plate."

Miss Honey slapped the counter and they all jumped. "Okay, Miss First Lady. It's a shame your prizewinning choir is more important than your family, but we're having a reunion next Saturday and you're going to help."

Violet pushed away from the table.

"Wait." Charley leaped to her feet. "This is crazy. Violet, you just got here." She grabbed Violet's hand. "Let's take a walk."

"No," Violet said. "Charley, I'm glad you're back. You look real good." Charley tried to follow but Violet raised her hand. "I'll let myself out."

At the front door, Charley said, "Don't go."

Violet pulled her close. "Don't worry," she whispered. "You'll be fine. You can handle it." The sound of clanging pots rang from the kitchen and Violet looked over Charley's shoulder, her expression filled with anguish. Then she touched the nape of Charley's neck. "I really do love your hair. I wish I had the guts to do it."

Charley wasn't the praying kind. She believed what her father always said: that God helps those who help themselves; that most people are too quick to slough off their responsibility like a pair of dirty gym socks, lay their problems at God's doorstep. And until recently, Charley believed she was doing everything she could to make the farm a success. But now she was beginning to think she needed a little help. She slid out of bed and dropped to her knees as the morning sun filtered through the curtains. *Please, God. Let this farming thing break my way.* She cradled her face in her hands and waited for the words. The floor was unwelcoming. The rug smelled of dust and feet, and a faint trace of Murphy's Oil Soap. *Please, God. Give me a sign. A flash of light. A burning bush. Jacob's ladder. I'm not picky. I just need to know you're there.* She strained for an answer, held herself still as she could, but heard only an empty silence, felt air so heavy it was a presence all its own.

Half past seven, and the kitchen thermometer already read eighty-six degrees. Charley wandered into the den, which was even warmer because Miss Honey insisted on running the space heater for her arthritis. Miss Honey and Micah sat riveted by *The Littlest Colonel.* Shirley Temple, in bows and lace, stomped into the stable, demanding Bojangles teach her to dance. "I got no time for dancing," Bojangles said, in an apologetic drawl.

Micah, her breakfast on a TV tray cluttered with saucers—grits on one, scrambled eggs on another, sausage on a third—said, "She looks like Bo Peep."

Charley scoffed. "She looks like a poodle." Bojangles's docile, child-like manner, the way he grinned—it sickened her, and after a few seconds, she said, "Isn't there something else you could watch? Something educational?"

"Like that police show you had on last night?" Miss Honey took a swig of her Coke. "I don't see what's educational about some man chopping a woman into a hundred pieces and stuffing her in a garbage bag. I don't see Shirley Temple running around with a hatchet."

"Yeah, Mom," Micah said. "Nice job of setting a good example."

Charley winced. First the ring, then the garden, and now this. Coming down here was supposed to bring them closer, but they only seemed to be growing farther apart. "You know what I mean," Charley said, wearily. The farm and her daughter—she worried constantly about both, was trying every trick she knew, and yet neither was improving. "All I came to say is I'm driving out to the farm after church. Micah, we'll stop by the nursery so you can pick the seeds you want for your garden."

"We're not going to church," Miss Honey said, as though the headline had been plastered all over town and only Charley had missed it. "We got a lot of errands to run for the reunion. So go in there and fix your plate."

Between the heat, the ridiculous movie, and this last announcement, all at once, the sight of Miss Honey nursing her morning Coke and Stanback was more than Charley could bear. "Isn't it a little early for that stuff?" She heard the edge in her voice and didn't care. "I mean, is it even safe to drink?"

Miss Honey held the Coke up to the light, swirled it like fine wine, and took a long, deliberate sip. "I've been drinking Coke and Stanback every morning for fifty-some years and it hasn't killed me yet. Now hurry up. We're going to Sugar Town."

On television, a pickaninny whipped out her harmonica and played "Oh! Susanna." Bojangles couldn't resist and started to dance, his eyes growing bulbous as he performed a noodle-legged jig and finally scurried out of the stable. Micah and Miss Honey looked at each other and laughed.

"That's it," Charley said. "You've got to turn that off. It's lowering your IQ." She marched over to the TV, punched the power button. "I'm sorry, Miss Honey, I won't— First, it's driving around without a map, then the reunion, now it's— I can't keep saying yes all the time. If I don't find someone right away—" Charley felt her mouth moving, heard her voice, saw Miss Honey and Micah staring at her, their expressions a mix of focused attention and concern. It was the same expression hospital orderlies had, Charley thought, right before they wrestled the crazy lady into a straitjacket. "I'm sorry, but you'll have to go without me."

"Mom? Are you okay?"

"You know what?" Charley said. The realization had dawned upon her and she surrendered to it. "I'm *not* okay. I can't breathe, because it's hotter than the Amazon rain forest in here, and my kid is taking social cues from a tap dancing minstrel. I can't find a manager to run my farm, and I've got some corporate thug threatening to run me out of business. All the black workers around here think I'm out to cheat them, I've got a stack of bills I can barely pay, and each day that passes, I'm this much closer to losing the whole goddamned thing." The absurdity of it all. She almost laughed; probably would have, if it hadn't been so serious.

After a long silence, Miss Honey said, "Well, good heavens. Why didn't you say that before?"

Alone on the porch, Charley stirred salt and butter into her grits as a delivery truck pulled up along the gully. Violet sat behind the wheel.

"I thought I'd seen the last of you," Charley said, jogging out to greet her.

Violet climbed down, brushed the back of her shorts. "Mother didn't tell you I was coming?"

"After yesterday? She threw you out, remember?"

Violet raked her fingers through her hair. She had replaced her ringlet hairpiece with a long, straight ponytail. "If I took every mean thing Mother said to heart, I'd never speak to her." She threaded her arm through Charley's. "Mother wants to have this reunion, I say let her have it. The quicker she throws it, the quicker you can get back to business with your farm. I brought the van so we could get everything at once."

It was actually more of a truck than a van, with "Frito Lay" stenciled on the side above a faded potato chip bag, TRUE VINE BAPTIST CHURCH arching over everything in bright red letters.

"Rev bought it at an auction in Baton Rouge." Violet slid open the driver's door and invited Charley to look inside. "He welded the bus seats."

"Impressive," Charley said, stepping down. "But I can't go. The farm. It's dying." Stunted cane overrun with weeds, rusting equipment, broken tools scattered on the shop floor, paperwork she couldn't begin to make sense of.

"It's Sunday," Violet said. "Everything's closed. All you'll do is wring your hands and make yourself crazy." She took Charley by the shoulders and shook her gently, as if trying to rouse her from a bad dream. "Come on, girl. Let your mind air out a little." Violet shook Charley's shoulder again and looked at her expectantly. "Just for a few hours. It'll do you some good."

Charley looked out over the yard, past the camellia bush with its explosion of juicy red blossoms, past the towering live oak whose branches filtered the morning's sunlight. "All right," she said. "Especially if it'll drag your mother and my daughter away from *The Littlest Colonel*."

Violet scowled. "Good Lord, I hate that movie." She crossed the yard, climbed the porch steps, then called through the screen door, "Mother, come out of there," as though she and Miss Honey had never argued.

"Girl, don't rush me." Miss Honey, with Micah close at her heels, stepped onto the porch wearing a purple dress and white sandals that looked good enough for church. Her face was freshly powdered. She struck a pose.

Violet laughed. "Mother, you kill me." She took Miss Honey's face in her hands, using her thumb to gently blend the rouge on her mother's cheek. It was a gesture of such familiarity and closeness, it took Charley by surprise.

They rumbled out of town at a steady clip, the sky electric blue, the cane fields almost unnaturally green, and Charley felt her spirits lift for the first time in days. First stop, Mr. Nguyen, who sat on a milk crate beside his battered pickup parked along the road. He rose as the van approached, and flashed a cracked smile. Earlier, Miss Honey had referred to him as the Chinaman, but Charley thought she heard Vietnamese as he chattered with his wife, who pushed back the lids of Igloo coolers packed with fresh seafood on beds of ice—three types of shrimp, oysters, and crabs. Live red snapper thrashed and gasped in a five-gallon bucket. Miss Honey bought shrimp, her manner cordial but firm.

Then it was on to the produce stand in Arnaudville, where Miss Honey sniffed and pinched for ripeness like a chief inspector with the Department of Agriculture. Okra, speckled butter beans and black-eyed peas, bowling-ball-size cantaloupes, tomatoes, and cucumbers thick as Micah's arm. Soon the van was cluttered with boxes, the air inside sweet from the bounty, sharp with the musk of red earth and Gulf water. West on Highway 90 and north on Route 26, past Elton and Oberlin, where cane yielded to rice paddies, which yielded to vast stretches of piney woods, a part of Louisiana Charley had never seen.

They rolled to a stop in a small turnout where a strip of multicolored flags hung over a sign that read WELCOME TO SUGAR TOWN. Stiff-legged, Charley helped Miss Honey to the ground, then followed her toward two wooden shacks. Sun fell through a blue plastic tarp strung between their sagging roofs, and variations in the blue light beneath reminded Charley of being underwater. She squinted into the shadows, smelled pine, saw watermelons strewn everywhere.

The little man in soiled overalls and rubber fishing boots hefted a melon onto a wooden table, rolled it over until the pale yellow spot faced skyward. With one stroke, he drove his blade through the center and sweetness filled the air as the halves tilted away, revealing flesh as red as beef filet. He stabbed his knife into the center of one half, cut rough square chunks. The heady aroma made Charley laugh. She laughed till her sides hurt and tears streamed down her face and they were all looking at her like she was crazy, and even then she could not stop. Because life should be as simple as a bucket of fish caught a few miles offshore and a van full of produce bought at a roadside stand. It should be as sweet as a cube of melon the color of your heart.

Back at Miss Honey's in time for supper, Charley and Violet unloaded the van as a deep rumble echoed from up the street.

"Oh, Lord," Violet said.

Charley looked. It was a Cadillac Escalade, with tricked-out hubcaps that spun counterclockwise, and a chassis so low to the ground there was barely room for a shadow.

"Rosalee Simon's boy." Violet set a pallet of snap peas and okra on the steps.

But it was the girl in the passenger seat who Charley focused on as the car glided past. Glassy black mane with a streaked lock the color of strawberry Kool-Aid draped over one eye. A gold hoop, large as a salad plate, grazed her shoulder.

"Would you look at that?" Violet said.

"Like she's sitting on a throne." So straight-backed and regal, Charley thought, and pulled her own shoulders back.

Violet shook her head. "Young women these days. I just don't know."

"What?" Charley said. "She looks happy." Thought, *I'd trade a lot for happy.*

"Happy, till she's knocked up. Happy, till the boy she thinks is so fine dumps her. Happy, till she realizes how much time she wasted."

A wood sliver came lose from the pallet. Charley picked at it. "Geez, Violet. That's awfully harsh."

The Caddy sailed past the stop sign and turned. A hush fell over the street. Seconds passed, but the silence hung between them.

Violet searched Charley's face. "Okay. Spit it out."

"It's nothing. Forget it."

"Sorry, sugar, but I can see it in your eyes."

Charley wasn't sure she had the words. Sometimes it was a small ache behind her breastbone and sometimes it was a heaviness, like a sopping wool cloak draped over her. It was a feeling that had come and gone since childhood, but she had married young, and lost her husband young, and it was like falling down an elevator shaft that no one else could see. Charley peeled a speckled butter bean shaped like a heart.

"I don't mean to compare my loss to yours," Charley began. She couldn't imagine the pain of losing a child.

"It's all suffering," Violet said, simply.

Behind them, the porch light flicked on and moths danced around the bulb. Charley could hear Miss Honey and Micah inside the living room, talking to each other in low tones.

"After Davis died," Charley said, "I would drop Micah at school, then come home and put on this old robe." Blue terry. So old, the dye had faded along the seams, with big square pockets hung by a thread. She'd close herself up in Davis's closet, which was safe and smelled like grass. She knelt with the hood over her head, and cried till she was snotty and had a headache. "I cried a lot," Charley said. "I didn't shower much." Eyes stinging, she looked at Violet. "I bet you've never fallen apart."

"Oh, *chère*." Violet wrapped her arm around Charley.

In the street, another car passed. Charley waved; it was second nature now.

Violet put her hand on top of Charley's, and for a few seconds, they both stared out into the yard.

Finally, Violet sighed. "Life does get daily."

"If it had just been me, that would have been okay." Charley took a breath and made herself say, "Micah's arm. That's because of me." And suddenly, her admission felt like enough, too much, even. Yes, Violet was her closest ally, but she didn't need to know everything. Yes, she was a preacher's wife, a good Christian woman, but she was still human, and even the most godly, well-intentioned human being couldn't resist a bit of judgment were she to hear the rest of the story. Violet must have sensed this, because she sat perfectly still, as though she knew the slightest disturbance would trigger Charley's retreat. She didn't make eye contact. She just waited.

Months passed and Charley still wore the blue robe. Micah began doing laundry, dishes, making both beds. Her one symbolic act had been dinner, but that slipped too: a baked potato where there'd been roast chicken and a fresh green salad.

She was in bed, listening to pots rattle in the kitchen, the night she gave up and asked Micah to cook. She heard a sound that she strangely recognized as a rush of air, and then a cry. Not a cry for help exactly; more a cry of surprise, and by the time Charley reached the kitchen, Micah was in flames—her whole left side lit like a column of red cellophane. Charley looked and saw the pot of water boiling over, the box of macaroni and cheese. She saw the bottle of cleaning solution overturned on the counter and the long, narrow river where the spill snaked toward the burner. She saw the fine red seam of fire creeping up Micah's T-shirt, feasting on the drenched cotton, which curled away and turned to ash.

Violet listened quietly. She still didn't look at Charley, for which Charley was thankful. And for a second, Charley thought she understood why Catholics revered the act of confession. There was something freeing about speaking your mind. There was a relief in sharing the secrets you'd tended like mushrooms in the darkest corner of your thoughts without having to meet another's gaze.

In the bedroom, Micah turned her back, pulled her T-shirt over her head. She covered her bare chest with one hand, but Charley could see where the smooth caramel-colored graft ended and the normal skin began. In another year, probably less, Charley thought, Micah would ask her to leave the room when she changed. Wanting to extend the small moment, she said, casually, "Today was fun," like they'd only gone for a walk in the park.

"Totally," Micah said. "Aunt Violet's van is cool."

"It is."

Charley picked Micah's clothes up off the floor and was happy to do it. She put Micah's camera on the nightstand and was happy to do it. She pushed their suitcases to the back of the closet, saw the package on the floor, and hoisted it onto the bed. Between the farm and reunion preparations, she had forgotten it was there. The packaging tape peeled away with a whisper; the butcher paper crackled as she folded it back and kneaded it into a ball. She unspiraled the sheets of bubble wrap until the first bits of bronze gleamed through. Richmond Barthé's *The Cane Cutter*. A familiar calm settled over her.

Micah buttoned her pajama top. "Yuck. Why'd you bring that?"

The figure—a black man, naked to the waist—swung a cane knife. He was only eighteen inches tall, but his power took Charley's breath away. She ran her hand over the Cane Cutter's broad shoulders, the knots of muscle in his arms, the burnished slabs of his pecs and back flexed with the force of his swing.

The day her father brought it home, he called Charley and Lorna into the living room. Charley got there first and saw the coffee table heaped with Lorna's silver-framed family photographs, many of them facedown, Lorna's prized Lalique vase, the one with the naked ladies following each other around the icy glass, resting on its side.

"So?" Her father placed his hand on her shoulder.

Charley heard her mother's footsteps in the hall behind them; heard her mother's humming stop as she entered the room. But she saw how excited, how proud her father looked and she did not turn around. She took her time studying the piece. The bronze man looked like he must be sweating. Something about him—his deep-set eyes, wide forehead, and square hands—seemed familiar. He stirred up a feeling she could not name.

"He looks like you," Charley said.

"I certainly hope not." Her mother, coiffed and buffed from a day at the salon, was already holding the Lalique vase. "What's next, Ernest? A painting of the garbage man?"

Charley looked from her mother to her father and saw his expression dim, his mouth move as if he tasted something sour.

"This is the living room," Lorna said. "Your laborer can go in the den."

"Move it," her father said, quietly, not taking his hand from Charley's shoulder, "and I'll break every piece of goddamned crystal in this house."

Now Charley touched a finger to *The Cane Cutter*. The curve of his back like he could lift ten times his weight, the rough drape of his pants, which she imagined as burlap or canvas; his determined gaze, as though he could cut a thousand acres by himself. He almost breathed.

Years later, after her parents divorced, Charley let herself into her father's condo. She found him staring at *The Cane Cutter*.

"Dad? You okay?" He was on his second round of chemo by then. Leiomyosarcoma. *Leios* from the Greek word for "smooth." *Sarx*, Greek for "flesh." Cancer of the soft connective tissue: bone, cartilage, muscle.

When she sat, he patted her hand and she saw that the treatment had turned his nail beds the color of walnut shells. But she was not going to talk about his nails. She was not going to ask him if he'd slept; he hated that.

"I love the way he stands," she said, tilting her head. Because it was easier to look at *The Cane Cutter* with his broad back and tapered waist and biceps all intact than it was to acknowledge how the muscles in her father's arms and legs had withered away; he'd lost so much weight, the hollows beneath his collarbones were cups of shadow. Because it was easier to appreciate how the track lights brought out the warm tones in the bronze—the rich rusts and golds—than to admit her father's complexion had turned the color of bile.

"What else?" her father had asked.

She'd reached for the words. "A quiet confidence." He seemed to approve. She went on. "And a defiance."

"Yes," her father said, nodding. "Exactly."

Now Charley stepped over the butcher paper and bubble wrap heaped on the floor. She slid *The Cane Cutter* onto the dresser, where she could always see it.

Micah popped a row of bubble wrap. "Did it cost a lot of money?"

"Sort of." No sense in telling Micah how much.

"Gross," Micah said, making a face. "It looks like a mud monster. Put it back in the closet."

Pop, pop. Like a cap gun.

"He's staying right here."

Micah draped her dirty T-shirt over *The Cane Cutter*'s shoulders, pulled it up over his face, went back to her bubble wrap.

"Don't touch," Charley said, pulling the T-shirt off. She needed to see him. "I'm not kidding." *And stop that fucking popping.*

Four months in the hospital and a year of physical therapy before the doctors said Micah would recover. Charley still put on the blue robe at night. It was her fault Micah wore only long sleeves to school, even when the weather called for flimsy summer clothes. It was her fault Micah didn't want to swim anymore or go to the beach. Charley cried in the dark, until one day, she came home to the little Spanish bungalow to find *The Cane Cutter* on *her* mantle. No sign of her father anywhere, not even a note. But she didn't need one. The message was clear. He was telling her, *Get up.* He was telling her, *Fight for your life.* He was telling her, *We are the same, you'll find your way, I won't let you fall.* She carried the blue robe out to the patio, dropped it on the poured concrete, and doused it with lighter fluid. Then she lit a match.

Micah dropped the bubble wrap and stepped over the air mattress. At the door, she paused. "Mom? This morning you said we were gonna lose every goddamned—"

"Hey," Charley said. "listen to me." She took Micah by the shoulders. "Don't worry."

"But you said—"

Charley stole a glance at *The Cane Cutter*. Years from now, long after her body had turned to dust, the elegantly sculpted chunk of wire and molded metal would still be here; it would pass from Micah to Micah's children. The sculpture made her aware of what she had to do. That farm would get going again, no matter what stood in its path. For her daughter, for her father. Charley smoothed Micah's hair. "Forget what I said," she said. "Your job is to have fun. Let me worry about the rest."

7

❧ A buckled sandwich board advertised the Blue Bowl's daily specials: seafood salad, Cajun pasta, shrimp étouffée on top of fried catfish on top of French toast, white-chocolate bread pudding with vanilla ice cream and homemade caramel sauce for dessert. Charley crossed the bridge that spanned the bayou and crunched into the gravel lot filled with monster pickups, pulled alongside a Chevy one-ton with a cracked windshield.

All week, Charley had been consumed with finding a manager. On Monday, she placed an ad in the *Louisiana Sugar Bulletin* offering a three-thousand-dollar signing bonus. On Tuesday, she posted flyers at the market and plastered them on every telephone pole in town. On Wednesday, she spent so many hours at the Ag station that Gladys, the receptionist, knew how much cream she took in her coffee and had a cup waiting at the front desk when she came back on Thursday.

"Try the Blue Bowl," Miss Honey had said when Charley said she'd run out of ideas for places to find a manager.

Friday now, and Charley brushed past artificial flowers woven into the lattice by the entrance as she entered, and tried to imagine coming here every morning for coffee. Maybe she would. The place had a certain charm if you didn't mind the late-seventies Country Kitchen décor: yellow curtains with white eyelet fringe that looked hand sewn, framed pictures of farmers in their fields dating all the way back to the twenties, miniature model tractors that cluttered the shelf running around the room's perimeter.

"Table for one, please," Charley said, and followed the hostess past the salad bar. In the main dining room, groups of white men, some dressed in khakis and starched button-downs, others in overalls and work boots, crowded around tables. To a man their posture—meaty arms folded over barrel chests, legs apart like they were sitting around a campfire—conveyed an easy comfort. And whether they sipped mugs of coffee or stabbed at plates of pork chops and rice, they all looked like they belonged there. This was the college football crowd, Charley thought, LSU, Alabama, and Ole Miss; tailgates in the stadium parking lot six hours before kickoff. Except for the three waitresses flitting from table to table, Charley was the only woman. Except for the cooks, whose faces she saw through the cutout in the swinging door, she was the only black person.

"I can put you by the window," the hostess offered, then launched into the maze of tables and chairs.

Charley tried not to bump against any chairs as she followed. Still, men glanced up, eyed her curiously as she passed. What made her think she could waltz in here and take up with this crowd like one of the gang?

From her seat by the window, she had a clear view—the bayou's far bank, dark with trees and lily pads, and beyond it, a wall of green cane leaves drinking up the afternoon light. Above, a turquoise sky.

Charley eavesdropped on a group of farmers at a nearby table. She caught words, snatches of phrases, something about a new strain of cane the Ag Department had just released, then talk of mill pricing. But it was a foreign language. The men's conversations only raised new questions. *Which* mills? What *were* the newest cane varieties? The longer Charley listened, the louder she heard Lorna's voice, then Denton's, then Landry's, telling her she was out of her league.

Charley couldn't imagine eating, but she ordered anyway, and ten minutes later she confronted a platter the size of a manhole cover heaping with barbecued shrimp just off the grill, shells a deep, rosy pink, doused with lemon and chili powder.

"Mind if I join you?" Prosper Denton ran the brim of his straw cowboy hat through his fingers.

"Mr. Denton." Charley pushed her chair away from the table and tried to stand. "No—I don't mind. Please, have a seat."

"Don't get up." Denton laid his hat on the windowsill.

They sat across from each other for a full minute, neither, it seemed, knowing quite how to begin.

"I didn't expect to ever see you again," Charley said, thinking she sounded more defiant than she intended.

"I see you ordered the shrimp."

Charley pushed the untouched plate across the table and told Denton to help himself. He held up his hand.

"I'm trying to watch my cholesterol. Doctor put me on a strict diet." In his thick accent, cholesterol sounded like cholester*oil*. When the waitress appeared, Denton ordered a green salad, oil and vinegar on the side, and a cup of seafood gumbo.

"So," Charley began. "How's retirement?"

"I stopped by Miss Honey's looking for you." Denton's house was far out in the country, way on the other side of Saint Josephine. A drive to the Quarters easily took forty minutes. "She said try your farm, so I drove out there. I was on my way home when I decided to stop for lunch. Surprised when I saw you sitting here by yourself."

Denton ran his tongue over his lips in what was not quite a smile, but Charley couldn't help but think he was amused by the situation. "Yeah, well," she said, thinking how ridiculous she must look sitting there. More like a tourist who'd lost her way than a farmer.

Denton plucked a package of saltines from the basket and opened it slowly. "A man can only do so much fishing," he said, more to himself than to her. He broke a cracker in half, brushed crumbs off the table. "I was in the cane business sixty years, and I can tell you, every man in this dining room has seen his share of troubles." He popped the cracker in his mouth and chewed slowly. "But I've seen the way these white fellas look out for each other, and it's no accident they are where they are."

Charley remembered the hard, dusty floorboards beneath her bare knees that morning she prayed. She remembered exploding at Micah and Miss Honey: *Every day I get this much closer to losing the whole goddamned thing.*

Denton swallowed. He tossed the wadded wrapper in the basket. "Then here you come. Smart young woman with enough land to actually do something."

The waitress appeared with Denton's salad and gumbo. "Here you go, sugar. And this is from Agnes." She set down a plate of smoked boudin.

"Please tell her I said thank you."

So courtly, Charley thought, as Denton bowed his head over his food, and so decent.

When he looked up, it was to offer her a link of boudin. "Like I was saying, Miss Bordelon, I thought you were crazy the day you showed up at my door, but something about your situation appealed to me."

Charley was like a puppy in dog obedience school. She saw the treat in her trainer's pocket and could barely sit still for all the anticipation, but her gaze never wavered. She watched Denton slip a piece of boudin in his mouth, watched him wipe his fingers on his napkin, watched him spear a chunk of iceberg lettuce and dip the corner of it into the little ramekin of dressing. She held her breath and waited. The boudin must have been delicious, because he took another piece.

Charley couldn't stand it any longer. "Mr. Denton, are you saying you'll work with me?"

"That's the wrong question." Denton chewed the boudin and swallowed, casing and all. "Question is, can you work with me? If you want this, Miss Bordelon, you got to trust my judgment all the way. Some folks find that hard to do. There'll be things that won't make sense to you. There'll be times you think I should do the exact opposite."

"I can live with that."

"You think that now," Denton said, "but can you really? Because I want to be up front, put it all on the table. I've found it's better that way."

"I like up front. Up front is good." Charley thrust her hand toward him, knowing it was the only contract the man needed.

Denton reached across the table to shake, then leaned back in his chair, smiling the first smile Charley had seen since she met him. But it didn't last long. "Now, I drove around your place a bit." He took a pen from his breast pocket and sketched a rough square on an extra napkin. "You've got a pretty good spread. Good, loamy soil, decent drainage. But you got a lot of work to do. You got cane out there that's been suckering since early May; that's not good. You got a pretty good stand of first- and second-year stubble—looks like Frasier planted some three ten and a little three forty-five—but that back quadrant is in pretty bad shape. Blackjack land. That three eighty-four you got out there tends to lodge. Most of it's third-year stubble so it'll be coming out soon anyway. Good thing is, all that land you own, you can use some of it for shadow plow."

"Shadow *what*?" Charley was drowning again.

Denton held up a silencing hand. "We'll worry about that come August. Right now, we need to lay new mother stalk, and long as it doesn't get boggy, you might be okay." He looked ruefully at his clean boudin plate. "Four months between now and grinding, Miss Bordelon. That's not much time. We've got a lot of hard work ahead of us."

All of a sudden, Charley was starving. She peeled a shrimp, and then one more. "Trust me. I'm not afraid of hard work."

Denton watched her, then picked up his salad fork again. "Good. 'Cause you're in for a whole mess of it. Like my daddy used to say: 'If hard work had killed me, I'd have been dead.'"

8

❋ Charley peeled the aluminum foil from the five-gallon pot where the gumbo had been simmering for hours. Chunks of chicken and coins of sausage, lumps of crab and shrimp floated in brown broth thick as a witch's brew. She took a bowl from the cabinet.

"Better not let Mother catch you digging in her pots," Violet said, breezing into the kitchen. Juggling three grocery bags in one arm, her purse and a large ceramic bowl in the other, Violet was all motion and sound—the slap of her strapless sandals as she crossed the linoleum floor, the rattle of her keys, the gospel hymn she hummed to herself.

"I can't help it," Charley said.

Violet set her load on the table. "Mother's got a sixth sense about food. Don't say I didn't warn you."

"Consider yourself officially off the hook." Charley hadn't seen Violet or even phoned all week, and she was about to apologize when Micah sauntered into the kitchen wearing a green sundress and metallic flats.

"Well, look at you," Violet said, taking Micah by the shoulders. "All dressed up like a country bride. Here, let your aunt Violet help you." She unknotted the bow at the back of Micah's dress and retied it, propping and smoothing, as though arranging a bouquet, while Charley stood by, not minding that Violet was undoing the bow she'd tied herself just a few minutes ago.

At the counter, Micah and Violet peeled eggs for potato salad, while at the table, Charley had arranged carrot and cucumber slices, delicate florets of raw broccoli and cauliflower on a platter, and was making the garlic hummus for dipping when Miss Honey walked into the kitchen wearing a new dress the color of blood oranges and the snappy wedge sandals with T-straps Charley bought for her at Walmart.

"Let me just say, you're burning a river today, girl," Violet said, warmly. "You look good."

Miss Honey gave a little businesslike nod, but Charley could see, from the way her eyes shone, that Miss Honey was pleased with the way the outfit had turned out. She strolled over to Charley's work station. "Why are you cutting up vegetables?"

"I'm making crudités," Charley said.

"Crude-a-what?"

"It means raw vegetables, Mother," Violet said. "It's healthy."

"Try some." Charley smeared hummus on a piece of broccoli and offered it to Miss Honey who just stared.

"Vegetables are supposed to be cooked," Miss Honey said, backing away. "When you need a burner, you can push the gumbo back." She drifted over to Violet. "Are you adding enough mayonnaise to that potato salad? Because you know I can't stand potato salad when it's dry."

Violet looked at Charley and rolled her eyes. "Here we go." She gouged out a heaping spoonful of Blue Plate mayonnaise and flicked it into the bowl. "Is *this* enough mayonnaise for you, Mother, or would you like me to add more?"

"And why aren't you using the cut-glass bowl? You know that's what I always use. Where'd this other one come from?"

Violet sighed heavily, then said, in a syrupy tone, "Is that what you'd *like*, Mother? Would you like me to use the other bowl? Charley—"

Charley held up her hands. "I'm out of it." One week ago, observing the storms that raged between them, she'd been unnerved. Now she understood it was just the way they expressed their love. They would never change. "You two want to kill each other before this reunion even gets started, it's fine by me." She set her knife down and went outside.

In the front yard, folding chairs circled tables covered with red-and-white-checkered cloths like an East Village pizzeria. Charlie pulled one out and sat down; looked across the street where Miss Goldie's German shepherd paced back and forth in its big chain-link cage as Miss Goldie and her husband came out of their house. They waved to Charley as they slid into their car and backed into the street. Charley waved back, watched them pull away, and was thinking how nice it would be to have one day, just *one* day, when she wasn't worried about her farm, when she could just go for a drive, when, from somewhere down the street, she heard the screech and howl of gospel preaching. A Ford Bronco came to a skidding halt behind her Volvo. The engine stopped, the radio went silent, and the passenger door swung open.

"Hey there, niece!"

Uncle Brother—the graveled voice, the round belly he seemed to carry proudly, like something cultivated on the finest Creole cooking— who else could it be? He trekked across the grass, then pulled Charley into his bear of an embrace. "You're looking good." In that cowboy hat, those cardboard-creased jeans and black alligator boots, he could be a regular on a country music TV dance show.

"You, too." Charley kissed his cheek, struck by how much he looked like her father.

"It's about time," Violet scolded, sounding like Miss Honey as she marched down the porch steps. "Give me those." She held the gate open with her hip as Uncle Brother hauled covered dishes and aluminum serving trays from the backseat. He handed them to a young man who came around from the driver's side. "Hey there, John," Violet said as he bent to kiss her. "How you doing, sweetheart? Take those salads in the house and put them on ice."

"I'm Charley." Charley shifted a tray to extend a free hand.

"For heaven's sake," Violet said. "I've got too much on my mind. John, this is your cousin. I'm trying to think if you were even born the last time she was down here."

"Hey, cuz." John towered over her. He smiled warmly. His grip was firm and he held Charley's hand a beat longer than she expected. His close-shaven hair, his thick neck and broad shoulders, his solid chest muscles pressing against his ironed polo shirt suggested a military tour.

"John's a guard over at Huntsville," Violet said, proudly. "No, let me say it right—a 'correctional officer.'"

"Guard'll do fine," John said, beaming, and smoothed an already-smooth shirt.

"I know you just got here"—Uncle Brother put his arms around Charley's shoulder and leaned in close—"but when things get too slow for you in this little fish pond, make Violet bring you across the border. Texas. Now, that's the big time."

Violet snapped her fingers. "That reminds me, John. Charley has a little girl, Micah. She's running around here somewhere; a regular little woman. I was thinking you ought to take Micah fishing."

"If it's not any trouble," Charley added. "If you're not too busy. She's never fished."

"No problem, cousin. I go all the time. I'll take her out to Cousin Bozo's fish camp."

"Oh, that's a great idea." Violet turned to Charley. "It's real nice. Right on the bayou. Big old cypress trees, Spanish moss hanging down; like something out of the movies."

"A fish camp." Charley marveled again at how different life was down here.

"We'll catch some bass," John said. "Some bluegill, a little white perch. You fish, cousin? Maybe you'd like to come along."

The way John said *cousin*, the way he smiled that smile, made Charley think of fireflies flickering at dusk, water bugs skating across the pond, warm nights on a screened porch. She thought of what Prosper Denton had said. *Nothing but you, that fish, and your thoughts.*

Uncle Brother clapped his hands then rubbed them together. "So, where is the old girl? *El Capitan?*"

"Inside," Violet said. "But watch yourself. I don't know why, but she's got a chicken to pluck with everybody this morning. She turned her nose up at Charley's crudités and got on me about some of the mayonnaise I used. John, you'd better get those salads in the house. I know your mama didn't work as long as she did to have them spoil. Brother, you fire up the grill."

Charley turned toward the house, but Uncle Brother called her back.

"Hold up. I got a surprise for you, niece." He opened the Bronco's back hatch. There was a lot of grunting and swearing, and he had to try three times, but he finally lifted out the enormous turtle, which, to Charley's immense relief, was already dead. Its head was the size of a football, and you could fit a whole honeydew melon in the gaping mouth. Its tongue was as big as a cow's and its shell was the diameter of Miss Honey's coffee table. Its tail, covered in what could easily be vinyl flooring, was as long as a Labrador's and four times as thick. Uncle Brother leaned backward as he struggled to balance the turtle on his knees. He grinned broadly at Charley and said, "Thought I'd make my special turtle soup in your honor. Welcome home."

It was eleven o'clock. It was noon. Relatives arrived in steady waves like a river's rising tide—Great Aunt Rose from Opelousas with her high cheekbones and Charley's same smile; Uncle Oliver and Aunt Madeline, with the same red tint in their complexions; cousins Screw Neck and Joe Black, Buzzard Gravy and Maraine, who, as a young woman, moved all the way to San Francisco, where she worked as a maid at the Mark Hopkins Hotel and saved enough money to buy the real fur coat that she was wearing in a photograph that showed her waiting on the corner for a trolley. People two-stepped to blues and zydeco humming through Uncle Brother's rigged sound system. In one corner of the yard, folks slapped dominoes on the rented tables, while in another, men gathered at the barbecue grill as smoke drifted into the woods. And Charley, struck by the wonder of it all, let herself be drawn in. She listened to Uncle Arthur's story about growing up in a share-cropping family on Old Man Hebert's farm, of shopping at Hebert's store, where a nickel bought a bottle of Hadacol or Woodbury After Shave Powder, and a dance wasn't a dance without a little Rose of

Sharon hair tonic to make a fella's hair look fine. And just before they ate, Charley joined in the moment of silence when the entire family paused to hold hands and say a prayer for Ernest, funeraled and laid to rest way out in California, may his soul rest in peace. *These blessings we say in Jesus's name. Praise the Lord. Amen.*

The afternoon stretched away. People gathered around Charley, between rounds of bid whist and second helpings of potato salad, to tell her how proud they were of her and to ask about the farm. How *had* Ernest made enough money to buy so much land? It felt wonderful, like being tucked in at night, to know people were interested in her story, to hear them express their concern and wish her well.

Charley had just helped Miss Honey rearrange a table loaded with lemon cakes and sugar cookies and popcorn balls made with real molasses, when a man who looked to be in his early forties, wearing a pith helmet and shabby army fatigues, pushed a lawn mower into the yard and parked it along the fence.

"There you are, Hollywood," Miss Honey said, her face brightening. "Didn't know if your mama would let you come."

"Hey there, Miss Honey. *Comment ça va?*" He took off his helmet and clutched it to his chest as he kissed her cheek. "You know I wouldn't let nothing keep me away."

"This is my great-grandbaby, Micah, all the way from Los Angeles of California," Miss Honey said, waving Micah over. "And this is my granddaughter, Charley. The one I was telling you about."

Hollywood bowed to Micah and kissed her hand. "*Enchanté.* I see Miss Honey gave you the camera. I found it in her back room when I was cleaning."

His accent—part French, part Southern, and something else too—reminded Charley of NeNee Desonier and her granddaughter. Only, Hollywood's skin was pale, his eyes blue, his coarse graying hair brushed back in gentle waves. He didn't *look* black, but she was sure he wasn't white either. "Nice to meet you." She extended her hand, ready to shake, but Hollywood saluted her instead. She looked for stripes on his sleeve, bars on his collar, then to Miss Honey for an explanation. But Miss Honey only took out her handkerchief and dabbed her forehead.

They stood awkwardly for a few seconds, then Charley pointed to the fence. "Nice mower." Someone had soldered banana bicycle handlebars where the regular lawnmower handle should have been.

"Hollywood has a nice business cutting lawns for people in the Quarters," Miss Honey said.

Hollywood glanced at Charley and blushed deeply. "Just a little something to keep me busy." He brushed grass clippings off his pants and turned to Miss Honey. "I just finished Miss Ivy's and came to tell you I'ma run home real quick, clean up, but I'll be back." He turned to Charley. "So you're Ralph Angel's baby sister."

Charley's breath caught. She was accustomed to being referred to as Lorna and Ernest's daughter, as Micah's mother, as Davis's widow. Since she'd been in Saint Josephine, she'd started to think of herself as Miss Honey's granddaughter. But she still wasn't accustomed to being called Ralph Angel's sister.

"Hollywood and Ralph Angel grew up together," Miss Honey said.

"We been knowing each other more than thirty years," Hollywood said.

"They were like brothers from the beginning. Ain't that right?"

Hollywood fingered his helmet and looked off toward the street. "I guess."

"Lord knows you've eaten enough meals at my kitchen table," Miss Honey said. "Which reminds me. When are you coming over to finish cleaning the back room?"

"Friday afternoon if that's okay. Right after I cut Miss Maggie's grass." Hollywood put on his helmet, preparing to go.

"Well, don't forget. 'Cause Charley and them are sleeping up front in Ralph Angel's room and I know they'll change their minds once they see how big that back room is."

Micah made a tiny sound and stepped on Charley's foot.

The afternoon they arrived, they followed Miss Honey through the den with the faux wood paneling and down the narrow hall, past a laundry room, past the half bath, and the sunporch with a washing machine and a deep freezer that hummed loudly.

"Won't have anything back here to bother you but the sound of your own voice," Miss Honey had said. She stepped into a darkened room where the air was noticeably cooler, and yanked the cord dangling from the ceiling. Harsh white light flooded the room. "It's the biggest room in the house," Miss Honey had said. "And it's private."

Standing on the threshold, Charley looked past Miss Honey into a room crowded with garden tools, old bicycles and vacuum cleaners, mountains of browning newspaper, boxes of old clothes, and shopping bags brimming with mismatched shoes. She spotted a king-size bed piled with clutter, just visible beneath a small window. And worse than the sight was the smell—ointment and mothballs, mildew and dust. Odors that lingered, Charley thought. Odors that would hang in her clothes and hair.

"It's so messy," Micah had whispered. "And it smells like old people."

"Don't mind this junk, sugar," Miss Honey said, and went on to explain that she'd hired Hollywood, her gardener and all-around handyman, to clear away all the boxes. "He only got to half of what's back here, but when he's through, y'all can make this your home away from home."

That's when Charley interrupted. Said, as delicately as she could, that it was too much trouble.

"Back here, you'll have room to spread out, get comfortable," Miss Honey had said, waving Charley's protest away. "I saw all those suitcases and bags you brought with you."

But Charley had pushed. "I remember another room." She'd pressed her finger to her lips. "Up front. It had a window that looked out onto the porch."

Miss Honey had hesitated. "Ralph Angel's room. Besides, there's but one bed in there."

That was the first time Charley had heard her half brother's name in years. "Really, we'll manage," Charley had said.

Miss Honey shook her head. "Mighty silly to crowd two people into that little room."

"I like that room," Micah had said. "I like *little* rooms."

"We'll manage," Charley said.

Miss Honey had sucked in her cheeks. "Big room like this going to waste, but if that's the way y'all want it." She gave the light cord another quick yank plunging the room into darkness.

Now, with Hollywood promising to finish the job, Charley imagined what might have nibbled through the stacked boxes, made nests in the piles of old clothes, given birth to litters of pink blind hairless babies the size of her thumbnail. She squeezed Micah's hand. She looked at Miss Honey and thought, She may be the ringmaster, she may be the Grande Dame, but there was no way in hell they were staying in that back room.

Uncle Brother's turtle soup and Miss Honey's gumbo had been devoured. There was still a wedge of Violet's lemon pound cake left, though it wouldn't last long, and the last carton of Blue Belle ice cream was melting. But Charley's crudités with garlic hummus sat untouched as the Impala cruised past Miss Honey's and parked.

Charley looked up from the clutch of older women seated on the porch and watched the latecomer as he stepped through the gate. She nudged Violet. "Who's that?"

And because it took Violet a long moment to answer, Charley thought she had forgotten the man's name, thought that the long afternoon of laughter and old stories and a beer or two had made her aunt a little tipsy and forgetful. But Violet said, clearly, "Good Lord. What's he doing here?" which made Charley and everyone else on the porch look again. Even Uncle Brother, who had planted himself at the bid whist table two hours ago and not gotten up once, put down his cards and stared in disbelief.

The man stood just inside the gate. A small boy called, "Pop, wait," from the car.

"Well, come on, then," the man said, and held the gate open as the boy climbed out, then broke into a gallop that was lighthearted and, Charley thought, a little desperate. They stood together in the grass, waiting.

"Pop?"

"Don't worry." The man threw his arm over the boy's shoulders, pulled him close. "This is your family." He cleared his throat and stepped forward, the child clinging to his wrist. "Well, hell. Somebody say something." He gave his son's shoulder a quick squeeze. "You all are making my boy here uncomfortable."

The boy's shirt, with a truck decal on the chest, was one long smear of chocolate fingerprints.

Uncle Brother balled his napkin and stood up. "What are you doing here, Ralph Angel?"

Charley was twelve the last time she saw Ralph Angel, and he was nineteen. He came to her parents' house for Christmas dinner, his first visit since their father sent him home, and he'd surprised her with a chemistry set—the small metal cabinet with a black leather handle and real glass beakers, copper sulfate, aluminum bicarbonate, and citric acid in brightly labeled bottles. He was a college freshman, he said, planned to major in engineering then work for a big oil company after he graduated. But what Charley remembered most clearly was that he gave her ten dollars. And it wasn't the money as much as the way he gave it: pulled a roll of bills from his pocket, licked his fingers, and peeled off a ten, which he folded in half and held between his fingers, flicking his wrist as if to suggest he had money to throw away.

The metal locker, Charley thought now. The roll of bills. Ralph Angel. Her big brother. Here he was.

A quiet had descended upon the yard.

Ralph Angel smiled at Uncle Brother, who had come down from the porch and stood on the walkway. "Now, c'mon, uncle. Is that any way to greet your favorite nephew?"

Ralph Angel took a toothpick from his jacket pocket and slid it into his mouth. He looked like a guy who wouldn't fight fair; not at all like the boy she'd followed around or the young man who gave her ten dollars.

And just as Charley was thinking these things, she saw John rise from his chair and walk to his father's side. His fingers grazed his hips, Charley noticed, though of course, there was no holster. He drew himself up to full height, spread his feet, squared his shoulders. "Is there a problem here?" His tone was respectful, but cautious.

"Well, I'll be damned," Ralph Angel said. "Look at you, man. All grown up."

They stared at each other, then John bent to shake the boy's hand. "Hey there, Blue. I need to talk to your daddy for a minute, okay?"

Blue. Charley wondered at the mother who would name her child something so sad. But his solemn expression, the way he looked up, pleadingly, at his dad—somehow, the name suited him.

Ralph Angel put his hand on Blue's shoulder. "Don't you worry about my boy, John. Blue is just fine." But when Aunt Rose from Opelousas hurried down the step and took Blue's hand, saying, "Let's get you some lemonade," Ralph Angel let him go.

Uncle Brother stepped closer to Ralph Angel. "I asked you a question. What are you doing here?"

Ralph Angel put his hand over his heart. "What makes you think I wasn't invited?"

In a fluid gesture, John put a firm hand on Ralph Angel's arm. He was twenty years younger than Ralph Angel but stood a foot taller, and was, Charley guessed, at least thirty pounds heavier. "Why don't we take this out to the street?"

Something flashed across Ralph Angel's face. Charley saw it. Ralph

Angel looked at John's hand on his arm and pulled away slowly. "I don't want to take this out to the street. I'd like to say hello to the rest of the family." He stepped forward, but John blocked his path.

"I can't let you do that, cousin. I'm sorry. Not before we straighten this out."

Ralph Angel stared at John. After a long moment, he laughed. "Come on, man. Why you want to hassle me?" He brushed past John, quick as a running back, and made his way up the walk. He stopped at the bottom step and looked up at Charley. "Hello, sis."

Charley recalled what Violet had said about Ralph Angel pushing Miss Honey. Something about the way he stood there with that toothpick in his mouth made her think he might be capable of it. Still, he'd held Blue's hand with great tenderness. That counted for something. A lot, actually. How harmful could he be? Charley moved down the steps. "Hello, Ralph Angel. It's good to see you." She heard Violet gasp behind her. Unsure whether to hug him or shake his hand, she took a chance and opened her arms. Their embrace felt wooden.

Ralph Angel broke away first. "Yeah. It's been a long time."

The screen door creaked, and Miss Honey, wiping her hands on her apron, stepped out onto the porch. "Why is it so quiet?"

"Hello, 'Da," Ralph Angel said.

"Hello, Ralph Angel," Miss Honey said. She barely blinked.

Ralph Angel tipped his head toward the side yard, toward the tables and chairs, the last of the food on dishes covered with crumpled foil. "Looks like I missed the celebration."

"Mother," Violet said, standing up now, "did you call Ralph Angel?"

Miss Honey looked almost dreamily at Violet, then out into the street, where a car—a dark blue Monte Carlo, Charley saw—approached. Music pulsed and young, defiant voices rang out over heavy bass. The driver honked and waved. Everyone looked, out of habit, to see who was behind the wheel. "That's sister Martin's boy," Miss Honey said, more to herself than anyone. "Where does he think he's going?"

"Mother, I'm asking," Violet said. She inched up to Miss Honey and held her shoulders just the way she'd held Charley's that day she'd begged her to go to Sugar Town. "Did you call Ralph Angel? Because someone did, and now he's here."

The music blaring from the car's speakers was swallowed by the heat. Miss Honey's yard fell quiet again. But Charley still heard layers of sound—the hiss of insects in the trees, the creature whine rising from the gulley, faint voices of neighbors up and down the block, and beyond that, the faint drone of cars whipping over the asphalt. She heard all of it, felt herself drawn down into the mucky clay and the stalks of cane.

Miss Honey pulled away from Violet's grip. "What if I did? What's wrong with wanting my family to come together? Yes, I called him, and now it's done. Now I want you and Brother to welcome Ralph Angel home."

Violet and Brother exchanged glances.

"No, Mother," Violet said. "I'm sorry."

Miss Honey glared at Violet. "I'm booking you, girl." She turned to Uncle Brother. Her voice was raw. "I'm going to say this one time, so y'all better hear me, because I've come to the end of my row. Y'all may be grown out there in the world, but when you come to my house, you better leave your manhood and your womanhood under my porch step. If Charley can welcome Ralph Angel, so can you." She paused to wave a finger across the porch and over the yard. "As a matter of fact, all y'all can."

Charley looked at her relatives, at Screw Neck in his workday overalls and Maraine, small and birdlike in her compression stockings and orthopedic shoes, whose name, Charley had learned earlier, was actually Clemence, but who went by Maraine, which meant "godmother" in French. She searched every face, waiting for someone to say something, wondering what they knew. No one moved.

"Forget it, 'Da," Ralph Angel said. "Don't force them."

And as Charley struggled to make sense of what was happening, Violet pulled the screen door open. "I'll see you later, Mother." She disappeared into the house, emerging a moment later with her purse.

"Where are you going?" Miss Honey called.

Down the steps now, Violet paused in front of Charley and took her hand. "I'm sorry," she said. "I'm sorry this had to happen today. I'm sorry this had to happen when you have so much on your plate."

"Violet," Charley said. "Whatever is going on, whatever happened before, I'm sure we can work it out." Who knew why Miss Honey never told anyone she had invited Ralph Angel to the reunion, but in the end, what did it matter? He'd stay for a couple days, and yes, it would be uncomfortable, but then he'd go back to wherever he'd come from.

Violet shook her head. "You're sweet. But no, darling, we can't. We won't work this out. You don't know that now, but you'll see." And with that, she walked past Ralph Angel, past Uncle Brother and John, and out of the yard. Charley felt desperate watching Violet drive away. For Violet was the one person she'd come to feel at home with in her new home. Violet was family. When she turned back, she saw Ralph Angel give a little shrug. Then he looked to her.

"So, sis, what's going on? Long time, no see. And by the way, I heard the good news. Congratulations on your farm."

The party was over. Charley tossed the empty bottles and paper plates in the trash, dragged the garbage can to the street, and was about to go inside when she heard someone call her name. Hollywood, walking fast down the street.

"Was that Brother and John I just seen?" he asked, breathless, pointing over his shoulder in the direction he'd just come from then peering into Miss Honey's yard. "Where is everybody?"

He'd showered and shaved, combed his hair and changed his shirt, though he still wore his shabby army fatigues and reeked of cologne, underneath which Charley smelled laundry detergent and the deep odor of armpit perspiration run over with a hot iron. "Gone," Charley said, and looked back at the trampled grass, the tables and folding chairs stacked neatly near the bottom step. Within an hour of Ralph Angel's arrival, everyone left.

Hollywood's face fell. Though he was certainly older than Charley— he had to be close to Ralph Angel's age—Hollywood's disappointment made him look much younger. "Aw, man. I thought y'all would be partying all night." He gazed down the street like a boy who had missed the parade. "Doggone," he said, quietly.

"I'm sorry," Charley said. Twilight had declared itself with a rush of cooler air, and though she wanted to sit by herself for a while, sit and try to make sense of the day, Charley said, "Why don't you come in? At least let me fix you a plate to take home."

"I don't know." Hollywood jammed his hands into his pockets. "I should go."

"But you walked all the way over here," Charley said, thinking of the compound three miles down the road. Miss Honey had pointed it out one day as they ran errands in town—the handful of ramshackle trailers scattered around the cleared lot like boxes of crackers; the children, barefoot and pale, who played on the broken-down swing or in the rusted-out cars or jumped on the old mattress they used as a trampoline. "That's the Arnaud Plantation," Miss Honey had said. "Hollywood, my gardener, the one who's gonna clean the back room, lives there," and she'd gone on to explain that the Arnauds were a clan of Creoles—a mix of African, Spanish, French, and Anglo—who stuck to themselves and intermarried to preserve their fair skin; had for generations. They owned a cemetery back in the woods where all of the black folks in town were buried, where she'd be buried when her time came. "Miss Honey won't like it if you leave without saying hello."

"Well, okay. I guess," Hollywood said, following her into the yard. "You know my *maman* don't like that I'm always over here in the Quarters, cutting grass for black folks, but I tell her I love spending time over here." He gazed at Miss Honey's house. "I can't imagine a day without seeing Miss Honey. She's more like a *maman* to me than my own."

In the kitchen, Charley tugged the cord that sent the fan blades whirling. The sink was filled with dishes and plastic trays, the counters cluttered with Barq's root beer cans, brown paper sacks of cracklins, and the remains of crawfish boudin that Joe Black brought all the way from Hackett's Cajun Kitchen in Lake Charles. While Hollywood sat at the table, Charley fixed his plate, tucked the last wedge of Violet's lemon pound cake on the side, and wrapped the whole thing in foil.

"Most days, by the time I get home, *Maman*'n them have already ate," Hollywood offered. "I eat over at my brother's sometimes."

Charley nodded, wondering again what it was about Hollywood that struck her as odd. Something was missing; some small thing, like a bearing in his mower, but definitely something.

"Hello." Micah, barefoot but still wearing her party dress, stepped into the kitchen. She held an empty bowl and a spoon. "Seconds," she said. "Miss Honey said I could."

"Go tell Miss Honey Hollywood is here," Charley said.

"Okay." Micah moved toward the freezer. "Ice cream first."

"No," Charley said. "Miss Honey first. Do it now, then you can come back."

Micah rolled her eyes. "*Tu me rends dingue. Va je foutre.*"

"Translation," Charley said. "I'm being snotty and rude and I don't want any ice cream."

"But I didn't say—"

Hollywood sat forward, said, calmly, "*Tu ne devrais pas parles à ta maman comme ça.*"

Micah froze. She gawked at Hollywood. Charley did too.

"*Une gentile fille dit pas de gros mots. T'es grande fille maintenant— tu peux plus faire comme ça! T'as pas honte? Dis-elle pardon.*"

Micah turned to Charley. "I'm sorry." She glanced at Hollywood, who nodded with stern approval. "I didn't mean to hurt your feelings or be impolite."

"Now," Hollywood said, gravely, and pointed toward the den, "go tell Miss Honey I'm here."

When Micah was gone, Charley gaped at Hollywood, asked, "What was *that*?" Micah's stunned expression still playing through her mind.

Hollywood shrugged. "I told her nice girls don't swear. And then I told her she was too grown to act that way, that she was embarrassing herself."

"Well, I owe you one," Charley said. "She's given me hell lately." She felt a sisterly affection for him, though she barely knew him, and hoped they could be friends.

Hollywood pulled a glossy movie magazine from his back pocket, set it on the table, and smoothed the cover. "Miss Honey says y'all lived in Hollywood."

"Not exactly," Charley said, and thought of the little Spanish bungalow south of Pico, not too far from the Jewish deli where elderly waitresses wore pink uniforms and wigs stiff with spray. There'd been nothing glamorous about it.

"I'm gonna get out there one of these days," Hollywood said, and gazed through the kitchen window. "Take one of them buses that goes around to all the movie stars' houses. I'm gonna find Marvin Gaye's house first." He flipped to a dog-eared article and read haltingly, running his finger beneath each word. "'On April first, nineteen eighty-four, at eleven thirty-eight a.m., the world lost a musical genius when Rhythm and Blues legend Marvin Gaye was shot at point-blank range by his father after a heated argument.'" He paused, stared at the article, then looked up at Charley. "Marvin Gaye was a great singer. He had everything a man could want, but he was still unhappy. Made everyone around him unhappy. I wonder if that's what his daddy was thinking when he shot him?"

"I wonder," Charley said, and couldn't help but think about Ralph Angel, who—if Violet's story was true, and why wouldn't it be?—seemed to be haunted by his own demons. Maybe he still was. A current of regret rippled through Charley for not knowing.

"Well, I'll be damned. Look who's here." Ralph Angel stepped into the kitchen.

Hollywood's face flushed as he turned toward the sound of Ralph Angel's voice. He pushed back from the table, stood up. "Ralph Angel. Where'd you come from?"

His question made Charley think back on the afternoon, how Ralph Angel had materialized at the gate as if out of thin air.

"Rolled in a couple hours ago," Ralph Angel said. He set his beer on the counter, walked over to Hollywood, and pulled him close. "Glad to see you, Peanut. What's going on, man?"

But Hollywood stood stiffly, and Charley remembered how he had hesitated, earlier, when Miss Honey said he and Ralph Angel were like brothers. He had the same uneasy look on his face.

Ralph Angel must have noticed too, because he said, "Relax, Peanut. It's just me," and laughed nervously. "Jesus Christ. You're as bad as the rest of 'em. Everyone's acting like I've got the plague or something."

"I'm just surprised, is all," Hollywood said.

Ralph Angel looked from Hollywood to Charley. "I see you met my best friend."

"I was just fixing Hollywood a plate," Charley said. "Join us."

Ralph Angel went to the refrigerator for another beer, then slid into a chair. He picked up Hollywood's magazine. "*Highlife*?"

"It tells what all the celebrities are doing," Hollywood said. "Miss Loretta down at the library gives me the old copies when the new ones come in. Just a little something to keep me busy." He watched as Ralph Angel flipped the pages, then added, tentatively, "I didn't know you were home."

Ralph Angel tossed the magazine back on the table. "Don't tell me you actually believe the stuff they write."

"Why wouldn't I? It's from the library."

Ralph Angel rolled his eyes. "Yeah, okay. But you can't go around with your head in the clouds. You've gotta learn to think for yourself."

He took a sip of beer. "So, how you doing, Peanut? Seriously. What's new?"

"Please don't call me that, Ralph Angel."

"I'm just messing with you, man. All in good fun. Say, are you still cutting grass with that funny mower?"

"Yeah."

Ralph Angel gestured to Charley. "That's one of the things you'll find down here, little sister; things never change. I come back after all this time, and Hollywood here is still pushing that same goddamned mower. Unbelievable."

"Who's swearing in my house? I thought I heard swearing." Miss Honey pushed into the kitchen, and Charley saw that she'd changed into her housedress and slippers. Miss Honey looked at Hollywood. "Well, I'm glad to see you finally made it. Folks were asking for you."

"Miss Honey, you didn't tell me Ralph Angel was coming home," Hollywood said, but Miss Honey waved the statement away as she moved to the sink and started washing dishes.

"So, how much you charging these days?" Ralph Angel said. "Ten dollars?"

Hollywood blinked. "Five dollars. That's what I charge. Five's fair."

"*Five dollars?* Holy shit!" Ralph Angel put his hand to his forehead. "Listen here, Peanut. Don't you know minimum wage is around seven fifty? Hey, Charley, what are you paying the guys who work for you?"

"I don't know. I haven't hired anyone yet."

"Well, be sure to put Hollywood on your payroll. He's a steal. I'm telling you, man, you ought to raise your price. Better yet, you should expand your operation. Seriously. Get some guys to work for you. You could rake in the big bucks."

"I don't know," Hollywood said. "I sort of like working by myself."

"Boy, I tell you," Ralph Angel said, and stared into his beer can. "That's the goddamned South for you. That's another thing you'll find down here, Charley. Folks bend over backwards to be polite, even when it's killing them. Why, this nigger here only charges five measly dollars to cut a whole yard. How long does it take you? An hour?"

Hollywood shrugged. "About that."

"Five measly dollars an hour," Ralph Angel said, glancing quickly at Charley. "Ain't that some shit?"

Hollywood winced, and Charley—seeing how he just sat there, looking as though his shoes were two sizes too small, picking at the threads of his army fatigues like the new kid on the first day of school—thought she should say something. But she didn't. Because she was trying to reconcile the Ralph Angel from Violet's story with what she wanted to believe about her brother: that a lot of terrible things could happen to a person in twenty years; a person could run off the rails, and that sometimes it was easier to pick on someone else's weaknesses rather than face the weakness in yourself. And she also understood, from the way Ralph Angel glanced at her as he spoke, that in his own awkward way, he was trying to impress her, make a good impression.

"Ralph Angel, watch your mouth," Miss Honey said. "Hollywood's built a nice business. Folks depend on him. Now, let the man be. He wants to charge five dollars, let him charge it."

"I'm just talking to him, 'Da. Offering constructive criticism. Ain't that right, Hollywood? We're just talking, man to man. And I'm trying to show Charley what she can expect down here."

Miss Honey glanced at Hollywood. "How you feeling, *chère*?"

"I'm okay," Hollywood said, feebly. "But I don't want to talk about cutting grass no more."

Ralph Angel nodded. "Fine by me. What do you want to talk about?"

"I don't know," Hollywood said. He picked at the aluminum foil covering his plate. "I'd better get on. *Maman*'s gonna be worried."

"You sure?" Ralph Angel said. He sounded surprised, and a little hurt. "You don't want to stick around and have a beer?"

"Naw," Hollywood said, standing. He went to the sink and kissed Miss Honey.

"Hey, we should go hunting like when we were kids," Ralph Angel said, excitedly. "Been years since I fired a gun."

Hollywood frowned. "It ain't hunting season. They'll arrest you."

"I'll walk you out," Charley said, and closed Hollywood's magazine, relieved to have an excuse to escape.

Outside, the air was cooler, the street filled with sounds of a summer evening in the Quarter's winding to a close: the easy groove of an R&B tune wafting from a nearby radio, the chime of people's laughter as they relaxed on their porches, the occasional crack of a screen door closing, the cicadas' manic winding up and winding down.

"Well, thanks for the eats." Hollywood started down the steps.

"God, Hollywood. I'm so sorry. I didn't know he'd act that way."

Hollywood blanched. "It's all right. Me and Ralph Angel go way back. I'm kinda used to it." He took his magazine from Charley, slapped it against his palm, then slid it into his back pocket. "You got a good girl there. Don't worry. She was just being a kid."

Charley stood by the gate as Hollywood made his way down the sidewalk. She thought he looked lost without his mower. The sun had dropped below the tree line, the sky pinking around the edges, and up and down the street, people's porch lights were coming on so that every few feet, the aluminum foil covering his plate glowed like a faint star.

Miss Honey's den was already cozy with her La-Z-Boy, and the sectional upholstered in faded blue plaid, the étagère overrun with her collection of salt and pepper shakers, and the framed pictures hanging askance above the TV, but now it was downright crowded. Stretched out on the couch, Blue slept with his feet in Ralph Angel's lap, while Micah, changed into shorts now, perched on the arm of Miss Honey's recliner.

"It's late, Micah," Charley said in a hushed voice. "Time for bed."

Micah groaned.

"So, Charley." Ralph Angel eased Blue's legs off his lap and sat forward. "Last time I saw you, you were stuffing Kleenex into your training bra and picking lettuce out of your braces. Now look at you."

"Yeah, well. Here I am," Charley said dryly.

Ralph Angel leaned back into the cushion. "Micah here's been telling me about your farm. Eight hundred acres. Congratulations. Aren't you the lucky one."

"I don't know about lucky," Charley said. "It's a lot of work. It could all come crashing down."

"I bet," Ralph Angel said. "But it must be nice knowing our daddy loved you enough to leave you a whole plantation. Something to fall back on, know what I mean?"

Charley wasn't sure what to make of his question. She glanced at the television, where trumpets blared and snare drums *rat-a-tat-tatted* as Shirley Temple sang the closing number of *Rebecca of Sunnybrook Farm.*

"Guess that makes you the star of the family," Ralph Angel went on. "I mean, you got 'Da here throwing a whole reunion in your honor, people coming in from Houston and Baton Rouge just to get a look at you; my best friend fawning over you. You must feel pretty special."

"Miss Honey did a generous thing," Charley said. "I'm grateful. I said *right now*, Micah. Time for bed."

"If you'd come when I called," Miss Honey said, "you could've enjoyed the reunion for yourself."

Ralph Angel picked at the foam sticking up from the couch cushions, then poked his finger in the hole, making it wider. "Why are you riding me so hard, 'Da? I told you I had to take care of some business."

"I'm just saying," Miss Honey said, unfazed by his tone. "It's your own fault you missed the reunion."

"Jesus. I can't drop everything because you pick up the phone."

"Well, good night," Charley said. She took Micah's arm.

"That does it for me, too," Ralph Angel said. "Think we'll turn in." He hoisted a yawning Blue onto his shoulder.

"Ralph Angel," Miss Honey said. "Y'all are sleeping in the back.

Hollywood's coming Friday to finish cleaning it out. Till then, y'all can sleep on the floor in here."

"The *back*? But what about my room up front?"

"I gave it to Charley and them."

"But that's *my* room." Ralph Angel sounded almost panicked.

"And seeing how she got here first, I told her she could have it. You and Blue can sleep in the back. It won't kill you. It's a big room and it's private."

"But 'Da—"

"If you got here when I called, it'd be yours to claim. But you didn't. The front room belongs to Charley unless she agrees to trade."

Ralph Angel offered Charley a conciliatory smile. "How about it?"

It would be a hassle for her to pack everything and haul it to the back room, Charley thought, but she could do it. Thirty minutes, an hour max, and she could give Ralph Angel his room. Charley looked at her brother, standing there with Blue slumped over his shoulder like a sack of potatoes. She hadn't wanted to listen to Violet when she said it wouldn't work out, or believe Violet's story about Miss Honey finding Ralph Angel's drugs. Because, and Charley realized it only now, standing there in Miss Honey's tight den with that annoying Shirley Temple singing her heart out, she'd sort of hoped she and Ralph Angel could be friends; sort of wished, secretly, ever since Miss Honey first mentioned his name, that he might protect her the way big brothers were supposed to. Because the truth was, without Ernest or Davis, or her mother, Charley was terrified. The farm, Micah, her future—the stakes felt so high. There were days, driving home from the shop, when she felt so alone she thought she might split down the middle. Oh, how she'd wanted to give Ralph Angel the benefit of the doubt! But after the way he treated Hollywood? Teased him like some schoolyard bully, even if it *was* just to impress her? She couldn't help but think twice. She'd reserve judgment for now; hold out hope. But in the meantime, she'd stay in the front room. Because you couldn't just roll over for someone like that, haunted or not, or he'd start thinking his behavior was acceptable. And just like Marvin Gaye, eventually, he'd spoil it for everyone.

"Actually," Charley said. "We just got settled."

"That's it, then," Miss Honey said, like a game-show host.

Charley tapped Micah's shoulder harder. "Let's go," and peeled her off the recliner. She was just over the threshold when Ralph Angel called after her.

"Hey."

Charley turned.

"Go ahead. It's all yours." Ralph Angel winked. "But just so you know, you owe me one, sis. I'll have to figure out some way you can repay me."

9

When Charley arrived at her farm on Monday morning, Denton was sipping from a thermos and leaning against his pickup, his shirtsleeves rolled up, a pen tucked behind his ear, an Ag bulletin poking out of his back pocket. The sight of him made the day seem suddenly brighter, and Charley kneed her door open, stepped out into the buzz of a thousand unseen insects and sultry morning air. "Good morning."

Denton set his thermos on the dashboard and shook her hand. You could tell a lot about a person from their handshake, that's what her father always said, and Charley could tell from Denton's solid grip that he was the real deal—a man of integrity and honor, steady and forthright—he would not let her down, and for the first time since Frasier quit, Charley thought she might actually have a shot, not just at making the farm work; she would make Micah proud.

"So, where do we begin?" Charley said.

"Let's have a look." Denton headed toward the shop, but not before he whistled and his two dogs, the same ones Charley recognized from his yard, came bounding out of the fields, the larger one flinging slobber in his excitement. Now the picture was complete, Charley thought; it wouldn't be a farm without dogs.

Charley slid the metal door back and felt along the wall for the light switch. She still breathed through her mouth for the first few minutes after she entered, but Denton didn't seem to notice anything. In fact, he inhaled deeply, as though he were inhaling the homey aroma of fresh-baked bread. He bent to inspect an air compressor Charley could actually identify because there was one just like it, but smaller, at the gas station near her old house. Denton had barely touched the hose when the nozzle came off in his hand.

"It's bad, isn't it?" Charley said. "I told you it was bad."

Denton wiped grease off the air compressor with an old rag. "I've seen worse, but I've seen better." He moved from one piece of equipment to the next, calling out each machine's manufacturer, model, and function—all for Charley's sake—followed by the list of parts he'd need to repair it, while Charley recorded everything on a yellow legal pad. The Baileigh drill press under a veil of cobwebs needed a timing belt, and they'd have to order a new output contactor for the MIG welder. They might as well pick up another workbench, Denton said, and a set of wrenches; and that bin of odd pipes under the window might come in handy. Denton moved methodically about the shop like a chef in his restaurant kitchen. He arranged tools by size. He tested the drill press for vibration and runout, uncrimped and rewound the spool of feeder wire for the welder.

"What'll it cost to get everything working?" Charley asked. "Just ballpark?"

"Too soon to tell." Denton had his doubts about the tractor out front; it had been awhile since he'd seen parts for a JD 6400, and he needed to take a closer look at her fields, but when he pried the lid off a metal drum and saw that it was still full, he nodded. "Least we've got enough NH Four to get started. Saved four hundred dollars right there."

By noon, they had taken inventory, and Charley's list of parts and materials was three pages long. But before they drove into town, they climbed into Charley's car and headed off down the narrow road that led to the back quadrant, Denton riding shotgun, his dogs in the backseat, panting and thrusting their heads through the windows.

Occasionally, as they rolled down the headland, a rabbit darted across their path, or swallows, like kamikaze pilots, swooped in front of them, while a hot breeze kicked up from the south, romancing the young cane on either side of the road. Theirs turned out to be a comfortable silence, the only sound the crunch and ping of gravel under the tires. And riding along, Charley fought the urge to say again how grateful she was—partly because she kept thinking about Miss Honey's warning: *Don't come apart like a ball of twine*, and partly because Denton's manner was so calm, so steady, she felt more at ease than she had in months, but also because if she'd kept going like she was going, a few more weeks and she'd have been back in Los Angeles, back in her mother's travertine castle, listening to Lorna say, *I told you so*.

And as far as Charley could tell, Denton seemed equally at ease. He pointed out different varieties of cane as they rumbled past the fields: Louisiana 90 with its aqua-colored leaves and creamy stalks; Home Purple, which started off pale as green tea but turned to Bordeaux in the sunlight; and Denton's favorite, Ribbon Cane, with deep-red-and-bright-green-striped barrels that reminded Charley of an all-day sucker. Each time he called out another variety, 310 or 321, Charley repeated it, hoping that saying the names out loud would help her remember, wondering if she should confess that it all looked like the same leafy green stalks to her.

"For instance," Denton said, "you got a lot of three eighty-four out there."

"Three eighty-four," Charley said. "Is that bad?"

Denton nodded. "It's what most farmers've been planting since '93. But you ought to think about mixing it up some. Maybe plant some five forty or one twenty-eight. It's only been out two years, but it's good. More sugar in it than three eighty-four, and you won't get as much rust."

"Rust. Hold on." Charley asked Denton to hand her the yellow pad.

"What for?"

"I need to write that down."

"All you need to do is listen," Denton said, tossing the pad on the dashboard. "This ain't something you take notes on, Miss Bordelon. You got to live it."

And so, as they reached the second quadrant, Denton told Charley to pull over. When she did, Denton got out, knelt down at the field's edge, and palmed a handful of dirt. "This is what I was talking about at lunch last Friday. This here's good, loamy soil. You can tell by how it holds together." He pinched a bit of soil between his fingers then put it in his mouth. "Not too much clay," he said, "but not too sandy. Now you."

Charley knelt. She pinched a fingerful of dirt and raised it to her mouth, but then she hesitated, thinking of all the creatures that had probably crawled or slithered over that spot.

"Go on, Miss Bordelon. It ain't gonna kill you. All that scribbling won't do you any good if you don't let this get inside you. It's the only way you're going to learn."

Charley guessed this was what Denton meant when he warned that she'd have to do it his way. She looked at him again, expecting his face to have darkened with impatience, but he only gave her an encouraging nod. Charley put the dirt in her mouth and swallowed quickly.

"Well?" Denton said. "What did it tell you?"

"Nothing," Charley said. "I didn't taste anything. I don't know what to look for."

"Do it over. Take your time."

Charley raised the dirt to her mouth again. She sniffed: wood smoke, grass, damp like a sidewalk after it rained. She tasted: grit, fine as ground glass, chocolate, and what? Maybe ash? She closed her eyes as soil dissolved over her tongue, and slowly, slowly, almost like a good wine, the soil began to tell its story. She tasted the muck, and the peat, and the years of composted leaves, the branches and vines that had been recently plowed under, and the faint sweetness the cane left behind. She swallowed: a moldy aftertaste she knew would stay on her tongue for the rest of the afternoon. And though she didn't yet know the terms to describe what she had experienced, she understood a little more clearly what Denton was trying to teach her. When she looked over at Denton again, he nodded approvingly, then, without another word, brushed dirt from his knees and walked back to the car.

. . .

Back at the shop, Charley had just discovered another envelope of invoices Frasier apparently hadn't bothered to pay, when Denton knocked on her office door. He held her yellow pad. "Here's what I've come up with."

Charley wheeled around from the desk she'd only partially cleared, gesturing for him to take a seat on the tattered sofa.

"Besides the replacement parts for the machinery," Denton said, "we've got to buy more mother stalk."

"Mother stalk?"

"That's the cane you plant at the beginning," Denton said. "You start by cutting a long piece of cane and laying it on its side in the ground. Every piece of cane has knots on it a few inches apart, sort of like eyes on a potato, and out of those knots, a new cane plant will shoot up. That first shoot, when it grows up tall like you see around here, is called your plant crop. That's what you harvest during grinding. The next year when that cane sends up another shoot, that's called first-year stubble. Next year after that, the shoot that comes up is second-year stubble, the next year is third-year, and by the fourth year, that original stalk you planted is pretty much worn out, so you dig it up and start again. You usually get four crops from every mother stalk."

"So mother stalk is like sourdough starter," Charley said. "I think I get it."

"Sort of, I guess," Denton said, looking puzzled. "You got a lot of third-year stubble out there that'll need to be replaced. We also need to dig those drains I showed you and fill those ruts in the front quadrant. It'll cost us, but we can probably find some local labor if we ask around."

"Local labor?"

Denton looked at Charley over the top of his bifocals. "Black folks." He flipped the page. "Now, I think I can save the John Deere out front, but you're gonna need a combine, a chisel plow, and at least two three-row choppers." He did some final figuring. "We're looking at one fifty-six."

"Excuse me?"

"One hundred fifty-six thousand. Give or take."

Give or take what? Charley wanted to say. *My kid? My life? My soul?* She felt her knees buckle even though she was sitting down.

"One fifty-fix should do it," Denton mused, tapping the pad with his pen. "That'll get us to October. Once grinding starts, we'll need at least four cane wagons, that's another twelve, but I saw one out in the yard, so we'll worry about that later."

Charley leaned forward, put her head between her legs. And now the ball of twine had not only hit the floor, it was coming apart fast, with little bits of fiber poking out everywhere. "Oh my God. Oh my God. Oh my God."

"Miss Bordelon?"

"Mr. Denton, I don't have one hundred fifty-six thousand dollars."

"How much do you have?"

Between her savings and what was left of the operating fund she had ninety-one thousand dollars—a lot of money if you owned a bakery or a bicycle repair shop, but a pittance, Charley realized now, if you were trying to run an eight-hundred-acre sugarcane farm. "Ninety-one."

"Ninety-one?"

"Ninety-one," Charley said again, but it may as well have been ninety-one thousand gum balls.

Denton stared at her a moment longer, then pushed his hat back on his forehead and squeezed his brows together. "What about a line of credit?"

Charley shook her head, no.

"What about cash reserves?"

"These *are* my reserves."

"Ninety-one thousand," Denton said, like she'd just handed him a stack of Monopoly money. "I told you this was no game."

Charley could practically hear Denton cursing himself for coming out of retirement, kicking himself for buying in. She was on the verge of apologizing, but stopped herself, sensing that if she uttered another word, a single syllable, she'd tip the scales and Denton would walk.

"You can hardly find a decent used combine for ninety-one thousand," Denton said. He sighed the heaviest sigh Charley had ever heard, and set the yellow pad on the floor.

On the other side of the window, a dragonfly bobbed along the glass.

"I understand if you don't want to work with me," Charley said. She pulled a crumpled Ag bulletin off the stack, folded the first page over, and stared at the columns of print, not reading any of it, because it was easier, less agonizing than watching the disappointment register across Denton's face.

Denton slid forward on the threadbare couch. He rested his elbows on his knees and let his head hang. He didn't say anything for a very long time. "Well," he said, finally, looking up, the skin around his eyes seeming to sag. "Put your thinking cap on, Miss Bordelon, and roll up your sleeves, because we're about to get real creative."

By five thirty, the air was heavy with the promise of rain, and every muscle in Charley's back ached as she slid the shop door closed. She had spent the afternoon cleaning out boxes of yellowed files, scraping crud from the windows, hauling hoses, and lifting crates of old parts. She'd swept the floors and dragged impossibly heavy barrels of solvent out into the yard. Oil blackened the knees of her jeans. Her shirt was streaked with soot. It would take the rest of the week to clean up everything, Charley decided, and she might as well burn her clothes.

"I'll stop by the dealer tomorrow to see if they can order that distributor cap," Denton said, standing aside as she looped the chain through the handle, secured the lock.

Charley nodded. She was more grateful than she could say that Denton had decided to stick with her, that he hadn't bailed out when he'd had the chance. She was even happy they'd accomplished so much on their first day. It felt good to be productive, to push herself to the point of exhaustion. But privately, Charley nursed the growing suspicion that it was all for naught because no matter how hard they worked, how much they schemed, she didn't have the money Denton said they needed. *I'll stop by the dealer tomorrow*, Denton had said. Two weeks ago, she would have considered the word *tomorrow* to be the loveliest she could utter, filled with possibility, and opportunity, and promise. But as far as she could tell, tomorrow only meant she'd had another chance to disappoint him.

"Have a good evening, Mr. Denton," Charley said, sliding in behind the wheel. "And thank you." She followed Denton's truck along the headland, past the fronts of untended third-year stubble until they reached the junction, then tapped her horn twice to wish Denton a good night before turning left and bumping over the drawbridge. Up ahead, the sky was the color of gunmetal, the clouds heavy with rain. Lightning slashed through them and their lining glowed white. Nine miles down the road, the sky opened up, soaking the road until it was black. By the time Charley pulled up at Miss Honey's, the Volvo's hood glistened like it had just been waxed, and steam rose from it in misty sheets.

Miss Honey was chopping like a prep cook at a roadside diner, scraps of bell pepper, garlic, and onion scattered across the counter, when Charley walked in.

"Where's Micah?" Charley asked.

Miss Honey gestured toward the window, and when Charley looked out, she saw Micah in jean cutoffs she must have made herself that morning, digging a long, rectangular plot in the grass.

"I convinced her to come in when it rained, but otherwise, she's been out there all day," Miss Honey said, and alongside the swell of pride Charley felt at Micah's industriousness, she felt a pinch of guilt. Since the reunion, Micah hadn't played with a single kid even though Charley promised, *swore*, she'd help her find some.

"How was your first day?" Miss Honey asked.

Charley turned away from the window. She took a Coke from the refrigerator. "Things keep getting better and better," she said darkly. "Denton says I need another sixty-five thousand dollars. Shit!" In Miss

Honey's kitchen, Charley felt the full weight of what she was up against. Sixty-five thousand dollars more, and that would only get them to October. Where would she get that kind of money?

"One thing I don't allow in my house is foul language," Miss Honey said without missing a beat in her chopping. "That and taking the Lord's name in vain."

Her mother was right. She was a dreamer; had always been. But where had it gotten her? "This is the stupidest thing I've ever done," Charley said. The kitchen was quiet except for the whir of the ceiling fan. "I know I sound ungrateful, and I don't mean to, but I wish Dad hadn't left me this farm. I was doing a good job fucking up on my own. Now I have eight hundred acres to remind me I'm a failure. I'm just making a fool of myself."

Miss Honey scowled and Charley realized she'd sworn again.

"You remember that first day when we drove out to your farm?" Miss Honey said. "That day Frasier quit?"

Charley nodded. Of course. How could she forget?

Miss Honey stopped chopping, wiped her hands on a dish towel. "Well, your daddy worked out there one summer when he was a boy."

"Out where?"

"Those fields you own. That same land. I didn't recognize it at first, it's been years since I was out that way. The trees are much bigger."

"Dad never told me about working cane," Charley said. She knew a lot about her father. For instance, she knew how much he hated the South. So eager to escape, he skipped his high school graduation dance and the parties, packed his clothes in a cardboard suitcase, and caught a ride to California with a woman from town who needed someone to share the driving and the cost of gas. He had sixty-three dollars in his pocket. He was seventeen. Years later, when she was a girl and her father brought her back to Saint Josephine for summer visits, he couldn't last more than a week before his mood curdled. He grew antsy, short-tempered. Small things—the sound of a train whistle, the sight of an old black man pedaling his bicycle down the road, weeds sprouting through cracks in the sidewalk—annoyed him. But cutting sugarcane? Even when they sat in his living room and looked at *The Cane Cutter*, he never said a word.

"Can't say I'm surprised he didn't tell you," Miss Honey said. "But soon as you said he bought the place from LeJeune, I put it together." She pulled a chair out from the table and leaned heavily against it. Charley had lived with Miss Honey for almost a month. She had watched Miss Honey with Micah and knew she could be gentle; had seen Miss Honey explode at Violet, then turn around in the next moment and allow Violet to help her up the steps; but she had never seen Miss Honey look so troubled as she did now, as though her inner fire, the feistiness, her *Miss Honey–ness,* had drained away.

"Those were tough times," Miss Honey said. She looked through the window. "I was taking in as much extra laundry as I could, cleaning for Miss Barbara on weekends. Pappaw was working extra shifts at the mill. All that, and we were barely getting by. Ernest was thirteen that year. He told me he wanted to work cane, but I told him no. I'd worked cane when I was a girl, and I knew how hard it was. 'Go ask Mr. Henry down at the gas station if he has work for you,' I told him. But Ernest didn't listen. He got up before dawn and walked four miles to where they rang the big black bell. Got himself hired onto one of the crews making a dollar a day."

Miss Honey fell silent, and for the first time, Charley thought she looked every one of her seventy-nine years, her skin thin as parchment, her shoulders slumping, her ankles swollen as popovers above her orthopedic sandals. "All that dirt is like an oven the way the heat rises up. You feel like passing out from thirst. 'Round ten, the supervisor set a water bucket at the edge of the field. Didn't seem to be any order to it. Seemed like, you got thirsty, you drank from the bucket. But not that day. When it came time to break, Ernest was first in line. Reached for the ladle when something caught him upside his face. Said it felt like a hunk of metal. Andre LeJeune, making his daily rounds. He'd hit Ernest with a shovel. *Let the white drink first.* Couldn't stand seeing a black boy drink ahead of him."

Her father had been thirteen, Charley thought. Just two years older than Micah.

When Miss Honey spoke again her voice brimmed with regret. "My son kept that job till school started because he knew how bad we needed the money, but he didn't tell me what happened till a month before he left for California." She asked Charley to get her a Coke from the fridge, then tore open a packet of Stanback. "I used to wonder what that did to him, but after that day we were out there with Frasier, I knew." Miss Honey took a deep breath, and Charley saw her mouth tremble. "It's an awful thing when a mother can't protect her own child."

"I know," Charley said. She would do anything to take back that day Micah burned herself. She would do anything, *give* anything, to have those hours back. Through the window, she heard the faint echo of Micah's shovel as it sliced through the layer of grass, cut into the soil beneath. Miss Honey was right. It was an awful thing, the worst. The very, very worst thing of all.

"Ernest bought that land and never said a word," Miss Honey said, looking small and frail sitting there with her hands in her lap. "Now he's gone, and I can't tell him how proud I am." She stood and moved to the sink, but not before Charley saw her wipe her eyes.

Out beyond the town limit, the Missouri Pacific's whistle announced midnight's arrival, while in the pitch black of the front bedroom, Charley thought about Miss Honey's story, imagined her father, just a boy, working the long rows of cane as the sun beat down, racing to the water bucket like any child would do. Charley rolled onto her side. She had to find the extra sixty-five thousand dollars. She had to get to October, then through to grinding. She slipped out of bed and walked down the hall to the kitchen, where the stove light threw off a soft glow. She flipped the light switch.

"Oh."

Ralph Angel sat at the table confronting a heaping bowl of Frosted Flakes. He wore a T-shirt and boxers, and Charley, in only shorts and a tank top, folded her arms across her chest, thinking this was far too intimate for a brother and sister who hadn't seen each other in twenty years. "Excuse me. I didn't know anyone was in here," she said, and was about to head back to her room when Ralph Angel spoke.

"Couldn't sleep either, huh?"

Charley hadn't seen much of Ralph Angel since he teased Hollywood the night of the reunion. But looking at her brother now, she thought he looked smaller without the warm-up jacket, almost harmless sitting there with the big box of kid's cereal. "The heat at night," Charley said. "It's the one thing I haven't gotten used to."

Ralph Angel poured more cereal into his bowl then pushed the box across the table. "Help yourself," he said standing up, going to the sink, holding his bowl under the tap.

Charley stared.

"What?"

"Nothing, I guess," Charley said. "It's just that I've never seen anyone eat cereal with water before."

"I been thinking." Ralph Angel turned off the tap and sat down again. "We sort of got off on the wrong foot the other night."

"Sort of, yes," Charley said, warily.

Ralph Angel dipped his spoon into his cereal and stirred slowly, but he looked as though he'd lost his appetite. "I mean, it's just a room, right? And like 'Da said, you got down here first." He seemed to be talking to himself, and for a second Charley thought he'd forgotten she was in the room, but then he looked up. "The room's yours fair and square."

As troubling as Violet's story was, as much as she disliked how Ralph Angel had treated Hollywood, people deserved a second chance. Because it was easy to make mistakes. "Thank you."

Ralph Angel nudged the box of Frosted Flakes. "Sure you don't want any?"

"I'm fine."

"At least you want to sit down?" He pushed a chair from under the table.

"For a couple minutes."

The kitchen was quiet, the stillness soothing. Charley wondered how long Ralph Angel had been sitting there, how many nights he spent sitting alone in the dark.

"It must feel pretty wild," Ralph Angel said, "you being down here, riding around on tractors all day, getting your hands dirty."

Charley shrugged. "I don't mind." Just this morning, under Denton's careful tutelage, she'd donned thick gloves and safety goggles and he'd shown her how to use the blowtorch. "It's interesting."

"Come on, sis. You can level with me. I mean, Saint Josephine isn't exactly Vail, Colorado, or some other fancy place. Even this—" And here, Ralph Angel gestured to indicate Miss Honey's kitchen. "I mean, it's not exactly the Beverly Wilshire. It's gotta be an adjustment, seeing how you were a debutante and all."

"I was never a debutante," Charley said. "It just looked like a fairy tale."

"Well, kudos to you for coming down here. I'm not sure I'd have done the same." Ralph Angel looked down at his own hands, turned them over to stare at his palms. "So, I was thinking. I'm going be down here for a little while. I've got some free time on my hands, maybe I could help you out on the farm."

Charlie blinked. "What do you know about sugarcane?"

"Well, nothing. But I was thinking I could manage the office or something."

"I already have a manager," Charley said.

"Yeah, I know. Prosper what's-his-name. Micah told me. But I was thinking about something administrative. I'm good with numbers. I was an engineering major in school."

"There's not really much to administer," Charley said.

"There's gotta be something I can do."

Charley looked around the kitchen still crammed with paper goods and cases of soda from the reunion. "I appreciate your interest. And if you knew something about sugarcane, I'd say yes, absolutely. But since you don't, it would sort of be 'the blind leading the blind,' know what I mean? And besides, I can't afford to pay you."

"I know we could work something out. I could build up some equity or something. Come on, sis. There's gotta be something. At least say you'll think about it."

Charley sighed. "I'll think about it. But I have to see how things go these next couple weeks."

Ralph Angel smiled. He picked up the cereal box and poured another bowl. "Take all the time you need. I'm not going anywhere."

10

It was a Wednesday morning, the third week of June. The sun had risen high enough to bake the fields and the air was warm, but still held a little of its coolness from the night's embrace. Charley had just settled into the ratty desk chair and was sorting through old bank statements and outdated copies of *American Truck* magazine when Denton poked his head in the office.

"Come with me."

"Where arc we going?"

"I'm going to teach you how to fish," Denton said. "Like I told you that day you came to see me, the time for laying-by has almost passed."

"Laying-by," Charley said envisioning the notes on her yellow pad. "That means cleaning up the rows." She felt like a kid at a spelling bee.

"Correct, and Frasier should have done it way back in May." Denton slid a finger under his baseball cap and scratched his scalp. "But if we work quick and double up on fertilizer, we might be able to catch up." He led her out into the yard. "I found an old disc plow behind the shop. The discs were rusted, but the iron case held up pretty good. I cut up some of that rebar you found in that box of pipes and made us this three-row. It's basic, but it'll get the job done."

Charley knelt before the length of extruded pipe. Denton had welded three metal spikes long as chef's knives along the length of it—one on each end and one in the middle. "I can't believe you made a piece of farm equipment," she said. With the circular patterns on the spikes, and the spray of rust along the extruded shaft, the contraption was more suited for a museum sculpture garden than a cane field. "How do we get it out there?"

Denton pointed to the tractor. "We hook it to the back and pull it through the rows where all the weeds are growing. I spaced the spikes far enough apart so they won't tear up the cane. Frasier should have gotten to the weeds when they were low. Now they done took us. You got stands out there that are tied up from end to end. That's lesson number one, Miss Bordelon. Never let them weeds get out ahead of you."

They rode out to the second quadrant, Denton on the tractor, the three-row clanging like church bells as he rumbled over ruts, and Charley following close behind in his pickup, the sun reflecting softly off the hood's dull paint, the dogs pacing in the truck bed, where they barked at every bird or insect that happened by and lifted their noses in the breeze. She gazed out over her fields. Almost a month, and she was still not accustomed to the way the land looked—no mountains or rolling hills, even, to break up the horizon; the sky lower somehow than it was in California; the land for as far as she could see flat as a sheet of paper—and Charley wondered how long it would be before the place felt familiar, how long before she felt in her bones that she was truly home.

Ahead of her, Denton signaled that they'd arrived. He pulled over, climbed down from the tractor, and stood on the headland. Charley joined him.

"See what I mean about this field being tied up?"

Charley squinted and, for the first time, noticed thin green vines dotted with bright red poppylike flowers twisting among the cane stalks. "Is that kudzu?"

"Tie vines," Denton said. "Also known as morning glory. And it'll smother your cane if you don't stay on top of it." He walked back to the tractor, lowered the three-row, and secured the hitch. "We'll go up and down the rows, pull up the grass first, then we'll come through with the fertilizer. The trick is to get down to the seeds and the roots so the vines don't come back again. I'll take the first row so you can see how it's done, then I'll turn it over to you."

"But I don't know how to drive a tractor," Charley said.

"Time for you to learn."

As Charley stood by, Denton climbed onto the tractor, turned the engine, and fishtailed back and forth until the three-row, like an enormous comb, was directly behind him, then he slowly guided the tractor into the field, being careful to line the tractor's tires up with the furrows so the cane passed underneath the chassis. He pressed the clutch, gave the engine a little gas, and the tractor lurched forward, the three-row's spikes sinking deep into the earth like a dog bite, pulling up the roots and turning over clots of soil in three rows as it dragged along. Brilliant, Charley thought, and her heart leaped as she watched Denton roll through the field. When he reached the far side, Denton swung around and came back.

"Amazing," Charley called over the engine noise. "Mr. Denton, you're a genius."

But there was no time for compliments. "You're up," Denton said stoically, and shifted into neutral, set the emergency brake. Heart thumping, Charley climbed into the seat. "Now release the clutch." Charley obeyed. "Now grab hold of that lever and switch into first, then release the brake." Denton was patient but firm, and Charley followed his instructions like a schoolgirl—*shift into first, release the brake*—letting out a small cry of delight as the tractor rolled forward. "Now look-a-here," Denton called, walking beside her, "as long as you keep the tires in the furrows, the three-row will do like it should. It'll follow behind like a duckling. Don't be hasty. Turn around and check every few yards or you'll tear up your cane. You get to the other side, swing around wide and come back. Understand?"

"I think so." Charley gave a tentative thumbs-up.

"Remember. Go slow. This ain't the Kentucky Derby." And then Denton stopped walking, stopped talking, and let her go.

Charley was halfway down the row and feeling light-headed before she realized she was holding her breath. Her hands sweated from gripping the gearshift so tightly. She exhaled, sat back in the seat, glanced quickly behind her to check that the three-row was still there, and was relieved to see that it was, the spikes cutting through the soil, tearing up weeds and roots, the earth folding in on itself like cake batter. Charley turned forward and straightened the wheel to keep the tractor in the row. From up there in the seat, she had a different view of her fields entirely. Overgrown as they were in places, scraggly and neglected in others, when taken all together, they still held a certain beauty; it was like floating on a sea of green tea, and she felt the tiniest bloom of satisfaction knowing that with a lot of hard work and some luck, she might, *just might*, be able to tease a miracle out of those plants.

When she returned to where Denton stood, he nodded approvingly. "Not bad, Miss Bordelon," he said, squinting up at her.

"Thanks." Charley beamed.

Denton tugged his hat brim lower over his eyes, and Charley thought she saw a smile curl in the corners of his mouth. "Just a hundred fourteen rows to go."

Lunchtime. Back in the shop, Charley and Denton dragged two folding chairs just inside the shop door, where, if nothing else, it was a few degrees cooler.

"Tomorrow, maybe the next day, we'll hit those rows with nitrogen," Denton said. He peeled the top slice of bread off his sandwich, which Charley had picked up on her way in, and regarded the remaining layers of sliced turkey, cheese, and tomato with disappointment.

"Do you not like it?" Charley asked, thinking she should have ordered the plate lunch.

"I remember when I could eat for twenty-five cents a day," Denton said. "Ten cents for a piece of ham thick like this." He held his thumb and forefinger a few inches apart. "Fifteen cents for a soda water. Now it's ten dollars and you can't even see what you got." He looked across the road where afternoon sunlight leached through the gathering clouds. "Truth is, everything cost more nowadays. Labor done doubled. Insurance done tripled, fuel done tripled. Meanwhile, the price of cane's been the same for the last seven years. You couldn't have picked a worse time to get into this business, Miss Bordelon."

Charley felt an ache spread through her gut. Her mother, too, was a straight shooter, often brutally so. "It's a cold world out there, Charlotte," her mother had said. "You have no idea. You go down to Louisiana trying to be a sugarcane farmer, all you'll be is a pretty face."

She turned to Denton. "Maybe," she said, "but anyone who tries to stop me," and here she thought of Landry, with his slick smile and flashy sedan, "anyone who thinks I can't do this, can go to hell."

Denton turned to look at her, and for a few seconds he didn't say a word, just stared. Then he smashed the top bread slice back on his sandwich and took a bite. "I like that you're willing to work hard," he said. "May turn out to be good at fishing after all."

Ten straight days of clearing the morning glories, and tearing out johnsongrass, and spraying double doses of fertilizer. Ten straight days of dirt and dust and sweat from places Charley never knew she could sweat. Ten straight days of rumbling up and down the rows—up and down, up and down, up and down—while the sun blazed overhead and heat rose from below, and finally, *finally*, Charley's second quadrant, and then the rest of her farm, was neat as a pinstriped suit. The cane was still stunted, much to her dismay, and in some places looked worse than it had before, but Denton assured her that now that the rows were clear, it had a chance to grow properly.

"What's next?" Charley asked, as they rode to the hardware store late one afternoon. An order of wrenches had come in.

"Time to run your drains," Denton said. "All that dirt we cleared between the rows has piled up on the ends. Have to clear it out or your fields won't drain right, and the last thing you want is for water to get hung up out there. Cane likes to be damp, but it hates to be flooded." He turned left at the junction and rolled down his window. "Good news is, most of your land is the perfect combination of sand and loam. It drains well. Go over it with a piece of equipment, you can hardly see where you passed. It's that black jack land, all boggy and filled with clay, that'll hold water and tear up your machines."

"Who knew laying-by was so involved," Charley said.

Denton nodded. "It's critical. You're giving the cane your final *Amen*. You're saying, 'That's it. I've done all I can do.' Everything goes like it should, it's the last time you're in your fields till grinding. After laying-by, you stand back and let Mother Nature take over."

From the passenger seat, Charley looked at Denton, and for the hundredth time was overcome with relief and gratitude. It wasn't simply the knowledge that she couldn't have done any of this without him. No, it wasn't simply that. It was the feeling she got in his presence, a sense of peace, a quiet calm, as though she were standing in the shadow of an old redwood. They didn't make them like Denton anymore; she couldn't have asked for a better mentor. She'd noticed that sometimes, whether it was driving the tractor or operating the drill press or mixing a batch of fertilizer, he seemed to hold himself back, forced himself to step aside so *she* could learn, rather than doing the work himself. At least three times she'd walked into the office to find him scribbling on a pad, sketching pieces of equipment he planned to make. And was she imagining things, or did he seem to be walking with a newfound lift in his step?

"So, we run the drains and then we're finished?" asked Charley. They were approaching the little town of Jeanerette, where LeBlanc's Bakery on Main Street had been baking French bread and ginger cakes since 1884. Over the front entrance with its big picture windows, the red light glowed brightly, signaling that fresh loaves had just come out of ovens and were ready for sale; all you had to do was walk around to the side door. The air was heavy with a sweet, yeasty aroma and Charley inhaled. She'd have to pick up a couple loaves on her way home.

"We won't be sitting around eating bonbons, if that's what you're thinking. Still lots to do before grinding." Denton scratched his forehead thoughtfully. "And that's if Mother Nature doesn't throw us a curveball."

"What could go wrong?"

Denton inhaled, as though he, too, was tempted to stop for a loaf and eat it right there in the car, if only they could afford the time. "What could go wrong?" He looked out over the hood then at Charley. "Plenty."

Charley called Violet on her way home that evening. "So, exactly how long do you plan to boycott your own mother?"

"Look who's talking?" Violet said. "When was the last time you talked to Lorna?"

"Touché."

"Besides, Mother is welcome at my house anytime as long as she doesn't bring you-know-who."

"Please come over, Violet," Charley said. "I miss you. You don't even have to come in. We can stand on the sidewalk."

Violet sighed. "I miss you, too, sweetheart, and I hate not seeing y'all. But if I give in, Mother will think she can always rewrite the rules for Ralph Angel. She never let us get away with half of what she lets him get away with. Someone has to draw the line. Speaking of which, how are you holding up?"

And so, Charley told Violet what Denton said about needing more money, about her father working sugarcane as a boy. "I never knew Ernest did that," Violet said, and Charley heard in Violet's voice the same sorrow she'd heard in Miss Honey's. And finally, she told Violet about Ralph Angel asking to work on the farm.

"What are you going to do?" Violet asked.

"I don't know," Charley said, as she pulled up in front of LeBlanc's bakery. The red light over the door was off but the side door was still open. "That's why I called. I thought you might have some ideas."

Mother Francisca's eyes looked like peppercorns behind her oversize glasses, the skin of her plump white face as wrinkled as a dried apple. While prices flashed at the bottom of the TV screen, Mother Francisca, beloved host of the Catholic Home Shopping Network, held up plaques,

Bible covers and wristwatches, coffee mugs, commemorative plates, and T-shirts, all emblazoned with the image of Padre Pio, the miracle worker, as the seconds to purchase each item ticked down to zero, and Charley, home from the farm late Friday afternoon, was horrified when she stepped into the den and saw Miss Honey sitting in her recliner and Hollywood on the couch, their expressions glazed over, their eyes fixed on the screen as Mother Francisca pawned her wares.

"It's about time," Miss Honey said, at the commercial break. "We were about to send out the National Guard. Where've you been?"

"Take one guess," Charley said, wearily, dropping her backpack.

"Well, I'm glad you're home," Miss Honey said. "Look who's here."

Hollywood stood, smoothed his hair, then wiped his hands on his army fatigues. "Hey there, Miss Charley."

"Well, hello," Charley said, and felt her spirits rise in spite of the exhausting day she'd had. She and Denton had power-washed the shop windows, and she'd climbed up and down an extension ladder at least thirty times, checking the roof for leaks. She crossed the den and started to shake Hollywood's hand, then changed her mind and hugged him. She needed a friend, especially now that Violet refused to come around. As they embraced, Charley caught a whiff of Hollywood's cologne, thick and spicy and a tad too sweet for her taste, but thought it was nice that he'd made the effort. When she stepped back, the scent clung to her clothes. "How've you been? How's business?"

Hollywood shrugged. "I been okay. Same ol', same ol'. Cutting grass, helping *Maman* around the place." He flushed pink, like a schoolboy, and looked at the floor.

It would be easy, Charley thought, to mistake his modesty for a lack of confidence, his simplicity for stupidity. But beneath that quirkiness and quiet demeanor, there was a current of strength, a sense of honor and integrity, and in his own special way, a clear-eyed view of the world. Charley thought back to the way Hollywood had talked to Micah, respectfully but firmly, and knew that was true.

On television, Mother Francisca was pushing Padre Pio salt and pepper shakers now; only ten sets left as the clock counted down.

"Hollywood finished cleaning the back room," Miss Honey said.

Charley nodded. "Then you must be exhausted. What can I get you to drink?" she asked, knowing she had only Coke and water to offer. She'd have to remember to ask Denton how his wife made that lemonade.

"Water if it's no trouble," Hollywood said, and moved to follow her into the kitchen.

But Charley told him to stay where he was. "No, no," she said, "sit down, I'll get it." When she returned, he was flipping through a new edition of *Highlife*. She handed the glass to him and watched him take a small, careful sip.

On television now, Mother Francisca had stopped hawking products and had moved to a different part of her studio. Ensconced in an overstuffed chair like a TV talk-show host, she took calls from listeners, offering tips on how they might avoid purgatory. "And how long have you been unable to feel love?" she asked, her hands clasped together as she stared into the camera.

"Hollywood's been waiting for you to get home," Miss Honey said.

"Oh," Charley said.

Hollywood dabbed his forehead nervously. He closed his magazine.

"Well?" Miss Honey said.

"I was gonna ask if—I wondered if you wanted—" He paused, and swallowed. He looked at Charley and blinked, as though waiting for the words.

But just as he opened his mouth to speak again, Ralph Angel burst into the den. "Man, those kids just about wore me out," he said, breathing hard. "I forgot how much I hated the park." He gestured over his shoulder, anticipating Miss Honey's question. "They're out front. They collected a bunch of rocks. I told them not to throw them against the house, or at any cars, which I could tell was exactly what they planned to do." He sat on the arm of the couch, "Hey, sis," then he saw Hollywood. "Hey, man. How's it going? I didn't see your mower."

"Hey, Ralph Angel," Hollywood said, stiffly.

"I was gonna call you. I could use a little grown-up playtime, if you know what I mean. I thought maybe we could hit the bars or go fishing tomorrow over at that place we used to go when we were kids. You know, across the bayou, near that barge slip."

"I gotta work tomorrow."

"How about this weekend? I know you don't cut grass on Sundays, right? And if I remember correctly, that joint Smitty's over in Tee Coteau draws a big crowd on Sunday nights."

"I don't know, Ralph Angel," Hollywood said, "that place is pretty rough. People always getting shot over there."

"Well, *Jesus*, man, when are we going to hang out?"

"Stop harassing him," Miss Honey said. "Hollywood didn't come here to see you anyway. He came to see Charley. He wants to ask her out on a date."

"Me?" Charley said.

"Who else?" Miss Honey said.

Ralph Angel looked from Hollywood to Charley. "I guess I made a mistake, then. I thought my old buddy dropped by to see me. Excuse me. I didn't realize."

Hollywood slid forward on the couch. "I'm sorry, Ralph Angel. Maybe we can hang out another time."

"Yeah, yeah. No problem." Ralph Angel waved his hand casually. "It's my fault. You two go ahead."

Hollywood looked at Charley as though he were about to propose. "I wondered if you wanted to go over to Sonic for a burger or something. I mean, we don't have to go there if you don't like burgers. We can go to Joe's on the Bayou or anyplace you want. We don't even have to eat. We could just take a walk." He rolled up his magazine. Then he unrolled it and smoothed his hand across the cover.

"That's sweet of you," Charley said, noticing now that Hollywood's hair was recently cut. "I'm flattered, but—"

Ralph Angel groaned and stood up. "Aw, Jesus, Peanut. You can do better than that. If you're gonna ask a woman on a date, you need to be more confident. You gotta look her in the eye. Here, let me show you." He slid between Hollywood and Charley. "Let's start again, sis. From the top."

"Ralph Angel." Miss Honey sat forward in her recliner. "Let the man be. If he wants to ask Charley out, let him do it his way."

"Relax, 'Da." Ralph Angel turned to Hollywood. "How much is a burger and fries? Three, four dollars? Only costs you an hour's work. You hear that, Charley? You're worth a whole lawn."

"You should stop," said Charley. And maybe it was because something in Ralph Angel's smile reminded Charley of Baron and Landry, but she decided she'd had enough. "You're being cruel."

Ralph Angel stepped back, his arms folded. "Well, look who's decided to take the moral high ground."

"What are you talking about?"

Ralph Angel looked at Charley for a long time. "Never mind, sis. Forget about it. But just so we're square, I'm not the only one who's being cruel."

JULY

11

What could go wrong? After twelve straight days of thunderstorms, Charley believed she knew. Each day she woke up and checked the weather report, and each day the meteorologist forecast more rain; not the occasional showers that were a welcomed part of summer in south Louisiana, but a steady downpour, unrelenting, with thunder like cannon fire, lightning strikes that made you wince and duck your head, and flooding that felt biblical. Now Charley stood in the shop door, staring out at rain falling so heavily she couldn't even see her fields across the road. Just yesterday, she sat in her car in the Winn-Dixie parking lot for twenty-five minutes, waiting for the storm to pass, then got frustrated, took off her shoes, and dashed the few yards to the entrance, only to be soaked to the bone by the time she burst through the automatic doors. *What could go wrong?* If she were superstitious, she would almost start to believe she'd brought this on herself.

"I can't take much more of this," Charley said, turning to Denton, who was busy soldering the plug on the generator. "Is this much rain *normal*?"

"Just be thankful we finished laying-by when we did," Denton said, matter-of-factly. "We were trying to finish that work now, we'd be up to our ears in mud if we could get out there at all."

And so, Charley waited.

While it rained.

And rained.

And rained.

In New Orleans, streets flooded and power lines went down. The state closed the highway for a time.

And then, as if it were tired of playing the practical joke, the sun appeared, just for a few hours the first day, shooting rays of weak light through breaks in the clouds before the rain started again, but then growing gradually stronger, so that by the second week in July, it was a bright yellow ball. In her little corner of the world, Charley rejoiced. She was sick of being cooped up in the shop, shuffling papers or playing Monopoly at home with Micah; sick of waking to rain and going to sleep to rain; sick of feeling damp as a cotton sock.

"I'm glad *that's* over."

"Don't get too excited," Denton said. They were driving along the far edge of the farm, checking to see how the drains had held up. "All that rain means we're likely to get more insects. Cross your fingers we don't have borers."

"Borers?" Charley said. The last time she heard Denton mention borers, he was pouring her a glass of lemonade.

"Little worms that burrow into the cane stalk," Denton said. "If they get into the heart of the cane, you lose the sucrose; you lose the sucrose, you lose your sugar content. Basically, your crop is worthless."

Charley sighed. "How do we know if we have them?"

"You have to pull down the cane sheath. That's where the parent lays the eggs. If the eggs have already hatched, you'll see holes in the cane."

"Let's get started. What do we need? Gloves? A flashlight?"

"I already sent someone out to check," Denton said. "Matt Thibodeaux teaches science over at the high school, moonlights as a crop consultant. He'll walk the fields, then write up a report. Turns out we've got an infestation, he'll draw up a site map and figure out exactly how much we need to spray."

"Sounds expensive," Charley said. "Who'll do the spraying and how much will it cost?"

"Bug work normally costs six dollars thirty-five an acre. But I told him we're on a budget. Best news is, his brother's a crop duster."

Thibodeaux's Flying Service was located in a low metal building beside the landing strip. When Charley and Denton arrived, Bradley Thibodeaux was sitting in a cushiony black office chair fit for a Wall

Street executive, behind a big oak desk cluttered with maps and aerial photographs similar to the ones Charley had studied all those months ago. He was talking on the telephone, and at the sight of Charley and Denton, he waved them in and placed a hand over the receiver.

"Y'all make yourselves comfortable," he whispered.

Denton motioned for Charley to take the empty seat by the desk. Another folding chair leaned against the wall, and he brought it over, sat down.

While she waited, Charley surveyed the office. The décor was spare and functional: linoleum floors, plastic blinds in the windows, a couple card tables and a watercooler in the corner—which lent to the industrial feel. The only object of interest, aside from the maps Scotch-taped to the walls, was a large gilt frame behind Bradley's desk in which hung a portrait, done in heavy oil brushstrokes, of a man in a blue suit.

Bradley hung up the phone. "I'm sorry about that, y'all," he said in a heavy Cajun accent. "I didn't mean to be rude."

He rose from his chair. "Prosper Denton. Well, hello, stranger," walked around the desk, and shook Denton's hand. "I wouldn't believe this if I weren't standing here looking with my own two eyes. How are you? It's been what, three years?"

"About that," Denton said.

"What'cha been up to?"

"Let me introduce you to Miss Charley Bordelon, from California."

Bradley shook Charley's hand and held on to it as he stood back to appraise her. "You look like you just got out of high school. What'cha doing with this old man?"

"I'm helping Miss Bordelon run her operation," Denton said, steering the conversation back to business. "After all that rain we just got, I figured I'd have Matt come out and check for borers. He said the report was ready."

Bradley nodded. "Just came in." He sifted through the stack until he found Charley's, then slipped the rubber band from a piece of rolled paper the size of an architectural blueprint, spread it over the desk, and pulled out a pair of reading glasses. "Let's see what we got," Bradley said, studying the field map like a three-star general planning his next attack. The map of Charley's farm was overlaid with a grid. Each one-inch square represented a section of a quadrant, half of which were highlighted in yellow marker. "Well, you definitely got you some borers," he said. "Everywhere it's yellow is infested."

Charley sighed.

"But don't worry," said Bradley, rolling up the map, sliding the rubber band down around it. "We'll hit 'em with a good dose of Intrepid. That'll stop 'em in their tracks. I'll write up the ticket today and get on it first thing tomorrow."

Charley reached for her checkbook but Bradley caught her by the elbow. "On the house." And when Charley objected, Bradley assured her this wasn't the last time they'd be doing business. "You'll be back come September."

"What happens in September?"

Bradley and Denton looked at each other, the long years of experience passing between them.

"That's when we gotta spray the crops with ripener," Denton said. "We'll be seeing a lot of this old Cajun."

12

❦ Until the 1970s, the few square blocks of ravaged ground known as Tee Coteau were strictly Cajun—poor farmers from the backcountry and scruffy fishermen who, nightly, blew off steam in the dingy bucket-of-blood bars. In the last twenty years the population had changed. First blacks moved in, then Mexicans, followed by Vietnamese in the early nineties, and in the last ten years, Laotians had staked their claim. But Tee Coteau had never lost its lower-than-blue-collar roots or seedy reputation, which was probably why Ralph Angel was so fascinated with the place; something about the narrow streets, the dingy bars, and dilapidated houses with junk cars parked in the yard felt familiar, comforting. And so, when Miss Honey came into the kitchen where he sat reading the paper, he couldn't help but mention the day's headline.

"You see today's paper?" Ralph Angel snapped the front page. "Some kid shot up that bar, Smitty's, over in Tee Coteau."

"That's what Hollywood was trying to tell you." Miss Honey, dressed like she was going to church, set her purse and three jars of blackberry jelly on the counter. "I'm dropping these off at Miss Ida's for the church rummage sale," she said. "Then I'm taking Micah to the garden show in Morgan City. We might swing by Bayou Chic on the way back. I saw a Crock-Pot over there last month but the lady wanted thirty dollars for it. If it's still there, she might sell it to me for fifteen. You and Blue are welcome to come."

"No, thanks."

"Well, don't sit around all day," Miss Honey said. "Make yourself useful. Hollywood left eight big boxes of junk out back. Be a good friend and take them to the dump for him." She opened the cabinet, pushed the glasses and tea cups aside, and brought out a Kerns jar stuffed with a fat roll of bills.

"I'll think about it," Ralph Angel said. What he really wanted to do was take a ride over to the crime scene, see what kind of memorial folks had put up. He liked to do that sometimes, drive around and look at the flowers and candles and stuffed animals people set out on the sidewalks. Sometimes they set out weird stuff—sneakers and bottles of liquor. He couldn't say why, but the memorials always moved him, not making him want to cry exactly, it was deeper than that; he always felt as though something solid inside him clicked into place, like tumblers in a lock.

"Cut the TV off, Micah, it's time to go," Miss Honey said, and Ralph Angel watched as she counted out ten singles, licking her fingers before she touched each one, then pushed the jar back and closed the cabinet. "You and Blue need to get out of this house. It's not good for that boy to spend so much time inside."

"I said I'll think about it." Ralph Angel knew he was being short with her and felt guilty. She meant well, had always been in his corner, and when it came to kids, no one loved them like 'Da did. She was always giving things to the children in town—books and money for ice cream. Every Easter since he could remember, she bought cheap white wash-cloths from the discount store and folded them like origami into the shape of bunny rabbits, glued on those funny squiggly eyes and little pink pom-poms for noses. That was how she'd met Hollywood. She had been driving around delivering washcloth rabbits to every kid in the Quarter when she saw him on the side of the road. He'd fallen off his bike and she brought him home, cleaned him up, sewed his pants. Gave him something to eat before she put his bike in her car and drove him out to where his family lived. *My grandson's about your age*, she'd said. But she had a way about her, a way of nagging when she got an idea in her head that got under his skin and he couldn't help himself. She'd start in on him with that nagging and all he wanted to do was get away. That's what happened the last time.

Charley left long before Ralph Angel had even considered waking, and with Micah and Miss Honey gone, now the house was quiet. He scanned the Tee Coteau article one last time, then folded the paper, grateful to have had something to occupy his thoughts, because the truth was he hated the mornings, hated to look out over the long hours of daylight with nothing to fill them. Charley still hadn't gotten back to him about the farm. He was trying to be patient, but the wait was driving him crazy. Nothing to do but sit around the house with Blue, watching the paint dry. At least back in Phoenix he'd had his buddies at the bar to help him kill time after he lost his job, but down here it was different; walk into the wrong bar and you could get your throat cut.

In the back room, Blue, in his undies and T-shirt, sat on the floor beside an enormous glass jar. "Look what I found," he said, and tipped the jar forward.

Ralph Angel recognized the marbles, Civil War bullets, old brass buttons, miniature porcelain teacups and saucers, crudely carved wooden toy blocks, and antique porcelain baby dolls' parts—tiny legs, heads, torsos, and arms—as the ones he collected when he was a kid and wandered out in the cane fields after the harvest. The fields were barren then, and the winter rains would have washed away the top layer of dirt so that all the objects left over from the 1800s, before the fields were planted in cane and farmhouses stood on the land, would just be lying there in the dirt. He'd take the objects home and wash each piece in the kitchen sink, then line them up on the windowsill. And when the windowsill was too cluttered, Miss Honey gave him the old jar.

"Where'd you get that?" Ralph Angel said.

"An old box," Blue said, vaguely.

"An old box *where*?"

"Outside," Blue said. "Am I in trouble?" He'd already sorted half the relics into piles.

Blue must be referring to the boxes Hollywood moved when he cleaned up, Ralph Angel thought, the ones Miss Honey wanted him to take to the dump. "No, buddy. You're not in trouble."

"Okay, good, because I really like this stuff. I think it's treasure," Blue said.

"Oh yeah?"

"From a pirate ship." Blue held up a cat's eye marble big as a golf ball and an ancient bullet. "Can I keep these?"

"Sure," Ralph Angel said. "Finders keepers. Keep all of it if you want. But that bullet's got lead on it, so don't put it in your mouth. It'll make you sick. Stay here. I'm going outside."

The boxes were leaning against the back of the house just where Miss Honey said they'd be, but as for the contents, Blue had found the best of it. Nothing left but old shoes and wire hangers. But his fishing poles stood beside the boxes, the hooks still on the lines, and his old tackle box, which gave Ralph Angel an idea.

"What are you going to do with those sticks?" Blue asked when Ralph Angel came back inside. Blue had set all the teacups on their saucers, arranged the doll torsos from largest to smallest, arranged the marbles by color.

"Sticks?" Ralph Angel had to laugh. "Boy, these are my old fishing poles. By the time I was your age, I was catching tons of fish—catfish, speckled trout, red fish—and I was cleaning 'em too." Thinking back on those old days, an excitement Ralph Angel hadn't felt in years washed over him; some of the best days of his life. He set the tackle box on the bed. "Tell you what. We're going to have some good ol'-fashioned fun. Get dressed." 'Da was right. They need to get out more. But more than that, he'd show Charley he could contribute, that he wasn't just sitting around with his hand out.

"Can I bring my treasure?"

"Sure. And grab Zach. I know he won't want to miss this."

It took Ralph Angel a while to find the ruins of the old sugar mill just outside town. When he was a boy, cane fields covered the acres, but since then they'd been subdivided, the cane cleared, and now, sprawling ranch-style homes dotted that stretch of the snaking bayou. But he found the spot eventually, and led Blue through a narrow stand of cherry trees and water oaks, cypress, wax myrtles, pecans and hackberries, until he found the barge slip, an inlet cut deep into the bank, where all through the 1800s, workers loaded barrels of molasses onto barges headed to New Orleans. Ralph Angel set down his tackle box. Across the bayou, the woods of Camperdown Plantation, just as dark and menacing as he remembered, inched right up to the bank, nudged the saw grass and elephant ears and water lilies deeper into the murky water. He was glad remnants of the old wooden Civil War bridge were still there, and as he baited the hooks, Ralph Angel tried to recall the details of the Battle of Irish Bend he'd learned in school; how Union troops had crossed over that bridge as they pursued General Taylor's rebels; how in just over a day, three hundred fifty Union soldiers were killed and buried in a trench somewhere nearby.

"Now watch me." Ralph Angel held the rod over his shoulder then whipped it forward and the line sailed out over the water. The red bobber made a small splash and sent a chain of ripples through the water hyacinths. "Like that," he said, and reeled in the line. "Now you try." He handed a pole to Blue.

Sitting on an overturned bucket, watching clumps of water hyacinths drift down the bayou, Ralph Angel had to acknowledge that he'd forgotten how good it felt to be outside. He liked the way the sun shone on the water and made everything look soft and sort of hazy, the way the water looked like it was sliding by in one long piece, like the whole bayou was on a conveyor belt. An egret landed on the old bridge and stood for a few seconds, perfectly still, looking for fish, before it launched itself back into the air.

From his seat on the tackle box, Blue looked up and said, "Did you come here when you were a little kid?" He took Zach out of his pocket and laid him in the dirt.

"All the time," Ralph Angel said. "Me and Hollywood. We were best friends." In his mind's eye, he saw the two of them as boys standing on the bank. The vision came to him as though through a telescope, their distant silhouettes hazy and dark. Still, it was enough to inspire a pang of longing for his old friend. Ralph Angel looked out over the water. Down the bank, a frog hurled itself into of the shallows.

"I'm hungry," Blue said.

"I figured that was coming," Ralph Angel said. He'd packed sandwiches—peanut butter on both sides, just the way Blue liked it, and salami for himself—and while they ate, they watched an alligator, a juvenile, Ralph Angel guessed, judging from the size of its head, drift toward Blue's bobber.

"Watch this," Ralph Angel said. He grabbed Blue's pole and reeled in the line fast as he could. The alligator gave chase, cutting through the water with alarming speed, its mouth open slightly, its snub nose almost touching the bobber until it was a few feet from them and Ralph Angel lifted the line out of the water.

"Pop!" Blue yelled. He fell backward off the tackle box and scrambled toward the woods.

Ralph Angel laughed. "Come back. Don't be scared. Long as you're up here and he's down there in the water, you're safe." He looked for the alligator and saw that it had dipped under the surface, and when Blue finally came back to stand at his side, still whimpering a little, Ralph Angel pulled his son next to him. "Pretty cool, huh? I used to do that all the time when I was a kid."

Way down in the curve of the bayou, a barge slowly approached. It sat low in the water and Ralph Angel guessed it was filled with sugar from Saint Mary's Co-op, heading to one of the refineries in Grammercy or Arabi where they turned raw sugar into white.

"Zach and I don't want to fish anymore," Blue said. "It's boring."

"Okay," Ralph Angel said. "Bring your pole over here, then y'all can go play." They should probably head back, but he wasn't ready to leave; not yet. Not when the air was so warm and the sky was all blue like that. Even the heat wasn't so bad. No, he wasn't ready to go.

When Ralph Angel looked up, he saw that the barge was still a ways down the bayou, but moving at a steady clip. He felt the vibration from its engine, like an approaching train, under his feet. He looked around for Blue and saw him standing at the head of the barge slip. He seemed to be talking to Zach as he held him over the water.

Amazing how quickly the barge moved. It was closer now. The engine rumble sent larger ripples, and across the water, Ralph Angel could see the captain high up in the towboat's wheelhouse, his small white face like a speck of white sugar behind the big glass window. As it approached, the barge sucked water into its enormous hull so that the current up where Ralph Angel sat seemed to flow in reverse and the water level actually dropped. Water hyacinths and lilies clumped together in the backwards flow and even up ahead, in the barge slip, the water seemed to be draining away. Blue still peered into the water. He leaned down, seemed to be looking at something.

"Not too close," Ralph Angel yelled.

Blue looked up, waved, yelled something back, but the barge was closer still, its rumbling engine louder, the vibration strong enough that Ralph Angel felt it in his bones, in his eardrums, and he couldn't hear what Blue was saying. He turned back to look at the barge, thinking he wanted to get the captain's attention, signal for him to blow the horn. Blue would get a kick out of that.

The front of the barge was directly before him now, and Ralph Angel walked to the edge of the bank, right up to where the saw grass and lilies were thickest. The vessel was even more imposing than he remembered from his youth; one hundred seventy-five feet of burnt-orange steel pushing through the water, the two-story wheelhouse glowing white against the tree line, the windows reflecting the sun's glare, the engine churning up the mud as it sucked the water in, turning the bayou from murky green to dark brown as it pushed water out behind it in a massive wave that washed over the banks. Ralph Angel could see the captain's face. He waved and the captain waved back. Ralph Angel signaled by balling his fist and pumping his arm up and down that he wanted the captain to blow his horn, and the man gave him the thumbs-up that he understood. Ralph Angel turned to look for Blue, to call him over so they could stand together. But Blue was not there.

"Blue!"

As the barge passed, the whole earth seemed to shake. The horn sounded and, for a few seconds, it felt to Ralph Angel as though he were standing at a railroad crossing as a train thundered past. He looked again and saw that Blue had climbed off the barge slip into water that was shallow now because of the barge passing by; he saw that Blue was inching around the far edge, out toward the bayou, holding on to the wooden slats that lined the slip's perimeter, and he seemed to be reaching for something.

Ralph Angel ran to the barge slip. He called Blue's name, just as the horn sounded again. He looked and saw what Blue was reaching for— Zach, bobbing like a twig on the water, carried away by the current, out into the bayou. The back end of the barge was coming up quicker than Ralph Angel had anticipated and he could see the dark water churning out of the hull, the gushing wake rolling back toward the bank.

Ralph Angel stepped to the edge. He looked down into the water and felt gripped by an old terror as he tried to judge its depth. He couldn't swim. Had never learned. In all the years he'd come out here as a kid, he'd never dipped in as much as a toe. But now the thought of losing Blue—he'd already lost Gwenna, couldn't rely on Hollywood—no, he couldn't imagine. He forced the thought from his mind. And so, before he could talk himself out of it, he held his nose and jumped. The water came to his hips as it flowed out toward the bayou, but when his feet touched bottom, the grasses and sludge held for only a second before giving way and his feet sank into the mud. And suddenly the water was at his waist, then up to his chest as he crept farther out. He slid his fingers between the slip's wooden slats, which were not just wet but slimy from having been submerged for a century, and with every step, his feet sank deeper until it was as though hundred-pound weights were strapped to his ankles each time he took a step.

Blue had inched all the way to the edge of the slip where it opened into the bayou. He still gripped the slats, but only with one hand now as he reached for Zach with the other, his small arm straining, his fingers spread wide. The back end of the barge had almost passed. Another few seconds, Ralph Angel knew, and the wave would gush back into the slip. He remembered the alligator and felt a clench in his chest as he scanned the water's surface.

And then the water was coming toward him, curling over itself in a frothy wake, the swell looking much bigger at eye level than it did from up on the bank, the water hyacinths and lilies rolling at him like a dark carpet. Water splashed in Ralph Angel's face, washed up his nose and down his throat; he tasted the bayou's earthiness, felt himself lifted as the water level rose, heard the wave splash against the slip's bulkhead, and a fresh panic ripped through him. The world went black. He was drowning for sure.

"Pop!" a small voice called.

Ralph Angel gasped for breath, wiped water from his face. He saw Blue dog-paddling toward him, his little body fighting to stay upright in the swirling current.

"This way, buddy," Ralph Angel called. He stretched his arm as far as he could. "Swim this way."

"Pop!"

"I'm right here." Ralph Angel leaned out even farther because he couldn't live alone in this world. "Just keep going, buddy. That's right, swim to me." He heard his voice catch in his throat. Water splashed in his face again and he wiped it away, and knew he wiped tears with it.

Blue was closer now and Ralph Angel was surprised by the look of fear, yes, but also determination on his son's face. He hadn't been able to save Gwenna because he was afraid, but he would save his son. Ralph Angel wiped his face again and reached across the water. "That's it, buddy. I'm right here. Just a little farther."

13

❧ Mid-July now, Friday, and after the rainy false start, summer asserted its full magnificence with velvety morning air and peachy skies that turned glacier blue by noon, then a brilliant marbled red and purple at dusk. Laid-by and borer-free, the cane grew lustily, the swordlike leaves thickened, the roots deepened, the stalks pushed eagerly upward in the generous sunlight until they stood eleven notches high. And as Charley rolled along the northbound highway—the *Polyester Power Hour*, sixty uninterrupted minutes of seventies funk played on radio K-AJN, a glass of Tang nested in the cup holder, and two buttered slices of raisin bread wrapped in paper towel on the dash—she marveled at how far she'd come. A month ago, she hadn't known the difference between a combine and a chisel plow. Now she read the *Louisiana Sugar Bulletin* like it was the *New York Times* and tuned in to Ag call-in shows with the same regularity she used to reserve for NPR's *Morning Edition*. And while she still couldn't spout the yield potential of 384 versus 321, she could eyeball a stand of cane and determine whether a wild boar had been in it; could tell the difference between Roundup and Paraquat. As the Kisatchie's piney woods studded the horizon ahead, and Saint Josephine's emerald cane fields shrank in her rearview, Charley thought she might be an honest-to-goodness cane farmer after all. It was enough to make a girl want to sing.

The auction was Denton's idea. So far, they had gotten by on his ingenuity and a few pieces of jerry-rigged machinery, but the serious work of grinding was still ahead of them, and at eighty thousand dollars for a new tractor, two hundred fifty thousand for a combine, new equipment was out of the question. On their measly operating budget, used equipment was all they could afford.

Turning off the highway, Charley followed the trail of neon flyers down the service road and pulled in beside Denton's pickup. She had assumed the auction would be held in some kind of warehouse or possibly an airplane hangar, but this place was no more than an open lot with patches of Saint Augustine grass forcing its way up through the gravel. Ahead of her, Charley saw rusted spray rigs and ditch diggers, fertilizer tanks and tires, tractors and level liners all arranged more or less by size and stretching out in long, ragged rows. The place looked like an enormous archaeological dig, the farm equipment like dinosaur bones baking under the unforgiving sun.

There must have been two hundred farmers in attendance, Charley guessed, as she got out of her car. She maneuvered through the roiling sea of men in cowboy hats and baseball caps, men whose necks and arms tanned a deep, brick red, and whose creased faces bore out their years of struggle and worry. She'd never seen so many discouraged and defeated white men; it was like Shiloh, Gettysburg, Antietam, and Verdun all rolled into one. She moved among them, nodding when her eyes met theirs. She passed a farmer who looked like he'd just learned his house had burned down with his entire family inside, while a beady-eyed man with a hyena's skulking posture stared into faces as if trying to identify the weakest in the herd. Strings of multicolored flags wagged limply in the morning heat, country music wafted over the sound system, and the air smelled faintly of hot dogs, but it was impossible to ignore the gloom underlying the carnival excitement.

At the far end of the lot, Denton, dressed in yet another pair of Liberty overalls, leaned under the hood of a battered John Deere 4840—a make of tractor Charley recognized from pictures at the Blue Bowl.

She knocked on the chassis. "You didn't tell me it would be so crowded."

"I'm surprised as you." Denton yanked an oily cloth from his back pocket and wiped his hands. "It's late in the season, but I guess everyone's looking for a deal. Got a lot of good equipment out here, but most of it'll go for a fraction of what they paid." He handed her a catalog. "Might want to flip through this before the bidding starts."

CHESTER GROVELAND AUCTIONS
Liquidations, Bankruptcies, Asset Recovery

"'We believe our commitment to God, ethics, and integrity can help turn your assets into cash,'" Charley read. She opened the catalog and studied photos of tractors and forklifts, sleek quarter horses and stocky Texas longhorns. "At least we can buy some cattle if we're outbid on everything else." It was a bad joke, Charley knew, but it was all she could manage. Truth was, she was nervous about their chances. They had budgeted thirty thousand for equipment, which was like strolling up to the high rollers' table in Vegas with a dollar in your pocket. God help them if they were outbid.

Every few minutes, a farmer recognized Denton, called out to him across the yard or came over to say hello. The men shook hands, slapped each other's shoulders. They exchanged news about other auctions, shrugged over interest-rate hikes for production and equipment loans, shook their heads mournfully over news of farmers who'd gotten out or gone under. Charley was surprised at how many people Denton knew. The younger farmers addressed him with respect, even admiration, while the older men greeted him like a brother. Though he was the only black farmer on the lot, he seemed at ease, Charley thought, carried himself with the quiet confidence of a diplomat, and while she couldn't quite forget the story Denton told about the sealed bid and inside baseball, she guessed that in the end, every man there was just struggling to survive.

"You register yet?" Denton asked, when the last man moved away.

"I wanted to find you first."

Denton stuffed his oily cloth in his pocket. "Well, hurry up. Things move pretty fast once the bidding starts."

Inside the office, a woman in floral capris and a flip-flop-wearing teenage girl—the only other women Charley had seen all morning—sat behind a card table sipping Big Gulps and fanning their necks with paper plates. Over the roar of the industrial fan, the older woman explained the buyer's premium and the 4 percent parish tax while the girl recorded Charley's license number and handed her a bidder's card.

Charley was on her way back through the crowd with twin cups of Community Coffee when she saw Denton a few feet from where she'd left him, talking to two men. She recognized Jacques Landry just as Denton saw her, waved her over.

"Good morning." Charley handed Denton a coffee.

"Nice to see you again, Miss Bordelon," Landry said. He flashed a big white Pepsodent smile.

"You, too," Charley said, coolly.

"I'd like you to meet my boss, Samuel T. Baron. He's the head of Saint Mary's."

Baron was twenty years Landry's senior. His hair was spun sugar. The skin on his neck hung loose like a Brahman bull's. "Welcome to Louisiana," Baron said.

"Well, gentlemen," Charley said, sipping her coffee, "if I'd known you were coming, I'd have baked a cake."

Baron and Landry laughed, but Denton stayed quiet. Charley glanced at him, struck by the change in his demeanor. Fifteen minutes ago he was shaking hands, slapping men's backs, now he stood with rounded shoulders and seemed to have taken a step back from the conversation. She tried to catch his eye, but he wouldn't meet her gaze.

Landry turned to Charley. "I understand you've hired ol' Prosper here. You've got a fine employee, Miss Bordelon. Worked for my daddy for many years." He laid a heavy hand on Denton's shoulder.

"Yes, sir," Denton said. "Your daddy was a fine man."

Charley's heart jolted. She stole a glance at Denton, whose expression had gone vacant, as though the man she'd been working with the last three weeks, the man who could recite every cane variety produced since 1957, and just yesterday had fashioned an oil filter from mesh screen and duct tape, had slipped out the back way.

"Hell, Prosper," Landry said, "if I'd known it was this easy to lure you out of retirement, I'd have asked you to come back to us. But to tell the truth, I'm a little disappointed. Of all people, I'd have thought you knew better than to mislead this lovely lady into thinking she could be a cane farmer."

Charley imagined Denton's wife in their tidy kitchen, where all the dish towels were folded neatly into thirds and the counters were clear. She imagined Mrs. Denton fixing her husband's dinner, arranging the food just the way he liked it, placing it on the table set with water in a pink Depression glass pitcher. She imagined her leaning through the side window and calling out to the garden, *Prosper, time to come in. Quick, before supper gets cold*, saw Denton raise a hand to let her know he'd heard as he staked the last tomato plant. And then Charley imagined the two of them—two decent, hardworking people—sitting down together as they'd done every evening for the last fifty years: napkins spread over their laps as they bowed their heads in prayer, eating and talking quietly, and maybe even laughing as the radio played.

"It's *Mr.* Denton," Charley said. She stepped closer to Denton, hoping to jar him out of his stupor.

Landry blinked.

The temperature was in the low nineties, but with the heat index it felt over one hundred. Charley poured the rest of her coffee in the grass, and when she wiped her forehead, Landry suggested they move into the shade.

"So, Miss Bordelon . . ." Landry squinted out over the crowd. "You sure are a long way from Los Angeles. You do much surfing when you were young?"

"Some," Charley managed. Her hands felt pasty. Sweat trickled down her back, into the waistband of her jeans.

"Well, now." Landry squared his class ring on his finger and looked right at her. "A black surfer chick." His gaze slid down to her breast and then down to her crotch and he grinned. "I'm trying to picture that."

Charley stood very still. She was hot and cold at the same time. She had wondered when this day would come, because you don't move to a tiny Louisiana town, way out in the middle of nowhere, and expect life to be a stroll through the park; you couldn't expect to be the only woman in an industry filled with men and not think someone would eventually say something stupid; you couldn't ignore the long, dark, tortured history of Southern race relations, or pretend everything would be fixed overnight. And maybe you couldn't force an old black man to stand up for himself, which was deeply disappointing, and not at all what you would have expected for someone otherwise so dignified, and something you'd think about for a long time. But you could be brave. Even while your heart threatened to split your chest open it was pounding so hard, and your ears were ringing, and the hair on your arms was standing up because you instantly knew, in a way you never knew before, what it meant to be black in the South, and this might as well be 1945 with Jim Crow and lynchings, and Ku Kluxers burning down black merchants' stores and running families out of town. Even then, you could draw a line in the sand. You could do that. Because it was like your father said, *You have to bring ass to kick ass.*

Charley pulled her shoulders back. "And I'm trying to imagine your tiny pink prick."

Landry's head jerked and for a moment it looked like Charley had won. Then the color came back to his face.

But before Landry could respond, Baron cleared his throat and stepped forward. "It appears we've gotten off to a rocky start," he said, in a deep buttery voice. He spoke slowly, as though he didn't have anywhere in particular he needed to be. "Please excuse us, Miss Bordelon. My apologies for Mr. Landry's behavior. I'm sure he didn't mean anything by that last comment, and I suspect he was only praising Mr. Denton's work ethic. But I'm sure you're already aware of Mr. Denton's stellar reputation."

"As a matter of fact, I am," Charley said. "I'm honored to have Mr. Denton as a partner."

"Partner?" Baron gave Denton a congratulatory nod. "Splendid. Then I hope you'll both accept my apology, our apology, and allow me to propose we start over." He offered his hand.

Charley stared at Baron then looked away. All around her, men were inspecting equipment, raising side panels, kicking tires. A few spoke in hushed tones as if they were in a university library. "Accepted," Charley said.

And suddenly, Denton was back. He took Charley by the elbow, said, quietly, "We should go."

But before she could follow, Baron cleared his throat again. "I'm sure Mr. Denton's already told you, Miss Bordelon, that cane farming is a tough business. Every day, there's a report of another farm going under, another mill shutting down. It's depressing after a while." For an instant, he looked genuinely mournful.

"Don't worry, Mr. Baron," Charley said. "We have a good idea what we're up against."

"I beg your pardon, but I don't think you do."

Denton leaned over. "You don't have to put a dog in this fight."

Charley ignored him. "I have no idea what you're talking about, Mr. Baron."

Baron's laugh had a serrated quality to it. "I tell you what. I'm going to make you an offer. I want you and Mr. Denton to go at this cane farming hard as you can. Give it everything you've got. And if there's anything I can do for you, anything at all, I want you to feel free to come to me. But I also want you to make me a promise."

"I'm fresh out of promises."

"Promise that when it gets to be too much for you, you'll come to us first. Mr. Landry was right about one thing, Miss Bordelon, you've got a fine spread. But it's like anything else. One can only exploit an opportunity with the right resources.

"What could you possibly know about my resources? My resources are fabulous."

Baron shrugged. "If your resources were so fabulous, you wouldn't be looking to buy one of these rusted heaps." He smiled with front teeth square as Mahjong tiles. "Come to think of it, I'll sweeten the deal. On behalf of Saint Mary's Sugar Co-op, we'll be glad to take that land off your hands whenever you've had enough. We'll offer a fair price, of course, and I may be able to convince our board to throw in some lagniappe for your efforts."

Charley looked at Baron. She should walk away, she knew she should. It was what Denton had been asking her to do for the last five minutes. But she couldn't. "Save your offers. As a matter of fact, you two can go fuck yourselves. Mr. Denton and I will do fine."

Baron looked at her without blinking. "Feisty," he said. "I like feisty. Don't lose that. But remember this: It's one thing for you to make that claim when you're working for someone else, Miss Bordelon. It's different when the land is yours. When, pardon the expression, it's your ass on the line."

"We'll see about that."

"Yes, Miss Bordelon, we will."

A voice over the loudspeaker announced the auction would start in ten minutes, and the noise level rose as farmers hurried to finish their appraisals. Charley waited for Denton to speak but he only cleaned his glasses on a napkin. The seconds dragged on.

"I didn't mean to speak for you, Mr. Denton," Charley said, unable to wait any longer. "I'm sorry—I just couldn't—"

"What's the best piece of equipment you reckon you saw this morning?" Denton's voice was quiet. He pulled the catalog from his back pocket and flipped through it.

Charley pictured the rows of machinery and tried to recall whether she'd noticed men gathered around any single piece. "I guess the John Deere you were looking at."

"Wrong." Denton slid his catalog toward her, a tiny, almost imperceptible gesture. "That one." He tapped a picture of an I.H. 1066. "International Harvester. That's the machine we're going to buy."

Charley studied the picture. "But you spent all your time at the John Deere. How can you be sure the I.H. is better when you didn't even—"

Denton shook his head like he wasn't surprised she was dumb

enough to overlook it. "It was right up front by the entrance. I know the farmer who owned it. His initials are on the chassis. He was a good man, a talented farmer, always took good care of his equipment. But his wife got sick, something with her heart, and he couldn't pay her medical bills and cover farm expenses. Pretty soon he was underwater." Denton shook his head. "It's a shame." He rolled the catalog into a scroll, slid it in his pocket.

Exactly on the hour, a pickup with a camper shell, a hole the size of a car window cut into the side, the auctioneer peering through it, pulled up at the far side of the yard.

"All right, boys," the auctioneer said, through a bullhorn, "let's get started so we can get out of here."

When the camper swung around, Charley saw the two women from the office perched on stools just inside the camper's back door.

At the sound of the auctioneer's voice, the men under the trees dragged themselves out into the open, where the heat rose off the gravel in waves, and that was when the reality of why they were there hit Charley hard. She and Denton were there to benefit from others' misfortune like everyone else, brotherhood and slapping backs be damned. And if the wind didn't blow in her favor, Charley thought, she could easily be back here in a year, standing at the back of this very same crowd while these vultures picked the last scrap of flesh from her bones.

A rap of the auctioneer's gavel started the bidding. "Lot ten-dash-four," he announced as if calling a square dance. "A Taylorway twelve-inch disc. Like new. We'll start at five hundred. Five, five, five hundred. Five hundred dollars. Come on, boys, let me see the money."

Men signaled their interest with nods and hand gestures. Charley followed along as best she could, struggling to decipher the auctioneer's warbling, making notes in the margins of her catalog. There was a new energy, a fresh excitement in the air. Suddenly, everything moved faster. The small stuff went first. Tools and farm implements, things,

Charley imagined, that would wind up in a roadside antique mall if they weren't put to some farm use.

An hour later, the lot was even more crowded, and the bidding was going strong. They'd moved to the large items. Charley flipped to the catalog page that showed the I.H., surprised at how anxious she felt.

Denton leaned close. "I want you to sit tight. Don't show your hand." He scanned the crowd, his gaze resting on one face and then another, as though he were sizing up their competition.

"Lot one twenty-four," the auctioneer called. "We'll start the bidding at eighty-five hundred. Eight five. Eighty-five in the back. Eight five, who'll show me nine?"

Without looking at her, Denton tapped Charley's leg. "Put up your card."

"But it's an Allis Chalmers," Charley whispered, consulting her catalog.

"Nine. Nine. Do I hear nine five?" The auctioneer's voice drove the crowd forward. "Nine five down in front. Who'll give me ten? Anyone gonna elbow in?"

"I know what it is," Denton said. "Raise your card."

"Ten down in front. Who'll give me ten five? How 'bout ten and a quarter?" Ten and a quarter, ten and a quarter for lot one twenty-four. Ten and a quarter in the second row. Let's have ten five."

Charley started to raise her card, then hesitated.

"Please, Miss Bordelon. Do like I'm telling you. Remember what you promised at the Blue Bowl?" The force of Denton's tone stung her. Charley raised her card.

The auctioneer nodded. "Ten five in the back. Who'll give me eleven? Eleven on the side, thank you, sir. Eleven for the Allis Chalmers. Can I get eleven five?"

"Keep going," Denton said.

Charley raised her card again. "But we don't want—"

"Eleven five in the back. Thank you, madam. Do I have twelve? Twelve on the side again."

Charley saw Denton glance over at the last bidder, a man standing on the far side of the lot with his arms folded. He didn't look in their direction, but something in his manner, the way he stared straight ahead, told Charley he was watching them.

"That's the rainmaker," Denton said.

"What the hell is a rainmaker?"

"Someone who bids just to drive the price up," Denton explained, and went on to say most times, they worked for the auction house, but sometimes for the person who was selling. "I wanted to put some bait out there, see what we caught."

"What did we catch?"

"Baron. Riding your tail. Bidding you up." Denton ran his hand over his face. "Give me a second to think."

The bidding was at thirteen thousand. The auctioneer scanned the crowd. "What y'all thinking, boys?"

Denton nudged Charley. "Sit tight."

He was gone before Charley could ask where he was going, and the Allis Chalmers sold while she waited patiently. The I.H. would be up soon. Charley tried not to look at the rainmaker, but when she glanced around for Denton, their eyes met. He nodded and touched the brim of his cap, a small gesture, one that could be mistaken for a bid if a person didn't know better, but Charley felt certain it was a signal for her—a threat, or worse, a promise—and for a moment, she couldn't decide who was more terrifying: Baron and Landry in their corporate uniforms, wielding their power in her face, or the rainmaker, looking like a KGB agent in his dark glasses and devil's goatee. And then Charley's mind cleared and she was annoyed with herself for being afraid. Maybe Denton had jumped to conclusions. Maybe the man wasn't a rainmaker. Maybe he was just being polite.

Denton reappeared. "We're changing up the plan," he said, slightly winded. "We're not bidding on the I.H. anymore."

"Not—what?" Charley said. The auctioneer was calling for lot one thirty-five now. The I.H. was lot one thirty-six. "You said it's the best tractor here. We need it."

"Next up, lot one thirty-six," the auctioneer called. "An I.H. 1066. Crank it up, Billy. All right, boys. Let's put a little money up. We'll start at seven thousand."

A man climbed up into the I.H. and started the engine. It was the closest thing Charley had heard to a machine purring. She got her card ready. Denton grabbed her wrist. "Just hold on." He leaned forward and stared at the ground as though he were trying to hide.

And suddenly, Charley disliked him. The slight hump in his back— his old man's back—as he leaned forward to rest his hands on his knees; his fingers with their wrinkled knuckles and nails like rinds of parmesan; his ridiculous pressed overalls and his old-fashioned shoes. They needed that tractor, *she* needed that tractor if she wanted anything close to a chance of making it, and she'd be damned if she sat back while some old man who was afraid of his shadow told her what to do. This wasn't 1945, Charley wanted to say. There was nothing to be afraid of. No wonder her father hated the South. No wonder he ran for his life.

"Eight thousand for the I.H.," the auctioneer called. "Who'll elbow in? Eight. Can I get eight and a half?"

"Here." Charley raised her card as all heads turned to look.

"Eight and a half, right there. Thank you, madam. Who'll show me nine?"

Denton glared at her. "What are you doing?"

"That guy's not the rainmaker."

"Nine down in front," the auctioneer said.

"There, you see," Charley whispered. "He didn't bid."

The auctioneer called for nine and a half. A man the next row over gave a signal.

"Nine and a half. Can I get ten?"

The auctioneer called for nine five again. The man in the next row bid. Charley raised her bidder's card. Denton grabbed her arm. "I'm trying to tell you," he said, but she ignored him. Denton never swore, but Charley heard him swear under his breath. "I'll be g'all damned."

"Ten five," the auctioneer said.

Charley kept her card raised. The tractor wasn't worth more than thirteen, that's what Denton said. Anything over thirteen, they'd agreed they'd walk away. The man in front dropped out of the bidding; it was just her and the man in the next row. Maybe she'd get it at ten five. Maybe eleven. The rainmaker hadn't made a peep. Charley turned to him. She stared him right in the eye, dared him to jump in. He seemed not to see her, didn't move or look in her direction, and she was flushed with relief. She was right. He was just another farmer, an ordinary man. The auctioneer asked for eleven and Charley's card was still raised. Another few seconds and the tractor would be hers. She'd show Denton that times had changed.

"Eleven, going once."

The rainmaker signaled—two fingers.

"Thirteen!" the auctioneer cried.

For a moment, Charley couldn't move. When she did turn her head, the rainmaker met her gaze and she saw that thing in his expression that Denton must have seen earlier: a coldness, a steely indifference that made her shudder, and she understood she'd done exactly what he knew all along she'd do.

"Thirteen." The auctioneer looked at Charley. "Do I have fourteen?"

If she continued, she'd be over her limit. She'd have paid more than Denton swore the tractor was worth. If she dropped out, Baron and Landry would have won.

Charley raised her card.

Fourteen. Fourteen five. Each time she bid, the rainmaker bid higher. Fifteen. Fifteen five. Denton leaned over and whispered something to her, something hot and blistering, though she couldn't make out the words for the rushing in her ears. Then he pushed his way through the crowd. And though she panicked to realize Denton was gone, Charley reasoned, somewhere in the back of her brain, that when it was all over and the tractor was theirs, he'd understand and agree she'd done the right thing. It all would have been worth it. She'd won.

"Sixteen thousand."

The auctioneer seemed to spot someone far behind her. "Seventeen thousand in the back. Come on, boys, somebody put me in the money. Can I get seventeen five?"

Charley stole a glance at the rainmaker. He didn't move or look her way, but she knew he was waiting for her, ready to pounce if she kept bidding. Now someone else had thrown his hat in the ring. For all she knew, it was another of Baron's cronies. Silence hung over the crowd. It lasted only a few seconds—but it was enough for Charley to realize the harm she'd done, the damage she'd cause if she continued this ridiculous game. She had no idea where Denton was, what he was doing, but she was pretty sure he'd given up on her. And who wouldn't? Who'd want to work with someone who refused to listen, refused to learn? Who had that kind of time to waste?

"Seventeen, going once. Twice."

Charley folded her bidder's card and shoved it deep in her pocket. There would be other tractors.

"Last call for lot one thirty-six. *Sold!* For seventeen thousand."

After the fiasco with the I.H., Charley tore up her bidder's card, then watched through a fog of humiliation and distress as the rest of the equipment, tractors included, sold for a fraction of what she bid. She barely noticed who bought what and stayed only because she would rather have slept on a bed of nails than walk through that crowd. Denton was right about one thing: one's heart went out to the farmer who once owned all that stuff. It was tough seeing a three-row chopper, probably eight or nine thousand dollars new, go for two hundred bucks. A whole life's work, years of struggling to make ends meet. How could farmers stand it?

Behind the office, the people at the hot dog booth were packing up. Someone had slashed through the prices with a red marker and hot dogs were only a quarter. Charley was not thirsty, but she bought a Coke, hoping the carbonation would settle her stomach. The air had that heavy, expectant feel, as though at any moment someone would shout or fire a gun. In a couple hours the regular afternoon showers would turn the sky a steely gray, and crooked fingers of lightning would illuminate the horizon. The storm would only last half an hour, Charley thought, but by the time she got back to Saint Josephine, it would be too wet and maybe too dark to do anything on the farm. Better to go back to Miss Honey and Micah, lick her wounds tonight and crawl back to Denton tomorrow.

The rainmaker, Landry, and Baron were long gone. Up and down the rows, farmers loaded air compressors, old sinks, and batteries into their trucks. Standing alone in the shade of a shabby oak, Charley was afraid to check the parking lot for Denton's truck. Just the thought that he'd quit made her light-headed with shame. She'd acted foolishly. Now she had to go home and tell Micah and Miss Honey how badly she'd blown it. She'd have to sit there while Ralph Angel laughed in her face.

The empty Coke can still in her hand, Charley walked toward the parking lot, braced for the sight of the empty spot where Denton's truck had been. But his truck was there, and yes, thank God, there he was, leaning against its door as he flipped through a stack of receipts, the ones, Charley recalled, he stuffed above his visor. She had never been so happy to see those Liberty overalls, the bald head, or that raggedy old truck, as she was right now. Her first impulse was to run over, hurl herself on the ground, and beg for forgiveness. She would apologize for everything: the bidding, the money, all the stupid questions she'd ever asked—all of it—if he'd just give her another chance. And she was just about to when Denton looked up, noticed her, and she saw something in his expression. Disgust? Disappointment? All Charley knew was that she had never seen him look so unfriendly. Denton stared at her for a moment, then went back to his receipts.

"I was afraid you'd gone," Charley said, chastened, and then, "Oh,

God, I'm so sorry. I'm such an idiot. You were right about the rainmaker. No. You were right about everything and I don't blame you for quitting." If she thought Denton wouldn't find it girly and manipulative, she'd cry. And for an instant, she thought she might. Her head was buzzing and there was that tightness again, like some gigantic, soggy wool sock was being wrung out inside her. But then it lifted. Just enough for her to say one word. "Please."

Nothing. No reaction at all. Denton turned away as though he hadn't seen or heard her, as though her plea was nothing more than an atmospheric disturbance. He leaned over the wheel and stuffed the receipts back onto the sun visor, then lifted himself into the seat, slammed the door, started the engine.

Well, Charley thought, that's it. It's over. She stood clear as Denton backed up and swung around. A furious spray of gravel flew out from the tires and there was that awful grating sound, the sound of spinning tires over loose rocks and dirt, the sound of someone who couldn't get away fast enough. She could barely see Denton's truck for all the dust and dry grass that blew up in her face, and she listened for the roar of his engine, wondering if she could hold off crying until he was gone. But the sound never came, and when Charley opened her eyes, Denton's truck was idling right there in front of her and he was leaning across the seat. And now he was reaching for the handle, and the door was swinging open. It wouldn't be until later that night, when she was at Miss Honey's and had time to think back on it, that Charley would understand there was a difference between kowtowing and letting people's assumptions work against them; that there was a beauty and honor in the Japanese bough that bent but didn't break, and she finally, *truly*, appreciated what a decent man Denton was. That just when she thought her life was over, just when she thought she'd screwed things up (*again*), forgiveness and grace would be bestowed upon her with two simple words: "Get in."

Given all that had happened, Charley knew better than to ask questions. For once, she was grateful Denton wasn't much of a talker, and barely dared to breathe as he threw the truck into drive. She had no idea where they were headed or how long they would be gone, and frankly, she was too tired to care. Normally, she hated not knowing the plan, but right now, she didn't want to think. As long as Denton didn't put her out of the truck, she was satisfied.

The drive turned out to be short—just a few hundred yards. Denton pulled around to the other side of the office, parked, then went over to talk with a white man who was busy strapping equipment down on a long goose-neck trailer. Charley couldn't see the man's face, just his two tanned arms sticking out from his faded red T-shirt, but she knew he was another farmer simply by the way he was dressed: the requisite baseball cap, Wrangler jeans stuffed sloppily into the tops of his work boots.

From the way he and Denton talked, the way they both nodded and stood back to admire the equipment, they must be friends. It was nice to see, Charley thought, the pleasure Denton could take in someone else's success; clearly the guy had done well. Just look at all the equipment he'd managed to buy: the Ampco flat chopper she and Denton had looked at, a shaver, and a ditch digger. Why, there was even the cultivator that went for one hundred and seventy bucks. Denton seemed genuinely happy despite the fact he was walking away empty-handed, and Charley wondered whether this wasn't part of his secret, the reason he'd lasted all these years. Because you would have to be forgiving. You'd have to have a huge heart. You'd have to insist on seeing the good in people to deal with all the Landrys and Barons and who knew who else, and not go a little nuts down here.

Eventually, Denton waved her over. "So it ought to run real good," he was saying by the time Charley joined him. "Something wrong, it'd be smoking in idle. A new hose and it'll run up and down the rows for a long time."

"Still can't believe I got that chisel plow for four seventy-five," Denton's friend said, wedging his thumbs through his belt loops. "The way it rakes up roots, turns them around? Oh, man. It'll be just like combing hair."

It was such a relief to see Denton in a good mood that Charley felt a surge of gratitude for his friend. Thank God. You're a lifesaver. You really have no idea, she wanted to say. But instead, she offered her hand and said, simply, "Congratulations."

"This here's Remy Newell," Denton said, a smile brightening his face.

Remy Newell looked at Charley strangely. "Congratulations for what?"

Charley looked from Remy to Denton, who gave a little shrug. "She never gave me a chance to tell her."

"Tell me what?"

"You mean she doesn't know?" Remy Newell shook his head and laughed. "Good Lord, Mr. D."

Denton massaged his forehead. "You mighta noticed she's not too good at listening, so I stopped talking."

"Tell me what? What's going on?" Charley stared at Denton.

"Like I was trying to tell you earlier. When I saw what Baron was doing with the rainmaker, I had to go to Plan C." He stepped aside. "I had Remy here bid for us. That's where I went after you bid on the Allis Chalmers. Congratulations, Miss Bordelon. All this equipment is yours."

14

❦ Evening. From his place on the ratty sofa, Ralph Angel watched Blue, on hands and knees, march Zach over a fortress of old *Reader's Digest*s and stacked cans of string beans.

"Got my Glock," Blue chanted, imitating a grown man's voice, "gotta get some money," and Ralph Angel thought he'd have to mix more pop radio, maybe some jazz, in with the rap music. Blue looked up at him. "My stomach hurts."

"Well, I warned you not to eat so much ice cream."

Across the room, planted at Miss Honey's feet, Micah looked up from her mystery and said, "When my stomach hurts, my mom gives me tea with lemon."

Ralph Angel blinked at Micah, thought she looked exactly like Charley when she was that age. And for a moment, as it had so many times since he arrived, time pretzeled back on itself and he was nineteen again. He had given Charley a Christmas present he couldn't afford—a chemistry set—along with a ten-dollar bill. He would never forget the way she'd looked up at him, her face aglow with gratitude and admiration, bright as the little white lights on the tree. *The best gift ever*, she'd said. A lot of good it had done him. Where was the gratitude now? Where was the admiration? All this time and Charley still hadn't gotten back to him about working on the farm. He purposely didn't come on like gangbusters with a lot of demands and accusations, even though the entire time they talked, he struggled against the darkness gathering like a storm inside him. He was polite. *Have some cereal.* Reasonable. *Of course you should talk to Denton.* Promised to be patient. *Take your time.* And for a few days, he'd thought the strategy worked. But lately, he'd begun to think Charley was avoiding him. She never had time to talk. Was always rushing out, saying she had to get back to the farm.

And when she was around, usually for a few minutes in the morning, he overheard her telling 'Da what she'd learned. It was always, "Mr. Denton showed me how to do this" or "Now I know how to do that," like he wasn't sitting around all day, killing time, going crazy waiting for an answer.

"Micah," Miss Honey said, waving the TV remote, "go get the pink medicine from under my bathroom sink."

Ralph Angel motioned to Blue, said, "Come here, boy," and when Blue climbed into his lap and folded himself over Ralph Angel's shoulder, Ralph Angel slipped his hand under his son's shirt and rubbed his back, trying to remember how Gwenna used to do it. "How's that?" He patted Blue's back.

"Pepto Bismol tastes like vomit," Micah said, returning with a bright pink bottle.

"That's very helpful," Ralph Angel said, dryly. "I can't thank you enough." He turned Blue around, poured a capful of the pink liquid, and held it to Blue's lips.

Blue eyed the bottle and whimpered. "I don't want to vomit." He pushed Ralph Angel's hand away.

"It won't make you vomit. She said it *tastes* like vomit, but it doesn't. It's just medicine. Come on now, open up."

But Blue pressed his hands to his mouth, turned away. Medicine sloshed out of the cap, dribbled down Ralph Angel's arm, across his pants, onto the sofa cushion. Ralph Angel drew in a shallow breath. It felt as though someone were picking a thread inside him, picking and picking, and now the stitch was coming lose, pulling through him in one ragged piece. "Goddamn it. Do you want to feel better or not?"

Which only made Blue start to cry.

"Good Lord, Ralph Angel." Miss Honey slid out of her recliner and pulled Blue into her arms. "The child doesn't know what he wants. Stop barking at him." She backed into the recliner, pressed Blue to her chest. "How about a hot water bottle, *chère*? You might like that better."

Ralph Angel looked at Miss Honey and felt his face get hot. He shouldn't have answered the phone that day he saw her number come up; shouldn't have let her talk him into coming back. He'd been fine out in Phoenix; okay, not perfect, but getting through the days, getting by. He'd managed to squeeze his life down into something small, something manageable, no more than he could handle. No big dreams. A postage stamp of a life. And to the extent he dreamed, it was of Billings and the life he'd make for them somehow. Why hadn't Miss Honey just left them alone? But he'd come like she'd asked. Okay, maybe he wasn't as good at this mothering stuff as Gwenna, but he didn't have to sit around and be insulted.

"I'll take it from here," Ralph Angel said, rising, because this was how things started between them last time, and he was trying to be good. Last time, she got in his face with all her questions, pressed and pressed him to explain about his stash, and he'd felt like an animal being poked with a stick. Then she said she was disappointed, that he'd let the family down, which was exactly what his father had said when he found out about the tuition money. It was as though she'd opened the levee and all that darkness had rushed in and he was sucked under. He hadn't meant to push her, but he couldn't breathe, had just been trying to get some air. "Come on, buddy. I'll read you a story." He pried Blue from Miss Honey's arms and ushered him out of the room.

In the back room, on the large bed, Ralph Angel pulled the sheet up around Blue's waist. "Go to sleep."

"But you said you'd read to me."

Ralph Angel looked at his son. Yes, he'd said that, but off the cuff, as an excuse to get out of the den. Gwenna had always been the one to read bedtime stories. That was so long ago, though, he wondered if Blue even remembered. But now Blue was looking at him, watching, his eyes wide and expectant, as though he were waiting for Ralph Angel to do a magic trick. "Right. Well, uh, let's see what we've got here." Hollywood had stacked the few remaining boxes in the corner and Ralph Angel eyed them warily. Just the thought of sorting through them made him tired. He pulled the nightstand drawer open, saw a Bible, black and solemn, lying among the buttons, old church bulletins, broken pencils and ballpoints, and felt a dull, heavy feeling roll through him. He didn't like to think about God. He glanced at the stack of boxes again, then reached for the Bible. "Scoot over."

Blue sat up. "It doesn't have any pictures."

"I know," Ralph Angel said, flipping the tissuey pages. "You'll have to use your imagination. I'll read an adventure story—about a boat." And so, Ralph Angel turned to Genesis and began to read, or rather, began translating the old language. *And it came to pass, when man began to multiply on the face of the earth . . . And God saw that the wickedness of man was great, and that every imagination of the thoughts of his heart was only evil continually . . .* "Once upon a time," Ralph Angel began, "the world was full of people doing bad things."

"Bad things like what?" Blue said.

"I don't know. Just bad things. Beating up on each other, stealing cars. Be quiet. Listen to the story." *And the Lord said, I will destroy man whom I have created from the face of the earth; both man and beast, and the creeping thing, and the fowl in the air . . .* "So God, who had made the earth and all the people and all the animals in the first place, got real mad and decided to start over. He decided to make it rain until the whole earth was covered with water."

"Could the people swim?"

"No, they couldn't swim."

"So they drowned?"

"Yeah. They all drowned."

"Even the animals?"

"Sorry, buddy. Even the animals."

"I don't like this story."

"Don't worry, it gets better. Just listen." Blue nuzzled against his arm, and he felt heat radiating off his son's limbs. *But Noah found grace in the eyes of the Lord . . .* Grace in the eyes of the Lord. Ralph Angel read the line again and looked up from the page. He'd had the thought for a while now that the world was divided into two kinds of people—those who believed they were worthy of God's grace and those who believed they weren't. It wasn't something to fight—it just was or wasn't, much the way some people were natural-born leaders while others were born to follow, or the way some people's bodies were built for long-distance running while others' were built for sprinting. Was it destiny? Was it fate? He didn't know. But reading the verse seemed to confirm that what he'd felt way down in the pit of his gut was true, and he knew, just like he knew his own name, what side of the line he was on, would *always* be on, and the same emptiness that opened within him as he stood in the minimart that day opened in him again.

"What happened next?" Blue shook his arm. "Why did you stop reading?"

"Sorry." Ralph Angel found his place and forced himself to read more. *And God said unto Noah . . . And thou shalt come into the ark.* "But there was one man who was God's favorite," he said. "His name was Noah and he was a good guy, and God decided to let him and his family live. So he told Noah to build a big boat."

"A speedboat?"

"No, a wooden boat. Bigger than this house."

In the winking hours, Ralph Angel startled awake. The light was on and the Bible lay open on his lap. The clock radio read 12:28 a.m., and for a long time he sat listening to the night—the refrigerator humming through its cycles, the buzz of the streetlamp, the faint croak of frogs in the gully. The minutes dragged. He'd planned to wait up for Charley so that he could ask her again about a job, but it was too late now; he'd try to catch her in the morning. Right now, he had to get out of this room, out of the house.

In the dark, Ralph Angel eased the Impala's door open, and was halfway down the block, past the old church and over the railroad tracks, before he turned on his headlights. On the open road, he picked up speed. Moths and beetles flitted across the narrow tunnels of his high beams, warm air spilled through the open window, the road unfurled like a length of movie reel.

At the junction, Ralph Angel headed east toward New Orleans, a two-hour drive, and was figuring where he could score when, in the distance, over the trees, the sky took on an eerie radiance. Gradually, the Indian casino came into view: gushing fountains that threw off a twenty-foot curtain of fine mist, the entrance a spectacle of neon lights and anodized metalwork. He rolled up alongside a Chevy Avalanche, its angular converted cab dwarfing the Impala.

The marquee flickered, and inside the slots rang nonstop, though the place wasn't very crowded for a Saturday night. Half-empty gaming tables ran down the center of the room. Along one wall, a man sat heavily on his padded stool as a dealer, looking bored in her sequined vest, tossed cards beside his short stack of chips. Ralph Angel touched his back pocket, where a withered five and a few singles nested in his wallet.

For the next hour, Ralph Angel lingered over the hunched shoulders of the last determined blackjack players, then wandered into the private room where Vietnamese high-rollers flung down twenties and fifties at Mini Baccarat, and finally, drifted into the arcade where three gangly boys stomped out a sequence of steps as the Dance Dance Revolution machine pulsed out a techno groove. He dropped a quarter into the Alpine Ski Jump, watched it roll down the narrow ramp and through the fifty-point slot in the turning wheel. The game machine spat out a length of tickets as long as his arm. Surprised, he dug in his pocket for another quarter and tried again. Bingo! Another stretch of tickets.

In the end, Ralph Angel blew two dollars on the ridiculous game. He chose a large stuffed monkey, a rubber spider, and a pack of plastic zoo animals from the display of prizes before exhaustion overtook him and he wandered back into the casino, set the monkey on the floor between his legs, rested his head against a quarter slot called Money to Burn, the spider and zoo animals into a plastic bucket at his feet.

"Looks like you got lucky."

Ralph Angel lifted his head. The woman before him held a cocktail tray against her square waist. She nodded at the prizes.

"I got 'em for my boy."

"Guess you win the medal for Father of the Year."

Ralph Angel eyed her. She wasn't pretty—a little pale for his taste— but she wasn't ugly either. Something about her, though, the way more teeth showed on one side of her mouth than the other when she smiled, reminded him of Gwenna. *They'd had a good life once. They never meant to cross over.*

"I'm just playing," the woman said, laughing lightly. "Actually, I think it's sweet." She took a small pad from her apron pocket. "What can I get you?"

Ralph Angel took a moment to think. He'd snuck a couple six-packs into the back room then waited until Blue fell asleep, but it had been a long time since he'd had a real drink. Not since Phoenix.

"How about an Old Havana?"

The woman winked. "Coming right up." Within seconds of her pressing the drink into his hands, Ralph Angel promptly drained the glass.

"My," she said. "Aren't we thirsty?"

He passed the glass back to her. "Can I get another?"

"That's the point, isn't it? Loosen you up so you'll throw your money away?" She smiled that crooked smile again.

"Exactly."

Another couple rounds of weak drinks, another hour of feeding the slots. Every time the woman came around to check on him, bring him a fresh drink, they'd talk for a few minutes. Nothing deep. Just bar talk. How big the last jackpot was, the last guy to get tossed out for counting cards, the most recent eighties has-been pop star to cycle through. She came by one last time before her shift ended.

"Nice talking to you."

"Yeah, you, too."

. . .

Three o'clock in the morning. Ralph Angel felt as if cinder blocks were strapped to his ankles as he pushed through the double doors, out into the neon glow.

The woman sat on the curb smoking. She'd traded her cocktail uniform for cutoffs and a T-shirt.

"Thought you'd be home by now," Ralph Angel said.

"My ride bailed on me." She waved vaguely and exhaled a stream of smoke. "I hate when this happens." Flicked ash away and stared into the dark. "One of these days, I won't have to put up with this bullshit. Gonna buy myself a little pickup, cherry red with a double cab."

The woman's skin looked ashier, rougher than it did inside. Sort of like Gwenna's right before she went to the hospital the last time. Gwenna had had smooth, clear skin once. Like chocolate milk. She wore nice clothes, fixed her hair. *They never meant to lose their house. They never meant to become junkies. They'd just wanted to take the edge off, get that warm feeling—pillows between them and the world.* The day they released Gwenna from the hospital, her skin had cleared up a little, but she was still thin. Weighed ninety-eight pounds; a goddamn sparrow. After their last run, her lungs had filled with fluid, collapsed with infection. *Close call*, the doctor had said. The morning he picked her up, she claimed she felt stronger, but she couldn't even lift Blue, who'd just turned four.

Ralph Angel looked down the service road for the flare of headlights. Nothing. He felt for his keys. "I can give you a lift."

"You sure?" But she was already stubbing her cigarette out on the curb.

At the Impala, Ralph Angel cringed, seeing the trash on the floor, clothes strewn across the seat. "It's a little junky."

"No worries."

He waited for her to set her purse on the floor before he closed her door.

. . .

Maybe it was some unarticulated relief at having secured a ride home, and maybe it was the feel of the velvety upholstery against her bare legs, Ralph Angel couldn't be sure, but the gap between them seemed to narrow the farther they drove from the casino.

"I never got your name," Ralph Angel said.

"It's Amber."

"Ralph Angel."

"Ralph Angel." She seemed to taste the words. "You a musician or something?"

"An engineer," he said, then held his breath, startled by the words that had come out of his mouth. He waited for her to laugh or ask where he worked.

But all she said was "Cool," and dug in her purse. Said, "You mind?" as she held up the cigarette. And when Ralph Angel shook his head no, she lit it, cracked her window, and blew a long stream of smoke as tendrils of her hair lifted in the breeze.

A jazzy melody oozed through the radio, followed soon after by the announcer's silky voice. Ralph Angel relaxed back against his seat, wondering at what had just happened. He hadn't planned to lie. All he said was what he *wanted* to be true, what *would* be true if his life had taken a different turn, and she'd accepted it. He didn't believe in the power of positive thinking or any of that mumbo jumbo, but he felt different having said what he said.

Amber laced her fingers through the rods of his headrest. "I don't know many engineers," she said, closing the gap between them. She looked at him again.

And just like that, he was pulling off the road into a clearing beyond the barbed-wire fence, past trees nailed with POSTED signs, and Amber was, *Jesus*, already pulling down her shorts, raising her T-shirt to reveal her pale breasts. She climbed into his lap and straddled him, her back arched against the wheel. Ralph Angel closed his eyes, turned his face into her hair. It was curlier than Gwenna's since Gwenna started giving herself perms, but had the same faintly floral smell. Ralph Angel remembered how once, during the good times, he came home from work and found Gwenna leaning over the kitchen sink, plastic gloves turned inside out on the counter, the lid off the jar of hair straightener.

"I thought that shit burned your scalp," he'd said.

"I'm used to it," Gwenna said, groping for the shampoo. He'd pushed the bottle toward her, then changed his mind, poured some in his hand, stood behind her, and massaged the shampoo into her hair, smelling lilac and honeysuckle. He felt her relax, letting him take over. Then he gathered a towel around her head and led her to the couch, watched as she pulled the comb through her hair, then plucked strands from the teeth and twisted them around her finger.

"We should take Blue to see your dad," she'd said. Beads of cloudy water hung from the tips of her hair.

"Why would I do that?" He'd wiped the drop of water running down the side of her face. "He wasn't interested in being a dad. Why would he be interested in being a grandfather?" But that was why he loved her. Because she saw his better self even when he couldn't; because she always pushed him toward the light. *I have more faith in you than I have in myself,* he once told her.

Sonny Stitt played on the radio as the Impala slid over the country road, and Ralph Angel felt that a new day had broken.

Amber lit another cigarette. "What are you thinking about?"

"A poem I used to know." Ralph Angel kept his eyes on the road. "My daddy taught it to me." It was really Gwenna's favorite poem. He'd memorized it when they were still dating and recited it the night he asked her to marry him. But he didn't think Amber would appreciate that little factoid, that he was thinking about his wife, after what they just did.

"Let's hear it."

"That's okay."

"No, honest. I want to hear it."

"Okay," Ralph Angel said. "Here goes. Don't laugh.

"*So live, that when thy summons comes to join / The innumerable caravan, that moves / To the pale realms of shade, where each shall take / His chamber in the silent halls of death, / Thou go not, like the quarry-slave at night, / Scourged to his dungeon, but sustain'd and sooth'd / By an unfaltering trust, approach thy grave, / Like one who wraps the drapery of his couch / About him, and lies down to pleasant dreams.*"

"Damn," Amber said.

"You didn't like it."

Amber shrugged. "I don't know. I kind of like the ones that rhyme."

They were on the outskirts of town when a car came out of nowhere and pulled on to the road, hung back for a while, but then closed the distance. In the rearview mirror, Ralph Angel made out rectangular headlights, a rack on the grille, the cruiser's white hood glowing in his taillights. The blue and white lights flashed.

"Shit."

Amber sat up straight, smoothed her hair as Ralph Angel steered onto the shoulder. He clamped his hands to the wheel, where he knew they'd be visible, watched in his side mirror as the trooper ran his plates then came up alongside the Impala, his palm resting lightly on the grip of his gun. He tried not to blink as the trooper shined the light in his face.

One Mississippi, two Mississippi, three Mississippi, four Mississippi. The arc of light swung past him, over the seat, across Amber's lap and up into her pale face. Five Mississippi, six Mississippi. Seven Mississippi, eight.

"You all right, miss? You need some assistance?"

"No, Officer, I'm fine," Amber said, her voice high and strained. Her accent thicker. "Just trying to get home."

Nine Mississippi, ten Mississippi. Lights in Ralph Angel's eyes again.

"License and registration, please."

"Yes, sir." Slowly, Ralph Angel reached into his back pocket. He thought about the car as he handed his license to the trooper and his mouth went dry as he played out the possibilities. Eleven Mississippi. Twelve Mississippi.

The trooper studied the photo. "California. You're a long way from home."

"Yes, sir." Ralph Angel cleared his throat. "I'm visiting family."

"This car belong to you?"

"No, sir. It's a rental." Thirteen Mississippi.

The trooper studied his license again. "And you drove all the way down here?"

"Yes, sir. Like I said, I'm visiting family."

Fourteen Mississippi. Fifteen. The trooper looked up the road. "It's a little late for you two to be out here, don't you think?"

"Yes, sir. I'm just driving this young lady home."

"You been drinking tonight?"

Sixteen Mississippi. How should he answer? Be careful. "I had one drink back at the casino, but that was awhile ago."

Amber leaned forward, raised her hand against the hard beam of light. "He's telling the truth, Officer. I work there. I'm the one who served him."

Eighteen Mississippi.

"Because you were doing seventy-two coming into town," the trooper said. "You know that?"

"No, sir, I didn't. I guess I'm more tired than I thought."

Nineteen Mississippi. Twenty. Twenty-one.

The trooper looked from Ralph Angel to Amber. He studied Ralph Angel's license again, then handed it back. "I'm gonna let you go this time, but I want you to pay closer attention, you hear me?"

"Yes, sir, Officer. Thank you."

"Y'all have a good night."

Ralph Angel waited until the cruiser slid back onto the road, watched the taillights flicker as it disappeared over the rise, then let his head fall against the headrest. His heart beat so fast he thought he might faint. He hadn't felt like that in a long time. Not since that night.

He and Gwenna had never bought from that house before, but word had it the stuff that came out of there was pure. Black tar. None of the cut-up shit those punks down on Central tried to pass off. They bought enough for a three-day run, then went over to the abandoned house down from the market. No gas, no electricity since the owners got evicted. A legless couch and a coffee table littered with stems, matches, and steel wool in the living room. Colder inside than out. They chose a bedroom facing the street so they could keep an eye on Blue, asleep in the car. Before he lit the pipe, he looked at Gwenna. Until the last run, she'd been going to meetings. She said the counselor, Linda, offered a lot of strategies for how to stay clean. *Stay busy*, Linda said. *Surround yourself with positive people.* He knew what that meant: changing the locks. He hadn't wanted to get clean, but he didn't want to be locked out either. So he begged her, took her hand. *Come on. Just this once, then get clean if you want.* He'd recited the poem and she'd smiled her crooked smile. He mixed the smack with a drop of water, flicked the lighter under the spoon and caught a whiff of vinegar.

When he woke, the room was dark. It took him a minute to remember where he was.

Baby?

No answer.

Hey, G, get up.

For a second, he thought maybe she'd left him, thought maybe she never took the syringe, drove off with Blue instead. He went to the window and saw the car on the street, its windows black beneath the streetlight. He turned back to the room and that's when he saw her.

In the car, Blue was awake and crying. He'd soiled his pants. Ralph Angel held him anyway, pulled off Blue's clothes and used a crumpled napkin to wipe the shit. He found one of Gwenna's T-shirts in the backseat—it smelled like her—and wrapped it around Blue's shoulders, dumped the soiled clothes in the gutter. He drove for a long time, not sure where to go. Kept thinking about the way she looked lying there on the floor— He shouldn't have pushed her. But then again, he'd been so afraid she'd leave him behind. She'd always been the stronger one when it came down to it.

Blue had looked up at him. *Where's Mommy?*

He shook his head. *No more Mommy. Just you and me.*

Ralph Angel and Amber rode in silence the rest of the way now, until Amber pointed to her turnoff.

"So maybe I'll come by the casino sometime," Ralph Angel said. "Take you to dinner after your shift." In the light of her open door, he saw red creases on the sides of her legs where they pressed hard against the seats.

Amber glanced at the house. "No," she said, "I don't think it'd be a good idea. It's nothing personal, honest. You seem like a nice guy." She tossed her purse over her shoulder. "Thanks for the ride."

"You bet." Ralph Angel watched her walk down the driveway, her purse bouncing against her hip. He could still smell her hair.

On the road again, Ralph Angel turned the radio dial, trying to find the jazz station. He still felt jumpy from the encounter with the trooper, couldn't believe how close he'd come. Nothing left now but to go home. They'd all be getting up soon, dressing for church. If he were religious, he'd say a prayer—*Thanks for keeping my ass out of jail just now*—maybe ask for a small blessing for Blue, ask Gwenna to forgive him. But he wasn't a believer, hadn't been for a long time. Ralph Angel rolled his window down and felt the early-morning air against his face. When he got home, he would ask Charley to cut him in on the farm. Because you couldn't sit around hoping to get lucky or wishing for a miracle. You couldn't sit around waiting for God's grace.

15

❦ Every day since the auction, Charley made a point to arrive at the shop before Denton, and every day she followed his instructions and recommendations to the letter. When he observed that they were low on Pennzoil and 2, 4-D, she was on the phone with the hardware store; when he suggested they tear out the third-year stubble along the highway, she had the three-row chopper hitched and the tractor refueled before he finished reading the day's farm bulletin. And when he announced, during lunch, they'd soon need lubricant for the drill press, Charley was off to Cyd's Tractor and Repair in Franklin before he finished his sandwich.

Now, with two gallons of lubricant in a box on the floor, Charley rounded the corner expecting to see Denton's truck but instead saw an old tractor, not too different from the one she owned, idling in front of the shop. Smoke belched from the exhaust pipe. Music leaked from the cab. As she pulled up, the tractor's engine sputtered and died, the door swung wide, and a man—muddy overalls hanging from his skeletal frame, clumps of strawberry blond hair sticking out of his baseball cap—climbed down the ladder like a spider at the end of its thread.

Charley couldn't help but think of Landry's visit as she stepped from her car. "Can I help you?"

"Where's Denton?" The man pushed his cap back and gave his forehead a furious scratch, then took one last drag on the cigarette that hung from his lips before grinding the butt into the dirt. "What time is it?"

"Two thirty," Charley said.

"Well, I sure as hell hope Denton shows up soon 'cause I got to pick up my boys at four," he said. "Damn day care dings you two dollars every fifteen minutes you're late. Tell you, I can't *wait* till September and I can put those two rascals in kindergarten. Don't care if they're five or not. Public school, you hear me? Only thing still free in this freaking country." He lit another cigarette, then squinted out over the cane through eyes the color of frozen pond water. "What time is it now?"

"Two thirty-two," Charley said.

"Come on, Denton, where are you?"

"I'm sorry," Charley said. "Exactly who are you?"

The man looked startled. "Alison Delcambre. Denton didn't tell you?"

"No."

"Well, I'll give him till three but then I got to go."

"Is there something I can help you with?" Charley said. Just then, she heard the low grumble of Denton's engine and there he was, coming down the road. He parked and ambled over, the same oily cloth from the auction dangling from his back pocket.

"Good to see you, Alison."

"You're late, Denton."

"Sorry. My wife needed a new filter for her car." He took a small square of fabric, from his front pocket this time, and cleaned his glasses, wiping each lens purposefully.

"Well, I'm delighted to hear you're such a devoted husband, but I got to be over at the freaking Magic Rainbow by four."

"How are those boys?"

"They're fine if you like raising wolf pups."

Denton slipped his glasses back on and looked at Charley over the rims. "Alison's wife passed last year and he's raising their two grand-kids. One's three and one's four."

"Their parents are dopeheads," Alison said. "Well, one's a dopehead. The other one's a plain fuckup."

Charley was surprised to hear Alison speak so harshly, she would never talk about Micah that way, at least not to a stranger, but then she saw Denton suppress a smile and guessed Alison's rants were a frequent occurrence; heard him say "So, I guess you met Miss Bordelon," as though Alison had just commented on the weather.

Alison removed his baseball cap. "Not formally, no."

"Me and Alison worked together over at Saint John back in '79," Denton said. "Till Alison quit and started farming for himself. Eleven hundred acres over in Saint Petersville. I asked him to come by."

"You mean, I *used* to have eleven hundred acres," Alison interrupted. "You forgot to mention I'm being forced out of business."

"That's one way to put it," Denton said.

"What do you mean, 'that's one way to put it'?" Alison said, flailing his arms. "That's the *only* way to put it. Go on, Denton, you might as well get used to saying it. I've sure had to."

"Alison's losing his farm," Denton said, soberly. "They canceled his contract after thirty-some years."

"I'm sorry," Charley said.

"He's one of the best farmers around," Denton said. He looked weary all of a sudden, like an army captain who'd lost too many men. "Knows everything there is to know about sugarcane and then some. Which reminds me. Guess who I saw up at Groveland's?"

"Don't tell me," Alison said, waving a hand. "I don't even want to know."

"Baron and Landry."

"Those sons of bitches? Jesus, Denton. Now you've ruined my whole day."

Denton winked at Charley. "Yeah, but we got 'em, didn't we?"

She smiled back, still embarrassed about the way she'd behaved at the auction, but he'd clearly forgiven her. Twice yesterday, he had shown her how to attach the spray rig to the tractor, and twice she'd backed the tractor into the fertilizer tanks. But he hadn't lost his temper, hadn't even raised his voice. Charley watched Alison pace an invisible cage. "Do you mind if I ask why you're losing your farm?"

"'Cause I can't ever get out of *debt*." Alison shook another cigarette from the pack. "Hey, look. When I first got into this business you had thirty-eight-cent diesel and cane was twenty cents a pound. Now diesel's over five dollars and cane sells for nineteen cents." Years ago, Alison went on to explain, a farmer could make twenty-five thousand dollars a year. "I didn't get rich but I made a living. Then they started messing with things."

"They?"

"The mills," Denton said. "They built warehouses."

"Sugar warehouses." Alison leaned against Denton's truck and gazed at some point in the distance. "Here's the way we work in this business. Say you're a roofer, and I hire you to reroof that barn over there. I say, 'I'll give you five thousand dollars.' So you say okay."

Denton broke in. "But then I say, 'I won't give you five thousand straight up. I'll pay half now and half next year.'"

"'Unless I have a bad year,'" Alison added, "'in which case, I'll only give you fifteen hundred now—that okay with you?' Meanwhile, you have all the cost of reroofing my barn. And you're paying interest at a percent and a half a month to stay alive."

"You see, Miss Bordelon," Denton explained, "these days, a farmer gets paid over a twelve-month period rather than all at once. The crop you're trying to get ready for grinding in the fall? The mill won't finish paying you for that until next September. It used to be the mill paid you within a month of delivery. By January, you had all your money. You'd pay everybody off—the bank, your suppliers—your cost went down. Now they've taken that money they owe you and stretched it out."

"They?" Charley said.

"The *mills*," Denton and Alison said in unison. "Guys like Landry and Baron."

Alison pulled his cap down over his eyes. "Freaking capitalist system. That's why I'm becoming a socialist a little more each day."

Denton had explained some of this before. It had made sense, but in an abstract way, as if he were explaining how electricity or the Internet worked, which was sort of unbelievable if you really thought about it. But now, hearing Alison's story, Charley was beginning to understand. "So the mills expect us to carry all the costs?"

"Exactly," Alison said. "Excuse me, Miss Bordelon, but it sucks." He turned away and stared out over the fields, as if looking back through the years. "This used to be a good business. You got your money up front. But forget it now. And that dimwit we had in the White House? Jesus. Between the price of sugar and whatever happened with CAFTA—" Alison shook his head. "Let's hope this new fella's got more sense."

"I asked Alison to come over," Denton said. "We're in good shape from the auction, but I got to thinking about what we still need. Thought Alison might be interested in striking a deal. And just so you know, he's hearing this for the first time, same as you."

"What kind of deal?" Charley and Denton had agreed on a sixty-forty split, assuming they brought in enough cane to make a profit. She wasn't sure they could afford another partner.

"The way I see it," Denton said, "we can help each other. Alison's got two combines, three tractors in pretty good shape, and a handful of cane wagons. That's equipment you won't have to buy, Miss Bordelon. We each give up seven and a half percent, Alison lets us use his equipment and comes to work here."

"Give me a minute to digest this." Charley walked over to the Volvo and put her hands on the warm hood. She let her head hang as she puzzled through Denton's scheme. On one hand, she'd be getting the full benefit of Alison's experience, and heavens knew, she needed his equipment. And why shouldn't she trust Denton? Didn't his decisions at the auction prove his judgment was sound? If he said Alison was an excellent farmer, then she had no reason to doubt him. A few yards away, Charley saw Alison light another cigarette. On the other hand, she'd be working with someone she didn't know, and there was no denying Alison was, well—eccentric.

Charley rejoined the men. "What do you say, Mr. Delcambre?"

"I can't *wait* to stick it to those sons of bitches over at the mill," Alison said. "Believe me, Miss Bordelon, it'll do me good to see those boys get licked. And just wait till they find out they got beat by a black woman. *That'll* raise a breeze."

Charley's heart skipped. If the situation were different, if Alison weren't having his land yanked out from under him, if he were wearing loafers and khakis instead of those filthy overalls and work boots, would he give her the time of day?

Charley tried to imagine what her father would say. *It's your land now.* She wished she could ask him, "By any means necessary?" but she knew she had to pull the answer from the ground herself. She turned back to the men and offered her hand. "If you're in, I'm in."

"Excellent." Alison took one last drag on his cigarette and looked Charley square in the eye. "Where do I sign?"

Holiday Hills, the subdivision where Violet lived in the next town over, had a golf course in the middle, with a small, man-made lake filled with water dyed a troubling shade of aquamarine, and a ribbon of walking path that wound past the empty guard booth and out to the patch of woods that stood between the development and the surrounding sugarcane fields. And since Violet still refused to come over to Miss Honey's, Charley swung by Tortilla Flats, the Mexican restaurant in the casino, and showed up on Violet's doorstep with shredded taco salad to share and two frozen margaritas.

It was after dinner now, and Charley sat in Violet's family room admiring her shadow-box coffee table. Violet had arranged an assortment of seashells and plastic crustaceans—lobster and crabs—and brightly framed sunglasses on a bed of sand underneath the glass top.

"First lady of the church *and* an interior decorator," Charley said, accepting the piece of lemon icebox cake Violet offered her.

"I love flipping through all those home magazines when I get my hair done," Violet said. "I always find good decorating tips. Then I run over to the Dollar Store to see what I can throw together."

Charley nodded. Violet's house wasn't large; in fact, it seemed to be the smallest home in the neighborhood of Acadian-style brick houses, but it was twice the size of Miss Honey's: a kitchen filled with shiny appliances overlooking the family room, and a decent-size patio with space for the Rev's barbecue grill and Violet's potted tomato plants.

"Mother was angry with me when we moved out here," Violet offered. "She wanted me to buy Mr. Delrose's house down the street from her. But I told her, I want to be exposed to new things, meet new people, get some fresh information."

"This certainly isn't the Quarters," Charley said. It was refreshing to sit in a room where every surface wasn't cluttered and where the air was breathable.

"May as well be the far side of the moon as far as Mother's concerned. But I like it out here. People are friendly. A group of us neighbors get together every week to watch that TV show where celebrities dress up in skimpy costumes and dance with the pros; you know the one. And the Rev is thinking about taking golf lessons if you can believe it. But enough about me, let's talk about you."

Charley had already told Violet about spraying her crops to kill the borers, about making a fool of herself at the auction, and agreeing to take Alison on as a partner, which was working out fine so far, as long as she didn't take his daily rants too seriously.

"You said something before about Hollywood asking you out on a date?"

"He did," Charley said. "Well, sort of. But Ralph Angel came home and started teasing him. It was terrible."

"Poor Hollywood," Violet said. "He's so sweet. A little slow, but a real sweetheart; always has been."

"He is," Charley said. "I'm surprised how much I enjoy his company."

"Well, you wouldn't be the first. Mother adores him. Treats him like he's one of her own. If you ask me, I think Ralph Angel is jealous."

"Or maybe he thinks he's being helpful," Charley said. "Tough love or something. It's the strangest thing."

Outside, beyond Violet's low picket fence, a golf cart rolled past and the driver, an older white man in a white polo shirt and baseball cap, waved. Violet waved back. She ran her spoon across her plate and licked at the last bit of icebox cake. "If Hollywood asks you out again, what will you say?"

Charley sighed. Hollywood had looked so nervous sitting there with his hair perfectly combed and his shirt ironed—like a schoolboy on picture day—and she'd been tempted to say yes, she'd go out with him, just to put him at ease. But that would have been a mistake. He'd have gotten the wrong impression and then what? The last thing she wanted was to hurt his feelings, but she'd been relieved, actually, when Ralph Angel walked in and interrupted. If only he hadn't started in with the teasing. Why did he always take it too far? "If I had the money, I'd pay someone to break the news that I just think of him as a friend." Charley said.

16

There were plenty of things for which Charley was prepared. She was prepared for the day Micah first kissed a boy (or a girl), and for the day she'd start her period. She was prepared for the day Micah got her learner's permit and accidentally drove through a neighbor's yard because she mistook the gas pedal for the brake; and though she hoped it would never happen, she was prepared for the day Micah got caught shoplifting strawberry lip gloss from the five-and-dime, and, God forbid, for the day she got busted for smoking cigarettes behind the high school gym. Charley had steeled herself for conversations with Micah about sex, and considered the advice she'd offer about colleges and careers, love, marriage, and parenthood. But Charley was not prepared when, after a long day at the farm and a quick stop at the Piggly Wiggly, she pulled in front of Miss Honey's and saw Micah standing in the yard, her Polaroid camera pointed at the sky.

"What are you doing?" Charley asked.

"I'm taking pictures of the gates of heaven," Micah said.

"The what?"

"The gates of heaven," Micah said. She pressed the button and the camera spat a dark square into her hand.

"May I see?" Micah handed her the square on which a fuzzy pronged circle of gold and white light appeared against a backdrop of sky the color of bleached driftwood, and Charley was flushed with a sinking sensation. "Exactly where did you get the idea you could take pictures of heaven?"

"Miss Honey," Micah said. "She always talks about God, how he washes us clean. How he always answers our prayers. She says after we die, God is waiting for us at the gates."

"I think that's Peter at the gates," Charley said, grimly. "Or Samson. One or the other."

"It's what she says."

Charley looked into Micah's face, which was so open, so hopeful and filled with innocence it was all she could do not to turn away. "Sweetheart," Charley said in her most patient voice, "I know you're curious about God, but those aren't the gates of heaven."

"They are." Micah pressed her finger to the photo. "You aren't looking at it right."

"I'm looking," Charley said. She studied the photograph closely, then handed it back, but when Micah aimed her camera at the sky again, something within Charley flared. "That's enough."

"Just a few more," Micah said, twirling away. She snapped another picture, quickly, and another. And another.

Ten pictures lay spread across the top porch step before Micah put down the camera.

"And you can really see the gates of heaven in all of them?" Charley asked, seated now and not reaching for the camera any longer, because the last time she tried to grab something from Micah, she wound up on her hands and knees, crawling through a cane field. She wanted to make sure she understood exactly what Micah believed she saw so that when she spoke to Miss Honey, she could thank her for exposing Micah to God, and could suggest, as delicately as possible, that a little faith was fine, Lord knew she could use some herself, but that religion was like vitamin A: a little bit every day was good, but too much left you sweaty and unable to see straight.

"Yeah," Micah said. "That's what I showed you." She knelt on the step a few inches from where Charley sat, but didn't look at her as she gathered the pictures into a stack, carefully aligning the corners like a deck of cards.

"What are you going to do with them now?" Charley asked, remembering how, as a kid, she was never good at cards or any other game for that matter, not Monopoly or Sorry or even Clue. She did play the Game of Life once, though, at her friend Carolyn's house. Carolyn Brewster, with hair the color of corn silk and eyes blue as a baby doll's.

They spread the board on the shag carpet in the living room, and she'd especially loved the tiny pink and blue "people" pegs tucked into the little plastic cars, how the twisting roads promised as much misfortune as triumph, how a spin of fate's wheel could set your make-believe grown-up life in motion, like a ship launched from a dock.

Micah responded to Charley's question with a half shrug, a gesture Charley found off-putting and slightly disrespectful, but she decided to ignore it. One day, months or even years from now, she'd find the pictures under the couch or scattered along the bottom of an old shoe box with other artifacts of Micah's youth, and she'd look back on these moments and wonder why she wasted so much time and energy worrying.

And so Charley decided to take a different approach. "Well then, let's get sno-cones," she said, even though she had just bought two boxes of Moon Pies at the market, and saw what they put on sno-cones: not just the usual assortment of artificially flavored syrups, but condensed milk, of all things.

"Can we?" Micah asked, unable to mask her surprise. "Right now?"

"Why not?" Charley said. "Take these groceries inside. We'll unpack them when we get back." She handed Micah a grocery bag. "And put some shoes on," she called, as Micah disappeared into the house.

While Charley waited for Micah to change, she poked around Micah's garden, where the first sprigs of carrots with leaves like the lace on baby's bonnets were just poking through the soil, and pea blossoms, fragile as tiny fairy hats unfurled against the fence. And walking up and down the rows now, Charley's heart broke even as it leaped, because Micah had done all the work without her help. Soon enough, Charley thought, even the garden would be forgotten as Micah's interest turned to boys and dating, and college after that. Up and out and on her own. Time moved too fast. Charley stared at the garden again. Time moved too fast and there was nothing she could do to stop it.

The late-afternoon sun lingered as though it were enjoying, far too much, shining its golden light over rooftops and warming the country roads to give way to evening, and Charley wandered about the garden, gathering up Micah's tools and empty seed packets, recoiling the hose, until she heard the screen door slam and walked to the corner of the house, thinking she'd meet Micah on the walkway. Only it was Ralph Angel and not Micah who'd stepped out onto the porch in his T-shirt and sweats, his hand raised against the afternoon sunlight, looking like he'd just woken up from a nap.

"Hello, Ralph Angel." Charley spoke politely but cautiously. She hadn't been in the mood for too much conversation since he teased Hollywood for asking her out.

"Hey." Ralph Angel yawned and stretched. "Micah said you were out here. But it's what—five thirty? You don't normally roll in here till after six."

"We finished early for once," Charley said. Privately, she was glad when Alison said the preschool called, one of his grandsons was sick, he needed to leave by three, and Denton had suggested they call it a day. The fields were looking good. The cane had grown another notch, which meant that it was almost as high as it needed to be for this time of year, and they'd nearly finished making minor repairs to the equipment they bought at the auction. But since Ralph Angel seemed to be in a good mood, she let her guard down. "I would have been home sooner, but LeBlanc's light was on, so I picked up a loaf," Charley said. "I bought some ginger cakes, too, if you want one. I told Micah to put them on the counter."

"Good to know," Ralph Angel said. He leaned against the porch rail and surveyed the garden. "'Da had a garden when I was coming up, but I always hated yard work. Too hard."

"Hard work builds character," Charley said, picking up a shovel Micah had left facedown in the grass.

"Maybe, but this here is plain old manual labor, which doesn't build anything but an aching back. Thanks, but no thanks. That's why I was an engineering major."

"What kind of work do you do, exactly?"

Ralph Angel seemed to hesitate. "Actually, I'm out of work at the moment, but my last gig was for the Department of Water and Power."

"Like designing power grids and reclamation facilities?" Charley asked, thinking maybe she'd underestimated him.

"Reading meters," Ralph Angel said. "But it's more technical than you think. Have to be extremely precise or customers complain."

"I see."

"Anyway, I've been meaning to talk to you. Sort of hoping you'd made a decision about me working on the farm."

But for the cereal bowls he often left in the sink or his sweat jacket she noticed slung across the back of a kitchen chair, Charley had almost forgotten Ralph Angel was around.

"Here's the thing—" Charley began, but then, thankfully, the screen door slammed again and Micah, and then Blue, holding a small action figure, stood on the top step. Micah took the camera from around her neck and slipped it over Blue's, helped him point it at the sky. He pressed the button and smiled as the camera churned a dark square into his hand.

"Now blow on it," Micah said.

"Micah, we need to go," Charley said.

"Those aren't the gates of heaven," Blue said, disappointment leaking into his tone. "That's a tiger's eye." And just like that, he and Micah were bickering like they'd known each other all their lives.

"Hey, now. Cool it, you two." Ralph Angel's voice was like a firm hand on the napes of their necks. "Here, let me see that thing." He studied the photo, asked Blue what he saw, and when Blue said he saw the tiger's whole body now, Ralph Angel laughed, and Charley laughed too, because wasn't it just like a kid to let his imagination run wild? "Now, show me those gates of heaven." He held the picture while Micah explained.

Charley tucked her keys back in her pocket as she watched Ralph Angel with the children. She thought he looked like a regular father playing with his kids on a Saturday afternoon, was impressed when he managed, somehow, to convince them the Polaroid could be both things, and no one cried or pouted or ran into the house.

"Uncle Ralph Angel has memorized the whole Bible," Micah said. She yanked his arm. "Say that thing about clean hands."

"What's this?" Charley said.

"Your daughter's overstating things," Ralph Angel said, looking sheepish. "The other day I told her I used to memorize Bible verses for Sunday school."

"Whatever," Micah said. "Just say it again, so Mom can hear."

"Okay. But one time and that's it." Ralph Angel took a breath, closed his eyes. "'Who shall ascend into the hill of the Lord or who shall stand in his holy place? He that hath clean hands, and a pure heart; who hath not lifted up his soul unto vanity nor sworn deceitfully. He shall receive the blessing from the Lord, and righteousness from the God of his salvation.' Psalm twenty-four, verses three through five."

Micah and Blue clapped, and Charley clapped too. "Impressive," she said. "I didn't make you out for the religious type."

"Yeah, well. The Lord and I aren't exactly on speaking terms, but some things are just hardwired, you know? 'For by grace are ye saved through faith; and that not of yourselves: it is the gift of God.' Ephesians, chapter two, verse eight."

"Nice," Charley said, and meant it.

"Say another one," Blue demanded.

"That's enough." Ralph Angel handed Micah the stack of Polaroids. "Your mother's ready to go."

Micah turned to Charley. "Can Blue come with us?"

Charley hesitated. She had talked to Ralph Angel more in the last ten minutes than she had in the last three weeks. She looked at him. "It's fine with me."

Ralph Angel reached for his wallet. "Uh—well, buddy, let's see."

Charley didn't want Blue to see his father fumble with his flimsy billfold. She didn't want Blue to see his father finger the two measly singles and grab for the smeared scraps of paper that fell into the grass, not that there was anything wrong with being broke, but she didn't want Blue to understand that Ralph Angel was broke in a particular and humiliating kind of way.

"That's all right," she said. "It's my treat."

The John Deere 3510 sugarcane harvester was designed for comfort and convenience with its forward-tilting cab and pressurized Clima-Trak temperature control that provided a dust-free environment, its air suspension driver's seat and optional DVD player with surround sound speakers. Lying on her bed that evening, Charley stared at the machine's picture featured in a two-page catalog spread with the same rush of desire as a high school boy staring at his first *Playboy* centerfold. All those hoses, gears, and bright green paint, Charley thought. Who knew a piece of farm equipment could be that sexy? She was reviewing the safety features for the second time when Ralph Angel knocked on her open door.

"Didn't mean to scare you," he said when she startled. "You busy?" He stood awkwardly, just over the threshold.

"Just reading." Charley invited him in, aware that she was sitting on the bed that should have been his.

Ralph Angel stepped into the room. He looked around, brushed dust off the lampshade, and drummed his fingers on the headboard. Charley expected him to say something about the way she'd maintained the room, but he didn't.

Instead, he laughed nervously. "Weird, you know. Never thought I'd be back here again." He drifted over to the dresser, lifted Micah's T-shirt off *The Cane Cutter.* "Something tells me you didn't get this at Walmart."

"It belonged to Dad."

Ralph Angel nodded, and again, Charley waited for him to say something about her being spoiled. But he lifted the shirt higher and studied the piece more closely, ran his finger along the cane knife, traced the pant fold. He stared into the figure's deeply carved eyes, then turned it around to examine the back, handling it with respect, even reverence.

"Micah said you talk to it."

"Micah said that?" Charley wondered what other personal tics and idiosyncrasies, what small moments, forgotten or overlooked, Micah had innocently revealed.

Ralph Angel gently turned *The Cane Cutter* around. "Kids. Boy, I tell you, nothing gets past them." He shook his head. "And, man, don't promise you're going to do something and then not do it. They never let you off the hook."

Charley recalled the recent promises she'd made to Micah: that she'd have her own room in the house they'd own one day, where she'd be free to hang her favorite posters and paint the walls any color she chose, because it would be their house and not some rental; that she'd help Micah find kids to play with and her afternoons would be filled with endless games of Capture the Flag and Kick the Can, because everyone wanted to know a kid from California. Charley thought of those promises and all the others she'd made to lure Micah into coming, and felt sick at how few she'd delivered on.

"On our way down here," Ralph Angel was saying, "I promised Blue I'd buy him a toy, some Power Ranger thing he saw at a rest stop. I thought he'd forget, but he must have asked me about that thing ten times. Probably stopped at twenty rest stops before I found it."

Ralph Angel's eyes met Charley's and she smiled in agreement. "Kids." An easy calm settled in the space between them.

"Kinda funny when you think about the two of us," Ralph Angel said. "We got the same daddy. My wife dies, your husband dies, and here we are, come to roost in the same house. To say we spent so many years apart, we're just alike."

Charley gave Ralph Angel a smile, but she felt a chill ripple across her skin. "Funny," she said, and thought he was almost right—almost but not quite. She wasn't perfect, far from it, but she'd never taken money from her father and lied to him about it. She'd never used drugs or pushed an old woman down. Were they minor infractions? Perhaps. And she believed everyone deserved a second chance, but she couldn't shake the feeling that there was more to her brother than he was letting her see.

Ralph Angel absentmindedly pulled the dresser's top drawer open a fraction, then seemed to remember whose room it was now and closed it. "Anyway, I just wanted to say thanks again for taking Blue with you this afternoon. He's still talking about it."

"It was just a sno-cone," Charley said.

"Not to him."

Charley nodded, understanding all that Ralph Angel couldn't bring himself to say. "My pleasure."

Ralph Angel re-covered *The Cane Cutter* and slid it back into position. He glanced around the room as though he were seeing it for the last time. "Well, I ought to let you get back to your reading. I just wanted to say thanks."

"No problem."

Ralph Angel turned to leave, and was over the threshold, pulling the door behind him, when he paused. "There was one more thing I wanted to ask." He leaned against the doorjamb. "You said you'd think about us partnering up on the farm."

"Well, like I said, I already have a partner." Two, Charley thought, and prayed Ralph Angel never found out about Alison.

"Yeah, you said that before."

"And there's not much—"

"To administer. You said that, too. But I've been thinking." Ralph Angel stepped back into the room and straightened the lampshade. "You've got to need help with something. I could drive a tractor, run errands. It wouldn't be permanent. Just till, you know, we figured out an arrangement."

"An arrangement?"

"For cutting me in on the action."

"What action?" Charley thought of the long hours she, Denton, and Alison spent in the fields, the black mold she scrubbed off the refrigerator shelves, the bird shit she chiseled off the shop windows. Tedious, boring work. And then there were the bills. Between the unpaid invoices and Denton's ever-growing list of parts and supplies, they were barely scraping by. Denton and Alison had agreed to take smaller draws till the harvest, but Charley still had to pay them something. As for herself, she'd budgeted sixty dollars a week for gas and her share of Miss Honey's food bill, but she still felt like they were eating more than their share. Charley looked at her brother in the glow of the bedside lamp and knew Ralph Angel was desperate; she could see it on his face. She knew that in her brother's eyes, she was seated at a grand banquet and that all he was asking for, *begging* for, was a morsel off her plate. But she had nothing to offer. Nothing to spare.

"I can barely afford to buy gas," Charley said. "If I can't afford that, I can't afford to pay you, and you can't work for free. If I could hire you now with the promise of paying you after the harvest, I would, but I'm not sure there'll be any profit. Hell, I'll not sure there will be any cane to harvest." Still, he was her brother—her *disinherited* brother. She reached for her purse and pulled her last twenty from her wallet. "It's all I have. I'm sorry." As she held out the money, Charley thought of the old black veteran who peddled newspapers outside her neighborhood market back in Los Angeles—not a fancy market, but still a decent one, with its crates of freshly picked produce, and bulk bins of grain, and cuts of meat laid between sheets of butcher paper. All day, every day, he stood there, politely, in his dirty veteran's cap, with his pulpy, smudged newspapers in one hand and frayed American flag in the other. She always thanked him as she bought a paper, slipped him an extra dollar. And sometimes she didn't buy a paper at all, just gave him the money. "It's all I have," she'd say.

Ralph Angel took the money. But rather than put it in his pocket, he let the bill hang limply between his fingers. "Twenty dollars," he said. "What the hell am I supposed to do with this?"

"I'd give you more if I had it," Charley said, and it was true. If Ernest had left her any unrestricted cash she'd have gladly shared it. For a moment, she thought about explaining the trust: that every expense had to be backed up with receipts; that if she made one false move she'd lose everything.

"Jesus, Charley. I thought we had an understanding."

Charley blinked. "What are you talking about? What understanding?"

"I gave you that damn chemistry set."

It took her a moment to realize what he was talking about. "But—" Charley counted back through the years. "That was ages ago. I was just a kid."

"I'm your brother, Charley. Your big brother. Your *only* brother. We're supposed to look out for each other." Ralph Angel stepped deeper into the room and began to pace the floor in front of the dresser. Back and forth, back and forth, slowly, with his hands on his hips. "You know, I've tried to be patient. I've tried to be nice about it, give you space. But I'm starting to think you're giving me the runaround."

"I told you. I can't afford to take on more expenses."

"Yeah, yeah, yeah," Ralph Angel said. "This is what I'm hearing." He bunched the fingers on his left hand together, pressed them against his thumb, then opened and closed his hand, pantomiming a mouth talking. "Just talk. Talk, talk, talk." He gripped the bedpost and leaned toward her. "You think it's easy for me to sit around here sucking eggs while you waltz off to work every day?"

"It's not the party you imagine, trust me." Charley felt her heart drumming. Her legs felt shaky even though she was sitting on the bed.

"I hear you talking to Miss Honey. I know you just bought a shitload of equipment, and that Denton taught you how to drive a combine. You think I can't do that stuff?"

"You don't like manual labor. You said so yourself."

"You think it's been easy for me, all these years, hearing stories about how good you had it? 'Charley got a new car for her birthday.' 'Charley's going to a fancy East Coast school.' 'Charley went to Hawaii on her honeymoon.' How do you think that made me feel, sis, knowing Dad loved you more?"

"How can you say that? That's not true," Charley said, but the truth was, even if he'd had a perfect childhood, whatever *that* meant, something told her he would always believe she'd had a better one, and she would never be able to convince him otherwise.

"Then how come he didn't leave me part of the farm? Come on, sis. Don't bullshit me."

"I don't know."

"You know what I think? I think you had something to do with it. I think you told him to cut me out because you wanted it all for yourself."

"That's crazy." Charley thought about her father's final months: the hospital bed like a barge docked in the living room, the cocktail of medications that coated his teeth with plaque and made his breath smell like metal and rotting meat, the gurgling tubes that sucked green mucus from his lungs, bones so brittle they snapped like matchsticks. Even with hospice there, she'd barely had time for her own life, for Micah. Charley threw her legs over the side of the bed. "I didn't know anything until he was gone and his lawyer told me."

When Charley looked at Ralph Angel again, she saw that something had changed. The man who'd played with the kids was gone, replaced by the person who'd teased Hollywood.

"Yeah, right. I bet," Ralph Angel said. "Just look at you, sitting there like Little Miss Perfect. Little Miss Rich Girl. And that daughter of yours, running her mouth all the time. She's a goddamn little know-it-all. She's going to grow up to be a spoiled brat, just like her mother. The two of you make me sick."

Before he went back to Houston, Uncle Brother had warned her the house would be tight with Ralph Angel in it. Charley thought about how Violet had said, as she left the reunion, that things wouldn't work out if Ralph Angel were allowed to stay. Now she understood.

"Maybe the reason Dad left you out of his will," Charley said slowly, "had something to do with money you stole."

Ralph Angel blinked. "He owed me that money."

"For school. Which, by the way, I know you didn't finish, so spare me all that talk about being an engineer."

"I am an engineer. Just a few more credits and I could get my degree if I wanted."

Charley knew she should stop, yet she couldn't stop herself, didn't want to, because he'd insulted Micah, and it was as though he'd opened the latch on an enormous steel door where every hope and fear and worry and secret longing she'd ever felt about her child was piled up on the other side, and it all came tumbling out. It was not fair to go after Micah; that was crossing the line. "What did you spend the money on? Drugs? Did you smoke it up? Snort it? Did you drink it away? Because that's what I heard."

"Violet and Brother should mind their own business."

"Were you on something when you pushed Miss Honey?" Charley said. "Or did you break her arm on purpose?"

"Shut up!" Ralph Angel said. "You weren't there."

"I didn't have to be," Charley said. "All I have to do is look at the way you treat Hollywood to know what you're capable of. He's supposed to be your friend, but you treat him like shit. But you can't help yourself, can you? You hate the fact that he has a business and you don't."

"I said, shut the fuck up!"

"You should be ashamed of yourself."

Ralph Angel lunged forward and grabbed Charley's wrist.

Charley looked down at Ralph Angel's hand. All the blood had drained from his fingertips, he was squeezing so hard, the skin under his nail beds had gone white. Charley's hand was slowly going numb. She looked up into Ralph Angel's face, expecting to see a monster, but to her surprise, she saw a man who was out of his mind with anger, yes, but also terribly, achingly, afraid.

"Pop?" a small voice said. "What game are you playing?"

Charley and Ralph Angel both looked and saw Blue standing in the doorway.

"Oh—hey, buddy." Ralph Angel's voice sounded strained and breathy. He let go of Charley's wrist. "You're supposed to be in bed."

"I woke up and couldn't find you. I kept calling you."

"Oh yeah? I guess I didn't hear you. Where's 'Da?"

"Watching TV with Micah," Blue said. "I heard you say a bad word."

"Yeah, well, uh—" Ralph Angel patted his pockets as though searching for his keys.

"He made a mistake." Charley did not look at Ralph Angel as she said this. "But it's okay now. Let him take you back to bed."

"Yeah," Ralph Angel said. "We'll finish our story."

When Ralph Angel was gone, Charley closed the door, and as soon as she did, a surge of adrenaline shot through her so that her whole body tingled and she had to lean her head against the door, close her eyes. Through the door, she could hear the faint sounds of the TV coming from the den, and behind her, through the open window as the warm air drifted in under the curtains, the sound of Miss Marti next door, dropping an empty bottle in her trash can and dragging it to the curb. Charley stood there until the anxious feeling passed, then she sat on the bed. She wasn't afraid of Ralph Angel, but she could never trust him. He wasn't the person she'd hoped he would be.

Charley woke in the night and saw that Micah was not on the air mattress. Nor was she in Miss Honey's bed, or on the moonlit porch, or in the den watching TV, and it was only on her way back to her room that Charley saw a sliver of light under the bathroom door, heard Micah's voice, and imagined who might be in there with her, doing God knew what, and she turned the knob, thinking the worst, ready to slay any monster, ready to kill her own brother if it came to that. And so it was with extravagant relief that she saw, immediately, that Micah was alone. Alone, but also naked, standing at the sink on a kitchen chair so she could see herself in the mirror. She had taped all of her gates of heaven Polaroids around the mirror's edge, propped the lookalike

Barbie doll—the bare-chested one with the nest of tangles and the crochet antebellum hoop skirt, the one Miss Honey gave her the day they arrived—on the counter beside a flickering candle, and—Oh my God, was that a Shirley Temple DVD cover on the floor?—so that now the bathroom looked like some kind of freaky voodoo shrine.

"Micah! What on earth—?"

"Mom!" Micah tried to cover herself. "Get out!"

"What are you doing?"

"I said get out! Please!"

Close the door, Charley's mind said, as she stood there gazing into the dark bathroom, where the mirror reflected the candle's golden glow and Micah tried to cover herself. *Just close the door. You don't want to know.* But then her mind cleared and she realized there was no way she could abide Micah's command.

Charley stepped into the bathroom. She closed the door behind her. "Not until you tell me what's going on." She spoke in a measured tone, like a tour guide, *This way, please. Everyone follow me*, even though inside, she was screaming.

And when Micah realized Charley was not leaving, when she saw that her mother had locked them both in, she jumped down from the chair and climbed into the far end of the bathtub. She sat with her arms wrapped around her knees, put her head down, and rocked slowly.

"Micah, please. What's going on? What were you doing?" The bathroom smelled like cucumbers and melon from the candle Micah had lit.

Micah shook her head, no. She covered her ears.

"Please, talk to me." Charley sat on the floor with her back against the tub and waited. She would wait as long as it took.

"I was praying," Micah said at last. "I was asking God—I was asking God to fix my arm."

The red flame had already spread up Micah's shirt by the time Charley reached the kitchen and she smelled the burning flesh, saw how the top layer of Micah's skin had already blistered, how under that top layer of Micah's arm was the same wet pink as her tongue.

"I was asking Him to make me pretty."

"Oh, babe—" Charley said. "But you are."

"I'm not. Not with my arm."

Charley climbed into the bathtub with an aching heart. "My sweet girl." She pulled Micah into her lap and felt where Micah's body was cold from leaning against the side of the tub. She wrapped her arms around her daughter. And that was all Micah needed. She burst into tears. She cried harder than Charley had ever heard her: anguished sobs with long breaths and choking in between, until she was spent and her body was hot and sweaty. And when she finally fell asleep, Charley covered her with a towel, then leaned back against the tub's sloping back and prayed to be forgiven.

17

Given Alison's contempt for the Blue Bowl crowd, most days, they ate lunch at Dina's out near Belle Island, where the dining room opened onto a view of the salt flats, the air smelled faintly of jasmine and boiled peppers, and five bucks bought a cold beer, a basket of cobbed corn, and all the peel-and-eat shrimp you could handle.

With Alison on board, their productivity had skyrocketed. One brilliant morning last week, they fertilized the back quadrants, and yesterday, under an enamel blue sky, they pulled the cutter through some of the coco grass that kept the cane from suckering.

At the table now, Denton peeled a shrimp and squinted out at the salt flats in a way Charley had come to know. "An idea came to me last night," Denton said, quietly. "I think we ought to pay eight dollars for common labor come grinding."

Alison drained his beer and snapped his fingers for the waitress to bring him another. "Going rate's seven and a quarter. You got money to give away?"

"We offer seven and a quarter," Denton said, "we'll be up against every farmer out there. Won't have nothing to set us apart."

"Hell, Denton, how much different we need to be? A black chick from California, an old black has-been, and a broken-down white dude? We're like freaking Barnum and Bailey as it is—*Jesus Christ.*"

Charley winced. It had been a month since Alison signed on, and she still hadn't gotten used to his frank appraisals and candid observations.

"In a way, that's what I'm talking about," Denton said. "It hurts me to say this, Miss Bordelon, but I've come to know it's true. The white man's ice is always colder." He paused for a moment. "Say you hire a man for grinding, tell him you'll pay same as the white man's paying. You give him an hour for lunch where the white gives him fifteen minutes, works him all day. You tell him all the ways you'll treat him better and he'll look you in the eye, shake your hand, and say he's coming to work for you. But come October first, you look up and he's gone to work for the white farmer down the road."

"Shit," Alison said. "I never knew that."

"I didn't either," Charley said, "but I'm not surprised."

"Now, we pay eight," Denton said, "we got a chance. We pay eight, men will come and they'll stay."

Alison tossed his cap on the table. "Denton, how's Miss Bordelon going to pay extra for labor when she barely has enough money for plant cane? LSU's charging three hundred a ton for the new variety. We'll be lucky to afford enough for ten acres."

But Denton had already taken his pen from his bib pocket and folded his napkin over. "Here's how." In his shaking hand, he drew a line from one end of the napkin to the other. "We tell 'em up front: you don't miss work, you get eight. You don't quit halfway through, you get eight. You get sick or need to go to a funeral, you get eight. Long as you stay to the end of December, you get eight dollars an hour." He looked up to make sure they were following. "Now, when grinding starts, we pay them seven and a quarter, every two weeks, just like everyone else. Come January we pay the seventy-five cents extra. The ones who keep their word can collect."

Alison leaned back scratching his head full of straw. "Damned, if that ain't the best idea I've heard in months. Where'd you get that from?"

"I come up with it last night," Denton said, modestly, "lying in my bed."

"Brilliant," Charley said. It was one of the things she admired most about him—his ability to puzzle through a problem and come up with not just *any* solution, but the *right* solution, to make all the other pieces fall into place. With Denton's plan, Charley realized, she could hire good workers and still afford fertilizer and plant cane.

Alison squeezed Denton's shoulder tenderly. "Man, Denton. If I didn't know better, I'd swear you were a freaking genius."

Charley looked at her two partners seated across the table, and rested her chin in her hands as a swell of gratitude and affection washed over her. Alison was right. The three of them were a sideshow, but she wouldn't trade their company for anything. As far as she could tell, they were beating the odds, if only just by a nose. In less than four weeks, they had whipped most of her fields into shape, almost eight hundred acres. They'd dug more ditches, cleaned more drains, had more arguments, and eaten more five-dollar lunches together than she could count. But come October, God willing, her cane would be ready for grinding.

And then it was time for Alison's daily lecture. To look at his uncombed hair and dirty fingernails, Charley would never have guessed he had a PhD in agriculture and an MBA from LSU. But Denton swore it was true. Today's class was a history lesson: Louisiana Sugarcane's Founding Fathers.

"Did you know," Alison began, "that in the 1790s, when Louisiana still belonged to Spain, farmers grew maize, rice, tobacco, and cotton? There wasn't a single stalk of sugarcane anywhere in the region. Their main staple was indigo."

"Indigo?" Charley set her beer on the table and imagined barefoot Bengalis straddling boiling vats, Gullah women in the South Carolina low country up to their elbows in blue dye.

But Alison said, "Yes, indigo, until 1794, when worms and damp weather destroyed their crops and drove most farmers out of business. The next year, on a plantation that is now Audubon Park in New Orleans, Étienne de Boré, planter, entrepreneur, and visionary, gambled his fortune on sugarcane. He figured out how to turn sugarcane syrup to crystal on a commercial scale."

And somehow, hearing that men and probably a few women had struggled with sugarcane for centuries and that the crop's history reached across the Atlantic to Cuba, Santo Domingo, the West Indies, and Brazil, Charley felt as though she were part of something larger, a worldwide movement. People had fought over sugarcane and died for it. They had married for it, prayed over it, and cursed its existence.

And then lunch was over. Denton and Alison wiped their mouths and balled up their napkins, while Charley cleared their baskets. And when she returned to the table, she saw that, for once, they both looked relaxed, their faces not etched with the permanent frowns that came with being cane farmers.

"You guys are the best," Charley said, overcome again. Because, for once, it had been a good day, and at least for a few hours there was nothing she wanted more than to be a cane farmer, and there was nothing more satisfying than sitting down with her partners over baskets full of peel-and-eat shrimp and washing it all down with a cold beer.

Every day around four fifteen, cicadas fell mute in the stifling heat, the cane grew eerily still, the sky, almost colorless all afternoon, turned to slate, the clouds from white to battleship gray. Thunder rumbled. A rush of wind. And within minutes rain fell in opaque sheets, the half-dollar-size drops exploding against the shop's tin roof so loudly Charley could barely hear the radio. Whatever fieldwork remained would have to wait.

It had rained for twenty minutes when Charley, sifting through a stack of new invoices, heard a truck pull up. Denton's dogs, which he'd left behind to keep her company, started barking. It couldn't be Alison, who left at three to retrieve his grandsons from day care, but it might be Denton, back from Lafayette, where he'd driven for an order of discs.

But Denton's dogs kept barking, and soon Charley heard a man's voice calling, "Mr. D.? Anybody here?"

Charley went to the office door. It was Denton's friend from the auction, the one who'd helped load their winnings onto the gooseneck trailer. "Come in, come in."

He stepped into the office, stamped his feet. "Man, I tell you," he said, brushing rain off his baseball cap, "it's coming down sideways." He wore the farmer uniform—T-shirt, dusty jeans, and boots—all of it darkened with rain.

Charley struggled for his name. "It's Ramon, right?" She'd been so embarrassed the day of the auction, she hadn't said much more than "thank you."

"Close enough. Name's Remy." His hand was damp and warm. "Remy Newell."

"Remy. Right. I'm Charley—"

"Bordelon," Remy said. His voice had an internal luster, as deep and rich as cherrywood. "I remember."

Charley waited for Remy to make a crack about the auction: how foolish she'd acted going up against the rainmaker; how silly she looked crying when Denton surprised her with the equipment, but he didn't. He just stood there. Dripping. She fetched a roll of paper towels from the bathroom. "Thanks again for loaning us your trailer. And for delivering all our new toys."

Remy dried his face and arms, which were pale under his T-shirt where his farmer's tan ended, then stooped to wipe the puddle on the floor. "Y'all cleaned up. That tractor you snagged only has eight thousand hours on it."

To her surprise, Charley could grapple with sugarcane math. Eight hours a day, one thousand days. Grinding season lasted three months, which was roughly one hundred days. If her calculation was correct, the tractor had been running for eight years. Not bad as tractors went.

She gestured toward the papers on the desk. "I couldn't do any of this without Mr. Denton."

"I've known Mr. D. since I was sixteen," Remy said, nodding. "I used to work cane every summer. Dug ditches and filled ruts till I worked my way up to driving a combine. Still don't know why he did it, but Mr. D. always looked out for me. Made sure I didn't lose a hand in the scrolls. Some of the old-timers don't want to admit it, but Mr. D.'s one of the smartest men around." He paused. "If I know half as much about cane when I'm his age, I'll have done all right."

"His mind is quick," Charley said. "I'm blown away by the ideas he comes up with. The other day our partner, Alison, said he was a genius. I think that's true."

"And he's got a good heart." Remy's voice went quiet. He looked at Charley as though there was a story he wanted to tell her. "I owe him a lot."

Outside, the storm had passed. For a few minutes they sat quietly, listening to the rain on the metal roof downshift into the softer syncopation of water dripping off the eaves.

"So—"

Remy snapped his fingers. "Almost forgot. I brought y'all a surprise." He invited Charley to his truck.

It had been a scorcher of a day with temperatures in the low hundreds, humidity close to 90 percent, but now that it had rained, the temperature had dropped, at least for a bit, and the air was breathable again. Insects resumed their chatter. The ground fizzed audibly where moisture evaporated, and the cane leaves were glossy and dazzling in the late-afternoon sun.

"Buddy of mine caught these earlier," Remy said, "but it's way more than I can eat." He opened the passenger door, and Charley saw that other than a cracked windshield, the cab was neat, with an empty ashtray and a gleaming cup holder. Three large sacks of shrimp sat on the front seat. "One for each of you."

Charley wished she had something to give Remy in return. "Thank you." She had seen the Vietnamese and Cambodian fishing boats docked at Dago's fish market near the Point. "I don't think I could get shrimp any fresher."

"I know you city folks think nothing happens in a place like this, but I tell you, it's a pretty good life."

Remy heaved the sacks over his shoulder, refusing Charley's offer to help, insisting the briny water dribbling from the corners would stain in her clothes. Then he lingered, though whether to wait for Denton or to talk to her, she couldn't tell.

Charley listened for Denton's truck but heard only the fizz of the ground drying.

"So, you getting the hang of this cane farming?" Remy cleared a place on the couch.

"It took awhile, but I finally learned to keep the tractor in the row," Charley said. She told him how they were slowly transforming the back quadrant, about the twenty-two-pound possum they trapped last week, and how Alison insisted on carrying a rifle in his tractor so he could shoot rabbits and other wild animals that ran out of the cane. Then suddenly, Charley paused. Remy was just being polite, she thought, making small talk and listening patiently until Denton arrived. "This is way more than you wanted to hear, I'm sure."

But when she glanced at him over the stack of receipts and catalogs, she saw Remy looking back at her with open, unfiltered interest.

He smiled. "Keep talking. I'm hanging on every word."

"I've talked enough. Tell me about your farm."

"You don't want to know about that. It's nothing special."

But Charley insisted that she did.

"I lease three fronts," Remy said. "Colette, over in Saint Abbey, is six hundred and fifty acres, and Emilie, out near the bay, is four hundred. The biggest, Genevieve, out near Four Corners, is almost a thousand, with the rest in bits and pieces sprinkled around the parish. All in all, it's about twenty-one hundred acres."

"Twenty-one hundred acres. That's enormous."

Remy smiled modestly. "It's respectable. Just wish I owned it."

Charley had grown accustomed to Alison, who yelled, and to Denton, who, while her partner, also projected a quiet authority that required a certain respect. But Remy's manner put her at ease. He talked to her farmer-to-farmer, in a way she found she liked.

"Colette, Emilie, Genevieve," Charley said. "Sounds like you're talking about your children."

"Not mine," said Remy. "Back in the eighteen hundreds, farmers always named their fields after their daughters."

And right then, Charley decided to name her biggest parcel Micah's Corner.

Where did the time go? Six thirty, and the sky was a sultry cobalt with clouds like wisps of orange sherbet. Everything tinted to gold—the shop's tin roof, the tangle of wildflowers that clung to fence posts, even the dirt.

"I can't thank you enough," Charley said as she walked Remy to his truck. "I mean it." She was thinking that Remy wasn't quite like anyone else she'd met. Not just his voice (though she could listen to it all night), or that he was thoughtful enough to bring them a whole truckload of shrimp. He had an up-from-the-bootstraps scrappiness she found interesting. And there was something else. Remy seemed to have come up *through* the land, seemed connected to it in a way other farmers weren't. Like when he described how the land changed with each phase of the growing season: "In January, there's just dirt," he said, "then by April, the new cane sprouts, and by July, you're surrounded by green fields. Come December, all the cane is cut again and, suddenly, you can see for miles. It's always changing," he said, "a new view every four months," and she wondered who else paid such close attention. "I would rather be out there in my fields than anywhere else," he said.

Remy started his engine. "Tell Mr. D. I'll catch him next time." He squared his baseball cap.

"He'll be sorry he missed you." In twenty years, Charley thought, he'd look like all the old farmers who gathered every morning around the back tables at the Blue Bowl, swapping stories and solving the world's problems. She waved as he pulled away, then stood in the middle of the road. He was probably married with a house full of kids, Charley thought. And besides, she had too much to do on the farm.

"Well, well," Violet said, when Charley called her that evening. "The plot thickens."

"It was only a sack of shrimp," Charley said. "And he didn't just bring one for me. Besides, he really came to see Mr. Denton."

"I bet," Violet said. "Let me fill you in on a Southern man. There are only three things he'll sit still for: football, duck hunting, and a woman who's caught his eye. Remy Newell may have stopped by to see Mr. Denton but he stuck around to talk to you. So, are you going to ask him out?"

"Violet!"

"What?"

"What kind of woman do you think I am?"

"Girl, you've got to loosen up. This isn't the 1850s. Women ask men out on dates all the time. It doesn't even have to be a date. You could meet him for lunch or a cup of coffee."

"Since when did you start working as a matchmaker?" Charley asked.

"Since when did you become such a stick in the mud?"

18

On Thursday morning, Miss Honey asked Ralph Angel to put gas in her car. "I have a prayer meeting tonight and I won't have time to stop," she said, handing him forty dollars. And since he had nothing better to do, Ralph Angel obliged. Rather than drive straight home after filling up (thirty in the tank, ten in his pocket), though, Ralph Angel drove in the opposite direction, followed the Old Spanish Trail all the way out to where he believed the turnoff led to Charley's farm. He didn't set out to do it. He just wanted to take a drive, get out of the house for a while, which he'd been reluctant to do in his own car since the trooper pulled him over. But out on the open road, curiosity tugged at him, the need to see with his own eyes what he'd been missing, what he'd been *cut out* of, like a cupped hand nudging him forward. He didn't know exactly what to look for, and had guessed, by piecing together little bits of conversation he'd overheard, where Charley's farm might be. He was about to give up when he spotted her car.

Ralph Angel parked. Far enough down the road that Charley wouldn't notice Miss Honey's old blue sedan if she happened to look up, but close enough that he could watch as she and two men in overalls stood talking, a large sheet of paper the size of a road map held between them. Ralph Angel watched as Charley studied the paper, then pointed across the road to the wall of sugarcane; watched, a few minutes later, as a biplane dropped out of the sky and swooped low over the fields, gray mist streaming out from beneath its wings; and twenty minutes after that, he rolled down the window to let a little air in and watched, with a growing sense of indignation, as the black man, probably Denton, worked a raggedy tractor, while Charley and the other man—*who could that be?*—schlepped back and forth between the yard and the shop, loading boxes into the back of a pickup. Ralph Angel watched and thought, *Fuck her.* Fuck Charley and her talk of needing time to figure out how best to bring him in, she couldn't afford him, there wasn't enough work for another man. It certainly *looked* like she had enough work. Ralph Angel peeled off his sweat jacket, leaned back. He didn't know how, but he'd show her he was good for something—he was practically an engineer, after all—and when he figured out a plan, his sister would realize what she had missed out on and come begging. Ralph Angel watched for a long time. And when Charley and the two men finally disappeared inside the corrugated metal building, he went back down the road the way he came.

On his way back to Miss Honey's, Ralph Angel drove through Jeanerette, past LeBlanc's bakery, where the red light signaling that fresh French bread was ready for sale glowed like a flare. He turned down the short gravel driveway that ran alongside the brick building. Folks used to say that Jeanerette had everything you could want, you never needed to leave town, and thinking back, Ralph Angel supposed that was true. As a boy, when he came to Jeanerette with Miss Honey, he bought candy from the two Sicilian sisters who owned Machioni's Fruit Stand. Vee's five-and-dime sold everything from school supplies to china to aquarium fish, and at Gomez's Army Surplus, clerks scaled tall wooden ladders to reach merchandise stacked to the ceiling. There'd been three movie theaters once, though he could remember the name of only one; the National Mercantile Company, where, when he visited, his dad always took him to buy blue jeans; Grisiaffi's Grocery, a little mom-and-pop operation where you could buy a slushy for thirty cents; Rose Culotta's liquor store across the street; and down on the corner, the Fitch Family Hotel and Restaurant, where you picked up to-go orders at the side window. All that was in the past, though. These days, Jeanerette was closer to a ghost town than a boom town, the bakery practically the only business still open on Main Street.

Ralph Angel slammed his car door, and even before he reached the entrance, the sweet aroma of French bread wafted out to greet him.

Just inside, a man in baggy shorts and a faded gray T-shirt stood at the cash register.

"Morning," the man said.

"How you doing?" Ralph Angel said, "How much is a loaf?" and saw that from his face to his sneakers, the man was covered in a fine dusting of flour.

"Three dollars," the man said and sniffed. "Ginger cakes are a dollar fifty."

Ralph Angel pulled out his wallet. There was nothing better than a loaf of LeBlanc's French bread hot out of the oven, maybe with a little butter, though you didn't need it. "Give me two loaves," Ralph Angel said. He'd buy one to eat in the car, all by himself, and one to take home. Blue would like that.

The man disappeared through the swinging doors, and when he emerged, he held two plump golden loaves, which he laid on the long wood counter. He wrapped each loaf in a sheet of crisp white paper, swaddling it like a baby.

"Plastic or no plastic?" the man said.

Ralph Angel looked at him, confused, then remembered that each loaf came with a plastic storage bag to keep it fresh if you weren't going to eat it right away. "One with plastic," Ralph Angel said. "And give me one of those ginger cakes."

The man tucked the loaves and a ginger cake into a paper bag. Ralph Angel held out the ten left over from Miss Honey's gas money, waited for his change.

But as the man put the bills in his hand, he frowned. "Don't I know you?"

"I don't know."

"You from around here? 'Cause I swear your face is familiar."

"Grew up in Saint Josephine," Ralph Angel said. "Went to Ascension High School, then my grandmother had me transferred to General Taylor."

"That's it!" The man snapped his fingers. "I went to General Taylor too. Man, I *knew* I knew you. Name's Ralph Angel, right? Man, it's me, Johnny. Johnny Fontenot."

Ralph Angel looked more closely at the man, tried to think back. The name registered vaguely; he'd gone to school with a whole bunch of Fontenots, but he couldn't place the man's face, especially not with all that flour on it. But the man was looking at him with such naked delight that Ralph Angel said, "Oh yeah, of course I remember you, man. What's up?"

They shook hands and Johnny Fontenot slapped Ralph Angel's arm playfully. "Man, it's been what—twenty-five, twenty-six years?" As he spoke, his Cajun accent thickened. "You ain't changed one lick. I'd know you anywhere. Where you livin' now?"

"Been out west," Ralph Angel said. "California first, then Arizona. Phoenix."

"California, man, that's a *loooong* way from here, I'm telling you. You like it out there?"

"Yeah. It's nice."

"I got out there once. Too big. It was pretty, though." Johnny ran his hand over his dusted hair and wiped it, absentmindedly, on his shorts. "So, you back home for good or just visitin'?"

"Haven't decided." Ralph Angel thought about Charley out there at her farm, how she'd stood with those two men, all three of them looking so satisfied as the plane flew over. "What about you? How've you been? How long you been working here?"

Johnny shrugged. "Since I got out of college. It'll be twenty-three years next week."

"No shit," Ralph Angel said. "You must really like baking bread."

"Ain't had a choice," Johnny said. "Daddy was ready to retire, my older brother joined the service, so it was up to me. Either that or let some of my coon-ass cousins run it."

"You *own* this place? But I thought your last name was Fontenot."

"Bakery is on my mama's side. Her people came from France, then down through Nova Scotia before they settled here. Been in the family since 1884, right here in this building. Five generations."

"I'll be damned," Ralph Angel said, and studied the framed black-and-white photos on the wall above the register. It was like looking back through time. "So how's business?"

Johnny shook his head wearily. "Pretty good till this morning. My best guy quit; said he's moving to Mississippi. I'm down to two guys, which would be okay, but we got to fill a huge order for that zydeco trail ride over at the old Fruit of the Loom factory tomorrow. Two hundred loaves on top of our regular orders. I'm usually up front in the office, not back here on the floor, but we got to get them loaves out of here."

Ralph Angel looked at Johnny, then through the entrance, out at the gravel lot, and felt another page turn. "If you're shorthanded, maybe I could help you out."

Johnny looked at the ground. He ran his sneaker across the floor, which was itself covered in a quarter inch of flour dust. "Naw, I couldn't ask you to do that, man. But thank you."

"What's the problem?" Ralph Angel felt a sudden urgency bloom in his chest. "I got the time and I'm good with numbers. Was an engineering major in college. You need the help."

"You serious?"

"As a heart attack."

Johnny thought for a moment. "Okay, then," he said. "You got a deal. And of course, I'll pay you." He shook Ralph Angel's hand, then hugged him. "Man, I sure appreciate this. You don't even know. I was sweatin' bullets trying to figure out how I was gonna get all this work done."

"What are friends for?"

"You're really saving my ass," said Johnny. He went to the register, counted out seven dollars and fifty cents. "Take your money. Those loaves are on the house."

Twelve thirty a.m., and Ralph Angel, back in Miss Honey's blue sedan, drove the twelve-mile stretch between Saint Josephine and Jeanerette, appreciating, for the first time really, how quiet the country could be on a summer night. He crossed the high bridge that spanned the widest section of the bayou and looked out over the dark cane fields and the mill lights twinkling in the distance. He'd heard a story once, about a man who was crossing the bridge on his bike when a truck came along and knocked him over the guardrail. The man fell thirty feet into the water, but managed to swim to the bank even though his right arm, his right leg, and three ribs were broken. Some people were just born survivors.

After his conversation with Johnny that morning, Ralph Angel had stopped off at Goodwill. He bought a nice white dress shirt and tie—navy with red stripes—stylish but not too flashy with the $7.50 Johnny gave back to him. He hadn't mentioned the job to Miss Honey, though he'd wanted to, and he certainly hadn't said anything to Charley when she got home. Thought he'd stay quiet till she started griping about how hard she was working and asked him to join her, then he'd spring the news on her. He couldn't wait to see the look of surprise on her face.

Everyone arrived at the bakery at 1:00 a.m., Johnny had said, which Ralph Angel thought was early to be starting office work, but he'd agreed. Now he pulled into the gravel parking lot again, past the two white delivery trucks he hadn't noticed earlier, and parked in the last spot near the fence. It wasn't one o'clock yet, but the lights inside the bakery were already on, and through the open windows, Ralph Angel heard men's voices and the clatter of machinery over the radio.

"Hey, good buddy," Johnny called as Ralph Angel stepped over the threshold. "Right on time." Johnny had showered and shaved, changed into a new pair of shorts, but wore the same gray T-shirt and sneakers, and looked surprisingly alert, Ralph Angel thought, considering the early hour. He gave Ralph Angel a puzzled look. "What's with the shirt and tie?"

Ralph Angel looked down at his shirt, then up at Johnny. "Can't go around the office looking like vagrant."

"The office?"

"Yeah," Ralph Angel said. "You said I'd be doing office work, right?"

Johnny's brow furled. "No."

"But this morning—you mentioned working up front. Said your best man quit."

"That's 'cause *I* work up front," said Johnny. "I was talking about my head baker quitting; a guy named Leroy."

"Oh."

"I moved Joe up to Leroy's position and got Billy to take over for Joe, but now I need someone to take over for Billy."

Ralph Angel stuffed his hands in his pockets. "What does Billy do?"

"He's on the mixer. Mixes up all the batter."

"I see."

"Hey, look, man, I'm sorry for the misunderstanding. I should have been clearer." Johnny put his hands on his waist and let his head drop. "I understand if you don't want to do this. A guy like you—a professional and everything—I can see how this would be beneath you. Actually, that's what I was thinkin' this morning when you offered."

Disappointment settled down around Ralph Angel like a shroud. He'd been so excited at the prospect of working at the bakery; had imagined himself up front, in an office right next to Johnny's (though smaller, of course), his shirtsleeves rolled to his elbows, the knot of his tie loosened after a full day of taking phone orders, jotting names and numbers on a small pad, entering figures into a computer. He'd looked forward to taking coffee breaks and maybe, after he earned his stripes, long lunches down at the café. Ralph Angel sighed. He thought of Charley, the expression on her face—determined, purposeful, focused—as she carried those boxes from the shop, *her* shop, to the truck, then he tried to picture himself dumping big sacks of flour into an industrial mixer. Not exactly what he'd signed up for. But it was still work; it was still a job. "No sweat," Ralph Angel said. "I'll do it. A deal's a deal." He unbuttoned his cuffs, rolled up his sleeves.

Beyond the swinging door, the bakery floor stood large and boxy, with white tiled walls around three sides and two enormous ovens built into the far wall. The other men were already at work, stacking long rectangular wood boxes on top of one another and sliding big metal trays into tall racks. Everything—from the radio to the portable phone and the long wooden table in the middle of the room, to the men themselves—was covered with a fine layer of flour so that it looked as though an early-winter snowstorm had just blown through. Johnny introduced Ralph Angel to the guys, then led him over to the mixer in the corner. It was almost as tall as Ralph Angel, with a large stainless steel bowl and a huge paddle inside that looked big enough to row a boat with.

"People don't realize, but baking is an art," Johnny said. "Which is why I usually start new guys making loaves. I learned the hard way it takes a new guy three months before he knows how to form a decent loaf. But since it's crunch time, and I can't stop to train you, I'm gonna have you jump ahead and work the mixer first. Once you get the hang of it, made enough dough, we'll see what needs doin'." Johnny gestured for Ralph Angel to follow him behind the mixer where six large plastic garbage cans, each labeled with a different ingredient, stood against the wall. On the floor in front of the garbage cans, twenty fifty-pound bags of flour sagged like overgrown sandbags.

"I'll do the first batch, then I'll let you run with it."

Ralph Angel watched as Johnny dumped a sack of flour into the big metal mixing bowl, then peeled the lid off the first garbage can, labeled MALT, and dipped a ladle into the dark syrupy liquid. He used a big scooper to measure out the salt and yeast, then poured in a pitcher of warm water and flipped the switch.

"It looks simple, and it is, as long as you get exactly the right amount of each ingredient. Screw up the proportions and that's eighty dollars' worth of product down the drain. After you put everything in, run the mixer for fifteen minutes, then take the dough over to the table. Billy will take it from there. Questions?"

"I got it."

Ralph Angel stood silently by the mixer while the paddle turned a figure 8 in the big stainless steel bowl, and the radio played, and the guy named Joe lined the long wood boxes with canvas while Johnny fired up the ovens. As they worked, the men teased each other like brothers, lobbing curses and light insults across the bakery floor, and it struck Ralph Angel, standing alone, that he'd never had that; had never worked with people he liked and who liked him enough to joke around. Gwenna had been the only person, but she was gone. He'd thought he might be able to have that with Hollywood—they used to joke around all the time when they were kids—but Hollywood didn't seem interested lately. Was always saying he had to work. It would be nice, for once, to be in a place where everyone was friends.

Three hours of mixing. Through the windows, the darkness seemed less dense. There was a hint of sunrise. Ralph Angel hauled the last batch of dough over to Billy, who reached his tattooed arms—Ralph Angel could see the designs and dark outlines under the layer of flour—into the metal mixing bowl and, with his bare hands, scraped the tacky glob onto the wooden table. He watched as Billy pulled off softball-size chunks of dough, ran them through the breaker to squeeze out the air bubbles, shaped each chunk of dough into a circle, then went back and formed the circles into perfect oblong loaves and laid them side by side in the long wooden boxes. Johnny was right. It was an art.

"How many loaves do you get from a batch?" Ralph Angel said, in a friendly tone. He leaned against the table.

"'Bout fifty." Billy didn't look up; his hands never stopped moving. "But they gotta rise for two hours in the proof boxes before we can bake 'em." He nodded to the wood boxes stacked ten high under the window. "The second batch over there is about ready."

Across the floor by the ovens, Johnny was baking the last of the first batch. Inside the oven, the rotisserie shelves revolved like seats on a Ferris wheel, and Johnny had just enough time to lift raw loaves out of the proof boxes and arrange them on each shelf before it was out of reach. By the time the shelf circled around and appeared again, the loaves had baked to the gold of dark honey, and Johnny lifted them out and slid them onto the cooling racks.

"What can I do?" Ralph Angel said, thinking he could do what Johnny was doing.

"Take those boxes over to the ovens." Johnny pointed to the stack of wooden proof boxes. "But be careful, they're heavier than they look."

"I'm on it."

It was hot in the bakery now with the ovens going full blast. Ralph Angel had already loosened his tie, unbuttoned his shirt, but sweat still trailed down his face. At the window, he stood on his toes to reach the top proof box. He lifted it from the stack, but stumbled backward. The box was awkward to carry at nearly six feet long, tall as a man, and heavier than it looked, loaded from end to end with balls of dough. Worn smooth as river stones from years of use, the sides of the box were hard to hold, and as Ralph Angel struggled to get his grip, the box fell forward and the front end crashed on the floor. Everything seemed to move in slow motion then. Ralph Angel felt himself reaching for the loaves as they slid on the strip of canvas, tumbled out of the box, and lay on the floor in a soft, doughy heap. He felt the box slip out of his grasp completely, and watched it knock against others. He saw the tower of proof boxes waver, then topple like Fiddlesticks.

"Whoa!" Johnny yelled, rushing over. "Lord Almighty," he said, grabbing his hair in his fists. "My orders!"

But it was too late. Nearly a hundred loaves lay scattered and smashed across the floor.

The red light over the bakery door wasn't on yet and Main Street was quiet and still as Ralph Angel drove back to Miss Honey's. Three little girls waved from the bed of an old pickup as Ralph Angel passed; an old man dressed in a brown striped suit and freshly shined shoes moseyed down the empty sidewalk. Ralph Angel had offered to stay till they made fresh batches to replace the ones he'd destroyed, but Johnny had declined his offer. They'd have to work double-time to get all the orders out, Johnny said; Ralph Angel would just be in the way. Johnny offered to pay him for the hours he worked, but as much as he needed it, Ralph

Angel couldn't accept the money. Even though it wasn't the kind of work he'd wanted, the hours he'd spent in the bakery had reminded Ralph Angel how good it felt to be needed, to be productive. Everyone needed to feel that their days had purpose, that they were moving forward.

There wasn't room for a car to stop on the high bridge, but since it was still early and no cars were coming, Ralph Angel stopped anyway. He stood at the guardrail and looked out over the cane fields, stretched out like a soft green carpet in the morning light, and the bayou sliding beneath him. It was a long way down. He thought again about how that man on the bike must have felt, falling through the air, then hitting the water. Was he surprised to discover he was alive or had he always known he would survive? Ralph Angel thought back to that terrible moment when Blue fell into the barge slip. He'd thought he would die and he'd felt—he'd felt relief that it would all finally be over. Almost wished it could be so. But then he'd thought of Blue, all alone in the world, and it had been enough to make him keep going. He had to keep going. Somehow.

Ralph Angel pulled his tie from around his neck, took off his shirt. For a long time, he stood there on the bridge in his undershirt, feeling the morning air against his skin. He held his new clothes over the rail until the breeze came up from underneath and then he stood there watching as they drifted down to the bayou.

AUGUST

19

🌼 August now, 5:30 a.m., and the temperature was already in the high seventies with 86 percent humidity. This late in the summer, anyone with money had escaped the asphyxiating heat and fled to coastal Florida—but not cane farmers. Because planting season had begun. There was no time to rest. And so, under a dawn sky aglow with misty pinks and purples, Charley, Denton, and Alison hitched planter wagons to tractors for the first day of planting, while crews of laborers—black locals and Mexican migrants up from Guanajuato—gathered around Denton's pickup, waiting for instructions.

"Do we really need all these men?" Charley asked. "Isn't there some machine we can rent that plants cane? Because my labor costs are going to shoot through the roof."

"There's no cane planting machine that I know of," Denton said. "And if there was, we couldn't afford it. You gotta trust me. Planting by hand is the way to go. Has been for the last two hundred years."

Since cane grew from cuttings rather than seed, they had to cut some of Charley's premium cane in the second quadrant that would ordinarily have been harvested—"mother stalk" Denton called it—and replant it in the freshly cultivated fields.

Yesterday, they had cut the mother stalk and loaded it into the cane wagons. Now, as soon as Denton gave the signal, each tractor would pull a wagon through the fields slowly enough for the crews following behind to yank the mother stalks off the back and lay them in the open rows. Later, another tractor would come along and cover each row with dirt.

Between now and early September, Charley needed to clear and cultivate 25 percent of her land—rid it of the oldest cane stalks, which were no longer producing, and replant the same ground with mother stalk.

In a few weeks, delicate shoots known as first-year stubble would sprout from knobs along the recently buried stalks, and twelve months from now, if all went well, she'd have a decent stand of new cane to harvest for the next four years. That's how it went: 25 percent new cane, 75 percent existing. It was a constant cycle, one made even more unforgiving by the brutal August heat. Planting season was fleeting; and between the thunderstorms and the equipment breakdowns, Charley couldn't stop for a minute if she wanted next year's crop in the ground on schedule.

By six o'clock, it was light enough to start. The last tractor was hitched, the crews assigned. They were about to head toward the back section, now known as Micah's Corner, when Romero, the most experienced of the Mexican laborers, told Charley one of his men was sick.

"Sick how?" Charley said, eyeing the thermometer she'd nailed to the shop door so she could warn the men when it got too hot to work. Last week she rushed a man with a core temperature of one hundred six to the clinic. Two more degrees, the doctor warned, he would have died.

"Fever," Romero said. The brim of his hat flared wide as a whirling dervish's skirt. "It's no good, I know. But if he works today, he will maybe make the others sick too."

"Shit," Charley said, but Romero was right, of course. After all the trouble she'd gone through to get the men up here—the H-2 visas and the bus tickets from Guanajuato, the expense of fixing up the workers' house behind the shop so they'd have a decent place to sleep—the last thing she could afford was for them all to get sick. "I'll drive him to the clinic." Charley dug in her pocket for her keys. She pulled a black man who went by Huey Boy off the crew and told him to drive the tractor, then radioed Denton and Alison, already on their way to Micah's Corner, that she'd return soon as she could.

It was after eight by the time Charley got back from town. In halting high school Spanish and with a series of hand gestures, she explained the prescriptions to the sick worker, set a bottle of water by his bed, then headed for Micah's Corner. When she'd first arrived in Saint Josephine, this quadrant was the worst section of her land—blackjack land, Denton had said, ominously—overgrown with weeds, johnsongrass, and useless fourth-year stubble, the rows crooked as witch's fingers and so deeply rutted they were almost beyond repair. But since they'd cleared everything out and started over, the rows were straight and evenly spaced. Every time Denton pulled the cultivator through, he'd climbed down from his tractor, shaking his head in wonder, saying, "If I hadn't seen it for myself, I wouldn't believe it. Cutter goes through there like a wind song."

Now, standing at the edge of those fields, under a sky that had already faded from blue to white in the rising heat, it was obvious what the morning's delay had cost her crew. The goal was to plant five rows at a time with each man responsible for a row. But with four men, not five, behind the wagon, they hadn't made much progress. The crew moved slowly, pulling cane stalks from the wagon with extra care to ensure each row was filled, but Charley saw gaps where there was still simply no cane at all. Those spaces would be empty once the cane grew, which meant a lower yield next year.

Without another thought, Charley ran out to the field. Huey Boy was doing a good job of driving, so instead of replacing him, she joined the crew, pulling armloads of cane stalks off the back of the wagon. The men looked at her as though she'd lost her mind, whispered in Spanish, but there was no time to explain. Piled ten feet high in the wagon, the cane was still heavy with dew. Leaves and dirt were mixed in with the stalks, as if an enormous hand had ripped a ton of cane from the earth and dropped it into the wagon. Which was pretty much the way it had happened: after Denton cut the cane yesterday, Alison had used the derrick, which looked to Charley like a gigantic claw, to scoop the cane off the ground and dump it into the wagon until it was close to overflowing.

Positioning herself behind the wagon, Charley was surprised to discover that the tractor bumped along at a steady clip, and it was all she

could do to pull a few stalks off and lay them end to end before the tractor was out of reach and she had to run to keep up. As she worked, she
thought of the rats, snakes, rabbits, even wild pigs that might, at that
very moment, be buried in each scoop. Chances were they'd outrun the
combine when it went through, or were sliced up as it passed, but who
knew for sure? She'd heard stories of rats leaping out of the wagon, of
men being bitten by snakes coiled among the stalks. Then there was the
broken glass and the cane leaves with their razor-sharp edges. That was
only the beginning. After just a few minutes, dirt had caked her arms,
her watch, and the front of her jeans and had even sifted into her pockets, and she wondered if she'd ever be clean again.

Every few minutes, the men whistled to Huey Boy, who flipped a
switch causing the hydraulic arm to shove cane from the front of the
wagon to the back, closer to where Charley and the crew were pulling
stalks. It felt to her that a tsunami of cane was coming at her. But there
was no stopping. Each time the cane got low, the men whistled and
more stalks got pushed back. At the end of the row, the tractor
lumbered onto the headlands, moved five rows over, and the work
began again. It was simple, mindless labor, but grueling and treacher-
ous all the same. As the workers grabbed armloads of cane, the long
stalks knocked Charley in the head before she learned she needed to
duck. When the men dropped the cane in the rows, it landed on her
feet and she stumbled. If she hadn't known better, she'd have thought
they were doing it on purpose. But there was no time to wonder. The
cane wagon kept moving. Men kept whistling. The hydraulic arm kept
shoving the cane to the back edge of the wagon, and Charley kept
working.

The sun rose higher, the temperature leaped by ten degrees in the
time it took to reach the side of the field where they'd started, and
Charley's clothes were drenched. One of the men stooped beneath the
wagon, grabbed a metal cup from the hook, and held it beneath the
watercooler strapped to the axle. When it was full, he offered it to

Charley and she gulped it down, not caring that she'd heard members of the crew hack and cough and spit before drinking from that very cup. The water was sweet and cold and trickled down the front of her shirt.

Every few rows, Huey Boy shifted the tractor into neutral, climbed out of the cab, and scaled the plant wagon to check on their progress, his expression, as he looked down at Charley, a mixture of amusement and admiration. Charley imagined what he'd tell his buddies when he met them for a beer after work: that he was working for a crazy black woman from California who not only *owned* the land, but got behind the wagon and planted cane herself. Then Huey Boy climbed back inside the cab and Charley heard the faint beat of hip-hop over the engine's rumble.

Finally, the wagon was empty. The men fell back. And as the tractor lurched away, the men gathered handfuls of leaves into small nests and sat down right in the middle of the field, cowboy hats shielding their faces from the sun, and Charley sat too, glad to watch the tractor roll down the headland and out of sight, grateful for the few minutes to rest. One man smoked, but the others took the opportunity to eat, ripping the outer husks off the cane stalks, gnawing at the sweet fibers, sucking and chewing, and finally spitting the pulpy wads in the dirt.

"You work hard," Romero said, offering Charley a length of cane.

Charley sucked the juice greedily and spat. "Where will you go after this?" The money Romero would make during these next four months was good, Charley thought, but it wouldn't last all year.

"Arkansas to pick apples," Romero said, "then home to my village. I have a small farm."

Charley thought of all the men like Romero—Native Americans and indentured servants from Ireland and Germany, Chinese, West Indians, and former black slaves—who, through the centuries, had left their families and their homelands behind, sometimes voluntarily but sometimes not, to work sugarcane. "I hope you'll come back next year."

It wasn't long before Huey Boy, pulling a full wagon, appeared and made his way along the furrows. Groaning as they rose, Charley and the rest of the crew didn't bother to dust off their jeans as they fell in line and the work began again.

By lunchtime, it was hotter than the Congo Basin, the air heavy with humidity, the few clouds flat against the sky, the trees at the edge of the field blurry through the heat rising from the field. Denton and Alison brought Charley's lunch from the shop, and the three of them camped out in the tractor's meager shade.

"I'm impressed," Denton said. "I thought you'd quit after the first row."

"My hat goes off to these guys," Charley said. Normally, the heat lessened her appetite, but the hours of work had left her ravenous and slightly dizzy. "I don't know how they do it." She thought about the sick worker she'd driven to the clinic. Whatever he had, she hoped it only lasted twenty-four hours because she doubted she could keep up this pace much longer. Still, as Charley looked at the progress they'd made that morning, there was no denying the thrill of it, no ignoring the simple delicious fact that she had reached this stage in the game.

"Looks like your plan worked, Denton," Alison said. Indeed, word of their pay package had spread. In addition to the men Denton had hired earlier in the summer, twenty-five more had stopped by the shop in the last week, interested in hiring on, and they'd had the rare luxury of handpicking the crews. "Keep up this pace, we'll have the back quadrant planted in ten days. Even the locals are putting out a hundred percent."

"What's that supposed to mean?" Charley said, though she knew exactly what Alison was saying. She'd stopped counting the number of times she'd heard people refer to black folks as "locals," and was weary of their suggestion, sometimes their outright declaration that black folks would rather sit home and collect welfare than put in an honest day's work.

"Nothing personal," Alison said.

"I get so tired—" Charley began, and thought, at least call them *pioches*, which was the term the eighteenth-century planters used in referring to their black slaves and more honestly captured the feeling of disdain, but Denton interrupted.

"Just heard on the radio they're talking about a hurricane."

Alison pushed his cigarette into the dirt. "Jesus, Denton. Why you want to go and jinx us?"

"I'm just telling you what I heard. Right now, it's a tropical storm off Haiti, but it's getting stronger. Next forty-eight hours it's supposed to hit between here and Port Arthur."

"That's almost a hundred and fifty miles," Alison said. "May as well say between here and the moon."

"Maybe," Denton said. "But it means we're east of it."

"What difference does that make?" Charley said, trying to imagine what a hurricane might be like. Earthquakes she knew; but with the exception of the one or two truly devastating ones that had occurred in her lifetime, she didn't think much of them, they were more of a nuisance, really, and she always laughed to herself when she talked to someone from the East Coast or Midwest who spoke of their unpredictability with what seemed to her an almost irrational fear.

"Winds are always stronger east of a storm," Denton said, "and there's usually more water. Has to do with how the storm turns." He looked out to the horizon and frowned. "I'm telling you now, that storm makes landfall, we're in big trouble."

Just after two o'clock, Huey Boy climbed down from the tractor and announced that the hydraulic light had come on. While the crews took a break, he tinkered with the control panel, and it was while she waited that Charley spotted Remy's pickup coming toward her over the headland. He pulled up in a cloud of dust. With their reflective lenses, his sunglasses gave his otherwise boyish face a menacing steeliness, but it was his dopey legionnaire-style sun hat with its mesh side panels and protective neck drape that made her laugh.

Remy slammed the truck door, took off his sunglasses. "What's so funny?"

"Nice hat."

He touched the brim as though he'd forgotten he was wearing it. "I know it makes me look stupid. But it keeps the sun off my ears."

For a second they stood awkwardly, and Charley didn't know whether to hug him or shake hands. "I actually need a hat like that," she said, touching the bill of her baseball cap. "This glare is killing me."

Remy took off his hat and put it on Charley's head, put her cap on his. "How's that?"

"Better. *Much* better." But when she moved to return it, Remy waved her off.

"Keep it. It looks better on you."

Two weeks had passed since Remy gave her the shrimp, and in that time, with all the work, Charley had thought of him less frequently. She'd forgotten how tanned he was, how gently weathered his skin, how carefully he watched her when she spoke. She adjusted the hat and caught the faint smell of him—musk and citrus and the faint fragrance of the Gulf coast; it was a clean smell, strong and good.

"How about if I borrow it for a day or two, till I get my own?" Charley said.

"Suit yourself." He gave a little shrug and put his hands in his pockets. "How's planting going?"

"Mr. Denton says there may be a hurricane."

"Yeah, I heard." The look on Remy's face made Charley more worried. "In the meantime, I brought you a little something." He led her around to his tailgate and Charley saw that the bed of his truck was filled with cane stalks.

"What's all this?"

"Ag station released a new variety this morning," Remy said, and lifted out a long, husky stalk. "They're calling it 'Energy Cane,' and it's supposed to be more resistant to rust and borers, plus it's got a higher sugar content. I thought you might want to try some."

"Mother stalk is three hundred dollars a ton at least," Charley said. "How much do I owe you?"

"Consider it a gift. One farmer to another." And when Charley protested, he offered a compromise. "Give it a try. If it works out, you can buy me a beer."

"Two beers," Charley said. "One for the cane and one for the shrimp."

Remy seemed surprised she remembered. He smiled. "Two beers, then."

And for a moment, he looked at her so intently, Charley worried that she had something on her face or in her hair. She almost reached up to wipe her cheek and then felt a rush of embarrassment that she would even care. This was crazy, she thought. She barely knew him. "Well, thanks again."

"You bet," Remy said, glancing up at the clouds. "And good luck this afternoon."

"Thanks." She looked over at Huey Boy, who'd lifted the tractor's engine panel. "If we can just get the hydraulics on that old clunker to work."

"Let's have a look." Remy climbed up onto the tractor's wheel. "Can't fix it," he said after a minute, "but I can patch it. Should hold till you get back to the shop and Denton can have a go."

"Make that three beers," Charley said.

Before Remy climbed down, he surveyed this side of Micah's Corner. "Looks good, Miss Bordelon."

"Please, I've been trying to get Mr. Denton to call me by my first name since we started working together, but he refuses. I understand why he does it, but it's so formal. I don't think I can take hearing it from someone else. Just call me Charley."

Remy nodded. "Okay."

"And thanks again. For everything." Charley shook Remy's hand. "So. How about you? How's it going?"

Remy smiled and looked at the ground.

"What? What did I say?" Charley worried that she'd offended him.

"It's not what you said, it's how you said it. Your accent. Like you're on a TV commercial or something. Next thing you'll be telling me you grew up playing beach volleyball."

Charley hesitated. The last time she told someone how she spent her summers as a kid, the conversation had ended badly. "Surfing, not volleyball," she said, cautiously. "If you have anything you need to get off your chest about that, you should say it now and get it over with." But there was just that long, meditative look again.

"I can't figure you out," Remy said, finally. He shook his head. "First it's farming, then it's surfing." He laughed. "Are they all like you out in California?"

They? Charley's heart sank. What did he mean, *they*? Did he mean all left-handed people? All women? All African-Americans? But when she looked at Remy, whose eyes, she thought now, were actually on the small side, and whose sideburns were grayer than she'd noticed before, she didn't detect an ounce of malice or irony in his question, nor cynicism in his tone. "No, not all."

Behind her, the crew was crumpling up sandwich wrappers, beginning to reassemble, slipping on hats and gloves. Charley consulted her watch. "I'd better get back to it. Thanks again for the hat—and the Energy Cane." She shook his hand, which didn't feel like enough.

Remy climbed into his truck and started the engine. Then he paused. "Hey, California."

Yes, California, Charley thought, that was who she was; that far-off place her father, still a boy then, dreamed of as he lugged those water buckets; the address he made up—6608 Sunset Drive—and practiced writing in the corner of his homework papers until he was seventeen and old enough to escape. California. The place her dad had asked to buried, in a plot facing the Pacific, rather than the red clay of his youth. She was all those things. Always would be. Charley turned to look at Remy, who sat in his truck with one arm on the open window.

"I know it's planting and all," Remy said, "but you can't work every minute of every day."

"Is that so?"

"Those beers you owe me." And here he hesitated ever so slightly, a look of doubt, as though it was occurring to him that he was being hasty, too forward, swept quickly across his face, but then it passed. "There's this zydeco place. They book some decent bands."

"Keep talking."

"You like to dance?"

"Will it help me lose my accent?"

"Maybe, maybe not. You'd have to give it a try."

"Sounds tempting."

"Yes, ma'am." Remy smiled. "Couple of beers, some good zydeco, you'll be talking like a Louisiana girl in no time." He turned the key.

Charley caught the last bars of the *All Things Considered* theme song before the local news began. "NPR?"

"What?" Remy said, smiling. "Cane farmers can't listen to public radio?"

On the fourth day of planting, the hurricane moved into the Gulf of Mexico, and though it wouldn't make landfall for two days, the outer rainband would reach Saint Josephine in twenty-four hours. Charley and her team had planted seventy-five acres, but they still had one hundred twenty-five to go. She'd given the crews the option of evacuating, but Romero and the others insisted on working until the last minute. In the morning, they managed to plant fifteen acres, but by noon, Charley was nervous. The weather was disturbingly good; the clouds white as chalk, the sky blue as a gas flame.

"Time to pack it in," Denton ordered over the walkie-talkie. There was no mistaking the concern in his tone.

Once they were all back at the shop, Charley, Denton, and Alison gathered around the old Zenith TV in her office. The forecasters downgraded the hurricane from a category four to a category three, which meant evacuation was optional. Still, there was no way of knowing where the storm might hit, whether it would swerve up the eastern seaboard or hover in the Gulf, gaining force; and in the meantime, they had to decide what to do with Romero and his men.

"I'm not sure that house out there will hold," Denton said. "We ought to think about letting them head up to Arkansas. They can stay at the apple farmer's place till this thing blows over. We might lose a couple days on the back end, but I think it's worth it. At least they'd be safe."

"Yeah, but who's going to pay to get them up there?" Alison said. "Even if we could afford their tickets, every Greyhound headed north is sold out."

"We could rent a van," Charley suggested.

"Can't afford the liability," Denton said.

"Look, Romero's offering to stay," Alison said. "He swears they all know the risk. I say, let 'em stay. They want plywood, food, lanterns, and they'll ride it out; we can do that. Hurricane passes, they'll be here, ready to work."

Eventually, they reached a compromise: If the hurricane rating stayed at three, Charley would loan them her car and they would drive to Arkansas; if it was downgraded to a two, they would stay.

For the rest of the afternoon, they went about strapping down equipment and securing the shop's doors and windows. Denton went out for plywood while Charley boxed up bills and receipts, mourning all the work she'd put into organizing her file cabinets. Alison brought over his portable generator. "It ain't fancy," he said, "but it'll run a fridge, a couple of lights, and a TV."

. . .

It was almost five when Charley got back to Miss Honey's, and the wind had just begun to disturb the trees behind the house. Micah's garden was in full flower, and before she went inside, Charley walked through it, inspecting the cucumbers and green beans almost ready for the taking, okra and tomatoes baking in the unwaving heat; the sunflowers with faces broad as a baby's nodding along the fence. Micah had even planted pumpkins, not bulbous yet, just long, groping vines beneath hooding leaves, and as Charley walked the last row then climbed the porch steps, her arms loaded with groceries they'd need whether they evacuated or not, her heart broke for her daughter. It would be a shame if Micah lost everything she'd worked so hard to plant.

The sky was still gloriously blue half an hour later. Charley was struggling to tie the porch swing to the railing when, to her great surprise, cousin John eased the Bronco along the gulley.

"What are you doing here?" Charley asked. John had called to check in on her a couple times since the reunion, but she hadn't actually set eyes on him, which meant she'd never seen him in his prison guard uniform. Now Charley hugged him, and smelled something institutional—Lysol, maybe—rising off his starched gray shirt.

"I brought y'all some plywood," John said. "Thought you could use some help putting it up." He held out a cordless screwdriver and a box of screws.

"Oh, John. With this traffic?" But Charley was grateful. With so much of her attention devoted to getting Romero and his men settled and securing the farm, she'd imagined how she, Miss Honey, and the kids would spend the long hours waiting for the storm to pass but hadn't considered the physical damage the hurricane might do to Miss Honey's house. Now here was John, thoughtful as always, coming to her rescue. And for the first time in a very long time, Charley was aware of what it meant not to have a man around the house. For all the time she spent with Denton and Alison, there was a limit to what she could expect from them. They were her partners, and yes, even her friends, but they weren't her family, they weren't her husband.

"As long as I'm back before they start the contra flow I'm okay," John said.

Just then, the screen door creaked, and when Charley looked up she saw Ralph Angel standing on the porch. He paused for a moment with his hands in his sweat suit pockets, then planted himself in the middle of the top step, leaning forward with his elbows on his knees. "Well, if it isn't Little John."

"Hello, Ralph Angel," John said.

Ralph Angel frowned. "Since when did you start calling me by my given name, boy? Show some respect."

Hot as it was, Charley shivered. She hadn't seen much of Ralph Angel since they'd argued over the farm, and to be honest, since then she had avoided him. It hadn't been difficult. Most mornings, she left before dawn, returning home in just enough time to talk to Micah while she worked in the garden before eating whatever dinner Miss Honey left out for her and retiring to her room, where she promptly fell into a deep and much-needed sleep. As best she could tell, Ralph Angel spent his time barricaded in the back room, doing what, exactly, she could only guess; that, or watching old war movies with Miss Honey.

"All right," John said and sighed. "Hello, cousin. How are you?"

Ralph Angel took a toothpick from his pocket and slid it into his mouth. "You've got the nerve to look like a real officer. What kind of uniform is that?"

"Texas Department of Criminal Justice."

"No shit. A real-life prison guard. Bet you can kick some ass when you feel like it, can't you, boy?"

"Only when I have to."

Ralph Angel motioned to Charley. "What do you think, sis? Think John here can kick my ass?"

"I'm not having this conversation," Charley said.

"Want to try?" Ralph Angel said. His body seemed to inflate inside his sweat suit.

"No, sir," John said. "I don't."

"Is that a real gun? Let me see it."

"No, sir. I can't do that."

Charley looked at Ralph Angel and thought she could track the anger coursing through him.

"Ah, shit, boy. I've held a gun before. Let me see it. I'm not going to fire it."

"I'm sorry, sir. I'm not giving you my gun."

"Well, fight me, then." Ralph Angel stood up.

"I didn't come here to fight." John pulled himself up to his full height, and Charley thought, *this* was the man the prisoners at Huntsville saw. *This* was the correctional officer. His voice remained steady and calm. "I just came to help Cousin Charley cover the windows. Make sure y'all are boarded up and ready for the storm."

"Yeah, right," Ralph Angel said. "You came around to make sure I'm not causing trouble. Did I pass the test? 'Cause I know you've been spreading rumors about me, talking about me behind my back."

"I don't know what you mean."

"Oh, cut the shit, John. I know y'all told Charley about my last visit. Told her I broke 'Da's arm. You and Violet and Brother, all running your mouths. I should kick your ass right now."

John took a step forward. "That's up to you, cousin. I'll play this thing any way you want."

"John, please." Charley pulled on John's arm. "Let's get this wood up before it gets dark."

The first sheet of plywood was screwed against the window and they were moving to the second when John said, "Lucky for him Daddy made me promise to stay calm, otherwise I *would* kick his ass. I don't care if he is my cousin."

The wind had picked up and every few seconds, Charley felt a smattering of rain against her face. She told John about the day Ralph Angel recited the Bible verses and negotiated Micah and Blue's bickering over the Polaroids, how he'd admired *The Cane Cutter*, how he treated Blue so tenderly. "It's like he's two different people," she said, and looked at the big sheet of plywood nailed against the window. She'd wanted so much to like Ralph Angel. She'd actually sort of resented Violet for not giving him a chance, thought, privately, that Violet was being judgmental, maybe even a little self-righteous. But she'd been the fool, not Violet. And after she and Ralph Angel argued, she called Uncle Brother to say he'd been right when he warned her. She called Violet, too, and apologized for ever doubting her.

John put his arm around Charley's shoulder and she felt how solid he was. "Be careful, cuz. That's the first thing they teach us in training. The charming ones are the ones you have to watch. They'll play you every time."

20

At seven o'clock the next morning, the forecasters downgraded the hurricane to a category two. Good news, but they still had to be cautious. In Miss Honey's den, Micah and Blue broke into the games Charley had purchased when she shopped for groceries, spreading Monopoly money and Uno cards over the floor.

"I'm going out," Ralph Angel announced, appearing in the doorway.

"But it's still too dangerous," Miss Honey said.

Ralph Angel looked past her to Blue. "Mind your grandmother." And when Blue asked where he was going, whether he could go too, Ralph Angel refused without explanation, which was something Charley had never heard him do. The front door slammed and she could just hear the Impala's engine below the wind.

By afternoon, the sky was a gray slab filled with a confusion of churning clouds. Wind flurries worried the trees, tossing leaves and small branches across the yard. The outer rainband dumped showers on Saint Josephine in twenty-minute bursts, and when Charley couldn't stand to watch one more newscast with its high-definition graphics and endless loops of storm footage, she retreated to her dark bedroom, where every few seconds the wind rattled the plywood she and John had nailed over the windows. She lay on the bed, listening to the wind. It really did whistle, she marveled, trying not to imagine how much havoc the hurricane was wreaking in her fields.

The storm made landfall in the dead of night. And though it was much weaker than first predicted, there was no doubting its power to destroy. For eight hours, it tore trees up by their roots, peeled roofs off stores and churches, shredded trailers like tissue boxes, and flooded the streets downtown with dark gray water. Out in the country, sediment churned in the rising tide, and hundred-mile-an-hour winds battered the cane fields until the proud stocks lay flat in submission.

At Miss Honey's, while she listened to the wind's high whine as it sliced across the yard, and a downpour that sounded like a thousand coins spilling on the roof, Charley said a prayer. *Please God, protect my family. Leave something behind on the farm so I'm not completely ruined. Let me have one chance to see what I can do before you take it all away.* As she whispered the words, Charley felt a sense of peace settle over the room.

By morning, the winds had died. The rains had ceased. Sun broke through the clouds in bold rays. Charley unbolted the front door and stepped out onto Miss Honey's porch to survey the damage

It was as if someone had plucked all the leaves from the trees, then systematically plastered them across the lawn and pasted them to the side of Miss Honey's house. Branches thicker than a grown man's arm hung perilously or lay cracked and twisted every few feet, from the woods all the way out to the street. In Micah's garden, all the plants had been ripped up by their roots. It was an awesome sight, proof of nature's ferocity and indifference, and standing in the yard, Charley knew she would remember this day for as long as she lived. The wind had torn the metal flashing off one side of Miss Honey's house and sections of the sunroom were flooded. All in all, though, they came through the hurricane intact. Or so Charley thought until the phone rang and Miss Honey shouted for her that Denton was on the line.

"Are you at the farm?" Charley mashed the phone to her ear and closed her eyes. "How'd we do?"

Silence. Then Denton sighed. "How quick can you get out here?"

On her drive out to the farm, Charley began to grasp the full extent of the destruction and appreciated, for the first time, why storms were named after the Carib god of evil, Hurican. Folks had already started piling their waterlogged possessions—splintered furniture and mattresses, sheets of soggy drywall and chunks of ravaged insulation, dead washing machines, sopping curtains, and parts of swing sets—in heaps along the roadside. To hear some people talk, Charley thought, you'd think only black folks lived in the buckled trailers and shotgun shacks with abandoned cars askew in the front yards, but no; as many poor whites scraped by on the back roads as poor blacks. Maybe that was the hidden blessing: the hurricane was the great equalizer; its wrath indiscriminate. In the end, the blessing, if there were one, was that for a short time, everyone would come together in order to survive.

Less than six hours since the storm passed, and Charley was amazed to see all the animal carcasses—raccoons, possums, and armadillos run over by last-minute evacuees, no doubt—that littered the roads. In the black bayous, fish were bloated into silvery balloons that reflected the morning's light. The air reeked of death, even with her window rolled up.

Heart punching, Charley turned onto what was once the dirt road leading to her shop but was now an obstacle course of branches and twisted metal scraps, and finally pulled up in front to find Denton and Alison waiting.

"Your houses?" Charley asked, looking from one tired face to the other as she slid out of her car. "Your families? Please tell me no one was hurt."

Alison stubbed out his cigarette. "A tree branch took out our bedroom window," he said, "which really burns me up because I was going to prune it this weekend. But the boys are fine."

Charley looked at Denton.

Ever the stoic, Denton wiped his glasses on his shirttail. "Nothing broke I can't repair." He opened his pickup door. "Get in. Let's take a drive."

Neither man had much to say as they rolled past fields where the cane lay flat as a bad comb-over against the ground, but Charley gasped at the sight, shook her head in disbelief, saying, over and over, into her palm, "Oh my God. This can't be happening." Two days ago, she couldn't see the trees across her fields, the cane was so high, but now she had a clear view. For the first time since that day Frasier quit and she'd looked out over the expanse of earth, she was struck by how much land she actually owned.

"I know it looks bad," Denton said, soberly. "But as long as the wind hasn't dislodged the stalks from their root boxes, we can get the combine through. All it needs to stand up again is a week's worth of sun. But we won't know for a day or two how bad it's bent."

"Bent or straight, what difference does it make?" Charley said, still grappling with the notion of six hundred trampled acres.

"Makes a huge difference," Denton said. "We're using some of this as plant cane over in Micah's Corner. Crooked stalks are harder to plant. How're you gonna plant a crooked stalk in a straight row?"

Alison scribbled on the back of an envelope to illustrate Denton's point. "Even if you can get most of each stalk in the row," he said, thrusting the envelope at her, "the ends stick up, which means the eyes on 'em won't sprout." Charley looked at his drawing: two parallel lines with squiggles jutting out from both sides. "Which means we've got to cut more cane to compensate, which means our diesel and labor costs are higher. Plus, any cane that's not covered with dirt dies soon as it gets cold, and that affects next year's yield."

Charley handed the envelope back and listened to Denton and Alison estimate what it would cost to repair the fields, the figure jumping by the thousands. "So, you're saying we're screwed," she said, and reached for Alison's cigarette. God knew what she would do with the damn thing since she'd never smoked before, but it felt good to hold something in her hand. She was down to twenty thousand dollars, which she needed to cover payroll and buy fertilizer, and every day more invoices arrived with the afternoon mail.

"Let's hope Micah's Corner didn't get the worst of it," Denton said. "If there's water hung up out there—" His voice trailed off.

"Just say it." Charley sucked on the cigarette, coughed and choked.

Denton shook his head. "Let's wait and see."

"Hell, I'll say it," Alison said. "Close as that quadrant is to the bay, it's bound to have some water on it. You heard about the tidal surge, didn't you? Everything south of Patterson is underwater. And don't get me started about the damage out at the Point."

Denton punched Alison's shoulder. "Shut up, Alison."

"Why you barking at me, Denton? Hell, I didn't do it. I'm just telling her what she's in for." Alison turned to Charley. "Brace yourself."

But there was no bracing herself for the way the tidal surge, the great wall of rushing water blown in from the Gulf, had had its way with Micah's Corner. Half the quadrant was under hip-deep water. Where it had receded, a thick layer of sludge and grit coated the fields, as though someone had dredged the Mississippi and smeared its sediment across her land. For a long time, the three of them could only stare.

"Jesus H. Christ," Alison said, a match trembling in his hand. "I thought this was a category two."

"It wasn't the wind," Denton said. "It was the water. Storms are getting wetter every year."

Neither man, normally strong-willed and confident in his own way, had the courage to look at Charley. And standing between her two partners, a peculiar coolness settled over her, a sensation similar to the calm she figured most people experienced just before they died. "I don't see any point in kidding myself," Charley said. She looked out over her fields and thought how her mother always accused her of being a dreamer. Well, she wasn't a dreamer anymore. "It's over. I'm ruined."

Yet, back at the shop, Denton insisted it *wasn't* over. While Charley wondered how she'd tell the crews she couldn't afford to keep them on, Denton retreated to her office.

"An extra twenty-eight thousand," Denton announced an hour later, tossing the yellow pad on the desk. They'd need pumps to drain the water, money for extra diesel and overtime, and a petty cash fund for spare parts since they'd be running equipment twice as hard. "We'll have to cut more premium cane to replant Micah's Corner, so that's less we'll have to sell come grinding. You'll have to include those lost dollars in your costs."

Charley looked at him blankly. "You know I don't have that kind of money."

"Got anything you can sell?"

For one criminal instant, Charley saw *The Cane Cutter*'s broad back and steady gaze. If she sold him, she'd be selling her father's memory; she'd have sold everything he cared about. "I've got nothing," she said. "I'm telling you, it's over." Denton pushed the yellow pad toward her. Without looking at it, Charley tore off the top sheet where he'd made his calculations and jammed it in her back pocket, saying, "I'll take care of it." She waited till Denton left the office, then she walked calmly behind the shop where no one could see, planted her hand on the side of the building, and vomited on her boots.

Tapped out. Finished. Done. That was what Charley thought as she slid into the Volvo and drove away from her farm without another word to Denton or Alison. In minutes, she was out on the road still littered with branches and debris. But for the devastation, it was a beautiful day with the blue sky wide open, the big yolky sun overhead, the dark trees lengthening along on the horizon. Charley increased her speed and felt the wind's moist breath on her face. She could drive out to San Francisco or New York, assume a new identity and start over. But what about Micah? How would she explain that they were leaving *again*, and not just leaving but running away? How could she look Micah in the eye and tell her she'd given up because cane farming was too hard; because she was exhausted and afraid and out of ideas; because the life she'd dreamed of wasn't turning out as she expected?

The gently rolling hills and golden pastures dotted with hay bales and the wide dry riverbeds of the East Felicianas looked nothing like the south Louisiana Charley had come to know, and as she crossed into the parish, northeast of Saint Josephine and an hour's drive from Baton Rouge, her eyes drank up the scenery. She followed the country road through Slaughter, where the ragtime legend Buddy Bolden lived before he moved to New Orleans and lost his mind, and less than an hour from the Mississippi state line, she stopped at the gas station in Clinton and bought a Coke, then sat in her car for a long time, watching people come and go from the courthouse in the tidy town square. The courthouse, made in the Greek Revival style and painted a crisp, gleaming white, matched the row of lawyers' offices across the street, their columns looking like matchsticks, the way they lined up so perfectly. The whole town looked like a picture postcard, Charley thought, so serene and unblemished, having never been touched by the storm; nothing at all like the wreckage she'd left behind in Saint Josephine. Why was it that some places had escaped nature's wrath while her small corner of the world seemed constantly tormented by misfortune? It didn't seem fair.

When Charley finished her Coke, she checked her watch—almost three o'clock, which meant it was almost one o'clock in Los Angeles. She took out her cell phone and dialed her mother's number.

Lorna answered on the first ring. "Charlotte?"

Charley heard glasses clinking in the background, silverware tapping delicately against bone china plates, the echoey voice of a woman speaking into a microphone followed by applause, and guessed that her mother was at a fund-raising luncheon for one of her charities. Until that moment, Charley had decided, stubbornly, not to call, reminding herself every time she was tempted that her mother had mocked her decision to move to the South. But Lorna's voice was like warm milk, and hearing it now, all of Charley's defenses and justifications fell away and all the rawness she'd worked so hard to ignore came right to the surface. Her eyes filled immediately with tears, her chest tingled with a silvery tightness, and just like that, she was five years old again, aching to be held and comforted.

Charley took a deep breath and wiped her eyes. "Hi, Mom."

"Where are you? Where's Micah? I've been watching the news. Please tell me you're okay."

"We're all fine," Charley said, thinking nothing could be less true, and heard Lorna sigh with relief. "John boarded up Miss Honey's windows, which I think made all the difference." She went on for a few minutes, but at some point it seemed pointless trying to describe what the hurricane had been like. It wasn't something you could sum up with words. It was like Mr. Denton said, you had to live it.

"Well, I'm glad you're okay," Lorna said. "I was worried. People here have been asking and I didn't know what to tell them," which Charley understood was Lorna's way of chiding her for not calling.

"I'm sorry," Charlie said. "I should have called before now. It's just I've been so busy since we got here. There's so much to do. But you can tell everyone we're fine. A little shaken and there's a lot to clean up, but I think we were lucky."

"That's very good," Lorna said. "I'm so relieved, because from here the news reports looked so frightening—all that rain, and the flooding, goodness. I really can't imagine."

"I know," Charley said, and swallowed against the tightening she felt in her throat. She pictured her fields, which looked like nothing more than a big brown pond now with the cane stalks barely poking through. "You have to see it to understand."

There was a long pause, which seemed to stretch out endlessly, and as she searched for something to say, Charley mourned that things between her and her mother had become so awkward and strange. The whole conversation made her feel antsy and agitated, as though she were trying to fit into a sweater whose sleeves were tight.

"And how are you, Mom?" Charley said, finally. "How've you been?"

"Oh, Charlotte, you know me. I always have a thousand things on my plate. Busy, busy, busy, all the time."

"That's good."

"As a matter of fact, I'm at a function right now."

"Yes," Charley said. "I can hear."

When she dialed her mother's number, Charley had not planned to ask for a loan—not exactly. She'd only wanted to hear her mother's voice and feel a little bit of the warmth she'd felt when she was young enough to sit on her mother's lap. Had she hoped her mother would ask about the farm? Yes, she had, and maybe even offer to help. But it seemed Lorna had no intention of asking or offering anything.

"Actually, things aren't good," Charley said. "I've had a setback on the farm. The hurricane flattened everything. My crop is probably ruined, three of the four quadrants, anyway, and Mr. Denton—that's my manager, I don't know what I'd do without him—anyway, Mr. Denton says even if we're lucky enough to salvage a few acres, we'll need additional capital to make it to grinding. Even more than we needed before." Charley paused.

"My goodness, listen to you," Lorna said. "Quadrants? Capital? Grinding? Good heavens, Charlotte, you sound like a real farmer."

"I guess I do," Charley said, and felt a small burst of warmth spread over her. "I told Mr. Denton I'd find the money, and I wondered—you know I wouldn't ask if I weren't desperate—but I wondered if you'd help me. I need a hundred and two thousand dollars total, but I'll take whatever you can spare."

Charley waited.

"My goodness, dear, that's an awful lot of money."

"Yes, it is." Charley thought of her father. He'd always told her she should never make assumptions about other people's time or their money, and that's the way she'd tried to live. The moment she asked her mother, she regretted it, but the question was out there now. "It would be a loan, not a gift."

"I'll take Micah," Lorna said, finally.

"You'll what?"

"Send Micah to me. That way you can focus all your attention on your farm without distraction. You can get a second job without worrying who'll take care of her."

In the late-afternoon sun, the courthouse cast off warm yellow light and looked even more stately than it had an hour before, with the row of columns throwing long shadows across the grass and the sky blue as a robin's egg. The air was warm and the breeze carried with it the faint fragrance of willow and pine.

"That's very generous of you," Charley said, biting back tears, "but Micah's fine right here."

"Very well," Lorna said, "but if you change your mind, you know I'll always take her."

Through the receiver, Charley heard another round of applause and the clatter of dishes being cleared. "I should let you get you back to your lunch."

"Yes," Lorna said. She sighed again, and Charley pictured her sipping coffee from the china cup, her lips barely touching the rim. "I almost forgot," Lorna said, "I sent Micah a party dress. You can tell her it's an early Christmas present. I hope it fits."

"I'm sure it will. I'll make sure she calls when it arrives."

"Very well," Lorna said. "I'm glad you called. And don't worry, Charlotte, you're resourceful, just like your father. I know you'll figure out something."

The loan officer at First Bank of Baton Rouge had hair plugs, and Charley, sitting at the corner of his desk in his padded cubicle, couldn't stop staring at the fine hairs, like chick fuzz, and the constellation of tiny punch holes laid out in even rows. The irony of the situation was not lost on her, and she almost laughed out loud because there was as much chance those plugs would take as there was of her getting the loan. Charley knew, because this was the tenth loan she had applied for in the last two days; the tenth time she'd sat across from a loan officer in a bad suit and pleaded her case, and it would likely be the tenth time she would be turned away.

As if on cue, the loan officer glanced up from her application. His skin was pale under the fluorescent lights, his expression grim as an undertaker's. He tapped his pen against his chin.

"And you're sure you don't have any collateral?"

"I'm sure," Charley said.

"Anyone willing to co-sign?"

Charley thought again of her mother. "No."

The loan officer flipped the pages and frowned.

"My credit is decent," Charley said, massaging her ring finger. "Not perfect, but certainly not the worst. I just need enough money to get through grinding."

But the loan officer closed her file. "I'm sorry, Miss Bordelon. Since the meltdown, banks are more cautious than they used to be. I'll do everything I can, but I can't see how underwriting is going to approve this without you at least putting up some collateral. I'm afraid you present—"

"I know," Charley interrupted. "Too much of a risk." Every banker she had talked to from Saint Josephine to Baton Rouge had used that phrase. She gathered her backpack. She had begged the first three loan officers to reconsider; she was tired. "Thanks very much for your time."

"I'm sorry I couldn't do more," the man said. "Good luck to you. And if you find a co-signer, I'd be happy to resubmit your application. My dad farmed sugarcane in the eighties, so I know what you're up against."

"I appreciate you saying that."

He held the door open for her. "Well, be careful out there. The roads are still pretty dangerous."

On the drive back to Miss Honey's, staring out over fields that only three days before looked almost tropical in their lushness, Charley knew she should be grateful. She had the best two business partners anyone could ask for; she had her family; she had her health; and yet she was overcome with a sorrow so great she feared her chest would crack open. She pulled over to the side of the road and laid her head against the wheel. If only her father or Davis were there to tell her to keep going, or better yet, say it was all right to stop and rest for a while.

By the time Charley got back to Saint Josephine, it was evening, and the Quarters, buzzing with neighborly activity all summer, were quiet,

Miss Honey's street hushed now that school had started and folks had shifted into their autumn routines. Charley pulled up alongside the gully and parked. The yard was still a mess. Miss Honey stood in the window. By the time Charley reached the porch, she had opened the door.

"I thought you were Ralph Angel," Miss Honey said, standing there in her faded housedress and slippers.

"Nope," Charley said. "It's just me." Miss Honey looked tired. Her eyes weren't bright as usual, her complexion washed out, her shoulders slumped. She tucked a wadded Kleenex in her pocket and Charley wondered if she'd been crying. "He hasn't been home?"

"No," Miss Honey said, sharply.

Two days since the storm and no sign of Ralph Angel; that was strange for a person who seemed interested in little more than hanging around the house. Driving home, Charley had noticed all the boarded-up stores and restaurants along Main Street, the owners still busy dragging tables and dishes, computers and racks of soggy clothes out to the sidewalk. Only the Winn-Dixie had opened for business. Charley set her backpack on the couch. "Where could he have gone?"

"How should I know?" Miss Honey snapped. "Do I look like a fortune-teller?" She took the Kleenex from her pocket and twisted it.

Stung, Charley stepped back. "I'm sorry." In all the months she'd lived under Miss Honey's roof, Miss Honey had never spoken harshly to her. Charley watched as Miss Honey went to the window again, pulled the curtains open, and peered out at the street. A little sigh of worry, almost a whisper, escaped her lips as she pressed her face to the glass.

"I know you're worried about Ralph Angel, but I'm sure he's fine," Charley said. "He's probably safe in a hotel somewhere, or he might even be driving home right now. I-10 is still jammed with all the people trying to get back from Arkansas and Mississippi. I should know—it took me twice as long to get back from Baton Rouge just now. How about if I call Hollywood? I'm sure he'd come over to clean up the yard."

"The yard ain't the problem! Can't you see that?" Miss Honey flicked the curtains closed and turned toward Charley. "Ralph Angel is out there alone. He could be hurt or dead, for all we know. It's time you starting thinking about someone other than yourself, girl. You're not the only one who has problems, so stop all that whining."

Charley was stunned. As many evenings as she'd come home from the farm with stories about her day, she'd never thought of it as complaining. If anything, she'd always thought Miss Honey was interested in her progress. "I didn't realize I was whining. I apologize."

"Well, you were," Miss Honey said. "And I'm not in the mood for it. Not tonight."

"Then I'll get out of your hair," Charley said, coolly, and thought of Violet, who *twice* had walked out of Miss Honey's house. Now, she understood more than ever what Violet must have felt—the hurt, the anger, the deep sadness at being treated so badly for no reason she could see. Charley picked up her backpack. She'd clearly overstayed her welcome. It was like her father said: *Never make people glad twice—glad to see you come, and glad to see you go.* Charley walked through the dining room, past the china cabinet filled with cut-glass figurines and milky green cups and saucers, the ones Miss Honey collected from oatmeal boxes decades ago, and was almost at the kitchen door when Miss Honey called out.

"I'm responsible for that boy."

Charley turned. "Ralph Angel is a grown man."

"That's not what I mean." Miss Honey sat on the edge of the couch. She closed her eyes, and for a moment Charley thought she was praying. "Lord, forgive me for what I've done," she said.

Charley walked back into the living room and sat down. Outside, the sun had set, and beyond the sheer curtain, twilight, soft and purply, pressed against the window.

They sat in the silence as the living room grew darker, until finally, Miss Honey said, "Ernest felt guilty for getting that girl pregnant and causing her to lose her scholarship," and it took Charley a few seconds to figure out that Miss Honey was talking about Emily, the girl Ernest had dated in high school, Ralph Angel's mother. "He wanted to marry her and stay here in Saint Josephine, but I wouldn't allow it," Miss Honey said. "I couldn't bear the idea of Ernest giving up his dream, especially after what LeJeune did to him. I told him to leave Emily, go out to California like he planned, and when the baby was born, I'd help her take care of it." Miss Honey dabbed her nose. "Ernest wanted to take Emily with him. But I knew she'd weigh him down. Something about her wasn't right—she was smart, but fragile as a little bird. Ernest needed a fighter, a woman strong enough to stand with him against the world. So I offered Emily's family two thousand dollars—all the money I had—to keep her away until Ernest left town. Emily's parents were sharecroppers. Two thousand dollars was a lot of money." Miss Honey stopped talking and stared out the window. "I think the strain of taking care of a child made Emily's condition worse."

"If you knew she was struggling, why didn't you help her?"

"I tried," Miss Honey said. "I wanted to keep my promise. But her folks told her what I did, how I sent Ernest away and paid them, and she was so angry with me, she wouldn't let me near Ralph Angel when he was born. Not for two whole years, and by then, she was having all kinds of trouble. They put her in Charity Hospital for a while and that helped, but she wouldn't stay. The only way I got to see Ralph Angel was when Ernest came home to visit. He brought Ralph Angel over here every day—such a pretty little boy. I'd hold him and rock him like he was my own. But when Ernest went back to college, he had to take Ralph Angel back to Emily, and I wouldn't see him again until the next summer. I heard about all the jobs Emily lost, how she struggled. It weighed on my heart. But she was Ralph Angel's mama. I didn't have custody."

"Does Ralph Angel know what you did?"

"No."

"Do Violet and Uncle Brother know?"

Miss Honey shook her head. "You're the only person I've ever told.

Back then, they were all too young to understand, and when they got older, well—I was too ashamed." She paused for a long moment, struggling to fight off the tears. "Besides, after Ernest and Lorna sent Ralph Angel back from California he came to live with us. All the reasons why and how didn't matter." Miss Honey looked at Charley, almost pleadingly, then reached for her hand. "So, you see, Ralph Angel is my responsibility. Whatever happened to him all those years he was with Emily, happened because of me. Whatever troubles he has now, he comes by them honest."

Charley looked at her grandmother, then she rose and stood by the window.

"I only wanted Ernest to have a chance," Miss Honey said.

Charley nodded, because part of her understood exactly why Miss Honey did what she did. If Micah fell in love with someone too frail or weak to help her stand against the world, would she interfere? She probably would. And yet, and yet. How many lives had Miss Honey ruined, and if not ruined, altered in a way that couldn't be fixed? Charley felt a small burst of fury, like a match being struck within her. Sometimes there was no fixing a life once it was broken; love, devotion, shortsightedness, *ignorance*—none of it mattered. Sometimes it was too late.

Charley woke early the next morning with a sick feeling. Her first instinct last night after hearing Miss Honey's confession had been to call Violet, but Violet wasn't home, and Charley had only said, in the message she left on Violet's voice mail, that she needed to talk.

The sun had barely risen as Charley climbed behind the wheel. She'd just turned out of the Quarters when she spotted Hollywood ambling along the road's shoulder, pushing his mower in her direction. The sight of him in his fatigues and baseball cap instantly lifted her spirits. She honked and pulled over.

"You think your regular customers would mind if I hired you for a couple hours?" Three days since the hurricane and Miss Honey's yard was still a mess. The sunroom wasn't flooded anymore—what water hadn't evaporated, she'd mopped up or pushed out last night before she went to bed—but underneath the half inch of sludge, the floor had buckled. "I have to get to the farm, but I'll drop you off so you can get started. I'll be back as soon as I can." Before she could ask how much he'd charge, Hollywood had lifted the Volvo's back hatch, tossed in his mower, and slid into the passenger seat.

Now it was later that evening and Charley, back home after a full day with Denton and Alison, leaned the push broom against the doorjamb, wiped her face on a strip of old bedsheet. Miss Honey's sunroom opened onto the side yard where just weeks before all the family had gathered for the reunion. It felt like ages ago. Charley stepped out into the warm evening. "Maybe Walmart sells linoleum squares," she called.

Hollywood had spent the entire day at Miss Honey's and Charley couldn't believe the progress he'd made. By the time she got home, he'd hauled all sunroom furniture into the yard so it could air out, pulled up all the waterlogged linoleum flooring—an enormous task—so the sunroom's pine plank floors could dry. Now he tossed another tree limb on the burn pile—a smoldering heap of trash and leaves and splintered branches—he'd made in the yard's far corner. "I reckon," Hollywood said. "They sell everything else."

Only now was Miss Honey's yard beginning to look normal. Charley glanced at her watch. Almost seven o'clock.

"If you're tired, I can finish up here," Hollywood said, walking over. "Walmart's open till midnight. I'll go over there later to see what kind of flooring they got."

Charley pictured Hollywood struggling to push a basket of linoleum squares all the way back to Miss Honey's. "Tell you what," she said. "We'll drive together, then I'll buy you dinner. It's the least I can do after all you've done today." She looked at Hollywood standing there in fatigues now stained with sludge and ash. "Where would you like to go?"

"We could go to Sonic?"

"I'd rather take you someplace you've never been. You've gone above and beyond."

Hollywood looked at Charley then back at the burn pile. "Well," he said after a moment, "I've always wanted to go to Shoney's in Morgan City. I've heard folks talk about the all-you-can-eat buffet. They say it's real nice. I've seen the commercials on TV."

"You got it," Charley said, and imagined the family restaurant just off the four-lane. There were at least three restaurants between here and there that served better food, but oh well. "We can take the highway or the back roads. You pick."

"I don't know." Hollywood's face darkened. "I've never been to Morgan City."

"Never been to Morgan City?" Charley laughed. "But that's just down the road; couldn't be more than twenty miles."

Hollywood slid his hands into his pockets and Charley knew he was reaching for the comfort of his movie magazine. "I'm sorry," she said. "I'm not making fun of you. I guess I'm just surprised."

Her apology was enough to set Hollywood at ease again. His face blossomed. "That's okay. I know you'd never do that."

At Shoney's, Hollywood spent fifteen minutes surveying the buffet choices, then joined Charley at the booth by the window. He tucked his napkin into his shirt collar and bowed his head to say grace. Charley put her fork down and bowed her head too, and when she opened her eyes, she watched with quiet amusement as Hollywood stared in wonder at the mashed potatoes, meat loaf, fried chicken, string beans, pasta salad, and fried catfish he'd piled on his plate.

"I think something's wrong with Miss Honey," Hollywood said, and took a sip of his Mello Yello. "She usually comes out to talk to me when I'm working. Today she hardly said a word."

And because Hollywood sounded genuinely worried, and because Violet still hadn't called her back, and she needed someone to talk to,

Charley confided in Hollywood. She knew she was betraying Miss Honey's confidence, but she repeated Miss Honey's story anyway, including the part about paying Emily's family. "I know she loved my dad, but I can't believe what she did."

"I remember Miss Emily," Hollywood said. "She lived in a little house on Saint Bernard, right before you get to the boat ramp. Liked to sit on her front porch and smoke cigarettes."

Charley sat forward. All these years and she'd never really thought about Ralph Angel's mother. "Ralph Angel never talks about her. Maybe one day you could take me to meet her. Or if you don't feel comfortable, just tell me where she lives and I'll go. She's part of the family. Miss Honey should have invited her to the reunion."

Hollywood set his fork on the table. "Miss Emily's dead."

Charley gasped.

"She killed herself," Hollywood said. "Jumped off the bridge. I remember 'cause she did it the same summer Ralph Angel went to live with his daddy in California. It was in the paper."

Half a dozen small children, snaggle-toothed and barefoot, ran up to the gate and stared at Charley's car as she pulled up to Hollywood's family compound.

"I had a fine time," Hollywood said. "Thank you. It's gonna be a long time before I have that much fun again."

"I'm glad we went," Charley said.

"Shoney's is even better than it looks on TV. Maman's gonna be jealous."

"Then it's a good thing you brought something back for her." Charley handed Hollywood the bag of takeout. "And thanks again for today. That was a lot of work to do all by yourself. You're a good friend to Miss Honey, Hollywood—and to me."

Hollywood wiped his hands on his fatigues. "Can I tell you something?"

"Sure," Charley said, and braced herself. Hollywood was looking at her with such urgency, such earnestness, she was afraid of what he might be about to confess.

"You know how I said I'd never been to Morgan City before?"

Charley nodded.

"Truth is, before today, I'd never been out of Saint Josephine."

SEPTEMBER

21

Thirty days of dry weather, that's what they needed. Thirty days with little or no rain, a whole lot of sun to bake the fields, an infusion of cash, and maybe, just *maybe*, they could save the farm—or at least that's what Denton told Charley when she arrived at the shop. Debris still littered the fields, new ruts needed filling, drains needed redigging, johnsongrass needed cutting where it had grown tall and thick amid the cane, and so, for the first few days of September, Charley, Denton, Alison, Romero, and the crew spread out across the farm. They worked from seven in the morning until seven at night with a quick break for lunch. In the evenings, Charley staggered into Miss Honey's to eat whatever she found in the fridge or whatever Miss Honey left for her under a covered dish by the stove. She showered before bed only because her own smell drove her to it.

After the first week, to Charley's astonishment, the cane in the nearest quadrants actually righted itself, stretching toward the sun as if pulled by invisible wires, and they were able to assess how much they could salvage for planting. By the end of the second week, over in Micah's Corner, the water had all but drained off the fields. Mud still made new planting impossible, though, and between the salt and the standing water, it was pretty clear the cane they'd planted earlier was ruined.

"Be glad we only dropped seventy-five acres' worth," Denton said as they ate lunch one afternoon, their sandwich papers smoothed out on the hood of Denton's pickup. He balled his napkin and tossed it on the dashboard. "Farmers who started planting before we did lost everything. The Dugas brothers lost a thousand acres."

Mid-September and still the weather held, with each day seeming a little better than the last. The humidity lessened, the nighttime temperature hovered in the mid-fifties, and for the first time, Charley thought she felt a hint of autumn in the air. Every day, she monitored their expenses, questioned each purchase, and sat on bills until the very last minute. She hadn't found a bank that would lend her money, but they were scraping by. *The Cane Cutter*, meanwhile, rested on her dresser, frozen in his labor, but she no longer lifted the T-shirt draped over him; she could barely stand to look.

And then, in the third week of September, Denton announced he had good news and bad news. The mills had postponed the start of grinding until the middle of October—that was the good news, because it meant they had two more weeks to plant and maybe a couple days to catch their breath. The bad news was that the 4840's engine had blown out, and since he couldn't find used replacement parts, they would have to order new ones; the cheapest estimate was eight thousand dollars.

"We can't plant without that tractor," Denton said. He picked through the crumpled papers stuffed above his sun visor and handed Charley the estimate. "Time for you to pull that rabbit out of your hat."

In her bedroom that evening, Charley folded the T-shirt Micah had thrown over *The Cane Cutter* and looked directly into his eyes. A braver woman would go ahead and sell, Charley thought; a more practical woman would add up the ongoing expenses and the unpaid invoices, consider the look of despair on Denton's face every time he scribbled figures on the yellow pad, and there would be no question. But Charley didn't think of herself as practical and she certainly didn't feel brave. She slipped under the covers, pulled the sheet over her head, and curled into a ball, but she couldn't get Denton's face out of her mind. On the phone the next morning, Charley asked the operator for the numbers of all the New Orleans auction houses. A queasy feeling settled over her as she dialed.

Friday evening now, and Charley eyed the pile of clothes on her bed— the black wool suit she wore to her father's memorial, the jeans skirt she'd owned since grad school, the yellow checked blouse with the Peter Pan collar that made her look too much like a schoolgirl. Everything she owned was too wrinkled, too heavy for the weather, or out of style. She stepped into her only pair of jeans that didn't have oil on the knees.

On the air mattress, Micah picked through Charley's makeup case, tested a lipstick on the back of her hand. "A date," she said, "that's gross."

"It's not a date." Charley shed the jeans and peeled a green halter dress from its wire hanger.

"If you're wearing that dress, it's a date, Mom." Micah drew a black line along her eyelid. "Are you gonna flirt?"

"Flirting is for cheerleaders," Charley said. "God, this dress makes me look pregnant."

"Then how'd you get a date?" Micah widened her eyes. The mascara wand licked the tips of her lashes. "Are you gonna go to second base?"

"Second—*what*? Okay, that's it. No more PG-thirteen movies."

In the end, Charley decided on a plain black skirt she used to teach in, and the blouse she wore when she visited Mr. Denton the first time. She looked at her reflection and sighed.

"Those shoes make your feet look huge," Micah said.

Charley snapped eye shadow pallets shut, scooped up lip pencils and pots of blush she hadn't worn in years. Other than the light coat of gloss on her lips, her face was bare.

"How late can we stay up?" Micah asked. She'd made two friends at school and had invited them over to watch movies.

"Ten thirty," Charley said. "But you have to help Miss Honey with the dishes."

Micah rolled onto her stomach and rested her chin on a pillow. "Moms shouldn't date. It should be illegal."

"And don't call unless it's an emergency. I'm not kidding," Charley said, and thought, *I'm too old for this.* But on her way out of the room, she touched the *The Cane Cutter* for good luck.

Remy Newell took a road that snaked lazily along the bayou where lily pads the size of elephant ears grew in clumps on the banks, and tree branches, willow and tupelo, dipped down to touch the slow-moving current. As the bayou turned, Charley caught a glimpse of a small aluminum boat anchored a few feet from shore and a fisherman gently lifting his pole and letting it fall as he tested his line. They passed plantation homes, old and grand, with sweeping verandas, tin-roofed Cajun cabins made of cypress, Creole cottages with gingerbread around the windows, and as the day's light waned, Charley leaned back, content just to ride.

"Your place is looking better," Remy said, breaking the silence. "That second quadrant is coming back real strong."

Charley looked at Remy. He'd traded his T-shirt for a striped oxford rolled to his wrists, his dusty Wranglers for a new pair, stiff and lightly creased down the front, but he still wore his work boots, which was sort of reassuring because it meant they weren't on a date after all. Just two farmers blowing off steam over a couple of beers. Still, he cleaned up well.

"Not fast enough," she said, and pushed thoughts of her low bank balance out of her mind. "This is the hardest thing I've ever done," she said, then added, softly, "Well, the second hardest."

"The first?" Remy said.

"Raising a daughter."

Remy nodded, and seemed to consider Charley's answer, but he didn't probe.

They crossed the bayou again as the road turned, and lost the radio signal. Remy toyed with the dial till he found a zydeco waltz; the melancholic whine of the accordion, the singer's voice full of resignation and longing, wafted through the speakers.

Remy sang along for a few bars. "You speak French?"

"I wish," Charley said, thinking of Micah. "Just some high school Spanish, and even that leaves a lot to be desired."

For a while, they discussed the benefits and challenges of hiring migrant farm labor, the rising price of health insurance and workman's comp, but eventually, just as Charley knew it would, their conversation turned to the subject of marriage and family.

"You have just one?" Remy asked.

"Just one." Charley scrounged through her purse for the single picture she carried: Micah leaning against a bright red door, grinning with permanent teeth that looked too big for her mouth. Charley handed the picture over. "She's eleven."

Remy steered with one hand as he held the photograph up to the window. "She's a pistol, I can tell."

"You have no idea."

He studied the picture again, then looked at Charley. "Where's her daddy?"

Remy was so easy to talk to that Charley was surprised the subject of spouses hadn't come up before now. "He died four years ago," Charley said. "We were coming back from the movies and two guys tried to mug us. He tried to be the hero but they had guns."

"I'm sorry."

Charley slid Micah's picture back into her wallet. With every passing day, that other world, her old life, felt as though it belonged to someone else. Three and a half months and there was so much about it she'd forgotten. Charley looked at Remy again. His hair was thicker than she'd noticed and the tops of his ears were sunburned. "What about you?"

Remy drummed the wheel with his fingertips. "Divorced," he said. "Didn't last long. She said she didn't get married to be a farmer's wife."

"What did she want you to do?"

Remy shrugged. "Business, I guess. Management, sales—hell, even politics, not that I have the stomach for it; I don't think she cared as long as it didn't have anything to do with farming." He looked out the window, forlornly. "But I've worked around cane since I was sixteen. You name it, I've done it. It's who I am. Used to come home from college every weekend during grinding just to smell the burned sugar in the air."

"Kids?"

Remy shook his head then wiped his face on his shirtsleeve. "Maybe one day, if I'm lucky."

. . .

Paul's Café was a tiny joint that sat back from the road. The parking lot was jammed with pickups, and the sign over the door read NO DANCING ON TABLES OR BAR. It looked as if it had always been there.

As they parked, Charley looked at Remy with concern. Music echoed faintly across the parking lot and a cheer went up. Charley frowned. "I have a bad feeling."

"Trust me, California," Remy said. He took her hand and gently eased her out of the truck. "All folks in there care about is how much you tip the bartender and how well you dance."

Charley was relieved to see that the crowd was a comfortable mix of blacks, whites, and everyone in between. In one corner of the dance floor, a middle-aged colored man of uncertain lineage wearing a cowboy hat with a turtle's head mounted on the headband swung a white woman whose freckled skin had lovely orange undertones and whose red hair was streaked with silver. An elderly Cajun couple, eyes closed, wrinkled hands pressed together, waltzed gracefully around the edge of the crowd to a melody only the two of them seemed to hear. Men in jeans and vests, girls in short, twirly skirts and boots; husbands and wives, uncles and widows, undergrads and retirees—they were all dancing, everyone shuffling and stomping and two-stepping, their troubles temporarily forgotten.

For a while, Remy and Charley sipped beers at the bar and watched the dancing. Then Remy grabbed her wrist. "Come on," he said, pulling Charley off her stool, excusing himself and begging people's pardon as he pushed his way, politely but firmly, to the middle of the dance floor. Remy took Charley's hand, wrapped his arm around her waist, then patiently guided her through a series of intricate steps, first turning her this way and then the other, then spinning her out on the length of his arm like a fly at the end of a fisherman's reel before pulling her back.

The band played one upbeat tune after another, and Charley worked to follow the steps. It wasn't difficult—just step together step, back, then front—but she had to concentrate. The moment she took her mind off what she was doing, looked at another couple, how they moved together, changed it up, she got confused and stumbled.

And then, just as she was getting comfortable, just as she reached the point where she could anticipate Remy's next move, the band threw her a curveball and downshifted to something slow. It was a sweet, lilting melody with an old-timey feel: Spanish moss, low-hanging mist, and pirogues slipping through the water. The accordion whined and the leader sang in French.

"This here's my song," Remy said, starting to sing softly. He took Charley's hand again, pulled her close. So close that she felt where the front of his shirt was damp from dancing; so close she felt his breath on her ear and neck as he exhaled and she smelled his citrus muskiness.

But every time Remy moved one way, she moved the other.

"Sorry," Charley said for bumping into him. "Sorry," she said for stepping on his feet.

"It's all right. Just relax."

They knocked knees.

"Oh my God. I'm sorry. I swear I'll get this." Charley's back and shoulders tightened. She started to sweat.

Over and over. She kept messing up and apologizing, until finally, Remy pulled his cheek away from Charley's just enough to look at her. He caressed her face and gave her that long, careful stare, then, in a calm, steady voice, said, "Listen to me, California. I know you're a strong woman and all, but you need to let me lead."

Charley's heart stopped. *Let him lead. Let him lead.* Yes. She could do that. For once in her life—okay, for ten minutes—she didn't have to be the boss or the handyman or the plumber or the activity planner. Or the short order cook, or the chauffeur, or the banker, or the disciplinarian.

"Okay," Charley said. "I'll try."

Remy pulled Charley close again and her shoulders relaxed. He pulled her closer still, so that his face was right against hers, his chest right against hers, and she felt the vibration of his quiet humming. The band played two slow songs in a row, and she tried to let go of everything but the music and the feel of Remy's body, solid and strong, moving with hers.

The set was over. The band took a break. Remy led Charley to a covered patio where strings of white lights draped like vines and darkness was broken only by a handful of torches staked in the grass. They ordered waters along with their beers, and then, because all the tables were taken, sat on the edge of the patio, where they heard insects chirping and frogs croaking along the bayou.

"Tell me one interesting thing about you," Remy said. "Something I wouldn't guess."

Charley looked at her beer. She had never thought of herself as interesting. Stubborn? Yes. Impulsive? Possibly. Patient? She was trying. But interesting? Charley sipped her beer and wondered if Remy would understand what she found interesting. But Remy was looking at her, waiting, so she gave it a go. "There was a little girl who came to the art class I taught. The neighborhood was pretty scary, but this girl, she was in the sixth grade, she drew like Raphael. You've never seen anything like it. Kids would be throwing markers at each other or drawing monsters or coloring the sky blue and the trees green, you know, stuff you expect kids to do in art, and she'd draw cities. Or women sitting on park benches, looking like angels." Remy was watching her closely, so Charley reeled out a little more trust and said, "You have to be able to see with different eyes to draw pictures like she drew. You have to see past what's right in front of you." Charley paused, thinking about the girl.

"And?" Remy said.

Charley shrugged. "And then she stopped coming. I tried to find out where she lived, but I never found her. But I still think about her. I hope she made it." She picked up her beer and drained the bottle. She looked at Remy, who nodded and seemed to understand. Then Charley laughed, to change the mood back, and remembered Remy's promise that zydeco dancing would make her sound like a Louisiana girl. "I think I still have my accent."

Remy stood. He offered his hand and pulled her up. "No problem, California. We've got plenty of time."

They danced through the third set and then the fourth, fast dances and slow ones, releasing each other's hands only when the band stopped playing and the house manager turned on the lights.

On the ride back to the Blue Bowl, silence sat easily between them.

The parking lot was empty when they pulled in. Remy shifted into park. "We should do this again. Soon."

"Soon. Yes." Charley was still filled with light. "Absolutely."

Remy gave her that long, careful stare then leaned toward her, and only then did she realize he hadn't kissed her yet. How could that be, after all the time they spent dancing? After they'd stood so close together?

Remy paused, said, "I have to tell you something."

"Uh-oh."

He laughed. "Nothing bad, don't worry." He hesitated. "I know we just met. And I may be overstepping my bounds here, but I have to tell you, I like you very much."

"Good," Charley said, "because I like you, too."

Remy shook his head. "I'm not saying it right." He looked at her again. The long stare. "I think you're wonderful, California."

"Thank you." The light from the dashboard made the gray hair at his temples glow silver.

He tilted his head as though trying to see her more clearly. "You're so—unusual."

"Unusual." Charley looked at her hands. She should have filed her nails. "What do you mean?"

Remy shrugged. "I don't know. Just different. The things you're interested in, the places you've been, the way you think. I mean, look at you, what you're doing with your farm. You came down here and jumped in like it was nothing."

"My farm." Charley laughed. "That doesn't make me different. It just proves I'm crazy."

"No. It doesn't. It means you've got guts. It means you're smart. It means you won't let anything stop you." Remy squeezed her hand. "I don't know. You're not like other black people; at least not the black people around here. It's almost like you're not black at all."

It took Charley only a nanosecond to realize what he was saying. Her face grew warm. "Oh." She felt all the muscles of her face freeze. Her skin was like glass; if she tried to talk it would shatter. But Remy's face was lit and he smiled tenderly. She should say something. "I see."

Remy leaned toward Charley and stroked her face with the backs of his fingers. Then he opened his door, walked around to open hers, and Charley knew when he would try to kiss her: outside, standing against the truck, where their bodies could melt together. But as she watched his easy stride through the windshield, she felt as if all the truck's air was slowly being sucked away. *Not like other black people.* Not like who? Miss Honey? Her father? Violet? *Almost like you're not black at all.* Not like Denton? Or Huey Boy? What did that mean? Where did that leave her?

Remy opened her door, reached for her hand.

"That's okay. I've got it," Charley said, holding her backpack with both hands and stepping down without his help.

"Hey? You okay?"

"I'm fine."

Remy took Charley's chin in his hand. "What's wrong?"

"Nothing." Charley lifted her chin.

"Did I do something?"

Charley looked out across the parking lot to where she knew the fields stood waiting for morning. She heard the cane stalks rustle. People didn't change their fundamental beliefs about how the world fit together. Charley knew this. Besides, it was too hard; the problem was too big and she didn't have that kind of time.

She took out her keys and was about to leave without saying anything. But Remy deserved an explanation.

"Here's the thing." Charley took his hand. She pulled her shoulders back, strangely grateful for her mother's constant reminders about good posture. The words came from some place deep within her but she didn't raise her voice. "Every morning when I wake up and look in the mirror, I see a black face and I love it. Sure, I've been to Paris and grew up surfing, and yes, I speak like I'm in a commercial. But I'm just like the women you see walking on the side of the road with their laundry baskets and their Bibles. I'm just like the old men pedaling their rusty bicycles. I'm no different from the men who drive your tractors or the woman who probably raised you. I'm just like them, no better and no worse. I'm black, Remy, which means everything and nothing."

Remy looked stricken. "I beg your pardon," he said, all the ease in his voice drained away. "I apologize, California."

"My name is Charley."

"I'm sorry. I wasn't—"

The moon shone through the bunched and graceless clouds. Remy reached for Charley's arm but she stepped back.

"It's late," Charley said. "I should go."

In her car, KAJN played a zydeco waltz. Charley turned it off.

Remy tapped on her window. "We should talk. I'll call you tomorrow."

"No. Please don't." Charley turned her face away, mortified that tears were standing in her eyes. "There's nothing to talk about."

"I don't care if he's Robert Redford," Charley said, pushing past Violet and heading for the darkened family room. She dropped her backpack on the coffee table and collapsed onto the couch.

"Good morning to you, too." Violet tied the sash on her robe, turning on the lights as she followed Charley. "You mind telling me what Robert Redford has to do with you breaking down my door?"

"Remy Newell." Charley put her face in her hands. When she looked up, Violet was leaning against the wall with her arms crossed, yawning. "Did you hear me?"

"It's two thirty. I don't usually start seeing patients till nine."

"*Violet.*"

Violet came around and sat next to Charley. "Okay, what happened?"

"I just thought—well, I guess—oh, I don't know what I thought. I can't believe I fell for it. Shame on my being charmed by all that Southern gentility bullshit he sprinkled around like powdered sugar." Charley pinched the bridge of her nose. "I thought he was different from the other rednecks because he listened to NPR."

"*What happened?*"

"Remy gave me that 'you're not like other black people' line."

Violet nodded. "So where's the news?"

Charley looked down at the shadow box coffee table. Violet had changed the scene beneath the glass top. Last time it was a summer motif—sand, seashells, and a red plastic lobster. Now it was a Mardi Gras theme with masks and beads even though Mardi Gras was still months away. "I guess I wanted to believe—I liked the possibility—but it's like there's an electric fence between us all the time—God! I hate having to be the race police."

"So don't," Violet said.

"You mean let him get away with it?"

"Why not see if he's capable of learning, if he seems good in every other way?" Violet took Charley's hand. "Why does a man have to be perfect before Charley Bordelon will date him? What do you care if Remy Newell thinks you're not black, or that all black people have to play sports to go to school? I'm not saying it's not troubling, and I'm not even saying you have to overlook it. But if it's not that, I guarantee, it would be something else. Meanwhile, you're in a wonderful position. Girl, you're free, can't you see that? You've got your child, you've got your family down here who love you, you've got your farm. You don't have to ask anyone for anything. You know how few women in this world get to say that, black *or* white?" Violet let go of Charley's hand, but kept her gaze trained on her. "You know why you're disappointed in Remy Newell, why you're so angry with yourself? Because you thought he was the complete package. Southern accent, progressive politics, and all. You forgot he's just a man. Now, don't misunderstand, there's nothing wrong with men; I like having them around. But you've already got what you need, sugar." And here, Violet reached for Charley and hugged her, and Charley felt the softness of Violet's neck, and smelled the lingering fragrance of her night cream and exhaled. "Just keep doing what you're doing, Charley," Violet said. "Take care of your child, get your fields planted, stay right with God, and you'll be just fine."

22

🌺 Dressed in waist-high waders and flanked by crates of rotting trash fish, Ralph Angel sat on the German's tailgate, trying to convince himself there was nothing wrong with pulling traps for $7.25 an hour.

The night of the hurricane, he took the last of Gwenna's check and headed over to Tee Coteau, where he asked around in the seedy bars and dark parking lots until he found what he was looking for. Then, drunk and stoned, he rode out the storm and a few days after in an abandoned house. But when Ralph Angel came to, sobered up, he found that he was plagued by the same dark thoughts as before: how he'd made a fool of himself at the bakery (*Go*, Johnny had said, bending to pick up all the ruined loaves. *Don't worry about it. Please, just go*); how Charley accused him of pushing 'Da on purpose ('Da shouldn't have gotten in his face like that; why wasn't anyone talking about that?), stealing his father's money (How could he steal what should have been his?), that he was jealous of Hollywood (You call that a business? Any idiot could mow a lawn.).

All told, Ralph Angel stayed gone five days. Blue refused to speak to him when he reappeared; pouted and turned his back every time Ralph Angel called him. That had been the worst part; he'd never left Blue behind like that before, but sometimes a man had to step away for a while. Blue only came around when Ralph Angel offered to read him another Bible story, and even that didn't ease Blue's fears entirely. He followed Ralph Angel around like a duckling, cried when Ralph Angel said he still had to go to school.

As for the rest of the family, coming home was easier than he expected. Charley ignored him, and 'Da was so happy to see him she smothered him with all her hovering and coddling until he told her to give him some space. She apologized and left him alone after that, which was good, because he'd come up with a plan.

While everyone was at church, he took the newspaper to his room, spread the want ads on his bed, and circled jobs he thought he was cut out for. After Blue went to sleep, he found Miss Honey's old Underwood and pecked out a cover letter, filling in the missing keystrokes with a leaky black ballpoint.

```
To Whom It May Concern,
I am writing to inquire about the position listed in
Sunday's paper. I attended Southern University where I
studied Civil Engineering. I have extensive sales expe-
rience resulting from my years with Rancher's Pride
Meat Direct and the Phoenix Water Services Depart-
ment . . . I am flexible about the salary and benefits. I
would welcome a chance to discuss my qualifications
further and explain the gaps in my employment.
                    Yours truly,
```

Each afternoon, he walked down to the post office, imagining that he would see, there among the bills and circulars in 'Da's box, a letter inviting him for an interview. One day, a thin envelope arrived.

Dear Sir,

Thank you for your interest in our sales position. At this time, we have decided your work experience does not coincide with the job requirements. Good luck in your continued search.

Sincerely,

Ralph Angel jammed the letter in his sweat suit pocket and walked across the street to the gas station, where he bought three Snickers and a king-size Baby Ruth before boosting a Schlitz forty-ouncer from the display near the door.

In the next round, he answered ads for home health care aids, security guards, dishwashers at the Waffle House where he worked the summer before he went to college. But no luck. Finally, he signed up with the job-training center in Lafayette, where the clerk looked at him as though he were a recent parolee and told him to take a seat until she called his name. Two hours later, he had the name of a crawfish farmer and a number to call. Which was how he wound up sitting on the German's tailgate next to a crate of rotting fish.

"You there," the German said, pointing. He was a large man with arms sunburned terra-cotta and fingers thick as sausages. "You ever pull traps?"

"I'm an engineer," Ralph Angel said. "Went to Southern." He wondered if the German had even graduated from high school and guessed he probably inherited this place from his father, who inherited it from *his* father, since that was the way luck worked down here.

The German squinted. "Well, then you're smart enough to know I can't pay you unless you put in a day's work. This ain't no beauty contest. Get off your ass and start hauling bait."

"I don't know what the agency told you," Ralph Angel said, sliding off the tailgate. "But I've got management experience."

The German held Ralph Angel in his gaze. "I don't care if you won the fucking Nobel Prize. I need a man to pull those traps. Can you do the job or not?"

The first two crawfish ponds bordered a strip of raised ground where the pickup was parked. Fringed with willows overhanging the soggy banks, each pond measured forty acres and looked bottomless beneath the willows' reflection. Twenty more man-made ponds just like this one were scattered through the woods.

A burlap tarp concealed the bait crates. Ralph Angel peeled it away and forced himself to look at the hollowed eyes, the gaping mouths, the maggots inching their way through the bloody gills. His stomach rolled as he hoisted two crates into his arms.

Down at the dock, two young men—one black, one white—stood by an aluminum bateau beached in the cattails along the bank. Ralph Angel eyed the bateau warily, and couldn't help but wonder how quickly he'd drown if it capsized. The black boy—chinstrap beard, wave cap over his cornrows—jammed his fists in his pocket and spat into the water while the white boy, in a guts-smeared T-shirt, baseball cap set sideways like a music video gangster, scratched his belly and exchanged a knowing glance with the black kid as Ralph Angel set the crates on the dock.

"'Sup?" said the white kid.

Ralph Angel had been around long enough to know how he had to play this. You couldn't come off as too aggressive with guys like this, since you were on their turf; but you couldn't come off as a pussy either. "Nothing, man."

"The boss is a hard-ass," said the white kid, "but he's a'ight. Don't ride us too hard long as we be filling sacks. Yo, it ain't personal, know what I'm sayin'?"

Ralph Angel nodded. Why did white kids think it was cool to talk like black kids from the 'hood? "Yeah, okay," he said.

The black kid carried the crates to the bateau, where he stacked them neatly, as if it mattered.

"I'm Jason," the white kid said. "That's Antoine." Antoine ignored them; someone, apparently, had to load the bateau. Jason kicked at the marshy ground; his rubber boots made a sucking sound in the mud. "This your first time?"

"Yeah," Ralph Angel said. "You know how it is, man. Got to make a little paper."

Jason laughed. "True, dat."

"What about you?" Ralph Angel ignored the swipe of a glance from Antoine, who was now retrieving crates from the pickup. "Been doing this long?"

"Since eleventh grade," Jason said. "I be making enough paper to get me a new truck and my girlfriend's teacup Chihuahua; paid eight hundred dollars for that damn dog. Boss says I keep working like this, one day he'll give me a percentage."

"What about school?" Ralph Angel said. "You ought to finish. Go to college. Get your degree."

"Fuck school, man." Jason rubbed his fingers together. "This here's the money."

"Wanna know the real money shot? A diploma, man. Got mine in engineering. Southern." Which, for purposes of this discussion, Ralph Angel figured was close enough to the truth.

Jason's gaze narrowed. "If it's all about the diploma, how come you ain't hooked up in an office?"

"This?" Ralph Angel looked out over the ponds. "This here is temporary, while I figure out my next move."

"I feel you," Jason said. He signaled to Antoine, who set down a crate, wiped his hands, front and back, on his shirt, and shook Ralph Angel's.

"Hey, man," Ralph Angel said. "What kind of fish is this anyway?"

"Shad," Antoine said, shrugging. "Maybe a little carp. Hard to tell when it's all rotted and shit. But that's how the crawfish like it. They go wild for this shit, man." He climbed into the bateau. "We grading 'em or just running?"

"Just running," Jason said. "Not catching too many number ones, so the boss says throw 'em all together." He tossed Ralph Angel a pair of black industrial rubber gloves.

The necks of the crawfish traps rose just above the surface of the water. The bateau's hydraulic engine turned the paddle wheel, whose blades churned up mud and grass as it pushed the shallow-bottomed boat deeper into the pond. While Jason steered and worked the pedals, Antoine positioned himself at the small metal table in the center of the bateau. Woven sacks, the electric green of Easter excelsior, hung along one side of the table. As the bateau rumbled through the water, it was Ralph Angel's job to lean over the side, snatch each wire trap by its neck, and dump the contents—crawfish, gnarled fish heads and backbones, baby snapping turtles and weeds—onto the table, then replenish the bait and sink the trap back into the pond, all before the bateau reached the next trap, a few yards farther on. At the table, Antoine picked out the crawfish. He tossed the smallest ones over the side and shoved the larger ones through the chutes into the waiting sacks until they bulged like udders. It was simple work, but there was a rhythm to it, and the rhythm was cruel. The first few times, Ralph Angel was too slow emptying a trap, or he forgot to refill the bait, or he sank one trap too close to another and the bateau had to make a wide sputtering circle back.

"People be making some cheap sacks, man," Antoine shouted over the engine. "Sacks keep popping." Rogue crawfish scrambled around at his feet.

"Keep it going," Jason yelled, and motioned for Ralph Angel to speed it up.

By noon, Ralph Angel's shirt was soaked with pond water, his pants speckled with mud, blood, and fish guts. His back ached from bending. His shoulders cramped from lifting and dumping. On the sorting table, crawfish, like chunks of carnelian, glinted in the sunlight. The sight of them writhing at the shock of warm air, tails slowly flapping, tiny claws mechanically grabbing for futile salvation, struck Ralph Angel as ecstatic. *Thou wilt shew me the path of life: in thy presence is fullness of joy; at thy right hand there are pleasures for evermore*, Ralph Angel thought, before he could stop himself.

When they broke for lunch, Ralph Angel dragged himself up the bank and sat alone in a half-circle of shade. He choked down his gummy cheese sandwich, struggling against the craving for a hit. Heat rose from the ground as he lay in the grass.

In his dream, he was back at the Piccolo Club with Gwenna and a stranger who had a marble for a glass eye. The marble rolled wildly in its socket as the stranger licked Gwenna's ear. Ralph Angel couldn't protest; his lips were stitched shut. He woke to see the German standing over him.

"Time's up, sleeping beauty."

Ralph Angel smelled rotten fish on his sleeve. Every muscle in his upper body had stiffened. He made his way down to the bateau.

On the pond, he worked the rest of the afternoon in silence. Jason and Antoine talked about girls, cars, and music, but Ralph Angel was too tired. What little energy he had, he used trying to forget where he was—pulling trap on some cracker's pond for minimum wage—until Jason steered the bateau toward the bank where the German waited for them to load the forty-pound sacks into his truck.

"Nice work," the German said, as Ralph Angel walked past him with the last sack.

"Thanks," Ralph Angel said.

"Tomorrow we'll hit the last two ponds on this side," said the German. "The front pond ain't producing as good as these. Still got some of that seaweed from the storm." He pulled out his keys.

And maybe it was the fact that the German had acknowledged his work, and maybe it was that he was being included in tomorrow's plan, but Ralph Angel felt himself buoyed. He followed the German to his truck. "Say, boss, I'd like to ask a small favor."

"What's that?"

"I wonder if I could get an advance."

"I pay on Fridays," the German said in a flat tone. He climbed into his truck, which dipped under his weight.

"Yeah, I know." Ralph Angel put his hand on the truck door. "But I'm riding on fumes. I don't fill my tank tonight, I can't make it back tomorrow." He didn't mean it to sound like a threat, but the German's face flushed. "Not trying to be a smart-ass. I'm just being straight with you."

"And I'm going to be straight with you," the German said. He dug in his ear with his key. "I don't give a shit where you went to school, or whether you wipe your ass with a silk handkerchief or the back of your hand. I pay out on Fridays; not Thursday afternoon, not Saturday morning. You want this job, Professor, you'd better figure out a way to gas up and get here by seven o'clock tomorrow. Not here at seven, I got ten other guys to take your spot." He pulled the door closed.

Ralph Angel stepped away as the German turned the engine over. "I'm not a professor."

Half a mile down the dirt road, the Impala sputtered then stopped. Ralph Angel sat behind the wheel, debating whether to sleep in his car, then got out and started walking. It had been years since he'd passed anywhere near a cane field. Now he cut through the rows. By dusk, he'd made it back to the Quarters and paused at the railroad tracks to look down into the dusty streets. The church, the school yard, the narrow road leading into the woods.

The screen door announced him. 'Da was at the stove. Blue, Micah, and Charley were setting the table.

"Where've you been?" asked 'Da.

"Got a job."

Blue ran over, then backed away. "Yuck, Daddy, you stink."

"A job," 'Da said, like he'd just told her he'd been elected mayor.

"I'm working with this guy. He's got a serious crawfish farm out past Bayou Duchein. Must have thirty-five, forty ponds." Ralph Angel hung his jacket over a chair as though it were a suit coat and looked at Charley. "He says if I keep doing what I'm doing one day he'll make me a partner, give me a percentage. What do you think about that, sis?"

"Congratulations," Charley said.

'Da looked at him expectantly. "What's he have you doing?" It was the same expression she had the first time he won the Junior Baptist Bible Verse Competition. He could still remember her, sitting there in the front row.

"Right now I'm out in the fields, managing the crew. He wants me to see how the whole operation runs, then he'll bring me inside."

"That makes two farmers in the family," 'Da said. "God is good all the time. I've been praying for something like this. All that talent you got?"

"I'm not sure the Lord has much to do with this," Ralph Angel said, "but thanks."

"What do you mean?" 'Da said. "The Lord's got *everything* to do with this. 'And all these blessings shall come on thee, and overtake thee, if thou shalt hearken unto the voice of the Lord thy God.' Deuteronomy, chapter twenty-eight, verse two." She wiped her hands on a dish towel, then slung it over her shoulder. "You're not sure what the Lord has to do with this? I know I raised you better than that."

"Denton says some farmers will lose as much as seventy thousand dollars if their cane doesn't stand up by the end of the week," Charley said.

Ralph Angel looked at Charley. On another day, her farm talk would have made him want to rip her face off. Could she *really* not see how much it bothered him? She *must* be doing it on purpose. But today, listening to her talk was like drinking castor oil: you wanted to vomit for a few seconds, but the feeling passed. "Speaking of money, 'Da," Ralph Angel said. "I need to borrow some. I ran out of gas; had to walk back."

"Why didn't you call? I'd've come get you."

"This place is way out. Walked half a mile just to get to the main road." Before he said another word, 'Da had reached for her purse. "Just enough to fill the tank. I get paid on Friday."

'Da pressed forty dollars into his hand. "I'll go to the bank tomorrow if you need more," she said. "Now go shower."

Ralph Angel turned to Charley. "If you can find it in your heart to help your brother, after dinner maybe you can give me a lift to the gas station then drop me at my car."

"So, one more week till grinding," Ralph Angel said as he and Charley pulled out of the Quarters. "Must be a lot of pressure."

"It'll be close," Charley said. She was quiet for a minute, then looked at him. "Congratulations on finding something. I'm happy for you. I mean it."

Ralph Angel looked at Charley and felt a small pocket of warmth—the same pocket of warmth that had first opened between them the day she took Blue for sno-cones—open again. For a moment, he considered telling her the truth about his job: that the German treated him like shit, *lower* than shit, actually, and that he'd never worked so hard in his life, didn't think his body would ever recover; that a kid young enough to be his *son*, for Christ's sake, had more seniority, was more successful than he was beginning to think he'd ever be; that if he thought about it too hard, he'd have to admit his life, other than Blue, was a total failure. He thought about telling Charley all that. It would feel good to confide in her, a load off his chest. But in the end, he just said, "Thanks."

"You've been pretty tight-lipped about the whole thing," Charley said. "I'd never have guessed."

Ralph Angel leaned back. "Yeah, well. I didn't want to say anything till I was sure."

Above the gas pumps at the Quick Stop, neon lights burned through the night. Charley cruised along the pumps, parked, then held out two singles. "Can you buy a bottle of water and some gum when you get your gas?"

"Sure thing."

Inside, Ralph Angel found the shelf of auto supplies, checked the price of a plastic gas can with a detachable funnel, and put it back on the shelf. At the counter, he set down Charley's bottled water. "You got any empty containers back there?" he asked the girl behind the counter. "Anything plastic? I need something to put some gas in and that gas can you're selling is a rip-off."

"No, sir. Not really," the girl said. She thought for a moment. "I guess you can buy a Big Gulp, but I'll have to charge you for the cup. Ninety-nine cents."

With Charley's singles, Ralph Angel bought the bottled water and the giant cup. He bought gas with 'Da's money, pocketed the change, fished a fistful of peppermint balls from the tub by the register, and tossed four dimes on the counter, then on the way out, when the girl wasn't looking, boosted a pack of Juicy Fruit.

"You can't do that," Charley said as Ralph Angel set the Big Gulp filled with gas in the cup holder.

"They wanted seven dollars for a stupid plastic gas can," Ralph Angel said. "The cup was practically free."

"I don't care. Not in my car."

"Here." Ralph Angel tossed the peppermint balls on the dash, where they scattered like marbles.

"It's completely illegal," Charley said. "What if we have an accident?"

"Then we'll be dead anyway. Chill out, sis. We're fine."

Out on the road, Ralph Angel crushed peppermint balls between his teeth while Charley, driving ten miles under the speed limit, glanced nervously in her rearview mirror. The country looked different at night and it took Ralph Angel a while to find the road where he'd left his car. Charley flipped on her high beams so he could see, but he still spilled most of the gas down the side of the Impala.

"I should get back," Charley called. So much for being happy for him.

Ralph Angel waved the empty cup. "Thanks. I got it from here."

When Charley was gone, he tossed the cup into the cane and stood in the dark. The night smelled of tea olive, swamp lily, and magnolia— the smells of his childhood—and for a moment, Ralph Angel understood why people loved it here, why no one ever left.

Seven hundred nickels, which was thirty-five dollars after he paid for the cup and the gas, and cashed in the rest, weighed far more than Ralph Angel expected. He set his plastic bucket on the stool next to him, balled his jacket on the floor. He fed the nickels one at a time into the slot machine, yanked the handle, and watched the numbers spin. When the waitress came back with his free drink, he asked for Amber.

"Who?" the waitress said, distracted. She stepped back, looked past Ralph Angel's shoulder to where high rollers were cheering at the craps table.

"Young girl," Ralph Angel said. "Wavy red hair." He could barely taste the alcohol in his Manhattan.

"Don't know her," the waitress said. She glanced at his bucket. "You're on the slow boat with those nickels, you know. Dollar slots or even the quarters, you'll have better luck."

"Thanks, but I got a plan."

"A guy won ten grand last night playing dollar slots five bucks at a time."

Ralph Angel rolled his drink around his mouth. "You're really working for that tip, huh?"

"I'm just trying to be nice."

"I'll keep that in mind." Ralph Angel set his glass on her tray. "But right now, I'll just take another drink. With some bourbon in it this time." He pushed another nickel into the machine.

Three coins left in his bucket. Ralph Angel's eyes stung from all the cigarette smoke, so thick the air looked milky. Hours of handling the filthy nickels had left his fingertips stained the metallic gray of trout scales. He could still hear the German's mocking voice. What he needed was something harder, a little horse to slay the beast. Ralph Angel pushed the last three nickels through the slot, yanked the handle one last time, and was turning away when the machine rang wildly and a spat a stream of coins into the tray. Three sevens bobbed on the centerline.

"I'll be damned."

Fifty dollars, crisp.

If he hurried, he could swing through Tee Coteau for a little nightcap and still be back at the ponds to catch an hour's sleep, maybe two. The German would be impressed. He'd recognize his potential, maybe apologize for the bad start. End of the week, he'd be talking to Ralph Angel about a raise, maybe benefits. Ralph Angel pushed through the glass doors. The guy from his old life, the professional, would be back in the game.

At the ponds, Ralph Angel turned on the radio and stretched out in the backseat, where he caught a whiff of Blue's urine each time he changed position and had to grip the edge of the seat to keep from rolling onto the floor. When he was comfortable, he lit his cigarette, then held the lighter under the square of aluminum foil until white smoke snaked into the air. In a few seconds, he was chasing the dragon, Delta blues providing an eerie sound track to his dreams.

Morning. The rumble of Jason's truck rattled the Impala. Ralph Angel crawled out of the backseat and urinated in the weeds, then trudged down to the dock, where Jason was already loading bait. He'd stopped chasing the dragon, but the last of its effects, the feeling of being inside a cocoon where nothing—not Charley, not the German, not even his father—could get to him, hung with him still.

"Holy shit, man. Who dug you up?"

"Hey, man," Ralph Angel said. He hung his jacket over a branch, then lifted two crates off the stack and dragged them over to the dock. "I want to drive."

Jason glanced back at the crates. "I don't know, dog. You don't look so good."

"No, no," Ralph Angel said. "It's cool. I watched you yesterday. I get it."

"It ain't that easy, man," Jason said. "You fuck around, run over them traps, the boss is gonna be hella pissed."

"I said I can handle it. Don't worry."

The sun had just risen over the trees as Ralph Angel stepped into the bateau. He slid into the driver's seat.

"I got a bad feeling about this, man," said Jason.

"Relax," Ralph Angel said, and practiced working the pedals.

Antoine came down to the dock. He shot Jason a look when he saw Ralph Angel in the boat.

"Yo, man." Jason tapped Ralph Angel's shoulder. "Just one time around. Then you gotta get up."

The bateau was surprisingly easy to maneuver and they slipped smoothly through the water, the pond's surface, this early in the morning, smooth as freshly blown glass. Everything in the world, Ralph Angel thought, seemed brighter, more intensely defined—the spiked yellow petals of the lily pad's flower, the silvery blue iridescence of a dragonfly's wing—it was all a miracle.

Ralph Angel worked the pedals while Jason stood at the bow and kept an eye out for clumps of grass and reeds that might catch in the paddle wheel, nervously calling out, "Right, yo!" or "Left! Left!" making angular gestures as they crawled along. As he got the feel for the steering, Ralph Angel leaned back. He closed his eyes and let the sun warm his face.

Then all at once, Jason was yelling, "Shit, man. Fucking A! Go back!"

Ralph Angel snapped awake in enough time to see Jason race to the back of the bateau.

"What'd I do?"

"Ran over a trap." Jason leaned over the stern, reached for the paddle wheel.

Ralph Angel heard a bump, then a scrape of metal under the boat.

"Turn off the fucking motor, man!" Antoine said.

Ralph Angel lunged. But before he could hit the switch, they ran over another trap. The engine whined crazily as it surged, ground through its gears.

"Cut the engine, motherfucker!" Antoine said again.

"I'm trying," Ralph Angel yelled back, fumbling. "Where's the switch? I can't find the switch."

Jason staggered forward. He reached for the switch and the engine died, but not before a third trap snagged on the paddle wheel and rose out of the water looking monstrous and strange. The crawfish inside the trap's bulbous belly scrambled and clicked like balls in a bingo tumbler, and as the paddle wheel continued to roll forward, it crushed the neck of the trap lodged against the stern. Smoke billowed from the hydraulic engine. It took almost an hour to paddle to the dock.

The German was waiting. "How the hell?"

"I can explain," Ralph Angel began, but the German pushed past him and leaned over the stern. "Who did this?"

"Give me a minute, Jesus."

But the German was having none of it. He plowed into Ralph Angel, knocking him out of the bateau onto the dock. "Get the hell off my pond."

"Just hear me out."

"Get off my farm before I fucking kill you." He grabbed Ralph Angel by his shirt and dragged him to the bank. "You piece of shit. I knew you were trouble. You have any idea how much you've cost me?" He took a wad of bills from his pocket, peeled off two twenties and a ten, and tossed them on the ground. "I'm making an exception. Consider yourself paid," the German said, then turned and walked away.

Ralph Angel knelt in the muddy grass, which was still wet with morning dew. He gathered the bills. Across the pond, morning fog had burned away, revealing storm-ravaged woods. Leafless branches, splintered tree trunks, underbrush littered with trash from the surge. At last, Ralph Angel stood up and walked to his car. He laid his head on the wheel. He felt himself falling through the blanket of damp leaves and steamy humus; through the horizons of loam, through clay and bedrock, and finally, through the fire.

OCTOBER

23

🌾 Still warm the first week of October. But it was the light, Charley thought, that had changed more than anything. Every edge was crisper, as if she were seeing the world through a freshly washed window. She loved how the sunlight cartwheeled through the leafy canopy along the Old Spanish Trail, how it made the cane fields glisten, so green now they looked to Charley like money in the bank. The seasons were changing, the light confirmed; grinding was about to begin. Which only made Charley more anxious to be finished, more desperate to get the tractor fixed and the men paid so she could be done with planting. She was almost there; just one hundred acres to go. Almost across the finish line. But they couldn't move forward in a real way, Charley knew, until *The Cane Cutter* sold at auction. Even if it sold for half what she knew her father had paid, she'd have most of the money she needed.

Late Thursday afternoon now, and as Charley turned into the Quarters she saw Micah and Blue waiting on the corner. They ran alongside her car, shrieking and laughing and waving pieces of paper, all the way down the block to Miss Honey's. She'd barely pulled the keys from the ignition before Micah pushed a flyer through the car window.

"It's for the Sugarcane Festival," Micah said, gasping. "It's only here until Sunday. Please, Mom. Please, please, please say we can go."

Downtown, on the nicer end of Main Street, Charley had noticed, in a back-of-the-brain sort of way, every marquee and billboard boldly announced, "Hey, Sugar!" or "Thank You, Sugar!" Now she knew why.

"There's a boat parade on the bayou," Micah added, trying to close the sale. "We can meet Queen Sugar."

"Yeah," Blue chimed in, barely able to stand still. His little body vibrated like a small pot on the brink of bubbling over.

"Queen Sugar," Charley said, trying to imagine. She handed the flyer back to Micah. "I wish I could, sweetheart, but—"

"I know, I know. Don't tell me," Micah said. "You have to work on the farm."

"That's right."

"But you promised we'd spend more time together," Micah said, bright tears pooling. "Why did you say that if you didn't mean it? I hate when you do that. You're such a liar." She tore the flyer to pieces and ran around the side of the house.

Blue clapped his hand over his mouth and stared at Charley.

"Yes, I know, sweetheart. She said a bad word." Charley gathered the pieces of flyer, then put her hand on Blue's slim shoulder. "Go inside. We'll be there in a sec."

Micah, thankfully, had not gone far. In her garden, using one of Miss Honey's old hoes, she hacked at the weeds around the lone soccer-ball-size pumpkin that had survived the storm. With every swing, she gave a small, furious grunt.

"Micah." Charley stepped closer then paused. She wouldn't lecture. She wouldn't press. Instead, she grabbed a rake and gathered the grass and weeds into a pile.

"I don't need your help."

But Charley kept raking. "A couple more weeks, it'll be perfect for Halloween," she said.

"Leave me alone. I told you. I can do this by myself."

"Sweetheart." Charley knelt beside the pumpkin and brushed dirt off the coarse orange skin, warm after a full day in the sun. She felt the urge to draw the pumpkin to her and let the heat seep into her bones. "I'm sorry. I know this is hard. Just give me—"

Micah stopped hoeing and glared at her. Then, without another word, she raised her hoe and chopped the pumpkin to bits.

By Los Angeles standards, the carnival was almost shabby with its rickety rides and crummy gaming booths and shady food stalls lining the perimeter. But there was something about it, too—the sound of folks screaming as the roller coaster clattered over the tracks, the bells ringing, the buzzers at the shooting range wheezing, the smell of funnel cakes and fried crawfish tails—that felt like pure magic, and Charley thought again, *yes*, this was exactly the distraction she needed.

She had not seen this many people in one place since she'd arrived in Saint Josephine. Teenagers moved about in clusters, laughing too loudly. Thin young men and their plump, soft-armed wives pushed strollers loaded with the oversize plush toys they won at the ring toss. A hodgepodge of people, black and white, Asian and Latino. Charley loved the rich mix of their voices, the lilting, sensuous phrases and singsong dialects. It was as though she were meandering through a tropical garden, a riot of color and sound, and she was grateful to be able to claim south Louisiana with its strange and extraordinary people.

Charley was Blue and Micah's age, maybe younger, the last time she went down a giant carnival slide, but she stepped into the burlap sack and scooted forward on her rear end anyway; and when Blue declared he would beat them to the bottom, Charley raised the stakes and said the winner got to choose the next ride; and all of a sudden, she wanted to win more than anything. And maybe it was because so many people had used the burlap sack before her that its coarseness had been worn away, or maybe it was because the slide was freshly waxed, but the speed took Charley by surprise and she screamed at the top of her voice. Micah and Blue screamed too, and Micah swore in French, which Charley heard but didn't scold her for because it was all in good fun and hilarious besides. At the bottom, they laughed so hard Charley almost wet her pants and they forgot to declare a winner, and then Charley tore three more tickets from the roll and said, "Who wants to go again?" Eventually, though, as the evening wore on, Charley surrendered: no more rides that spun or twisted or flipped. "I'll get the food," she said, and agreed to meet the kids at the exit from the Tilt-A-Whirl.

The crawfish pie line was the longest, which meant, she hoped, their food was the best. Charley listened to the conversations around her as she waited. Behind her, a couple argued about how they'd stretch their Christmas budget and still get their car fixed. One person ahead of her, Charley watched a man carry a small girl on his shoulders while doing his best to hold the hands of two little dark-haired boys. The boys were Blue's age—five or six—and just like Blue, they couldn't stand still. Charley noticed how patient and gentle the man was as the line inched forward. He didn't scold the little boys when they kicked up dust with their cowboy boots; he didn't raise his voice at the little girl when she whined that she was getting hungry. Charley was tempted to tell him how nice it was to see a father take time with his children.

"Y'all want to get something for your mama?" the man asked. "What would she like?"

His voice was steady and warm and strangely familiar. How did she know that voice? Charley watched as they stepped up to the window; how, with one easy movement, the man swung the little girl down from his shoulder; how he peeled the boys' small hands off the ledge as they tried to peer into the booth as he placed his order, which took a while, since the little boys kept changing their minds. Finally, the man stepped aside.

"I beg your pardon," he said, apologizing to the man standing behind him, and when he looked back, Charley saw his face. It was Remy.

For a moment, neither spoke.

Charley stared at Remy while the children squirmed and the woman at the window shouted for people to pick up their orders. Then Remy seemed to draw himself up, discomfort replacing the surprise in his expression.

"Hello, Charley."

"Remy," Charley fumbled. "I didn't see you—I mean, I'm surprised— what are you—"

The man in front of Charley placed his order.

"Step up, please," said the woman at the window. "Who's next? Please, ma'am, step up to the window or move to the side so the people behind you can order." Charley heard the woman, but didn't move until Remy took her gently by the elbow, easing her out of line.

"How've you been?" He held her elbow for a moment longer than he needed to, then released her, but it was enough to remind Charley of the way he'd held her at Paul's Café.

Charley blinked. "How've I been?" *Not so good. Terrible, in fact. Don't get me started.* "I'm okay—I mean, I'm fine—busy." She looked down at the boys, then back at Remy. "How are you?"

"Good," Remy said. The boys started bickering and he ruffled their soft curls. "Y'all stop fooling around and say hello to Miss Charley." He patted their heads. "This is Trevor and this is Braxton." The little girl yanked Remy's pant leg and he lifted her onto his shoulders again. She held on by a tuft of his hair, which was longer than Charley remembered. "And this is Annabel."

"I'm four," Annabel said, holding up her small hand. She had olive skin like her brothers, and her hair was divided into two long braids.

"Four years old means you're a big girl," Charley said. She smiled at the boys. If Remy said these children belonged to his new girlfriend, even though he was entitled to date whomever he wanted and she was the one who dumped him, Charley knew she would have to excuse herself politely and walk away. Her heart squeezed a little as she held her breath and waited for him to say more. But he didn't. "So," she floundered.

Remy hesitated. "Y'all getting through planting okay?" He looked thinner, tired. But that easy way—it practically rose off his body like vapor.

"More or less," Charley said. Thought, *More like less.*

The woman at the window called Remy's order. He ignored her. "That's good. You're lucky." He seemed genuinely relieved. "Lot of farmers lost half of what they planted."

"Lucky. Yeah, that's me." Charley looked away. "And you? How are you doing? How are your fields?"

"I'm okay," Remy said. He paused and they looked at each other across the awkward silence. "Hey, look. There's something I want to—"

But the woman at the window was calling again—angrily, this time—and Remy reluctantly stepped forward. Charley watched as he handed drinks to the boys, balanced the food tray in one hand and clasped Annabel's ankle with the other. Wobbling, he turned back to her, gesturing to his full load. "I'd better go. It's good to see you, Charley." He tried to smile. "Tell Mr. D. I said hello."

Charley stepped aside so Remy could pass. "You, too," she said, and forced herself to watch as he moved through the crowd, looking, with Annabel on his shoulders, like a stilt figure in a parade, the two boys following behind. She hoped he would turn around. Just one glance to show the door was still open. But he didn't. The woman at the window called for another pickup, and Charley realized she'd never ordered, and now the line for crawfish pies stretched on forever.

Pulling up to Miss Honey's, Charley's mind raced with all the things she could have said, *should* have said, to Remy: that while she didn't like what he'd said—no, she didn't like it at all—she'd been too quick to judge. Because who in this life was perfect? Who said everything right, *did* everything right all the time?

"Bedtime," she said, turning off the ignition. "No fooling around. Lights out in ten minutes." The words came out in the sharp tone of a drill sergeant. "Blue, honey, you can sleep in one of my T-shirts. And don't forget to brush your teeth." When no response came from the backseat, Charley turned to look and saw that both kids were asleep. Micah slumped against the door with her mouth hanging open. In the plastic bag in her lap, the goldfish she won at the Ping-Pong toss swam in frantic circles. Blue, curled up like a kitten beside her, clutched his bag of cotton candy now crushed to a hard pink wad the size of a baseball.

Charley came home the next evening and stopped short when she stepped into the kitchen. At one end of the table, Blue sprinkled bread crumbs into the coffee can he'd converted into a fishbowl, and at the other, Violet, yes Violet, helped Micah frost a cake shaped like a crawfish. For a moment, Charley just stood and looked.

"You should have seen how high up we were," Micah was saying. She dipped her spatula into a bowl of red frosting. "And then they dropped us. I almost barfed."

At the sink, Miss Honey scowled. "Barfed?"

Violet wiped food coloring off her hands. "That's California talk for vomit, Mother."

"Hallelujah!" Charley walked around the table and hugged Violet tightly, whispered, "Welcome back," in Violet's ear.

"We'd better hurry, Micah," Violet said when she and Charley let go. "Judging starts in an hour and we still have to decorate the base. And Blue, baby, that's enough bread crumbs. You're gonna kill that little fish."

"Judging for what?" Charley said.

"The baking contest," said Violet. "You can bake anything, long as you use Louisiana sugar. I told Mother she should make her pralines."

"And I told Violet, baking contests are for white ladies," Miss Honey said.

"Micah, don't listen to your great-grandmother." Violet opened the festival guide. "It says here, 'community invited,' Mother. That means you."

"Say what you want, Violet, but I've seen those garden club ladies with their matchy-matchy suits and not one of them is black."

"Grandmother Lorna wears matchy-matchy suits," Micah said.

"I don't say anything about joining, Mother," Violet said. "Besides, once they see Micah's crawfish cake, they won't care if she's green with purple stripes."

"Keep living, Violet," Miss Honey said. "You'll see what I'm talking about." And though her tone was harsh as always, Charley saw Miss Honey smile after she spoke and knew that for all her blustering, Miss Honey was happy Violet was back.

Violet turned to Charley. "How about we take the kids to the boat parade after we drop off Micah's cake? It starts at seven." She leaned closer. "Then you and I can go to the *fais do-do* on the plaza. Jimmy Broussard Jr. comes on at nine."

All along Main Street for as far as Charley could see, green sugarcane stalks tied with bright red bandannas festooned every light post and telephone pole. At Beads and Baubles, the Dew Drop, and the other boutiques lining the square, proprietors had decorated their big picture windows with shiny red wagons, hay bales, and scarecrows dressed in overalls and straw hats looking neater than most farmers in town. Even the side streets were packed with people. Zydeco music blared from the speakers in the plaza, and over at Evangeline's, Saint Josephine's fanciest restaurant, the bartender handed out free frozen margaritas from a sidewalk bar. The sky above the bayou glowed pink from all the spotlights and the sun dropping down to make way for evening.

Charley, Violet, and the kids fell in with the throngs. They staked out a spot near the drawbridge just as the boat parade began, and watched as old wooden pirogues, motor boats, and party barges trimmed with colored streamers and strings of lights, their reflection on the water like a thousand fallen stars, drifted down the bayou. Along the banks, where people's backyards opened onto the water, folks cheered and hurled fistfuls of candy at the boats.

The last boat was a slick, double-decker cabin cruiser. As it approached, everyone cheered louder, and Charley couldn't figure out why until she saw Queen Sugar and her court—all young white women dressed in heels and baby-doll dresses, their legs perfectly tanned— smiling their biggest debutante smiles and waving giddily from the deck. This was the best day of their lives, their smiles seemed to say. Queen Sugar wore a massive crown of green rhinestones fashioned into a ring of sugarcane stalks, and as she passed the spot where Charley, Violet, and the kids stood, she waved with one hand and pressed the other to her head to keep her crown from toppling.

"That's quite a crown," Charley shouted over the cheering.

"Honey, that's nothing," Violet shouted back. "Last year, the Shrimp Queen from Cameron wore a crown that was twenty-four inches tall. Must have weighed five pounds. It's like they say, 'the smaller the town, the bigger the crown.'"

For all the excitement, Blue couldn't care less, it seemed. For most of the parade, he searched the ground for loose candy and stuffed it in his pockets. But when Queen Sugar waved again and blew a kiss, Micah waved back, her face bright, then she leaned over the rail and pointed her camera.

Half an hour later, the boats had circled around and were chugging back toward the drawbridge. Charley looked at Micah's narrow back as Micah studied the Polaroids she'd taken of Queen Sugar, and thought she'd grown strangely quiet.

"So what do you think of all this?" Charley said. "Is this what you wanted to see?"

Micah looked up from her pictures. "They'd never let me be Queen Sugar here, would they?"

Let? Charley's heart sank. Why, in God's name, hadn't she seen this coming? She looked out at the bayou where the cabin cruiser, with its streamers and strings of lights, was gliding past. Couldn't there have been at least *one* black girl on that boat?

"Child, you don't miss a thing, do you?" Violet said.

Charley laid her hand on Micah's shoulder. "Some things take a long time to change. But you know, you'd make a great Queen Sugar."

"That's right," Violet added, defiantly. "With all you got going for you? By the time you're seventeen, you'll be a terrific Queen Sugar, if that's what you want. You'll knock 'em dead."

Micah sighed. She sifted through her stack of Polaroids again, then flicked the picture of Queen Sugar over the rail. They all watched it flutter down to the water and disappear under the drawbridge.

On the stage, as strobe lights pulsed and trumpets blared and drums rolled, Jimmy Broussard Jr. adjusted his cowboy hat, flipped his long black braids over his shoulder, and stepped to the microphone. "Are you ready?" he shouted, and the crowd erupted in applause. Broussard waved his hand toward the audience like he was sprinkling holy water, then, as the band launched into song, the guitar and horns, harmonica and accordion wound up the melody, he attacked the washboard hanging from his broad brown shoulders, raking spoons over its corrugated ridges. Within seconds, everyone on the plaza was dancing. Violet grabbed Blue and spun him 'round. Charley dipped Micah then kissed her sweaty cheek. And when it seemed as though the energy level couldn't go any higher, the crowd couldn't get any more excited, Broussard dropped his washboard and shimmied, gyrating and shaking his high firm behind as the guitar player strutted across the stage.

As the next song began, everyone switched partners. Charley danced with Violet and Micah danced with Blue.

"I didn't know you had all this in you," Charley shouted.

"Just 'cause I'm a preacher's wife doesn't mean I can't get funky." Violet broke out a dance move involving quick pelvic thrusts that made Charley clutch her sides, she laughed so hard. Which was why she wasn't paying attention when Remy Newell stepped up and asked Violet if he could cut in.

This time, there was nothing reserved or uncertain about Remy. He looked directly into Charley's face, and then down into the depths of her soul, where she had stuffed every bit of hurt and pain and disappointment and even the self-loathing, and it was as though he saw it all and wasn't afraid of any of it. He took her hand and guided her deeper into the crowd. And just as at Paul's Café, he placed his hand on the small of her back and pulled her into him, leading her through the music.

"You've been practicing," Remy said.

"No, I just had a good teacher."

And that was it. They didn't talk about farming or the coincidence of bumping into each other at the fair. They just danced.

Eventually, Violet appeared to say she was taking the children home. Micah looked from Remy to her mother. "Aren't you coming?"

"No, she's not," Violet said, before Charley could answer. "Your mother's staying out a while longer." She winked at Charley. "Just call when you're ready and I'll come back."

"I'll take you home," Remy said.

"Mom?"

"I won't be long," Charley managed.

"But *Mom*?"

And then it was just the two of them.

Across the plaza, in front of Evangeline's, Remy ordered two frozen margaritas and they found a spot on the curb.

"You must be a big fan of Jimmy Broussard to come all the way down here by yourself," Charley said, but it was the only thing she could think to say that sounded nonchalant, and not at all like someone who'd spent every last minute of the last twenty-four hours cursing herself and praying she'd have a chance to say what she should have said.

"He's my best friend," Remy said. "We were in college together. Those were his kids with me yesterday. He's got another one, but she's older. I'm their godfather."

"Your best friend's kids," Charley said, and felt the door swing open again.

A group of college boys, laughing loudly, stumbled out of the bar next door.

"Your daughter's beautiful," Remy said. "Looks just like you."

Charley smiled and said that if it weren't for Micah, she would have missed the entire festival. "She would have driven herself down here if I'd let her," Charley said, then added, "I haven't spent much time with her lately." She told Remy about Micah chopping up her pumpkin and how she threw her photo of Queen Sugar off the drawbridge.

Remy nodded. "It's hard with a farm. But don't worry. It'll be easier once grinding's over." He placed his hand on Charley's knee. "You're a great mother. The way y'all were dancing together, I could tell." Remy consulted his watch and stood up, saying, regretfully, "It's late. I should get you home."

The concert ended and people spilled out of the plaza onto the street. Police lights flashed, the sour odor of beer rose up from the asphalt, trampled cups and food wrappers littered the sidewalk, and Charley couldn't think of a place she'd rather be.

The porch light was on when Remy pulled up in front of Miss Honey's. He walked around and opened her door.

"It really is good to see you, California. Excuse me, I mean, Charley." He helped her down. "Maybe we could have lunch sometime, once grinding's over."

"Lunch. That would be nice. And really, California is okay."

"One last thing." Remy searched Charley's face. "I wanted to say it when I saw you yesterday." He took her hand. "I owe you an apology. For what I said. I wasn't thinking."

"It's okay."

"No. It's not. I was an ass."

"Yeah," Charley said, "you were. But then again, all men are."

They both laughed. How could they not?

Then Remy's smile faded. "But seriously, I'm sorry. I was a fool. I got to live with that." He stepped closer and kissed Charley. One light kiss on the corner of her mouth. "Well, good night."

"Good night," Charley said. "Thanks for the dance." Miss Honey's walk never seemed so long.

"California?"

Charley turned.

"See you soon."

Charley looked at Remy, standing by his truck looking wistful and forlorn. "I hope so," she said, and meant it.

. . .

In the den, Miss Honey sat in her recliner reading her Bible.

"What are you doing up?" Charley said.

"Waiting for Ralph Angel." Miss Honey took a moment to mark her page. "That job must be working him hard, 'cause he still ain't home."

"Must be."

"Violet said you bumped into a fella at the plaza."

"I did," Charley said. "Just a friend."

"Y'all hurry up!" Violet called, "or we won't get good seats!" It was only seven thirty in the morning. The sugarcane parade didn't start till ten. But yesterday evening after the concert, Charley noticed how people had already staked out their spots along Main Street, set out their folding chairs, assembled their Weber grills, and roped off sections of the sidewalk like a presidential motorcade was coming through. On the sprawling lawns of the stately mansions on East Main, the owners had already erected pristine white tents and set out rows of white wooden chairs, and black caterers in black aprons and white toques were unfolding tablecloths and arranging regiments of chafing dishes.

Charley had just dumped a second bag of ice in the cooler when there was a knock at the door. She and Micah got to the living room at the same time. Micah lunged for the knob. A young white woman stood on the other side of the screen. She wore a flowing white gown covered in pearls and Belgian lace, opera-length white gloves, and a crystal necklace with matching crystal earrings that dangled from her ears like a trail of stars. Her dark hair was swept into an elegant chignon. Charley recognized her crown. Now that she was close enough to get a good look at it, Charley appreciated the intricate design. Three rows of emerald rhinestones made up each sugarcane stalk. The leaves, also made of emerald rhinestones, bent gracefully, touching only at the tips, and were inlaid against a field of clear rhinestones so brilliant that the light bouncing off them cast tiny sparkles that shimmered and danced over Miss Honey's porch every time the girl moved her head.

"Good morning. My name is Ashleigh Marie Broussard," the young woman said, like this was the final round of pageant judging and it all came down to this moment. "I'm the reigning Queen Sugar. Does Miss Micah Bordelon live here?"

Micah gasped. For a moment, she couldn't speak. She gazed up at Queen Sugar. "I'm Micah."

Violet, more impatient than ever, came marching through the living room and up behind Charley. "Girl, why's it so quiet up here? I'm telling y'all we got to go if we want good seats. What's going—?" She stopped when she saw Queen Sugar. "Oh my Lord."

Queen Sugar smiled like Glenda the Good Witch. Somehow, she managed to balance her crown as she bent down to talk to Micah. "I'm here to see if you'd like to be my special guest in the Sugarcane Festival Parade. I'd like you to ride on my float and be an honorary member of my court."

Something like a squeal leaked from Micah's throat. She ran in a circle, then grabbed Charley's hand. "Oh, Mom, please, please say yes. Please say yes. *Please* say yes."

"Yes," Charley said. "Of course. Absolutely."

The Fifty-sixth Annual Saint Josephine Sugarcane Parade began at exactly ten o'clock. The Petite Shrimps, infants and toddlers dressed in tights and tutus, and seated in wagons pulled by their parents, led the way. Next came the junior cheerleaders with pom-pom balls tied to their white sneakers, backflipping and somersaulting in unison, followed by the Saint Josephine Rifle Club, the Boy Scouts, the baton twirlers, and the first-place winners of this year's 4H rabbit competition. And finally, here came Queen Sugar on the front of a float that looked like it was made of whipped cream. And beside her sat Micah, beaming.

Charley put her hand to her mouth, and for a moment, she could have sworn her heart would burst through her chest. She looked down at her hand and was surprised to discover that her fingers were wet from crying. But who cared? Because how often, really, do you get to see someone's dream come true? How often, on this great spinning ball where we're all just struggling to lead our tiny lives, do you get to see evidence of God's grace and know, the way you know your name, that at least for a little while, maybe just a few seconds, you can stop worrying, and take a deep breath, because things are all right? The float approached and Charley yelled Micah's name. Beside her, Violet waved and screamed, and Blue jumped up and down while Miss Honey, Coke in hand, looking proud and slightly amused, watched it all from the comfort of her folding chair. As the float approached, Micah looked down and saw Charley. She waved and grinned and blew a kiss. And then the float passed by and glided down the street, and it was just another small-town parade.

While Violet walked Miss Honey and Blue back to the car, Charley dumped the last of the cooler's ice in the gutter then went to fetch Micah from the staging area. Micah was waiting for her. She still wore the banner across her chest just like all the other princesses, and Charley knew it would be weeks before she would be able to pry it from Micah's shoulders.

"You ready?"

Together, they turned away from the rush of activity, people congratulating them as they passed. And that was when Charley saw Remy Newell across the parking lot, talking and then hugging Queen Sugar. "What's Queen Sugar's last name again?" Charley asked.

Micah frowned. "Broussard. Something like that."

Broussard. The singer down at the plaza—Remy's best friend. *He's got another one, but she's older. I'm their godfather.* She hadn't thought of it until now.

That night, no matter which way she turned, Charley couldn't find a comfortable position. She threw off the sheet, turned on the light, and was pacing the floor when—what was that? Remy's hat. The one he'd loaned her in those first days of planting. How could she have overlooked it all this time? It was practically begging her to go home.

. . .

"Ralph Angel? Is that you?" Miss Honey looked sleepy and startled.

"It's just me," Charley said. "I didn't mean to scare you." She set Remy's hat on the counter, stepped into the den. Miss Honey's Bible had fallen on the floor. Charley placed it back in her lap. "Go to bed. You won't get a good night's sleep in this chair."

"I'm fine." Miss Honey looked at her. "Where are you headed at this ungodly hour?"

"I need to deliver something. I won't be long."

At the edge of the cane fields down from Oaklawn Manor, Martin's Grocery was the shabby country store that, at first glance, looked more like a barn with its cypress doors flung wide. But the Drink Jax sign hanging out front and its shelves of Campbell's soup, condensed milk, Morton's salt, creamed corn, cane syrup, and toilet paper, plus the bottles of Jack Daniel's and Chivas Regal, the meat slicer, the Toledo scale, and the American flag were a signal to come in and sit a while. And if it weren't for Martin's Grocery, Charley never would have found the lane leading to Remy Newell's place. Would have driven right past it. But the little store was where she pulled off the road and bought a pack of gum, just to be polite, then asked the old Cajun who sat at the long wooden table playing chess with a young black man for directions.

"Remy Newell?" The old Cajun pushed his red hat back on his forehead. He glanced at the clock on the wall, and Charley knew he was wondering what she could want with Remy Newell at this time of night. He spoke French to the young black man, who moved his knight twice, lifted a pawn, then led her out to the weather-worn porch and in a sing-song accent she never got tired of hearing said, "You gotta go all the way to the end of this road and make a left. Another mile beyond that, make a right. He lives about half a mile down."

Charley got back in her car, and a few minutes later came upon a house tucked in among the trees, its windows four squares of soft yellow light hovering in the darkness. But it wasn't till she walked toward the house and noticed the pitched tin roof in silvery moonlight, and caught the fragrance of night-blooming jasmine, and stepped onto the porch of wide cypress planks, that Charley wondered if she was in the right place. Even in the dark, she saw it was no ordinary house. For a moment, she stood still, taking everything in: lanterns whose gas flames flickered quietly, red double doors with glass panes like slow-moving water, green shutters flanking windows that ran the length of the porch, potted ferns and a banana plant rising from an antique cane kettle. She got a pleasing sense of order and couldn't help but marvel at the man who would take that much care.

Charley knocked on the red door. She waited. And waited. And waited some more. And when no one answered, she stepped back and wondered what she must be thinking. What made her think Remy would be home on a night like tonight when there was so much fun to be had? He was probably at Paul's Café, dancing with someone who recognized a good man when she saw one. Charley could barely hold on to Remy's hat as she made her way down the steps. But rather than go back to her car, she took a chance and followed the gravel path around the side of the house. A lawn stretched out and away. Somewhere out there, the bayou was sliding past. She smelled it, heard it softly gurgling, felt a breeze rising like a whisper off the water.

One more step and Charley was at the back porch, which stretched the length of the house. Gaslights threw soft yellow light, an old fan circled lazily. And there was Remy, on a swing at the far end of the porch. His head was lowered, and Charley saw that he was reading. It was quiet, peaceful. She moved closer, out of the shadows.

"Remy?"

Remy looked up. He closed his book and stood. "Hello, California."

"I thought I should return this." She held up his hat.

"I was just missing that very hat." He lowered himself onto the swing. Patted the space beside him. "Come sit."

The steps creaked as Charley climbed them. The whole world seemed to be waiting.

In the yellow light, the wrinkles around Remy's eyes were more pronounced. His eyes were darker brown than she'd noticed before and there was still that calm in his presence, like the few seconds between one breath and the next.

Charley ran her finger over the hat's brim. "Thanks for what you did."

"You're welcome."

"It took me awhile to figure out. Broussard. Your best friend Jimmy's oldest daughter."

"The three little ones you met yesterday are his. Ashleigh's real daddy is white, but her mama divorced him when she was a baby. Jimmy's raised her since she was two years old. It was just a matter of asking."

"I can never repay you."

"You just did."

Charley looked down at Remy's hands. "What are you reading?"

Remy put the book in her lap. It was about Southern gardens. "I try to plant flowers that would have grown around here when this house was built," Remy said. "Out there at the base of all the trees—you can't see them now, of course, since it's dark—but a whole bunch of oxblood lilies are just coming up. Because of the hurricane and all."

"Of course," Charley said, because why wouldn't something as fragile as a lily come up after a storm? "I love what you've done here."

"I found this land on my twenty-fifth birthday and cleared it myself. Took me almost a year." He looked embarrassed. "A buddy of mine told me about this old house. It was abandoned, way out in the middle of a cane field, and the mill was about to tear it down. We dragged it over in pieces. It was built in the 1830s."

Charley shook her head in wonder.

"Would you like to see?"

"Now?"

"Why not?" Remy stood and offered his hand.

Charley closed the book and tucked it under her arm. Then Remy led her into the dimly lit central hall, where an antique clock ticked softly. He escorted her from room to room, drawing her attention to the framed landscape in the dining room, to a mahogany chifforobe from a New Orleans estate sale, to notches in the kitchen door frame where the previous owner stuck his cane knife after long days in the fields. With every step, Charley felt the outside world fall away.

"No television?"

Remy smiled. "Just a radio and a computer."

Charley laughed. "Micah would hate it here."

"But I just bought an iPod for my music," Remy said. "Tell the truth, I don't know how I lived so long without it."

"Well, maybe there's hope for you."

In the front hallway again, Charley marveled at the sepia portraits. The floorboards creaked as she walked.

"I love the sound of you walking on those old cypress boards," Remy said.

Charley tried to remember the last time she'd heard footsteps on old wood, any wood. "I didn't know wood sounded like anything."

"Oh sure," Remy said. "Every wood sounds different. It's like people; every type has a personality. But cypress sounds the best. When I built this place, I used the oldest boards I could find. Spaced them so they'd have room to talk."

Charley shifted her weight and the boards creaked. "What are they saying now?"

"They're saying—" Remy cocked his head. "They're saying, 'Don't blow it this time, Newell. Keep your mouth shut and maybe she'll give you a second chance.'"

"I bet she will," Charley said.

Remy crossed the hall. When he was standing right in front of her, Charley shifted her weight again. "What about now?"

He looked at her intently. "They're suggesting that I ask you if you'd like to see the second floor."

. . .

By the glow of a lamp, in a bed made a hundred years earlier, Charley ran her finger along the book's spine. "A book about gardens. Who'd have thought?"

Remy eased the book out of her hands. "That's enough." He turned it facedown on the floor. "I've read that book a hundred times. That's not what I'm interested in now."

"I bet you know those chapters by heart," Charley said.

Remy smiled. "I probably do."

"Well?"

Remy paused. He studied Charley's face to see if she was kidding, then he ran his finger along her shoulder. "'In the garden this season should be the climax of bloom. Rich in a beauty of its own.'" He kissed her neck. Then he stared at her.

Charley waited for him to say something about her dark skin, something predictable and disappointing. But he didn't. He just leaned closer.

"'After the intense heat diminishes, flowers revive.'" He unbuttoned her blouse. "'The grass is green again.'" He kissed her collarbone. "'Colors are deeper.'" He tongued her ear. "'We should make more of this season than we do.'" He kissed her mouth.

"Lovely," Charley whispered. Along the roads these last few days, she had seen crimsons and golds and coppers flare up like bursts of flame. How many names were there for red? Carmine, scarlet, rose? How long must one practice peeling back the petals of an oxblood lily? Charley put her hand on Remy's chest, where she felt the strong and steady *thunk* of his heart beating.

Remy ran his hand over her breasts. All around Saint Josephine Parish, the cane was finally standing tall, the stalks wavering in the faint breeze, the leaves glistening in the sun. He unzipped her pants, eased them off her. His hands roamed over her shoulders, her legs.

Charley closed her eyes. The blue-green ocean of cane, the fields of eager stalks pushing through the dark earth, offering themselves up for harvest. How much patience and tenderness was required to loosen the roots?

Remy slid his hand across her belly, traced the satiny stretch marks beneath her navel, and for a second, Charley's body seized, fearful that he would be repulsed.

But he was not. "Gorgeous." He leaned closer still, put his mouth on her pelvic bone.

"Remy," Charley said, but, overcome, couldn't say any more. Because who wouldn't be besotted with the quick color that flared up as suddenly as a flame? Who wouldn't be enchanted by the rivers of cane flowing across the dark, damp ground? Who could possibly resist the subtle stirrings of new growth or the glorious climax of fall?

24

❧ The mid-morning glare had turned the sky the color of weak tea, and Charley was late for mass. She was supposed to meet Denton and Alison for the Blessing of the Crops, half an hour ago, but Micah cornered her in the bathroom, blocked the door, and demanded to know where she'd spent the night.

"And don't tell me you were at Violet's, because I called."

"I was at the farm," Charley lied, taking extra time to floss so she wouldn't have to talk.

"Hollywood came by looking for you after the dance," Micah said. "I told him you were on a date."

Built in the mid-1800s, Our Lady of Perpetual Sorrows was the fourth-oldest church in Louisiana, and the largest building in Saint Josephine except for City Hall. It rose up from the center of the town square like a gigantic salt lick; although for a Catholic church, its design was decidedly understated: just a modest, two-story structure with a clock tower like stacked shoe boxes, the whole building covered with a layer of creamy-smooth plaster like fondant on a wedding cake. Still, if one was Cajun and had a little money under one's mattress, Our Lady was the church to belong to; the church where the daughters of all the rich cane farmers got married.

Charley waited in the rear of the sanctuary where the Knights of Columbus, half a dozen wizened old white men—one of whom appeared to be napping on his feet—adjusted their feathered hats and flipped their purple satin capes over their shoulders. They arranged themselves single file, then, on someone's cue, marched soberly down the aisle as if heading off to battle. When they reached the altar, they drew their swords, touching the blade tips together to form an arch through which

Charley expected the entire high school football team to come running.

"Sorry I'm late." Charley opened the gated pew and slid in next to Denton. "What did I miss?"

Alison, on the other side of Denton, leaned forward. "It's about time," he whispered loudly. "I didn't put on this monkey suit to sit here by myself."

Denton cut Alison a warning look, then handed Charley an order of service. "You look nice."

Coughs and shuffles rose up toward the cavernous ceiling. Charley recognized many of the farmers from the Blue Bowl and once again got the feeling that she was the only one who didn't know the secret password. "Is there a cane farmer in Saint Josephine who *isn't* Catholic?"

They stood as the priest and altar boys floated down the aisle, trailing a thick cloud of incense.

"Man, I wish they'd hurry up," Alison said, coughing and waving his hand.

"Quit complaining," Denton said. "This was your idea, remember?"

"Jesus Christ, Denton, can you blame me? I'd eat my shoe if it meant we'd pull through this."

Denton turned to Charley. "You sure you don't want us to come with you to New Orleans?"

According to Dupry, Brown & Associates, the auction house Charley chose, *The Cane Cutter* was worth forty-five thousand dollars and would likely fetch more. Denton's tone was relaxed, but his expression was less certain; as though he doubted she could pull this off.

"I'll be fine." Charley patted Denton's arm and offered a weak smile. When her father left the statue on her mantle, he hadn't left a note but she hadn't needed one. She knew what *The Cane Cutter* represented. It was more than a family heirloom; more than a rare piece of art. It symbolized generations of struggle and perseverance in the face of seemingly insurmountable odds. Yes, it told her family's story but it could just as well have told the story of any other family—black, white, brown, yellow, or whatever—whose forefathers (*and mothers*) had stayed the course. He'd meant for her to have it, to own it, to be inspired by it, and to pass it on. And here she was selling it like a quaint collectible at a tag sale. But grinding season started *tomorrow*. The auction was scheduled for Wednesday, three days from now, at one o'clock sharp. And the only way they'd know if her scheme worked, whether their ship would float or sink, would be if she followed through on her plan. Meanwhile, with the John Deere 4840 still out of commission, the crews were planting cane by hand. It was slow work, horribly inefficient, and the men seemed to be losing their morale. In three days, they'd planted only twenty acres. The 4840 would have covered four times as much ground. She had to sell or they were sunk.

The priest motioned for the congregation to sit, then welcomed everyone in the name of the Father, Son, and Holy Spirit. He wasn't so much thin as soft, with wisps of dull brown hair and oversize glasses that made him look gooberish. As he shook holy water over a bundle of cane stalks leaning against the wall, Charley wondered if his blessing would be powerful enough, because from where she sat, it looked like he'd have trouble asking for extra mayo on his sandwich.

"I'll call you as soon as it sells," Charley said, the thought of the auction once again making her insides churn.

Denton looked at her.

"What?" Charley said.

"You look different. Your skin's shiny."

"Shiny?" Charley touched her cheek, wondering whether Denton had picked up Remy's scent. Until a couple hours ago, a part of her still refused to believe she had spent the night with him. Even this morning, when the sun came up and she looked down into Remy's yard, where, indeed, bunches of oxblood lilies were erupting beneath the trees— even then she didn't believe it. Only when Remy walked her to her car and leaned in through the window to kiss her again did Charley know for sure.

Watching from the pew as Denton and Alison stood in line for communion, Charley sensed their anxiety—about the farm, about the future, about nature's hand in how well they did. They were like her, their fears were her fears, but they didn't show them. As she sat there, Charley said a prayer for her partners. *Lord, if you can hear me, please bless Mr. Denton and Alison, who have already done more for me than I could have ever asked for. Bless them and keep them strong.*

Outside, after the service, Alison lit a cigarette and tossed the match into the little cemetery where the first Acadian pioneers were buried. A fine layer of lichen coated the oldest vaults, which pitched sideways after decades of sinking into the soft ground.

"Well, thank God that's over," Alison said, smoke streaming through his nostrils. "I better get back before my grandkids set my neighbor's house on fire."

"You might want to take Highway 90 on the way back from New Orleans tomorrow," Denton said. "It's prettier than the interstate and it's not that much longer."

"I'll try to remember." Charley looked at Denton and thought he would be a better priest than that other guy. Even with uncertainty in his eyes, the way he held himself suggested an old battleship pushing through deep water. She dug through her purse until she found her checkbook, then scribbled a check for six thousand dollars. Now she was not only maxed out on her credit, she was officially broke. She folded the check and handed it to Denton. "That should take some of the pressure off. Tell the crews we'll square up in January after the numbers are in. There's enough there for you and Alison to pay yourselves, too."

Denton protested and tried to hand back the check.

"Absolutely not," Charley insisted. "In your wallet." She noticed, at the far end of the cemetery, a statue of the Virgin Mary that someone had vandalized. The side of the Virgin's shapely stone head had been bashed in; part of her face was missing. "I think maybe Alison was right."

"About what?"

"I thought the Blessing of the Crops would help, but I feel exactly the same." *Maybe worse.*

Denton leaned against the wrought-iron fence. "This is a long walk in a dark wood, Miss Bordelon. Don't psych yourself out just yet."

Back at Miss Honey's, Ralph Angel's car was parked along the gully. Inside, though, there was no sign of him. Micah and Blue, still in their church clothes, sat at the kitchen table eating large wedges of Micah's crawfish cake.

"I didn't win," Micah said, glumly.

"I'm sorry, sweat pea. I know how hard you worked." Charley kissed the top of Micah's head, then, in a moment of sheer zaniness, grabbed Micah's fork, broke off a chunk of cake, and stuffed it in her mouth, saying, "But now there's more cake for us."

Blue and Micah stared at her, then Micah said, "You're nuts," and smiled even as she rolled her eyes. And for the next few minutes, Charley sat at the table with the children, listening as they recapped the day's Sunday school lesson and trying not to think about Remy Newell or the auction.

"Y'all take your cake outside. I need to talk to your mama," said Miss Honey, stepping from the den into the kitchen. When the children were gone, she pulled out a chair and sat down—something she rarely did in the kitchen unless she was eating. She leaned in conspiratorially. "Ralph Angel is home." She tilted her head toward the back room.

"I saw his car."

"He's in a foul mood."

Charley thought, but did not say, *What else is new?* and instead patted Miss Honey's hand. As much as she wished she could sit longer, she had come home only long enough to change, then she needed to get out to the farm, check on how the crews were doing with planting.

"He's in a real bad place," Miss Honey said. "Worse than I've seen in a long time." Before Charley could ask, she added, "The boss let him go."

"Oh no." Even without the specifics, Charley knew what this meant: more sulking, more flare-ups, all of them walking on eggshells.

"Something about him being overqualified," Miss Honey said, rubbing her knuckles distractedly. "You know how that is. Some of these white folks don't like to see a black man get ahead." She looked at Charley for confirmation. "I knew something was wrong when he stopped coming home. I've been praying every night for the good Lord to keep him safe. You don't know how hard I've been praying."

Charley took Miss Honey's hand, which was warm and soft, like it had been marinating in buttermilk. "It'll all work out. Don't worry. You'll see." But when she started to rise, Miss Honey tightened her grip, and pulled her back down into the chair.

"I want you to give Ralph Angel a job."

"A what?"

"On your farm."

Charley dropped her grandmother's hand. "No. No, no, no, no. Bad idea."

"There's got to be something he can do, Charley." Miss Honey's tone seemed too controlled, too practiced. "Just to tide him over till he finds something else."

Charley pulled her hand away from Miss Honey's and stood. "I know you're worried. And don't get me wrong—I'd like to—it's just that—" She backed away from the table.

"Come back here. It's just *what*?"

"It's just." Charley took a breath and started over. "It's just, I can't even pay the men I've got. Even if I could pay Ralph Angel, he doesn't want to work for me. He doesn't *do* manual labor. He said so himself."

"What about a job in the office?"

Charley pictured the shop. The broken-down sofa, the piles of telephone books they hadn't had time to throw away, the refrigerator that sent a tingling current of electricity through her fingers every time she touched the handle. "There *is no* office." The suggestion was so absurd, she laughed before she could catch herself.

Miss Honey gave Charley the look she reserved for people who bumped into her shopping cart without apologizing. "You mean to tell me—you mean to tell me you got all those Mexicans and that crazy white man out there working for you and you can't find a way to help your own?"

"With what money?"

"You mean to tell me, you got your own flesh and blood right under this roof, and you can't find a way to lend a hand?"

"Miss Honey, please listen. Alison isn't working *for* me, he's one of my partners. He's made a huge investment. His time, his equipment." Charley felt her argument dissipate like smoke. Nothing she said would make sense now.

"Last spring when you called to say you were coming down here, you remember what I told you?"

Tears flooded Charley's eyes. "You offered to let us stay here. You said it was silly to rent a house when we had family."

"That's right. Family. This is about family. Ralph Angel is smart. All he needs is a chance. I know you can find something for him."

"Miss Honey, please. Things are tight. I'm on the verge of losing the farm." Charley took her checkbook out of her purse and flipped to the register. "Look. It says thirteen dollars. I just wrote Denton a check for the last of it. I'm broke."

Miss Honey drew herself erect. Her eyes bored into Charley. "'And the Lord said unto Cain, where is Abel thy brother? And he said, I know not. Am I my brother's keeper? And he said, what hast thou done? The voice of thy brother's blood crieth unto me from the ground.'"

Charley felt something slip inside her. "Maybe once grinding starts, if I need some extra help. That would be better."

"Charlotte Bordelon, I never thought I'd hear these things coming out of your mouth. That farm isn't just yours. Yes, Ernest bought it, and yes, he left it to you, but you're part of this family. Have I charged you rent?" Miss Honey leaned forward in her chair, but Charley could not speak. "When someone in a family needs help, it's up to everyone to see that he gets what he needs. I know Ralph Angel would do the same for you."

"*Thirteen dollars.* You're not listening. I don't have any money!"

Miss Honey stood up then. "I've heard everything I need to hear, and I'm telling you what you're going to do. You're going to find a job for your brother. I don't care if he digs ditches or scrapes cane kettles. He's coming to work for you until he gets back on his feet and you're going to find the money to pay him. And when we get finished with that, we're going to talk about giving him what is rightly his. If that takes till the end of grinding, if it takes the next ten years, then so be it."

The room, as far as Charley could tell, had tilted ninety degrees. Everything seemed to be sliding off its surface, crashing to the floor. Cabinet doors swung open, dishes tumbled, and silverware flew from the drawers, and Charley almost reached for the salt and pepper shakers to hold them in place. She swore she couldn't hear her own voice for all the noise, but when she looked around again, the room was quiet. Just the soft whirring of the ceiling fan, the steady dribble of water from the faucet.

"You can't force me to do this," Charley said, still dazed. "And anyway, the trust imposed restrictions on who can own it."

Miss Honey pointed an indicting finger. "'And now art thou cursed from the earth,'" she said. "'When thou tillest the ground, it shall not henceforth yield unto thee her strength; a fugitive and a vagabond shalt thou be in the earth.'"

The counter was littered with vegetable scraps. Charley stared at Miss Honey's broad, silent back, listened to the hiss from her skillet. Outside, Micah and Blue screamed as they played hide-and-seek and Charley knew they were still high on all the cake they'd eaten. They would run through the woods for an hour and come back panting and spent and hungry all over again.

Charley threaded her belt through the loops of her jeans. "I'm going to work," she said. "I won't be back till late."

"We're having pork chops," Miss Honey said. "I'll leave yours on the stove."

Charley recognized the gesture. Food was love. Food was Miss Honey's weapon, her sword and her shield. Charley knew she could accept the olive branch, and put the whole incident behind her; she could surrender, hire Ralph Angel, and in turn, receive the nourishment she'd come to cherish and crave.

Or she could reject it.

"No, thank you," Charley said, coolly. "I won't be hungry." She wouldn't eat Miss Honey's cooking if someone paid her. Not tonight, not for lunch tomorrow, not as leftovers later this week.

Miss Honey flinched, almost imperceptibly. She stirred something in the skillet and the hiss flared into a roar. "Then I guess you'd better go on."

Charley was still shaken when she pulled up to Violet's church, and for a few minutes she just sat staring at the words TRUE VINE BAPTIST CHURCH, which were painted over FRANK'S STICK 'N STEIN. Violet said the place used to be an old pool hall, Charley recalled, and she surveyed the row of dilapidated storefronts. Taped to the door, a piece of poster board meant to function as a marquee read TODAY'S SERMON: DON'T BLOCK YOUR BLESSINGS!

Charley stepped out of her car and leaned against the hood. Soon, the door swung open, piano music wafted out to the street, and a handful of people streamed onto the sidewalk trailed by Violet, stunning in her bright yellow dress and hat like a Victorian lampshade.

"Oh, my Lord, would you look who's here." Violet strode over to Charley and seized her hand. "What's going on? I can tell by your face this isn't a social call."

Charley leaned forward and buried her face in her hands. She told

Violet about deciding to auction off *The Cane Cutter*, about writing Denton her last check, about her blow-up with Miss Honey.

"I can't work with him," Charley said. "I know he's my brother, but he's—"

"Combative? Erratic? Manipulative? Has an inflated sense of his own worth?"

"I'll take door D, Monty, all of the above," said Charley. "She wants me to give him a share of the farm, but she doesn't understand I'm not allowed to. Either it's mine or it goes to charity. Some legal thing."

"So you get to support Ralph Angel while he works. Or, more likely, doesn't."

Charley's eyes filled. "Yes. And Miss Honey is angry. She quoted a lot of scripture. I think she put a hex on the farm."

"Girl, Mother always quotes scripture. She'd quote scripture in front of the Supreme Court if she thought it would help her win her case."

"Yeah, but she quoted that passage about being your brother's keeper. That last part about being a vagabond on the land was creepy."

"Hmmm." Violet went quiet for a moment, and Charley could practically see her scanning the biblical reference book she had in her head— it was the same edition Ralph Angel owned. Her lips moved as though she were reading to herself, her soft mumbling growing steadily louder. "'A fugitive and a vagabond shalt thou be in the earth,'" Violet said. "Oh. I see what you mean. Most people leave out that last part." She nodded, reverentially. "Mother's good."

"So I'm cursed?"

"Who can say for sure? This *is* Louisiana."

"Violet, you're not helping."

"I'm sorry, darling, but this one has me stumped. I have to say, I don't envy you." Violet gave her arm an encouraging pat. "Don't worry. You've managed to get this far, you'll figure something out. I have faith in you."

Just before Charley pulled away, she had a thought and rolled down her window. "How come you don't have a Blessing of the Crops service here?" she said. "Because if you did, I promise I'd come." She gazed again at Violet's church with its hand-painted sign and poster board taped to the door. Violet looked up and down the street and sighed. "'Cause none of our members own any crops to bless, I suppose."

Mr. Guidry's tiny shack was tucked far back in the woods, back beyond the dam where the local high school kids smoked pot and blasted the Black Crows from their car stereos, past the POSTED sign and the little lake covered with a thick quilt of algae, and standing on Mr. Guidry's creaky porch where every other cypress board was missing, Charley thought only a fool would venture this far back in the woods by herself with no invitation and no idea what to expect. How she'd found Mr. Guidry's still confounded her, but she had, just where Violet said it would be. "This is going to sound crazy," Violet had called to say, not long after Charley got home from her church, "but, there's an old man, a *traiteur*."

"What do you mean, a *traiteur*?"

"A healer."

"As in *voodoo*?" Charley had held the phone away from her ear. "You're right. You do sound crazy. I'm desperate, Violet, but I'm not *that* desperate."

"Now, hold on. Just hear me out before you say no. It's not voodoo. *Traiteurs* do good things like heal snakebites and get rid of warts and cure colicky babies, but they do other things too. Mother used to go to Mr. Guidry. Swore by him. I don't even know if he's still alive, but it's worth a try."

Now Charley knocked on Mr. Guidry's door—just one knock—and when he answered, she stood facing a blackberry-colored, rheumy-eyed man no taller than Micah, and older, it seemed, than time. Charley almost turned and ran. But Mr. Guidry invited her in as though he'd been expecting her, and before she knew it, she found herself sitting on an old wooden stool in a corner of his one-room cabin.

"You're a Bordelon," Mr. Guidry said. "I remember your daddy." He was soft-spoken and frail, but moved about the cabin with relative ease.

Charley watched as he pulled herbs and feathers, dried chicken feet and scraps of leather from dusty bottles on the shelf beneath his window.

"You knew my dad?"

Mr. Guidry nodded. "Long time ago."

He laid all the objects on the table, then rubbed each of them while he muttered an incantation, and when he finished, he touched his hand to Charley's forehead. What she felt was something between falling and flying. She wasn't sure when he removed his fingers, but when she opened her eyes, he presented her with a necklace—just a piece of string, really, with nine equally spaced knots—which she let him tie around her neck. Violet said he'd refuse to take any money and would even consider a thank-you unnecessary, so Charley shook his hand and offered him the fig cake she'd baked. She was already through the woods when she realized he'd never asked her why she'd come—he seemed to know— and that she'd forgotten to ask what he'd done for her father.

25

❦ Standing under a sky that had yet to break, Charley marveled at how different the air smelled. Mixed in with the usual mildew and damp earth was a carbony sweetness, and Charley knew that from this day forward she would always associate mid-October with the smell of burnt sugar. She took a final swig of coffee, dumped the rest in the bushes, screwed her thermos cap on tight, and crossed Miss Honey's yard, her breath pluming in a small cloud of white vapor, the frost on the grass crunching under her boots. In the car, she turned on the radio. And the heater. Mornings were cold now, and while the car warmed up, Charley listened to the first few minutes of *Morning Edition*. Sluggish economic growth, congressional logjams, unrest in the Middle East. Nothing ever changed.

Two minutes later, the car was toasty. Charley honked, then honked again, and was about to get out, when Ralph Angel tripped down the front steps carrying his shoes.

"Sorry," he said, sheepishly, sliding into the passenger seat. "I was looking for my gloves."

Charley threw the car into drive. "Let's just go."

By the time they reached the drawbridge, night was peeling away from the horizon, amethyst and plum replaced by a rising line of tangerine light. Fog swirled across the asphalt. The bayou was the blue-gray of a Confederate coat.

Ralph Angel rode in silence, which was fine with Charley. He looked out the window and picked at a blister on his hand. But every once in a while, he seemed to hear something on the radio that troubled him and he stared at the dashboard as though the announcer had insulted him personally.

"You'll be on Romero's crew," Charley said, not because she wanted to talk, but because once they got to the fields, there wouldn't be time to explain.

Ralph Angel looked over at her.

"His men work fast," Charley continued. "It'll be hard to keep up."

"Gotcha."

"And you'll want to keep your jacket on all day, even when it gets warmer. Those cane leaves will slice you up if you're not careful."

Ralph Angel reached into the well and lifted a book to the window. "*The Southern Gardener*." He flipped the pages, bending them slightly at the corners.

Charley cringed. He may as well have been rifling her underwear drawer. "Careful with that," she said, "it's not mine," and practically snatched the book from him.

Even in the near-darkness Charley could tell, by the height of the headlights and the rhythm of their bounce, that the approaching vehicle was a tractor. As they got closer, she saw that it pulled an enormous V-shaped trailer loaded to the top with cane. Stalks jutted through the metal rails and spilled over the sides. Charley slowed. "Will you look at that?" Gazing up at the creaking wagon, Charley couldn't help but smile. It was the second sign, after the burnt-sugar smell, that grinding season had officially begun.

When the tractor passed, Charley touched the necklace Mr. Guidry gave her, fingering each of the nine tiny knots.

"Where'd you get that?" Ralph Angel asked.

"It's nothing."

"Please tell me you don't believe in all that hoodoo shit."

Charley pressed the necklace to her throat. "It can't hurt," she said, her mind drifting back to the dark woods. Maybe she was imagining things, but she felt different—still anxious about their chances, still nervous about how much *The Cane Cutter* would sell for, knowing that it was her last hope, still furious with Miss Honey—but there was a quiet calmness too, one that had not been there before, as though a co-coon, loose and silky, had been spun around her.

Ralph Angel rolled his eyes.

"You only break when the cane wagon is empty and goes to reload," Charley said. And since she was at it, added, "You have an hour for lunch," and thought of the plate covered in tinfoil—last night's pork chops—still on the stove where Miss Honey left it for her. She would ask Denton to pick up an extra sandwich if he went into town.

"Aye, aye," Ralph Angel said and saluted. "No breaks unless the wagon is empty; an hour for lunch; clock out at seven."

If she weren't so angry with Ralph Angel, Charley thought, his response just now would be funny. Which is what Ralph Angel must have thought too, because he smiled to himself, and Charley felt a quick softening around the edges of her disgust. From the corner of her eye she watched Ralph Angel slip his hands into his gloves. They were extra large and looked cartoonish on his hands.

"It was the only size left," Charley said. "One of the guys might trade with you."

Ralph Angel shook the gloves into his lap, and for the next mile, they rode with just the radio playing, until Charley glanced over and said, "When I told Miss Honey I didn't want to hire you, you know it wasn't personal, right?"

Ralph Angel looked at Charley. His expression was cold. "Every-thing's personal," he said, then turned to the window.

At the shop, Denton and Alison had built fires in two empty oil drums and the crews huddled around them, warming their hands as the flames licked their fingers. Charley saw half a dozen new faces, men Denton recruited back in July, in addition to Romero and his crew. She introduced herself, asked the new men's names, what towns they were from, and welcomed them to her farm.

"You ready?" Denton zipped his jacket. He stopped, puzzled, when he saw Ralph Angel.

"I'll explain later," Charley said, though she still hadn't decided what she'd say.

"Hey, Denton," Alison called, the first cigarette of the day bobbing from his lips. "Why're we standing around?"

"Take it easy."

"I can't help it. First day of grinding always gets me fired up. Feel like a damned jitterbug."

Denton called for everyone to gather 'round and mapped out the day. Romero's men would keep planting while he, Alison, and Charley drove the tractors and the combines through the fields that were ready for harvesting. The new guys would replenish the planting wagons and haul the cut cane to the mill.

"Bayonne is taking four hundred tons a day," Denton announced. "We got eight cane wagons, but we really need ten. That means we got no time to waste. Longer that cane sits once it's cut, more likely it goes sour. Got to keep things moving. It's all got to flow." He reached into an old duffel bag, doled out walkie-talkies, and told the men to check in on the hour. "Questions? Anyone got anything they want to say?"

"Yeah." Alison raised his hand and stepped forward. "As some of you know, I ain't too high on organized religion." He glanced at Charley and Denton. "The Lord hasn't exactly been good to me these last few years, but that's beside the point. I think we should say a prayer, just to be safe. I'll lead it if you want."

All heads bowed.

"Gracious Lord," Alison began. "You know if there's ever been a sadder group of folks just trying to do what's right, it's this group of misfits right here. Why Miss Bordelon came down here and teamed up with us two old goats continues to be a mystery. But if you want my opinion, I think we done a pretty freaking good job pulling her farm together. The way I see it, we got a chance of bringing in a decent crop. So Lord, I'm asking you to cut us a break. You don't have to perform any miracles or nothing, though that'd be nice. All I'm asking is that you let us do what we do best, what each of us was born to do. Let us be the best damn cane farmers we can be. Help us get to the end of this grinding season, and maybe even live to do it all again this time next year. Oh, and stick close to Miss Bordelon when she goes to New Orleans tomorrow. Amen."

Amen.

The sun had risen in earnest, the fog lifting off the fields to reveal a carpet of solid green so thick Charley couldn't see between the rows. In the combine, she fingered the knots on her necklace and waited for the signal. Another minute, and the walkie-talkie on the dashboard crackled—*Jose to Missus. One-two-three.* Through the window, she gave Jose the thumbs-up, turned the ignition, and the combine lurched forward, the massive scrolls on its front end slowly turning. Down on the ground, cane stalks trembled. The machine moved forward, chewing through the rows. She made sure to stay a few feet ahead of Jose's tractor so that the combine was in line with the cane wagon he pulled as they moved along the row. Choppers inside the combine stripped leaves from stalks and cut the cane into billets, carrot-size pieces that traveled up the conveyor belt into a chute that spat them into the cane wagon. As Charley drove, shredded leaves and dirt fell around her like rain.

In an hour, the first two cane wagons were full. Jose pulled the tractor onto the headlands and waited for a driver to unhitch him. In the combine, Charley's walkie-talkie sputtered, then Denton's voice came in clear. He was sending Huey Boy out to relieve her.

"But I'm fine. I've got a rhythm going out here."

"Okay, but I thought you'd want to be the one to haul the first load to the mill."

Set back from the road, the Bayonne Sugar Mill was a jumble of geometric shapes—triangular warehouse roofs, cylindrical smokestacks, boxy square buildings housing the boilers and evaporation tanks, parallel rows of bulging cane wagons waiting in the yard to be unloaded. In

Pittsburgh or Milwaukee, a mill like Bayonne Sugar would have closed years ago, dismantled and shipped piece by piece to Cuba or Santo Domingo, or converted into a sprawling indoor shopping mall with a food court and a metroplex. But this was Louisiana, and Bayonne Sugar was the largest, most powerful sugar mill of them all. *Take that, Landry and Baron!* Smoke and steam billowed from the stacks while the windows in the main building glowed orange as *bagasse*, the shredded cane pulp, burned. The air vibrated with the muffled roar of furnaces and the drone of gears turning. Twenty-four hours a day, from now through the end of the year, Bayonne Sugar would roar and growl and hiss until it pulverized, ground, and boiled every stalk of cane to crystal.

A convoy of trucks and tractors hauling cane stretched a quarter mile down the road, and Charley, strapped into the passenger seat of the bull-nose semi, smelled burning sugar even through the closed windows. She rolled hers down and inhaled deeply, not caring that she drew some of the white ash falling like fine snow into her lungs. She had dreamed of this day, this moment. For the first time she saw the true connection, saw the chainlike links of iron between herself, her father, and grandmother, and their fathers' fathers before that. She was bound to this place, this small patch of earth; it was she and she was it. She thought of Ernest, who must have died praying—believing, crazily—that his daughter could do this. She thought of Micah, at school, where the scent of burning sugar must be seeping into every classroom. She even thought of Norbert Rillieux, son of a white plantation owner and free woman of color, who turned sugar processing on its head when he invented the muliple-effect evaporation system. Charley turned to the driver, a middle-aged black man whose nickname was Mule. His dark face was a map of scars and pockmarks. He hadn't said more than two sentences for the entire ride—out of respect, Charley guessed; after all, she was the boss. Charley didn't care. As he shifted gears and the truck inched forward, she put her hand right on top of his.

Mule looked startled.

"It's okay," Charley said. "I just wanted to say thank you."

"We got trouble."

Charley's boots had barely touched the ground. "What happened?" she asked, but thought she knew.

"Your brother. The men won't work with him." Denton pulled her aside. "He got angry. Thought the men were making fun of him; thought they were working fast on purpose, stepping up the pace to embarrass him."

"I told him Romero's team works fast."

"I'm not done. He didn't like that the men spoke Spanish. Thought they were talking behind his back. Or, I guess you could say, way out in front of him."

"Where is he?"

"Hold on. Somehow, he found out what everyone's making; that he's making less."

"Well, of course he's making less!" Charley shouted. And just like that, she was back in Miss Honey's kitchen, standing there like a stooge while Miss Honey shoved Ralph Angel down her throat. If she could, she would call Miss Honey right now and scream, *You're killing my farm!* "Damnit. I knew this was going to— This is exactly what I—"

"Easy there, killer," Denton said, raising his hands. "Calm down."

"I am calm. But I can't fire his ass without my grandmother throwing me out."

"I broke up a couple of fights while you were gone. I was going to suggest you talk to him, but maybe I should be the one."

If only getting rid of her brother were as easy as handing him off to Denton. "That's all right. I'll handle it."

To Charley's relief, Romero and his men were hard at work across the field, pulling cane from a freshly loaded wagon. Charley scanned the field for Ralph Angel and saw him camped out in a small patch of weeds and low shrubs. His sweat jacket was off, draped between the branches to form a crude shelter.

"What's the problem?" Charley stood over him, her shadow canted out to one side.

Ralph Angel squinted up at her. "Where do I start?"

"I need you to do your job, Ralph Angel. That's all I ask."

"Job? Don't you mean slave labor?"

"I'm on a deadline here."

"You pay them twice as much as me." Ralph Angel broke a cane stalk in half, then turned his gaze out toward the fields. Romero's men were approaching the end of a nearby row. He cupped his hands and yelled, "Speak English! *Comprende?*"

Thank God the tractor was so loud his voice didn't carry. "I pay for experience," Charley said. "You've got two hours of it counting the fights you started. They've got years."

"Yeah, but I'm an—"

"Engineering major. I know."

Ralph Angel looked at up Charley and she was surprised to see a wounded expression soften his face. He glanced down at his hands and stared. "Come on, sis. It might not seem like it, but I'm trying. This isn't easy for me, you know? I'm not young like those other guys. I'm struggling just to keep up." He cleared his throat. "If I can't do this—" Then he looked away, wiping his nose on his sleeve. "I'm dying out there."

Charley felt an ache of guilt deep in her chest as she looked down at her brother, who seemed older than she'd ever noticed before. Another place, another time, she could afford to handle the situation differently. But when she looked across the field, she saw that the tractor had made the turn and was starting down a new row. The clock was ticking. The cane would not wait. She turned back to Ralph Angel. "I'm sorry. And I hear you. But right now, the only thing that counts is how fast you plant."

Ralph Angel leaned back stiffly. "Well, listen to you, Miss ACLU, Miss Equal Opportunity."

"Are you going to work or are you going home? You call it, Ralph Angel."

Ralph Angel glared at Charley, and she thought he'd say he was quitting. Instead he rose and crammed his arms through his jacket sleeves, hobbled off toward Romero's crew.

But Charley took Ralph Angel off the planting crew just to be safe. She radioed Alison—a bad idea, she knew, but she couldn't think of anywhere else to put him—and pulled Denton's truck up to Alison's combine in the middle of the field. Unlike the combine Charley drove, Alison operated an old-fashioned soldier harvester, which looked like a garbage can on rollers. No metal scrolls or vacuum chutes to suck, cut up, and spit out neat billets. Instead, the soldier harvester moved through the field like a pair of cutting shears, clipping stalks at ground level and laying them side by side across the row.

Charley handed Ralph Angel a cane knife. "All you have to do is follow behind the harvester and cut the cane he misses." Scrapping cane was the most menial, most mind-numbing of all jobs; it required no skill. In the old days, it was the job reserved for women and children.

"Jesus, Charley. A man has his pride."

"Take it or leave it."

"Yeah, yeah, yeah," Ralph Angel said darkly, and slammed the truck door.

But pairing Alison and Ralph Angel was like throwing water on a grease fire. In less than an hour, Charley's walkie-talkie crackled again.

"What the hell were you *thinking*?" Alison's voice was a lightning strike, and by the time Charley made it to the front where she'd dropped off Ralph Angel, Alison had called her twice more.

"Sorry, Miss Bordelon, but I can't work like this," Alison said, stomping over freshly cut cane. "He's impossible. I told him to swing the cane knife closer to the ground, but he won't listen."

"*Me?*" said Ralph Angel. "All I was trying to say was that maybe if you adjusted the blade, you'd cut more cane to begin with."

"All right, that's enough!" Charley yelled. "Ralph Angel, you're out of line." They started up again and she stepped between them. "Hey!" she shouted. "Cut it out. Alison, please, go to lunch." She dragged Ralph Angel away from the combine. "Are you *trying* to cause trouble? Is that your plan?"

"It wasn't me," Ralph Angel said. "That guy's a whack job."

"Because I'm warning you. This is strike four by my count."

"It wasn't my—"

Charley raised her hand. "After lunch, you're going back to the office. You'll sweep the floors or shovel dog shit for all I care. I swear to God, Ralph Angel, this is your last chance."

Six thirty p.m. now, and night crept forward along the sky's hem. A mother-of-pearl crescent moon hovered above the tree line, and out on the road, the steady flicker of headlights confirmed tractors were still hauling cane to the mills. In her combine, Charley touched the knots on her necklace. *Thank you, Lord.* She had survived the first day of grinding.

Ralph Angel had, miraculously, swept the floor and stacked Denton's tools along the ledge when Charley returned to the shop. He looked up when she entered, seeming to search her face for approval.

"The others are on their way back," Charley said, tossing her gloves down. "You should clock out. Denton and I need to go over tomorrow's schedule, then we'll head home."

Ralph Angel nodded, but was quiet otherwise, and Charley figured maybe the time alone had done him some good.

From out in the yard came the sound of truck tires rolling to a stop and, over its idling engine, the faint echo of zydeco music. A man's voice, then Ralph Angel's saying, "Straight through that door." Charley poked her head out of her office. That weathered face; those eyes that looked at her as though she were the only woman in town. "Remy." She would never get tired of saying it.

"Hey there, California." Remy took off his baseball cap then leaned forward to kiss her. He ran his hand down her arm, lightly squeezing her biceps, and said, "Those pretty arms," then took her hand. He smelled of motor oil and grass and sweat, and underneath, citrus. "Thought I'd swing by, see how you did today."

"A few setbacks," Charley said, "but overall, good. And even better now."

Remy was about to kiss her again, but over his shoulder Charley saw Ralph Angel hovering just inside the shop door. The thought of him witnessing so private a moment made her pull away. She motioned, reluctantly, for Ralph Angel to come over. She introduced him to Remy. "This is my brother."

"Hey, man. How you doing?" Remy said, warmly, extending his hand.

Ralph Angel responded with a halfhearted shake. He looked Remy over, openly sizing him up. "So, how do you know my sister?"

"We met at an auction," Charley said. "Remy's a farmer."

"Oh yeah? No kidding. How many acres?" Ralph Angel said.

"Twenty-two hundred, give or take," Remy said. "Mostly over in Saint Abbey."

"Twenty-two hundred. I'm impressed."

"Plenty of farmers a lot bigger than me." Remy smiled and gave a modest shrug. "So, you're Charley's brother." He sounded relieved to be asking the questions now. "You driving a combine or something?"

Ralph Angel slid his hands in his pockets. "Actually, my sister's got me scrapping cane."

Remy laughed. "Get out of here."

"Why would I joke?" Ralph Angel said.

Charley winced. His tone had darkened, reminding her of the way he sounded the day John brought the plywood for the windows.

Remy looked from Ralph Angel, who stood by with a sour but satisfied look on his face, to Charley, and Charley was tempted to offer an explanation. She hated that Remy was looking at her with a confused expression, as though he were wondering who she was, really, way deep down; wondering if she might be some kind of monster to make her brother do such lowly work.

"Mr. Denton should be pulling up any minute," Charley said. "We can wait out front."

"That's okay," Remy said. The confused expression vanished. "You're the one I came to see. I thought maybe we'd have a drink to celebrate. A quick one, since we both need to be up early."

Nine o'clock at Paul's Café. Just one drink. Charley would drop Ralph Angel off at home first.

In the car, Charley was about to turn on the radio when Ralph Angel reached for the book she'd wedged between the seats. This time, he practically tore the pages as he turned them. "This belongs to that guy you introduced me to back there?"

"As a matter of fact, yes."

Ralph Angel closed the book. "Sort of sleeping with the enemy, don't you think?"

"What are you talking about?"

"You know, fucking a white guy. A Southern white guy at that."

"It's none of your business." Charley's heart was racing.

"I mean, there must be at least *one* black man down here who's good enough for you. There must be a doctor or a lawyer in one of these towns who meets your high standards."

"You'll be plugging drains tomorrow," Charley said.

"Just tell me this: what makes Mr. Twenty-two hundred acres so special?"

"There's a five-acre stretch over in Micah's Corner that had some water on it. Mr. Denton will show you what to do. Don't forget your gloves."

"I mean, what makes you think he sees anything in you but a piece of black ass? That's the way they do it down here, you know? They always have a little dish of chocolate on the side."

Charley's whole body went rigid. "You should plan on driving yourself from now on."

"You humiliated me out there today. I have my pride."

"We don't have time for pride. You brought this on yourself."

"Making me walk behind that cracker's harvester was bad enough, but then to make me pick up dog shit around the shop?"

"It was the only job left. If you don't like it, talk to Miss Honey since she forced me to hire you."

"And then to be fucking a *white* boy? I wonder what Micah will say when she finds out what white men in Louisiana have done to black women for centuries. Hell, why limit it to Louisiana? All over the South. I mean, what kind of role model are you?"

It was as though Ralph Angel had dipped a long stick into the dark pit of her private concerns and stirred up all the muck. And now, all the questions Charley had asked herself about how she and Remy could ever possibly work given the South's complicated history; given her worries about what people would say—white people but also black people—considering both sides' sensitivities and prejudices; what her own father would say given all he'd suffered—all of those anxieties rose to the top. This wasn't the 1950s. She was free to love whomever she wanted. Still, Charley felt as though she was breaking some cardinal rule. She knew Ralph Angel understood her fears, the obligation and the burden she felt. She knew her brother was hurting, that he was desperate, and would likely apologize later, but she hated Ralph Angel for saying what he said just to get back at her. Charley pulled the car over to the shoulder. "Get out."

"You could have put me in the office from the start. Let me file papers or something."

"I said get out."

Ralph Angel stared at Charley for a long moment, then opened his door. "Tell 'Da I missed my ride."

"Tell her yourself."

Ralph Angel stepped back from the car, but he didn't close the door. "See you at work tomorrow, sis."

"I don't think so," Charley said, leaning over to pull the door closed. "You're fired."

26

✳ In the back room, Ralph Angel stared through the darkness, his body aching after the day's labor and the long walk home, his mind cycling through memories of all that had happened—Ernest, Miss Honey, Johnny at the bakery, the German, Charley—and the more he thought, the more his stomach churned with the fresh waves of bright, cold fury. It might take a while to find what he needed. The punks he met in Tee Coteau, the ones he bought from after that mess with the German, were better than nothing, but they were small-time operators. He might have to leave town to find guys who could hook him up for real, sell him what he needed to stop the darkness he felt within him from spreading. He slid out of bed.

"Pop?" Blue raised his head and reached for Ralph Angel's arm.

"Go back to sleep." Ralph Angel dragged the clock radio to the edge of the nightstand. Midnight. He turned it toward Blue. "Don't move from this bed till you hear the man on the radio say it's seven o'clock. I mean it."

'Da's purse was on top of the refrigerator. Ralph Angel took it down, then cleared a place on the table, his heart bucking as he pulled at the tarnished zipper. Inside: old tubes of lipstick, a packet of tissues, an envelope stuffed with store coupons. Everything smelled like her, the sweet, powdery fragrance he'd known since he was a boy. He twisted the clasp on her pink wallet and it yawned open, but there were only two crumpled bills and a handful of coins.

"Think," Ralph Angel said to himself and paced the floor. Next door, Miss Marti's rooster crowed. In a few hours, steel-blue and orange light would bleed through the kitchen window to fill the shallow sink and spill over the lip of the counter.

The Kerns jar was shoved all the way to the back of the cabinet. Ralph

Angel untwisted the rubber band, straightened the stack of small bills, and counted them with a bank teller's speed. One hundred sixty-five dollars. He closed the lid and slid the empty jar back into its place before jamming the roll in his pocket. One hundred sixty-five dollars wasn't much but it was good for a seven-day run.

On the way out, Ralph Angel paused. Charley's door was open but the light was off. Holding his breath, he moved closer and saw, through the doorway, Micah asleep on the air mattress. Charley's bed was empty.

In her room, he swept his hand across the dresser, feeling for any coins or bills Charley had left behind, until his fingers grazed the cool base, the square feet. Ralph Angel paused, considered his next move, then eased *The Cane Cutter* toward him, mindful of its weight. Charley shouldn't have embarrassed him the way she had. She always had it so easy. Everything given to her while he'd struggled for the crumbs. *Pride goeth before destruction, and a haughty spirit before a fall*—the passage came to mind before he could stop it.

On the air mattress, Micah mumbled in her sleep. Ralph Angel froze. He waited. And when all was still again, he slid *The Cane Cutter* off the dresser and backed out of the room.

Beyond the porch, the street was alive with shadows. On the porch, the Bible passage came to him. *Grace in the eyes of the Lord.* Ralph Angel paused. Some people believed they were worthy of God's grace and some people didn't. Then he stepped into the darkness, stepped back across the line.

27

❀Miss Honey's living room was New Year's Eve before the ball dropped with all the party hats and plastic kazoos, the spiraled tin sparklers and colored streamers draped in scallops, and mylar balloon bouquets everywhere. Charley taped the HAPPY BIRTHDAY banner over the window before everyone hid, until Micah, still sleepy but dressed in her school uniform, opened the bedroom door and headed for the kitchen and they all jumped out and yelled *Surprise!*

"But you told me we weren't celebrating until this weekend," Micah said when she recovered from the shock. She had asked her two new friends to sleep over, and Charley had agreed to let the girls do beauty makeovers, have cake and an ice cream bar.

"I couldn't let your real birthday go by without doing something special," Charley said. "And since I won't be home until late tonight, I thought we'd celebrate now." She would drop Micah at school, then head to New Orleans.

"Open your presents," Blue said. "Mine first." He handed Micah a wad of newspaper tied with string. "It's Zach," he said before Micah could untie the knot. When she did, Charley recognized the action figure he played with the day he arrived. It was his favorite, she knew, and gave Blue a hug. "You're so sweet. Thank you," she said, knowing Micah would give it back to him.

Miss Honey gave Micah a new Bible with a bright white cover and real gold leaf on the edge of each page. "Every child who goes through confirmation at Mount Olive gets a Bible just like this. I order them special." Micah opened the front cover and saw her name in gold letters. "I still have mine, from when I was a girl," Miss Honey said.

Then Charley set a large present on the coffee table and they all held their breath as Micah lifted the lid off the cherry-red box and held up the Leica IIIf "Red Dial." "It has a self-timer," Charley said.

"Mom." Micah stared at the camera. "This looks expensive. Are you sure?"

Charley nodded. "It's used. And the man at the camera store said I can pay in installments. He said it still has a lot of life left. I thought you might need something more advanced since you're in the photography club."

Miss Honey made grits and eggs, Micah's favorite breakfast, and they were passing the camera around, taking turns looking through the viewfinder, when Violet, in paint-splattered overalls, on her way to re-paint the church bathrooms, rushed into the kitchen. "I wanted to catch you before you went to school. Happy birthday," she said, and set a box of Meche's glazed doughnut holes with two containers of choco-late dipping sauce on the table. The doughnut holes were still warm, light as air, and Charley stuck a candle in every one and they sang "Happy Birthday" and Micah made her wish. They passed the dough-nuts around and everyone took two, and Micah announced this was her best birthday ever.

Charley looked around the table. She saw her grandmother, she saw Blue, she saw Violet, she saw her daughter, who looked happier than she had in months, and Charley thought, *yes*, this was what she wanted. This was what she'd been hoping for.

"I just wish Ralph Angel were here to celebrate with us," Miss Honey said. She shot Charley a dark look. "He was pretty upset when he came in last night."

It had not occurred to Charley until that moment to wonder about Ralph Angel. Last night, she met Remy for a drink at Paul's Café and managed to put Ralph Angel out of her mind. She came home late to a quiet house, and this morning, rose extra early to decorate the living room. She didn't feel like thinking about Ralph Angel; not today, not ever. Charley looked at her watch. In a little while, the sky would be filled with great mushroom clouds of gray smoke as farmers burned their cut cane before loading it in the wagons, and she would see, along the bayou, where the tupelo trees donned leaves of orange and yellow where they had been green before, the China rain trees ablaze in a crown of red blossoms. "We should get going. I want to beat the New Orleans traffic."

"I'd like to eyeball that statue one last time since it'll belong to someone else tomorrow," Violet said.

Charley sent Micah to fetch *The Cane Cutter* from the bedroom, but Micah came back empty-handed. "It's not there."

"It has to be there," Charley said. "Look again. On the dresser."

But when Micah returned empty-handed a second time, Charley went to look herself. She looked on the dresser and in the closet and behind the door. She flung clothes and shoved aside the stack of farm catalogs. She lifted the mattress.

For the next hour, they searched the house—every shelf, every corner, every box—the whole time the voice in Charley's head repeating over and over, *This can't be happening*, until finally, she told everyone to stop looking. *The Cane Cutter* was gone. Charley collapsed into a chair. She laid her head on the table. She cried and didn't think she would ever stop.

Three hours after Charley discovered *The Cane Cutter* was gone, she still sat in Miss Honey's kitchen, clutching a wad of paper towel after having cried until she was spent. Hollywood still looked a little crestfallen after learning about her date with Remy, was trying, Charley could see, to put on a brave face. He had stopped by to say hello to Miss Honey and to wish Micah happy birthday, and heard about *The Cane Cutter* disappearing. Now he held Charley's hand and tried to comfort her. He refilled her water glass and encouraged her to drink; whispered, "Don't worry, Miss Charley, I won't leave you," which was sweet and kind, but Charley barely heard him. Meanwhile, Violet and Miss Honey debated whether to call the police. Like Charley, Violet was sure Ralph Angel had taken *The Cane Cutter*. She was sure that if they called the police right now, they could get it back. But Miss Honey kept saying, "No, Ralph Angel didn't take it; leave the police out of this."

"But he did!" Charley said, and blew her nose into what was left of the paper towel, looking for a piece that wasn't shredded. "No one else knew it was there. No one else had a reason to steal it."

"No police," Miss Honey said, like she was directing traffic. "No police. I won't allow it. No police. No."

"Mother." Violet's voice was calm, reasonable. "We have to call the police. If Ralph Angel is innocent, calling the police won't matter."

"Ralph Angel didn't take it," Miss Honey snapped. "He is a lot of things, but he's not a criminal. We had a house thief is what we had."

Charley leaped up from her chair. "Why wouldn't he take it?" She pounded her fist on the table. "I fired him, remember? Why wouldn't he get even?"

"You were brave, Miss Charley," said Hollywood. "It took guts to stand up to Ralph Angel."

"I'm calling John," Violet said, taking out her cell phone. "He'll know what to do."

"Call John if you want to," Miss Honey said, "but we're keeping this in the family."

"By tonight, he'll be across the Mexico border," Charley said. "He's probably a hundred miles from here already."

"The day you call the police on Ralph Angel," said Miss Honey, her voice low as tires on gravel, "is the day you are dead to me. Police don't ask questions. They just shoot. We're giving Ralph Angel till tonight and that's the end of it."

In the evening during grinding, the sky took on an orangey glow. As night approached, out in the fields, farmers continued to burn their cane before loading it in the wagons, so that it looked to passersby as though long red whips were snaking over the ground. And without the noise of daily life, without the *boom boom boom* of car stereos, and people calling across the street, Charley heard the mill chugging away in the distance—the low drone of the boilers and a faint whistle signaling the end of each shift. It was a comforting sound that meant people were doing the right thing. It meant life kept rolling forward.

It was six o'clock when Miss Honey's front door slammed. Brother stormed into the kitchen like a category three hurricane, all howling winds and thunder. "I knew it would come to this!" He threw his keys on the table. "I tried to warn you. I told you there'd be trouble." He wore his fast-food uniform—white shirt, white pants with a blue stripe down the side, a little button pinned to his chest that said "Service with a smile."

Violet punched Brother's arm. "Quiet. You'll scare the kids with all that noise."

Seconds later, John stepped into the kitchen. He looked handsome and serious in his prison guard uniform. He hugged Violet, said hello to Hollywood, then knelt down to Charley. "How you doin', cuz?"

"I want him arrested," Charley said. "Why aren't we calling the police? You know people, right?"

"What took you so long?" Violet said.

"Cut us some slack," Brother said. "We drove as fast as we could. Even stopped at some bars where we thought he might be."

John laid a comforting hand on Charley's shoulder. "When was the last time you saw him?"

"Around seven last night. I kicked him out of my car." Charley consulted her watch. "We've wasted enough time." She picked up the phone.

Miss Honey, in her pink robe and slippers, emerged from the hall. "Hang up that phone, Charley. I told y'all before. No police. They'll only hunt him down."

"Hello, Mother," Brother said.

"And don't come in here with a lot of foolishness, Brother." She went to the refrigerator and took out a Coke, poured in her Stanback. "I don't know what crazy scheme y'all are cooking up but I don't want to hear it. Can't none of you prove Ralph Angel did this."

"But Mother—" Brother began.

"And shame on y'all for judging when Ralph Angel's not here to defend himself."

"That's the point," Violet said. "If he were here, we wouldn't be having this conversation."

"Don't be fresh, Violet. 'Judge not, that ye be not judged. Why beholdest thou the mote that is in thy brother's eye, but considerest not the *beam* that is in thine own?'" The scripture made everyone stop.

Charley went to the cabinet. She flung the doors open. She pushed the glasses over to the corner and pulled out Miss Honey's money jar, held it up to the light. Nothing in it but air. "What about this? How do you explain this?"

Miss Honey regarded the empty jar like she'd never seen it before.

"For God's sake," Charley said. "How much proof do you need?"

"Well, well. Would you look at this? The gang's all here." Ralph Angel stood in the doorway.

He looked, to Charley, as if he'd been rolling around in the woods the way his old sweat jacket hung open. Under it, his T-shirt looked like it could use a good bleaching.

Charley went over to Ralph Angel, stood right in his face. "Where is it?"

"Well, hello, sis. How are you? Fired anyone lately?"

"There, you see?" said Miss Honey. "Ralph Angel doesn't know what you're talking about."

"Oh, you mean that statue?" Ralph Angel held up his hands. "I have no idea what they did with it. It was beautiful though, a real masterpiece. I see why our daddy gave it to you." He started to cross the kitchen. "Now I need to talk to my boy."

"One second, cousin." John reached for Ralph Angel's arm.

"Take your hands off me, John. I'm not fucking around this time."

"Where's Charley's statue?"

"I said let go."

That was when everything got scary, scrambled like eggs and grits and bacon all mixed together in one pot. It happened fast. And so slow. One minute, John had Ralph Angel by the arm and Ralph Angel was pushing him away. There was lots of shouting, rolling on the floor, and John had Ralph Angel pinned. He smashed his fist into Ralph Angel's face and Ralph Angel's cheek split open. And for a second it looked as though John had won. But then Ralph Angel slipped away, and Charley heard popping like firecrackers, and she saw that Ralph Angel had John's gun. He waved it around as he stood up, breathing hard, yelled, "Get the fuck back! Get the fuck back!" Violet and Brother were pressed up against the cabinets, and Miss Honey was saying, "Lord have mercy, Lord have mercy." And then Micah and Blue ran in, saying, "What's going on? Why is everyone yelling?" and then they stopped too, when they saw Ralph Angel waving the gun. Charley dropped the Kerns jar then, because the kids had run in, and because John was lying on the floor and blood, like a big dark flower, was blooming across the side of his uniform.

And then everything got quiet, except for the ceiling fan's soft whirling.

"Ralph Angel," Charley said, her heart pounding so hard she could hear it. "Put the gun down."

Ralph Angel looked at Charley. He still breathed hard, but not, Charley realized, from wrestling with John. "How come you always got everything?" He sniffed, wiped his eyes. "Who said you got to have Dad *and* the farm *and* the family?"

Charley looked at Ralph Angel—at the grimy stripe that ran down the arm of his warm-up jacket, which sagged across his shoulders, the pockets gaping like fish mouths; at his worn-out sneakers and the outdated cut of his jeans; at his hair, which was short when he first arrived, but had grown out unevenly because he couldn't spare the money to keep it cut; and finally, into Ralph Angel's face, which was a kind face, actually, and hadn't changed all that much since he was a kid, but looked so very tired now. Charley looked at her brother and for the first time saw just how broken and desperate he was.

On the floor, John groaned.

"Answer my question," Ralph Angel said.

Charley sighed. If she could turn the clock back twenty years and alter Ralph Angel's fate, she would. Gladly. "I don't know," she said. It was an unsatisfactory answer, but the only one she could offer.

But Ralph Angel nodded, as if she'd confirmed something. He reached over, then, and turned on the radio, tuned the dial away from Miss Honey's church music, and stopped at Marvin Gaye's voice, smooth as cane syrup.

Charley couldn't believe what she was hearing: the some song that played the first time she and Hollywood sat in Miss Honey's kitchen after the reunion. She glanced at Hollywood and their eyes met.

And that's when Hollywood inched forward, perhaps emboldened by the song on the radio, held his hand out. "Come on, Ralph Angel," Hollywood said. "Put down the gun."

If this were one of Hollywood's movies, Charley thought, police would be creeping around outside. Men on the roofs across the street, calling each other on their radios. Charley closed her eyes. No one was going to burst through the doors.

Ralph Angel blinked. "I'll be damned. Look who's decided to be the hero."

"Please, Ralph Angel," said Hollwood. "I'm asking you nice. You done enough already. John's hurt. Give me the gun."

Charley watched as Ralph Angel.checked the clock. He wiped blood off his cheek. "Shouldn't you be out cutting somebody's grass? You ever take my advice and raise your price?"

In the background, Marvin Gaye sang low and smooth.

"We got to get John to the doctor," Hollywood said.

"Of course you didn't," Ralph Angel said. "Why would you listen to me? You know, Charley thinks I'm jealous of you." He turned to Charley. "Ain't that right, sis? Ain't that what you said about your boyfriend here?" Then he turned back to Hollywood. "You know, we used to be best friends. In fact, I'll even admit you were my *only* friend. But then you got all chummy with Charley, and where did that leave me?" He tapped the gun's barrel against his temple. "Hey. I just got an idea. Since you two are buddies now, why don't you tell Charley how you got your name."

Charley saw Hollywood's face change. He looked confused.

"My name's Francis. After my granddaddy."

"Not your real name. Your nickname."

"My nickname's Hollywood."

Ralph Angel rolled his eyes. "Jesus Christ. Not that one. Tell her how you got the name Peanut. Hey, Charley, you want to hear a funny story?"

Hollywood shook his head. "No. No, no. You can't tell that story."

Ralph Angel looked at Charley. "A bunch of us boys used to work for this man, Mr. Sam. He owned a pharmacy downtown."

Hollywood put his hands over his ears. "Stop talking, Ralph Angel. Stop talking."

Charley put her hand out. "Don't do this."

"What's wrong? I'm giving you your big break. You get your chance at stardom." Ralph Angel turned back to Charley. "Mr. Sam used to hire a lot of the black boys from the Quarters to work on the loading dock after school. Thing was, he had this wife, see? Tits like cantaloupes. Mr. Sam liked to take us home with him on our breaks. Used to like to watch us fuck his wife."

"Shut up, Ralph Angel," Brother said.

"So, one day, Mr. Sam took ole Hollywood here. But when it was his turn—"

Charley knew there were only two ways for action movies to end. The hero either died or he didn't. She looked at Hollywood. But what if you weren't the hero? What if you were only a guy who lived with his mother and cut people's grass for five dollars? What if you were the guy who stood on the sidelines while someone else got the girl? "Ralph Angel," Charley said, and it sounded like she was begging because she was. "You have to stop."

"When it was Hollywood's turn, he got scared," Ralph Angel said. "Couldn't get it up. Mr. Sam called him a nancy boy. Threw him out. When Hollywood came to work the next day, Mr. Sam told him to take his peanut-sized dick and get off his dock." He turned to Hollywood. "Am I telling it right, Peanut? Ain't that the way it happened?"

Charley didn't have to look at Hollywood to know he was crying.

Ralph Angel had finished his story. Everyone stared at the floor.

"I guess that does it for me." Ralph Angel sighed wearily, as though he were relieved to finally set down a heavy box he'd been carrying. He looked at Miss Honey, his whole demeanor softening, and Charley saw the little boy reemerge. "Well, 'Da, it looks like Violet and Brother were right. Things didn't work out like you wanted. But before I go, I wanted to say I'm sorry I pushed you last time. I feel real bad about that. Violet and Brother won't believe me, but I really am. You've always been in my corner and I hate myself for hurting you. I know I've let you down." He walked over to Blue. "Time to go, Buddy."

Blue whimpered as Ralph Angel picked him up.

Charley took a step forward. "Leave Blue here. I'll take care of him."

Ralph Angel looked baffled. "And let you have the last thing that means something to me? No, thanks." Then he turned and walked out of the kitchen.

No one moved until the front door slammed. When they heard Ralph Angel's car pull away, Violet and Brother rushed to John's side. Charley grabbed Micah, who was crying, then she called 911 for an ambulance. After that, she called the police. And after that, she walked over to Hollywood, but he wouldn't look at her.

Miss Honey, meanwhile, stood by herself against the wall.

28

❉ Out on the road, Ralph Angel rolled down his window. The night was cold, the air stung his face. He turned on the radio and settled back into his seat. A two-hour drive to New Orleans. They'd lie low for a couple nights and then what—Orlando? Miami? Maybe they'd try Atlantic City. He looked over his shoulder. Blue was stretched out on the backseat, where he'd cried himself to sleep.

Ralph Angel blew past the Indian casino, all bright and glowing, and for a moment he thought about Amber, wondered if she ever got that cherry-red pickup. He had just passed the turnoff where she lived when a car pulled out and sped to catch up with him. Another second and the icy blue and white lights flashed. Ralph Angel slowed, pulled onto the shoulder, cruised to a stop.

"License and registration, please."

Ralph Angel recognized the voice. His heart drummed.

One Mississippi.

"Good evening, Officer. I've got my license right here." His hands started to sweat.

Two Mississippi. Three.

The beam of the officer's flashlight swept over Ralph Angel's face, swept over the dashboard, swept across his shoulder, and hovered for a few extra seconds above the passenger seat.

"Step out of the car, please." The officer's voice was tense. Tenser than it had been before.

Ralph Angel squinted into the harsh light. He shielded his eyes. "Is there a problem?"

Four Mississippi.

"I said, step out of the car, please."

"If it's about the rental, I can explain." Ralph Angel laughed nervously. "You see, I was going to turn it in. I got the contract in here, somewhere. I'll pay what I owe. I swear." His thoughts shifted to *The Cane Cutter*. After he took it from Charley's dresser, he wrapped it in a towel, put it in the trunk. In the end, he hadn't given it away; couldn't bring himself to do it. He'd just wanted to give Charley a good scare. Hold on to it for a couple days then give it back.

"I said, step out of the car. *Now*."

Five Mississippi.

Ralph Angel saw the trooper pull his gun from its holster and take a measured step to the side. He listened as the trooper called for backup on his walkie-talkie, and it seemed like only seconds before he heard sirens in the distance. Ralph Angel reached down, slowly, to unbuckle his seat belt and saw what the trooper saw: John's gun on the passenger seat where he'd tossed it. He heard a click as the trooper released his gun's safety.

"I won't tell you again, sir. Step out of the car. Do it now. Right. Now."

Six Mississippi.

"Please, Officer. It ain't how it looks. I got my kid with me, see? Just give me a second. *Jesus*. It's not what you think. I swear to God." Without thinking, Ralph Angel reached out his hand. "Please. I can explain." And then he heard the trooper's gun fire.

29

❦ In the last week, Charley did everything she could think of to save her farm. She called her suppliers and pleaded for extensions. She went back to the banks. Miss Honey loaned her twelve hundred dollars. Violet asked her congregation for donations. Micah and Blue sold lemonade and baked cookies using Violet's secret recipe. Denton and Alison insisted on forfeiting their cuts of the profits. Remy tried to work out a deal with the mills.

But nothing helped. The numbers were nowhere near adding up.

And so, on a beautiful, crisp Saturday in October, when a light wind rustled the cane and the roads were clogged with tractors hauling loads to the mill, Charley prepared to meet Landry and Baron.

In the kitchen, Micah's Polaroids were spread over the table. Charley gathered them into a stack. Here was a picture of her standing at the edge of her fields looking exhausted and overwhelmed the first day they arrived; here was a picture of Miss Honey at the stove. Miss Honey didn't like being photographed and Charley guessed Micah took it when she wasn't looking. Here was a picture of Micah and Violet and Micah's crawfish cake, and here was a picture of the cake that won first place, though they all agreed Micah's was better. Here was a picture of Micah and Blue that Ralph Angel must have taken. Micah looked so serious, Charley thought, but she liked that she could see Miss Honey's house in the background and that if you looked close, you could see where all the Christmas lights were still strung across the porch from last year. Blue must have taken the next two, because they were all blurry and out of focus. One was a picture of Ralph Angel's car, the next, a picture of the bike Blue wanted for his birthday, which Charley remembered was still on sale downtown at the five-and-dime. Here was a picture of Blue and Ralph Angel, both of them smiling the same smile as Blue sat on Ralph Angel's lap and Ralph Angel wrapped his arms around him. And finally, here was a picture of Micah standing in her garden the week she started it, the ground in the background dark and bare, the newly dug rows evenly spaced. Charley was tempted to ask Micah if she could keep it, but put it back on the table. There would be plenty of time for gardens; plenty of years left for pictures. Charley picked up the picture of Ralph Angel and Blue again, and felt a squeeze in her chest. Her brother was dead. She still couldn't quite believe it.

At last, Charley slid the picture of Ralph Angel and Blue back into the stack. "I guess I'd better go," she said, and slung her backpack over her shoulder.

"I just hate the thought of you having to cut a deal with those devils," Violet said. "I still wish we could have done more."

Charley loved that Violet wanted to keep fighting, even when it was clear they'd lost. "Three or four years, once I've paid off the debt, maybe I'll try again," she said.

The hardest part had been breaking the news to Denton and Alison. The morning after Ralph Angel shot John, she found them in the fields setting fire to the acres of dried cane leaves the combine had left behind. There was something unexpectedly beautiful about watching the cane burn.

"She sure looks better with her clothes on," Alison had said, and after a few startled seconds, Charley realized he meant the cane looked bare without its leaves.

"Guess I'd better dig out my old fishing pole," Denton had said, stoic as ever, and that was when Charley broke down.

Now Charley patted her pocket for her car keys. She hugged Violet and they stood by the sink, holding each other tightly before Charley pulled away. "This shouldn't take long. I'll meet you at the hospital."

Someone knocked at the front door.

"I got it," Micah yelled, and in a minute, she walked back into the kitchen followed by Hollywood.

Charley had not seen him since the shooting. Remembering the way he stood with his hands in his pockets looking down at the floor rather than at her, she understood why he hadn't come around. But her heart swelled at the sight of him and she didn't hold back.

"It's great to see you," Charley said. "How've you been?"

Hollywood shrugged. "I'm okay." He wore his helmet instead of his baseball cap. "I was just on my way—I was heading over to—I mean, I thought I'd—"

"It's fine," Charley said, and gave him a look that said all of it—the awful peanut story, his tears of humiliation—was forgotten. "I'm just happy you stopped by. I've missed you." She stepped toward him, extended her hand, pulled him close. When she stood back to give him space, she saw his face had flushed.

"We've all missed you, man," Violet said.

And just then, Miss Honey stepped up from the den. "Is that Hollywood?" She marched over and swatted his arm with a rolled-up *TV Guide*. "Where've you been? My yard looks awful."

Hollywood beamed then. "I've been missing y'all, too. How is everybody? How's John?"

"He gets out of the hospital today," Charley said. "We're meeting Brother over there in a couple hours. As soon as I—" Her voice trailed off.

Violet looked at Hollywood and sighed. "Charley's losing her farm," she said, and explained that without *The Cane Cutter*, there was nothing for Charley to sell at the auction.

"Without the money I would have made from selling the statue, I don't have money to get through grinding," Charley said.

Hollywood looked at Charley. "How much do you need?"

"Fifty thousand dollars. At least." She shook her head. She was tired of saying the number.

"I got fifty thousand," Hollywood said.

Charley looked at Hollywood standing there in his T-shirt and faded fatigues and sneakers. She looked at his pale blue eyes that always seemed to be searching, and his doughy, open face. She opened her mouth to speak, then closed it.

Finally, it was Violet who said what they all were thinking: "Hollywood Ancelet. How in the world do you have fifty thousand dollars?"

"It's my grass-cutting money," Hollywood said, like *what do you think I been cutting grass for all those years?* "It's just sitting down at the bank, collecting dust." He looked right into Charley's face. "You can have it. You've been a good friend to me since the day you got here. I don't have any use for it. I got everything I need. You don't even have to pay me back."

Charley looked through the window into the powder-blue sky and imagined her fields, the rows of cane—her cane, her father's cane—looking lush and orderly like the fields she passed when they drove in all those months ago. She allowed herself, maybe for the first time, to think her dream would come true. She thought of Micah. She thought of her father.

"You know what *Maman* used to say about cane farming?" Hollywood said. "She used to say, 'Cain killed Abel but I ain't gonna let it kill me,'" then he waited for them to get the joke.

"Of course I'll pay you back," Charley said. "I don't know what to say."

"How about 'Thank you, and praise the Lord,'" Miss Honey said. "Why don't you start with that?"

APRIL

30

❧ The dam was across the bay from the Point; out past the state park and the enclave of camps that folks called the Cajun Riviera; out past the marshlands and the cluster of small islands choked with Chinese tallow. Actually, the dam was just a sandbar covered with rocks and sun-bleached oyster shells and railroad ties forming a bridge that straddled the narrow channel. But there was enough space to moor three or four boats if you did it right, and Remy Newell's boat was tied up with the others.

Grinding season ended on New Year's Day. After the freezing rains of January and February, the weather was warming, fields were drying, and across Charley's land, cane was already twelve inches high. She, Denton, and Alison were back at work. They'd spent all of March off-barring, and in another week, it would be time for laying-by.

But today, Charley lounged in a beach chair on the highest point of the dam, Remy's goofy hat shielding her face from the sun, the Igloo cooler open for anyone who wanted a soda, and the hibachi hissing and crackling each time a link of andouille or crawfish boudin dripped on the coals. A few feet away, at the dam's edge, Remy helped Micah and Blue tie turkey necks to their crab nets, and showed them how to drop the nets over the side, where they sank in the ocher-colored water.

Micah wiped her hands on her shorts. "How long before we catch something?" She was two inches taller than this time last year, Charley guessed, appraising her daughter's long legs and feet she'd have to grow into. It wouldn't be long before Micah was tall as her.

"We'll check in fifteen minutes," Remy said. "Got to give the crabs time to find the bait and get comfortable." He took off his watch and handed it to Blue. "Okay, buddy. You're our official timekeeper. Come back when the long hand gets to the twelve. Think you can handle that?"

Blue nodded and stuffed the watch in his pocket.

"Y'all can go across to the other side if you want," Remy said, "but stay out of the water. Alligators like to lay out in the sun when it's warm like this."

While the kids explored the opposite bank, Remy took his cast net to the water's edge and, in one fluid motion, hurled it underhand. Charley watched it spiral, like a big silvery white web, out over the water. As it landed, the net made the most beautiful sound Charley had ever heard; like the gentle patter of rain. For a few seconds the net floated on the surface, drifted with the current. And just as it disappeared under the water, Remy pulled it in, his arm muscles lean and sinewy as he reached, hand over hand. The whole thing was like a poem.

"How'd you do?" Charley asked when Remy came over to her chair. A stream of water trailed from his net, and the front of his shirt was damp and dark where he held it against his chest.

He shook the net and a dozen translucent shrimp, big as Charley's palm, fell into the galvanized bucket. "Finish what you were saying. What else did the doctor tell you?"

Charley looked across the sandbar to where Micah and Blue were chucking oyster shells into the water. "There's not much more we can do." She looked at Blue, who, as far as the doctors could decipher, woke up after the trooper pulled Ralph Angel over and heard everything, and saw everything, and had hardly spoken since that night. Now Charley was in the process of adopting him. "There's nothing physically wrong with him," she said. "He just needs time. And love. And patience." Charley looked at Blue and felt responsible. She thought of Ralph Angel and felt responsible. She suspected she would be an old woman before the knot in her gut loosened and she forgave herself for the part she played, large and small, in what happened to her brother.

According to the police report, the trooper saw the gun on Ralph Angel's seat and believed he was reaching for it, so he shot Ralph Angel first. "Justified use of deadly force," the police report said. Charley had her doubts. For everything that Ralph Angel ever did, for all the problems he caused, she couldn't imagine him threatening a police officer. From birth until the last day of his life, he'd been caught up in the world of injustice. That Ralph Angel died on the side of the road before the ambulance arrived seemed like the latest injustice in a life full of it.

During the investigation, the detectives found *The Cane Cutter* in the trunk. After they closed the case, they returned it to Charley, and Charley had given *The Cane Cutter* to Blue with the promise that she would hold it for him until he grew up. But she knew that even if it tripled in value, which it probably would, it would never be enough.

Two hours later, the andouille and crawfish boudin were gone. The children had caught their limit and the galvanized bucket overflowed with ten dozen blue crab, a handful of mullets that got caught in the net, and four pounds of Remy's ghostly shrimp.

"That's one nice thing about crabbing and shrimping," Remy said. He loaded the bucket onto the boat. "Kids get tired, you pack up and go home."

On the ride back to shore, Micah and Blue hung their legs over the bow, which dipped and bucked and splashed spray so that they were all soaked. And a hundred yards from shore, Remy killed the engine and they glided.

"Who wants to go swimming?" Remy asked.

Charley sat on the deck as Remy and the kids leaped off the side. The cups of yellow sunlight on the water were ridiculously lovely. The smell of the bay, the gentle *glup, glup, glup* of the water licking the side of Remy's boat—for a moment, Charley couldn't believe her good fortune. She closed her eyes and felt the sun on her face. This was her life now.

"We'd better get a move on," she called at last.

Micah and Blue dog-paddled to the side of the boat.

Remy hoisted each kid onto the deck then climbed up. Charley tossed each person a towel.

"We'd better get started if we're gonna get these kids fed," Charley said. "What time does the show start again?" Jimmy Broussard was playing at Paul's Café. The show started at nine.

Remy dried himself off, then leaned down close to her face. He kissed her. "Don't worry, California. We've got plenty of time."